---------------------- ★ ----------------------

"Hannah, what is it?" Karen put her arm around her partner and held her close. Hannah Marsden swallowed hard and pointed her head toward the trunk. Rotted material that looked to have been bright red moiré crammed the trunk. The awful stench from the fabric oozed from the interior.

"Harry, shut that thing. The smell is awful." I moved toward him. Only from a few feet away did I see what Hannah and Harry had seen. Behind the folds of the tattered material was the unmistakable form of a skeleton. My vision blurred. I squinted to focus and regretted the attempt. The people on stage around the trunk faded, but the contents floated forward without sense of purpose except to escape confinement. I felt my arms raise and open to embrace the moiré-draped skeleton. I stretched out my hand, remembering another time when I had touched the skeleton of a long-dead woman.

"Grace." His voice slowed my steps. Harry's face filled my line of vision. *When did he move there?*

"Everyone stay where you are and don't touch that trunk."

---------------------- ★ ----------------------

THE
STATION MASTER

LUISA BUEHLER

W🌐RLDWIDE®

TORONTO • NEW YORK • LONDON
AMSTERDAM • PARIS • SYDNEY • HAMBURG
STOCKHOLM • ATHENS • TOKYO • MILAN
MADRID • WARSAW • BUDAPEST • AUCKLAND

To Gerry and Christopher,
who are always there, offering love and practicing patience.

Recycling programs
for this product may
not exist in your area.

THE STATION MASTER

A Worldwide Mystery/May 2013

First published by Echelon Press.

ISBN-13: 978-0-373-26849-8

Copyright © 2005 by Luisa Buehler

Acknowledgments

This is a work of fiction, but like the pearl that grew around a single grain of sand, this story developed around a modicum of fact. I am grateful to Kris Guill, owner of Jefferson Hill Tea Room, John Reeder, owner of Book Nook News, and Carl Grumbles, past president of the Lisle Heritage Society, for sharing their stories. A special thank-you to Officer Cindy McNaney of the Lisle Police for clarification on procedures. The "armchair sleuths," reference librarians at the Lisle Library, rate high marks and thanks for the details they gathered. It is in the details that a story comes to life.

All Aboard!

Magic music of the iron rails humming, engaging the imagination, changing to desire for adventure.

Holidays, honeymoons and homecomings, each beginning with a ticket to ride. The end of the line is a beginning in reverse....

Unless the ticket to ride is *one way*.

ONE

THE NIGHTMARE HARDLY came anymore. Mornings dawned sweet and rested, most mornings. Not this one. The gut-wrenching fear, the prickly sweat tore me from a sound sleep. I slipped from under the covers to the floor panting through the residual panic of the nightmare, hoping I wouldn't wake Harry.

My breathing calmed. I gently lifted my side of the covers and slid between still-warm sheets. I lay awake waiting for the time to pass and my nightgown to dry.

"WE FLY HOME in three days, Grace. It's time. We can't hide here any longer."

The pain at the thought of home still gripped my heart. It was crazy to think rushing off to another continent would heal me. I feared leaving, afraid that the healing joy I'd felt these past months would vanish if I crossed borders. My mind had created a "Brigadoon" and now I panicked at the prospect of crossing that bridge back to my life.

"Grace? I said we're leaving in three days. Is there anywhere else you want to visit before we go? Any church jumble you haven't plundered? Any brass rubbings you've missed?"

My husband's attempt at gleaning a smile from me failed miserably. I hated myself for the topsy-turvy emotions that plagued me even during idyllic outings with Harry and his family. They had been patient and loving through these past months.

Harry and I arrived on their doorstep with one day notice

and one suitcase. The maniac who once had been Harry's friend, but who had stalked me with deadly intent, had destroyed our home. Harry's parents, William and Dorothy Marsden, swept us into their hearts and life in the blink of an eye. They had readied the entire upstairs for us. We slept in Harry's old room and used his sister's adjacent bedroom as a sitting room. Both rooms had been left as they had been all those years before. Hannah's room still held the fragrance of lavender sachets in the drawers and armoire; Harry's room so typically *boy* even to his initials carved onto his desktop with his first Swiss Army knife, *H.N.M.,* Harry Nicholas Marsden.

Tears welled up in my eyes and my hands sought the comfort of a length of yarn tied to my belt loop. I kept my eyes on my hands while I looped and braided ten series of knots hoping the routine would calm my nerves and give me time to master my emotions.

Harry tipped my chin up and looked into my eyes.

"Pansy-purple," he pronounced. He leaned forward and brushed his lips against my cheek.

Even without the tears my mood would have been apparent. My personal physiology reacts to high emotion by changing the color of my eyes from a lavender shade with gold flecks to a deep pansy purple hue. My personal barometer makes it difficult to lie or hide much. Everyone who knows me can read me like a book.

"Gracie, please. We have to put this behind us. We did it once before. We can do it now."

Harry turned his cornflower-blue eyes away from my face and glanced out the window past the flower boxes attached to the sills bursting with color and tumbledown charm in the form of verbena, petunia, and celosia. His gaze continued across the neatly manicured lawn to the stone pillars at the macadam road that marked the Marsden entrance.

"It's lovely here, no doubt, old girl, but it's not our home.

We need to make peace with where we belong. Only way for that to happen is to go home, Gracie. And what about those job offers? People are waiting on you, love." He teased me now. "You would make a wonderful event planner. Ask your family. Your brothers told me you were always planning their lives."

Harry's emphasis on *planning* brought a smile to my face as I remembered the countless birthday parties, prom parties, school events that I had planned and participated in with the reluctant help of my brothers.

"Even Barb sent you a letter about joining her on some project."

Our neighbor in Pine Marsh had mailed me a notice about a position for an event planner/marketing designer for a Naperville PR firm that would be handling a big event in Lisle for their Depot Days celebration. Barb, as vice president of the Heritage Society, the group hiring the PR firm, had already talked me up with the firm.

"Yeah, everyone thinks I ought to get a job. Even Karen suggested I look into teaching a writing class at Trinity. Does my unemployed status annoy people?" I was being facetious since my full-time job was writing children's books. I had finished the fourth in my "Mick the Monster" series shortly before our lives had been slammed into the Twilight Zone by a maniac bent of revenge.

"People care about you. They love you. I love you. That's why we need to go home."

"Why? We can stay here, not this house, but in Arundel or maybe Bath. We could open a bookstall on the river. You were a publisher in England before, you can do it again. Or you could finish writing your book on plants. Plants are better here. Roses, you could grow wonderful roses here."

Harry placed two fingers against my lips to halt the torrent of wishful thinking spewing from my mouth. I took his hand in mine and kissed the top. His hands had been burned in the explosion that damaged our house.

They had healed remarkably well especially after we arrived in Arundel. A great aunt, Mildred, knew a lady friend who bottled the most marvelous honey from healing bees. I scoffed at the story. Harry's response had been different. My cosmopolitan husband listened and followed her instructions. It was imperative that he travel with her to the hives and thank the bees for their help. I stood in amazement as my world-traveled, high-tech gadget guy, agreed to drive an hour then walk the three miles to the recluse's cottage to thank the bees. Harry told me the bee lady knew the honey would work because the bees' "voices" grew hearty in the hive when Harry thanked them.

Those bees deserved Harry's heartfelt thanks and mine, too. Within weeks of using the honey salve, the tops of his hands had grown smooth and supple. The tightness and pain he had lived with had lessened.

"I want to go back to the bee lady and thank her bees." I looked up at Harry and tried a true smile.

"I've already thanked them, darling."

"I want to thank them for helping you and I want to ask her if I can thank her in advance for someone else." I stood up and walked to the window. With my back to Harry I lobbed my request over my shoulder. "Karen sent me a note on things back home. She mentioned that Ric is still in rehab. The department is forcing him to retire on full disability. She says the therapy isn't going well; so much scar tissue. I thought I'd bring home the honey for him to try."

Ric Kramer, my best friend's brother, had been injured in the same blast that hurt Harry. Ric owed his life to Harry. An awkward balance since Ric and I had once been close. Each time Ric reentered my life my marriage seemed to suffer from the encounter. I now mentioned Ric for the first time in three months. I felt I needed to act now. I turned to catch Harry's reaction.

"Of course we'll bring him the honey. I'll ring Aunt Mildred this morning and arrange the outing. Wait until you see the bee lady, Gracie. It's like she's from another time; like when those Druids you're so fond of telling me I'm related to ran amok."

He left the room to call his aunt from the kitchen, the only room in his parents' home with a telephone. Harry's good humor at my suggestion surprised me. The line from the Snoopy comic strip ran through my head, *You're a good man, Charlie Brown.* A good man indeed. Six foot tall, a trim, athletic build, blond hair streaked platinum from summer sun, and a dazzling smile. A young Roger Moore, of the Simon Templar era, my friends had decided when I first met Harry. His crystal-cut English accent nailed their choice.

Harry walked toward me from the kitchen. "Aunt Mildred says we can motor out there tomorrow with her. She'd like a visit with Morgana."

"The bee lady's name is Morgana? Wasn't she Merlin's nemesis?"

"I'm joking, darling. Her name is Maeve Flood. Thought 'Morgana' would amuse you."

My husband's sense of humor still escaped me at times.

"Maeve? Doesn't sound like an English bee lady. I thought her name would be something like Hyacinth or Minerva."

"I think it's a perfect name for her; a touch exotic for the English recluse. She's one of those 'inner sight' people, according to Aunt Mildred," he added. "Some people think she's a bit odd, talking to the bees and all, but I found her charming. She was thrilled to find out I lived in America; asked more questions about Pine Marsh than a Realtor. Said she'd always wanted to visit Illinois; don't know if she was being kind or casting for an invitation for lodging. I told her to contact us through Aunt Mildred if she ever made plans. Wait 'til you meet her; she's going to absolutely eat you up."

Harry's infectious smile didn't touch my heart. I kept thinking about the fairy tale *Hansel and Gretel* and the witch in the woods.

"I told Aunt Mildred what you wanted to do. She thought that refreshingly generous of you. She doesn't think your thanks will be enough, but the honey will still help somewhat." Harry's face grew somber. "Maeve told her before that only the person who needs the healing or someone who loves that person can thank the bees."

I'm certain my eyes flared purple as I realized what Harry implied. The mere mention of Ric a few minutes earlier had wedged him between us again. I felt guilty for feeling that I qualified. "I'll be sincere and hope for the best with the bees."

"Don't worry. I'm certain the bees will hum beautifully for you."

His quiet voice reminded me again that he has never felt truly certain of my heart of hearts since that time so many years ago when I found comfort in another man's arms and heart. After being told that Harry was dead, I had turned to Ric.

"Harry, please. Then you thank the bees. You saved his life. That should count for something with the damn bees." My voice faltered.

"Don't insult them or they won't help no matter how much you, uh, care for the good Inspector Kramer. They may have scouts sucking nectar from the petunias, checking you out." Harry waved his hand toward the window box where a bee busily visited each bloom.

My husband's mood shifted as quickly as a stray cloud across a beaming sun. His mood swings had swelled and crested about eighteen months after his "return from the grave." The doctors had warned me and his family that his mind was trying to balance itself from the horror he'd been through after a South American gang he was trying to break kidnapped him. Harry had lived a different life before our marriage; a life I didn't suspect until he disappeared on a "business trip" to Rio de Janeiro.

I recognized this adjustment and decided not to belabor the point. "All right, then. Let's sneak past their sentry into the kitchen and put some lunch together for a picnic. I'd like to walk to the ruins you showed me last month."

"Excellent idea."

"What's an excellent idea?" Dorothy Marsden walked into the room from the kitchen.

"Good morning, Mum." Harry planted a dutiful kiss on his mother's cheek. Dorothy beamed at her son. She appeared to have grown more animated and younger with each passing day since our arrival. Her soft gray eyes gleamed and her gentle mouth seemed less pursed. Dorothy wore her silver hair in a soft chin-length bob. Even her hair shimmered as though lit from within with its own light source.

I knew my presence wasn't the cause of her metamorphosis. Harry's effect wasn't limited to his mother. William Marsden seemed to also have strengthened in his son's presence. William had suffered a heart attack several years earlier, when the erroneous news of his son's death had reached him. Each time we visited them since Harry's rescue, William had seemed buoyed by the time we spent with them. This visit had lasted much longer. I'm sure they felt as though their son had moved back home.

"Gracie and I are planning a walk to the ruins." He smiled at his mother. "First, we are planning to cop the Edam, sourdough, pickles, and a tiny bit of that sausage we bought in Bath. And some fruit. Those pears from the market. And the cherries. They were sweet. Anything for you?" He arched an eyebrow in my direction.

I laughed at his bill of fare. Harry could snack all day and never gain an ounce. I came from a corned beef and pasta genetic coupling. My mother's lean, Irish genes were most apparent in three of my brothers. My father's Morelli genes settled in me and my older brother Mike Jr. He looked exactly like our father. We always pushed away from the Morelli *tavola* well before our siblings Joseph, Glen, and Marty.

"I thought you'd want to enjoy the day outdoors so I had Mary pack a hamper for you. You'd best check if the pickles are in there." Dorothy's soft voice filled with warmth as her maternal instincts were satisfied.

Mary was a local lady who worked in the neighborhood for several older couples. She would come in and do housework and some cooking. She had been a godsend when William had first become ill.

"Pickles are gone. Ate the last one last night." William Marsden spoke from the front porch. Posed in front of the window box, he looked every inch the English Cottage Gardener. For the umpteenth time I wished for my camera.

Dorothy chided him. "Then you've eaten half a jar of pickles, William, 'cause that's what I put up after supper. Your blood pressure will be sky high and I won't be rushing you off to hospital when you faint away."

"Nonsense, I'm fit. I have this minute returned from a brisk walk into town and back. I've been to the chemist. They've one of those blood pressure machines. Took my turn. 132 over 80. Shows what you know."

He certainly did look fit. William Marsden, at seventy something, looked like an older version of Harry, or rather, Harry a younger version of William. He was not quite as tall as his son, but every bit as ramrod straight. At his age, his build was trim and his bright blue eyes as clear as a mountain stream. I smiled as I recognized Harry thirty-odd years from now.

"Sorry, son. I left those olives Hannah always sends. Don't care for them, myself. Don't know why she keeps sending them."

"I'd best check to see what else you've devoured. Your appetite hasn't been this hearty in years. I'll have to remind Mary to buy an extra hen for tonight's supper." Dorothy finished her sentence more to herself as she bustled into the kitchen.

"Your mother loves fussing over the two of you. She's planning some sort of dinner tomorrow night for the only people left in Arundel who haven't met you, Grace." William stepped into the room and removed his lightweight fedora. His close-cropped gray hair bore the slight indentation of his hatband. He ran his hand over his hair. "Come to think, that dinner is a surprise. Your mother will have my hide if she finds out I let it slip. Be surprised when she tells you. There's a good pair. I'd best be back to my chores." He smiled as he turned to leave.

William's chores, I had discovered, consisted of walking their Yorkie, Duncan, and puttering in his vegetable garden. I vowed to follow him around and take pictures of his garden. My dad planted a garden every year. I'd have to show him people plant things other than tomatoes, bell peppers, Melrose peppers, sport peppers, zucchini, and eggplant.

A thought occurred to me. "You haven't told them we're leaving, have you?"

"Not yet. I didn't want to spoil the fun they're having fussing over us. I was going to try to tell them tonight."

"Try to tell them? We're leaving in three days, Harry. I thought I was the last to know."

"I've had a hell of a time telling anyone. I knew you'd be nervous about going home and I knew they'd be disappointed that we're leaving. We have to go home."

It almost sounded like a question. I shook my head in resignation. "Yes, we have to go home. We'll tell them tonight after supper, but before your mom starts playing the piano and we all start singing. I couldn't do it then."

"Agreed." Harry put his arms around me and rested his chin on top of my head. I snuggled into his arms.

A good man indeed.

A loud crash from the kitchen broke the mood and our embrace.

TWO

"NAUGHTY, NASTY BOY!" Dorothy Marsden admonished the rotund Arlo, swiping at the spot he'd recently occupied with a flyswatter. Arlo's timed retreat from the tabletop to under the potato bin where Dorothy couldn't reach him was not rushed. The imperturbable orange short hair never scampered. His dignified escape lacked decorum as a length of sausage hanging from his furry mouth muffled his loud chirp of accomplishment. "Nasty old thing. I don't know why William tolerates his tomfoolery. Never see Annabelle or Star causing mischief."

Harry and I stood in the doorway of the kitchen. The room, generous by Arundel cottage standards but tiny by comparison to the kitchen I barely used in Pine Marsh, gleamed spotless in the morning light. I marveled at all the delicious dinners and scrumptious baking Mary and Dorothy produced in this tiny space. The oversized wooden farmer's table dominating the room served as prep area and staging area for all the meals served from this kitchen. The wooden expanse, usually scrubbed to a pine shine, looked like an unscheduled dinner prep was underway.

Dorothy turned to face us after realizing she couldn't reach the triumphant tomcat even with the aid of the swatter. "That animal is exasperating. Your father knows he's a trouble-maker, but he insists on letting him have the run of the house. Why do I put up with him?"

"Arlo or Dad, Mum?" Harry's question caught Dorothy off guard and she narrowed her gray eyes before she answered.

"Don't make me choose, not right this moment."

Harry and I burst into laughter. Dorothy couldn't stay angry long; it wasn't in her nature. She laughed with us and moved to clean up the mess *William's* cat had made.

"Let me get those." I stooped down and retrieved the scattered fruit from under the table, careful to avoid the shards of crockery smashed on the floor. I collected apples, pears, and a kiwi and placed them in the sink to be washed. Harry brought out the broom and dustpan and swept up the broken crockery.

"Harry dear, dump that under the downspout at the corner please." Dorothy indicated out the back door. "We're trying to keep the puddles away from the foundation. Since your father lured that awful animal home last year, we've been adding to the pile on a regular basis."

Her comment caused another round of laughter. "You won't be laughing when you see what's left of your lunch."

Dorothy pointed to the overturned straw hamper on the table. The basket, similar to the ones I'd purchased for my sisters-in-law for Christmas presents, lay on its side with the contents mindlessly pulled from the interior. Arlo had shredded the wrapper on the cheese. The olives, ripped from their plastic wrap, lay strewn on the table unappetizingly coated with orange fur. A few pieces of fruit were deemed eatable; the rest traveled to the compost bucket under the sink.

"There's still plenty, Mum. Don't worry, we won't starve," Harry assured his mother. She seemed appeased. I thought the fare looked a little skimpy for two appetites, but then I always ate more than my husband.

After we had been married a short time Harry had announced to my dad, *I'd rather clothe her than feed her, Mike.*

In retaliation I had asked Karen, my best friend, to take me shopping; a dream come true for my 5'10" pal with great fashion sense who had been itching to outfit me for all the years we'd been friends. There had been no comment when

I handed Harry the receipts from Nordstrom and Saks. He still refers to that spree as the day Oak Brook Mall declared Gracie Marsden Day and established a shopping scholarship in my name.

"Plenty," I echoed. I'd eat my sandal strap before I admitted there wasn't enough for me. When Dorothy turned away from the table to ask Harry when we planned to return, I surreptitiously stuffed two breakfast rolls from a basket on the sideboard into the picnic basket. Harry spotted my sleight of hand and grinned.

"We'll be back around three; will we be in time for tea?" Since Harry's return he'd fallen comfortably into his old habit of afternoon tea. It was a lovely custom, giving everyone an opportunity to relax and catch up with each other. The Marsdens had been dears to stock their pantry with coffee for me. They unboxed a relic of a percolator from the fifties, when post-war American influenced a trend. It worked beautifully. I remembered a similar one that my dad used when I was young.

"Of course, dear. We'll wait tea for you and Grace." Dorothy beamed at her son. I hated the thought that we would shatter her happiness later this evening. *She knew we couldn't stay here forever. We have a life across the pond. We have problems to work out back home.* I shook my head slightly to stop the thoughts.

Harry noticed my movement. "All set, love?"

"Yes." I smiled at him. "All set."

"Excellent. Then we're off." He lifted two lightweight slickers from the peg near the back door. "Might sprinkle." He held one out to me and draped the other over his arm. I dutifully took my "second skin" and slipped a water bottle holder over my shoulder. Our basket held a tasty Riesling, but I wanted to chug not sip when I became thirsty.

"Oh, wait. I want to get my camera. I'll be right back." I

hurried through the living room to the back hall and up the stairs. I swooped into our room and stopped in my tracks. There on our bed lay a resplendent, snoozing Arlo flanked by Annabelle and Star. Apparently William's tomcat didn't repulse Dorothy's two calico ladies. My camera lay under Arlo's sizable head, being used as a pillow of sorts. This would make a great picture. Not to be. I quietly approached the bed. Star lifted her head and meowed hello. Arlo's eyelids opened cautiously. Two tawny eyes apprised me. I moved closer and explained my situation.

"Arlo, I need to take my camera. Nice kitty boy, let me get this hard lumpy camera out from under your head." I'm not sure why I talked to the orange mound except that the two girls had been extremely friendly toward me even spending some nights on the bed while we slept. Arlo had shown no signs of liking me.

"Gracie. What's the hold up?"

Arlo's head snapped up at Harry's voice. "Okay, Arlo. You heard him. He'll be up here any minute." Arlo stood and stretched insufferably long, never moving from his spot. A second before Harry appeared in the doorway the cat lumbered to the edge of the bed and plopped to the carpet. He brushed against Harry's leg as he left the room.

"Hullo, big boy. So here's where you've gone off to." Harry looked at the two remaining felines. "Can't blame you, old boy," he called after the retreating tomcat. "C'mon Gracie, no time to play with the cats now." Harry walked to the bed, patted each calico, and picked up the camera. I followed him down the stairs hoping the rest of the morning would be normal.

IDYLLIC, MORE LIKE IT. The well-worn footpath we traveled led us through meadows teeming with wildflowers blooming with abandon. I recognized the small, white flowers of feverfew and marguerite, and the bright purple and pink of dame's rocket, although those weren't their English names. Harry identified all of the flowers and pronounced their botanical names.

"Did your firm publish a book on wildflowers once? Where did you learn all this? And why do the English have different names for everything? Seems snobby of them to change our names."

Harry smiled at what he referred to as my American view of the world. "Could it be possible that those pesky colonists changed the names? Did you ever think of that possibility?"

I hadn't. "If they did, it makes perfect sense. Why would anyone call something as pretty as a Christmas Rose, Hellebores?" I smirked and crossed my arms in a position of *case closed*.

Harry laughed and threw his head back, shouting up to the skies, "I love this nutcase, Grace Elena Morelli Marsden."

Idyllic indeed.

THE TIME FLEW by and we found ourselves back at the cottage shortly after three o'clock, scurrying in the back door like a pair of truant children. Our intention was to freshen up in our room before tea.

"My sister is here," Harry said, pointing to a travel bag on the floor next to the table. It was indeed Hannah Marsden's travel bag; a gift from us last Christmas. We burst into the living room expecting to hear chatter and laughter. The scene was not at all what we expected.

Dorothy and William Marsden sat side by side on the burgundy and tan striped sofa while their daughter sat opposite them in one of the taupe-hued wingback chairs. The silence and serious faces frightened me. Harry spoke first.

"Hanns, what are you doing here? It's great to see you,

isn't it Mum, Dad?" Harry looked from face to face waiting for someone to say something.

"What's wrong, Hannah? Is it my dad?"

Hannah reacted then. "Oh, no. Everyone is fine. Sorry, didn't mean to give you a fright." Hannah looked at her parents, oddly quiet across the room. Dorothy should have been fussing around her daughter. They looked sad instead of elated at her arrival.

"I didn't know they didn't know you were leaving tomorrow after next. I wanted to get to you before you went home. Didn't mean to jinx your timing."

"Not your fault, Hanns." Harry moved toward his parents. He sat down in the other wingback chair. "I didn't know how to tell you, Mum. Grace and I owe you so much for taking us in. I felt like we were betraying you by leaving."

"Tish. Owe your parents for taking you in? Is that the nonsense they teach in America?" William's voice sounded husky with emotion. Dorothy's eyes welled up with tears.

Her voice trembled a little. "We knew you'd have to go back. We didn't want to face that time. It's been grand having you here. It's wonderful that Hannah has come visiting, too. I can't remember the last time you were both at home." She paused; her face lost some color as she probably did remember the last time her children were under her roof. It had been during Harry's convalescence. She seemed to push the memory from her mind and turned her face to Hannah. "Come along, Hannah, help me with tea. Goodness, look at the time." Dorothy stood up and motioned her daughter toward the kitchen. "William, Duncan needs his afternoon walk. Oh, Harry dear, will you nip upstairs with your sister's bag?"

Everyone had their assignment. Except me.

I saw the look exchanged between brother and sister. I

knew Hannah well enough to realize that she wanted to talk to Harry alone.

"Dorothy, let me help you, and Hannah can settle in before tea." I smiled at Hannah. She understood my ploy.

"Thank you, dear. How thoughtful. Actually tea is no bother but my mum always said, 'Tea made by two is twice blessed for the rest.' Come along, then."

Now I knew why Harry came up with what I called "britcoms," anecdotal phrases with a British flavor.

Hannah and Harry were up the stairs before I walked through the kitchen door. I wished I could be a fly on the wall, but I knew Harry would fill me in later. I hated waiting until later.

My curiosity was bursting when ten minutes later the family gathered in the living room. Dorothy carefully poured each of us a cup of tea. It was a pleasant ritual, anticipating the taste of the delicious aroma wafting from the ceramic spout as it released its brew *du jour*. The filling of Dorothy's cup signaled us to begin. Harry and Hannah stayed too quiet for my taste; something was wrong. I was dying to ask but I knew better. Dorothy apparently didn't notice their changed demeanor as she regaled Hannah with all the news of the district, news that would have been in her next letter.

I had already heard the update. My mind wandered to what news Hannah could have shared with Harry. I tried to catch his eye but he avoided looking in my direction. Usually, teatime with the Marsdens was fun for me; reminiscent of English Country House mysteries I'd read. I could imagine myself a great niece of Miss Marple, visiting St. Mary Mead. Today, I could hardly wait for teatime to be over. I sat staring off into space, idly twirling a lock of my shoulder-length hair around my finger.

My twirling, twisting and braiding had started in childhood. A diagnosis of Obsessive Compulsive Disorder at least identified my dysfunction and allowed my family to find a way to live with my quirks. I usually kept a length of yarn with me at all times, but hair would do in a pinch.

Harry's first words since he sat down prompted a small yelp from me. I jerked my hand down forgetting it still held my hair. My surprise was genuine.

"What did you say?"

His face showed no emotion.

"We're leaving in the morning. Our flight leaves from Gatwick at ten o'clock."

Dorothy and William looked crestfallen. First, they thought they had two days left with their son; now he would be snatched away after only a few more hours. I felt sorry for them. A lump formed in my throat. I hated to see them upset; such sweet, wonderful people. My father-in-law's brave voice interrupted my thoughts.

"I guess our girl brought you some news. You do what's best, son." William reached out a hand and placed it on Harry's shoulder, giving his approval. Dorothy's reaction was another thing. She looked miffed. I remembered what William had let slip earlier, the party she had planned.

"Harry, couldn't we put it off one more day? I mean, we're visiting the bees and all tomorrow and we'd still be home one day earlier than planned. We could be all packed and ready to leave first thing."

Harry's face clouded over at my suggestion but then lifted as he too must have remembered his dad's comment. He looked at Hannah. She shrugged her shoulders. Harry looked at his mother's hopeful face and made his decision. "One more day won't change much back home." He lifted his hands, palms up, in a sign of compliance.

Change much? What changed? If someone wasn't dead or dying, how much could have changed?

"WILLIAM, WHERE'S HARRY?"

I had helped Dorothy and Hannah carry the cups and saucers into the kitchen. I fully intended on getting the whole story out of Harry as soon as we were alone.

"He's making a quick run to town to pick up a few items for me. Good lad."

Good lad, my foot! He ducked out on me. I still have Hannah. I thanked William and went back to the kitchen.

Déjà vu.

"Dorothy, where's Hannah?"

"She's gone into town to look up a friend. Likes to keep in touch when she can."

I was a victim of the Katzenjammer Twins. I wondered how many times they had pulled this stunt or a variation on their parents and friends. I underestimated the "twin factor," as their friends called it; a natural plotting mechanism perfected by twins. Harry had the Marsdens' car and Hannah had her rental. Which left me on foot.

Wait a minute.

"Dorothy, may I borrow your bicycle? I'd love a ride. It's such a lovely day."

"Of course, dear. It's right out back."

Three could play at this game. I shot out the back door of the kitchen and stopped short. Dorothy had gone on and on about her trusty Schwinn that Harry had sent one year for her birthday. I assumed a top-of-the-line ten-speed. A light green, no-speed bike leaned up against the chestnut tree in the backyard. *Geez. Which birthday was it?*

I gritted my teeth and silently apologized for my thoughts. I hopped on and wobbled out of the yard. Down to the lane I rolled, frantically squeezing the handlebars as I approached the stone pillar at their entrance until I realized I needed to backpedal to stop.

It's a bike, for pity's sake, not an eighteen-wheeler. Relax. You had one of these when you were ten.

I pulled out into the lane. *Oh, darn. They drive on the wrong side. Bikes go the same way.* I moved to the left side of the road, certain that each revolution of the tires brought me closer to a head-on collision with the one tourist that didn't get it.

After a white-knuckle kilometer, I relaxed and began to enjoy the fields of recently mowed and rolled hay, the rill running parallel to the road with its sluice gate raised, and the mounds of wild Marguerite as I pedaled by on my green traveling machine. I actually felt giddy with excitement at my plan to catch those two in a conspiratorial huddle. I spotted their cars in front of the local pub, The Sword and Goatherd. I knew they'd be in there sipping warm beers and smiling about giving me the slip. The pub, a two-story limestone building with a whitewash veneer around the concrete sills and door lintels, had been listed in the county registry since the year 1798.

I hadn't thought of what to do with Dorothy's bike once I arrived at my destination. I didn't have a chain or lock. *Grace, this is Arundel not Naperville.* I guided the bike into an open space in the bike rack out front and entered.

It took a moment for my eyes to adjust to the low lighting and haze of pub smoke. The Sword and Goatherd boasted an outside wall and partial cellar that predated the Crusades. This part of the establishment sported the usual pub amenities. A long bar ran the width of the room on the inside wall. Regulars occupied almost every stool, the friendly bantering of lifelong friends and habits filling the room. Tables lined the opposite wall under the three mullioned windows which were minimally effective since heavy vines covered the outside like a blind allowing only a hint of light to penetrate. Along the

back wall near the hearth and fireplace I spotted two familiar heads. They were both half-turned away from the front.

Perfect.

"The house is rebuilt—it's fabulous. It would be ridiculous
for you and Grace to move," is what I heard as I approached.

"Why would we move?" They both craned their necks
around so fast I think I heard a *pop*. I smiled sweetly.

"Gracie, I, we, uh, here, darling." Harry recovered, and
he stood quickly to give me his seat. "Sit down. What would
you like to drink?"

"One of those lovely rum drinks would be wonderful." I
smiled up at my confused-looking husband.

Hannah looked as confused. "Grace, how did you, uh,
how are you?"

"You forgot the bike." I grinned at her expression.

Harry placed my drink in front of me and sat down. "She
took Mum's bike." The twins burst out laughing.

"I should have known."

"I wouldn't have had to bounce along that country road if
you two had leveled with me."

"Sorry, darling. Old habit."

"Fine. I'll give you that 'twin thing,' but why would we
move?"

Hannah and Harry looked at each other. Hannah's glance
slid away and refocused on the dart game in progress a few
feet away. Two opponents balanced pints of ale, feathered
missiles, and a running commentary on each other's ability.

"Now, once again, why would we move?"

Harry looked toward Hannah who hadn't turned away
from the dart game, but seemed to have us in her peripheral
vision. He turned back to face me and reached across the
table to take my hands.

Oh, Lord. How bad could this be?

"You're scaring me. What's going on? Why did Hannah have to tell you in person?"

He released my hand and gulped his scotch. "Gracie, there is no easy way to tell you." He paused for another swig and realized he had drained his drink. He looked frantic for another scotch. Hannah turned to the table.

"I'm going up. Can I get anyone a refill?" Harry shot her a grateful look. She seemed more relieved to get away than pleased to serve.

"Ric Kramer moved in with Lily."

I stared at his mouth trying to see the words that had escaped in that burst of a sentence, because I couldn't believe the ones I'd heard. The man whom I became involved with when I thought Harry had been killed, had taken up residence, a scant one half mile from our home, with the woman whom Harry had been in a relationship with before he met me. My silence signaled more explanation.

"I guess Lily felt some guilt about Ben and her father. She talked to Karen a few times and found out that Ric was in rehab at Marionjoy. Karen told her about his difficulty in getting to and from his appointments. So..." Harry stopped and gratefully accepted the drink Hannah placed in front of him. She sat down facing us apparently ready to join us now that the news was out.

Yes, I was surprised to hear about Ric. Yes, I hoped that Harry's gorgeous ex-lover would have moved out of Pine Marsh. Yes, somewhere in my woman's heart of hearts I felt a twinge of jealousy that he had found someone. I mean, Ric never went for long without a beautiful woman on his arm but he had never moved in with one or allowed one to move into his Oak Park brownstone.

"Okay, so Lily is a Good Samaritan and housing Ric for his convenience while he's rehabbing. The house has several bedrooms." After I spoke, I realized how petty that sounded.

"Apparently it's working out better than that." Harry paused to choose his words. I knew he did that when he didn't relish what he had to say.

Good grief, could he be upset about Lily taking in Ric? Harry never forgave him for falling in love with me. Was he upset with him now for taking up with Lily? Upset with Lily? For turning to Ric—like I had?

I remained silent.

"Ric finished his rehab weeks ago. He and Lily have a deeper interest in each other. He's moved in with her on a permanent basis."

Hannah hurried to fill in more details. "Ric is selling his share of the brownstone to me and Karen. We're redoing his apartments into office and meeting rooms. I'm moving my business to the States."

"Hanns, you didn't tell me that."

"Sorry, chap. Was about to before Gracie came in. That's another reason I wanted to do this in person. Mum and Dad say they don't see me enough the months I'm in London. I haven't told them I'm giving up my flat and moving to Oak Park."

Hannah Marsden appeared wistful in that moment. I knew she had always carried the responsibility of being the child that stayed *home.* Now she'd have to tell her parents that she was leaving even though she'd been living in London for years and traveling to the States more frequently since she'd met Karen.

"Anything else you wanted to tell me." Harry arched one eyebrow at his sister. A mirror image shot back at him.

"Good God, isn't that enough?"

"Quite."

I didn't know what to say. I couldn't think beyond the old Western cliché, *this town ain't big enough for the two of us,* make that the four of us. The paper coaster under my drink had disappeared into my hands during Harry's explanation. It reappeared as bits of white confetti on the table.

Harry put his left hand over mine and tipped up my chin with his other hand. "That's why we should consider moving. I can't live that close to Kramer." Harry kept my chin up so he could look into my eyes. "And it's not because he's with Lily. That was over and it will stay that way. I believe Kramer is using Lily to get closer to you. I don't know what I'd do, Grace, if he tried to come between us."

The word *again* went unspoken, but was as clear as if he had shouted.

Harry grew agitated. The worst was over. Why wasn't he calming down? He knocked over his drink when he pulled back his hand. I sopped up liquid with my shredded coaster. Hannah's napkin was more effective. *Harry doesn't easily frazzle. Not this easily. Something's not right.* I looked from one set of cornflower-blue eyes to another. *Oh, yes. There's more.*

"What else?"

Hannah started to rise to replenish the spilled drink. She seemed to prefer the role of barmaid today. I touched her arm.

"Stay. You brought this news; maybe you can tell it easier."

Hannah sat back down and nodded her head. "Lily has a child."

"Lily's having a baby?" I interrupted, looking from face to face. *A baby. That explains all this.* "Ric got her pregnant?"

"Grace, listen to me." Hannah's voice broke into my thoughts. "I said Lily has a child, a boy."

"Look, I may not have majored in science but even I know it takes nine months and Ric's only known her for six." My jovial comment crumbled like a three-legged stool with the wobbles as I understood.

Words of a madman during his attempt to kill me came

back to me with startling clarity, *They belong together; a bond you might say.*

I turned my eyes to my husband. His face told me what I already knew; I asked anyway.

"How old?"

"He's ten."

THREE

My CHIN SLUMPED to my chest. Wings of thick brown hair swept down each side of my face like curtains closing across a darkened stage.

"Gracie?" Harry's voice came low, and close. I could sense his movement across the table to lean near me. The scotch on his breath reached my nostrils. His hand rested on my shoulder.

I heard the scrape of his chair and realized he was getting up. "Let's get out of here, Grace. C'mon. I'll help you out." Without lifting his hand from my shoulder he moved out of his chair and squatted down next to me.

I knew I had to lift my head and look at him. I didn't want to. My whole world with Harry had shifted precariously near to shattering. We couldn't have children because of injuries Harry suffered years before at the hands of his kidnappers. We had accepted that circumstance; had talked recently of overseas adoption.

Now he had a child. A son with Lily.

"Why didn't you know?" I spoke into my chest.

"I stopped seeing Lily the month after I met you at Regina. We were moving in opposite directions in our lives. She left for New York. I never knew. I'm not accepting this claim at face value. I've a call-in to David. He'll sort this out. I've not seen documents, blood tests, anything."

I slowly raised my head. Tears slipped from the corners of my eyes creating paths down my cheeks. "Is there a chance he isn't your son? Why would she lie about it? Why didn't she tell you when she first saw you?"

"Grace, slow down. I don't know any more than you do. I'm not committing to anything until I see proof."

Hannah cleared her throat. I'd forgotten about her. She reached into her bag and pulled out an envelope. "I hadn't a chance to give you this before Gracie arrived." She slid the pale yellow envelope toward Harry.

I recognized the design on the back flap—Lily's wildly popular stationery, "Wee Uns." A panda cub snoozed, his head resting on oversized paws.

Harry's hand trembled slightly as he slipped his thumb inside the flap to slide out the contents. He held the photo still and stared at it until his vision must have blurred from the tears that filled his eyes. He brushed at his eyes with his left hand and carefully turned the photograph toward me.

I've seen this before. What's Hannah trying to pull? Harry at age six, astride a pony. Proper riding breeches, jacket, his head thrown back in laughter. The photo is on Dorothy's piano.

Something's different. Color. This one's in color.

"Oh, God," my voice barely above a whisper. I looked at Harry. He had turned the photo so he could still see the little blond-haired boy laughing into the camera. An expression I'd seen before moved across Harry's face like sunrise rolling over the landscape touching every corner. First his mouth lifting slightly at the corners to reveal a grin, then his cheekbones rising with the impetus from his lips and finally his eyes widening and reflecting the joy in his soul.

Unconditional love; offered to a select few. Our circle had expanded to include the sunny child in the photo. Now the need was Harry's. A child, a son. I turned over the photo and read the inscription out loud, "Will at Brighton."

"His name is Nicholas William, but he goes by Will."

We both turned our eyes from the photo to stare at Hannah.

THE MOVEMENT OF the 747 on its descent pattern to Boston's Logan Airport nudged me from borderline snoozing to fully awake. In the few seconds that transition took, my brain leaped from happy to be coming home to remembering why I didn't want the metal behemoth to land.

Harry and Hannah decided to wait until after the dinner party to talk to their parents. The party was lovely. I don't think any of the guests noticed how edgy the Marsden siblings acted. To the casual observer they were charming and attentive to their guests. I braided, knotted, or shredded anything that caught my eye or touched my itchy fingers. I'm certain my marks for the evening weren't that high; one of those "colonists" with minimal manners.

Our behavior had not gone unnoticed by Harry's parents. Before the last guest reached the lane, Dorothy had caught each of her children with a foot-tapping, "don't you fib to me," arms-crossed-on-her-chest look.

In that moment my throat tightened as I realized it mirrored the exact stance I'd seen my mother take a hundred times with my brothers. Well, maybe me too, now and then; usually because of one brother or the other. I swallowed hard to break the lump forming in my throat; even five years after her death, the lump in my heart never lessened.

The double-barrel news of Hannah's moving and Harry's son had devastated and elated the elder Marsdens. Harry and Hannah had taken an hour to explain. If they thought their parents would toddle off to bed after the bombshells they dropped, they were so wrong. I excused myself at midnight. They must have stayed up until at least two in the morning because that's the last time I looked at the clock on the nightstand before sleep overtook me.

Harry touched my arm as the plane landed. "No sense rushing off," he said. We sat quietly amid a stream of hurrying humanity. People jostling each other, bumping elbows, banging overhead bins shut, dragging oversized luggage up the aisle to the exit. We had a two-hour layover in Boston before United Airlines would deliver us to O'Hare. That would give us enough time to go through customs here and find our new gate. My brother Mike had volunteered to meet us. I knew my family; I'm sure a welcome-home party lurked somewhere in their plans.

Normally, it would be wonderful to see everyone I'd missed all summer. But nothing would be normal anymore. I looked up to find the plane almost empty, the last few scurrying travelers moving toward the flight attendant for their final "bye-bye." We pulled carry-on luggage from the overhead and deplaned.

We left the plane in search of bathrooms. When I came out of the crowded ladies' room Harry stood at one of the food kiosks. I accepted the cup of coffee and pulled some napkins out of the container. We moved to a table several feet away; one of those high tables, bar height, no stools. Standing felt good after seven hours of sitting.

We tapped our paper cups in a mock toast. "Almost home," Harry said.

"Almost home," I echoed. "Let's not tell my family about the...I mean your...about him. The last thing they knew, we were looking into adopting a little girl from Eastern Europe. Karen and Hannah have already made their appointment to be interviewed. I thought we'd be doing the same. I hoped we could bring our daughter home for Christmas."

"Darling, I'm not saying we won't. I need time to sort this out. We shouldn't be rushing off to adopt a child when we haven't even met the one we already have."

"You have," I interrupted.

"Gracie, if he's my son, he's our son. It won't be any other way."

I drained my coffee to avoid answering and then stuffed my napkin into the empty cup. "We'd better get to customs." I moved slowly, short and stiff, like I had to conserve my strength to keep the scream building inside me from bursting out.

Harry tried to take the cup from my clenched fist to throw it away. He gently closed his hand over mine and finally won the cup's release. He must have sensed how close I was to snapping. He didn't try to soothe me; instead he turned in the direction we needed to go. I followed.

Dammit, Grace. Be there for him. This is tearing him apart too. Remember the shock when the family learned that Joe had a daughter. We didn't stop to ask questions, point fingers. We scooped up Jolene and loved her with all our collective hearts. Isn't this the same? We don't know, but we'll love him. I'll love him. He's Harry's; how could I not love him? But Lily. She'll always be his mother, always be there.

I went through customs on automatic. The short line allowed us to be checked, stamped, and approved more quickly than we had planned.

"If I needed to get through that line quickly it wouldn't have happened." Harry picked up my carry-on and swung it onto his left shoulder. "Let's head for our gate and wait there. I'll track down some snacks for us."

Our gate was, of course, the farthest away. "I'll take my bag. It's not like we're skipping cross the hall." Harry relinquished the leather tote and took the lead toward Gate 26. Somewhere around Gate 22 I became aware of a figure waving from across the carpeted gate area. She moved toward us at a fast familiar pace.

"Karen? What are you doing here?" My best friend, Karen Kramer, rushed over to us. "What's wrong?"

"Nothing's wrong. You have got to get some help with that Italian dark side of yours. Can't a friend meet friends?"

Harry and I both fixed her with a "yeah, right" look. Harry spoke first. "Hanns isn't on this flight, but you knew that. So...?" He left his question hanging.

"All right. I wanted to come ahead to let you know that everyone knows."

"Everyone knows?"

"She means, the 'Barnum and Morelli' circus is forming, the vultures are circling, there's no turning back, the world will never be the same, they *know*."

I couldn't have sounded more unhinged if I'd ranted about little green men. I must have looked as bad. Harry and Karen stared at me as if my outburst made me certifiable. Karen's slack jaw, openmouthed expression caused me to gingerly check my lips for foam.

I tried a small smile to let them know the crazy person they'd heard had left the building or at least, my body. "Sorry. I guess I overreacted."

"See. That's why I flew out to meet you. I know her, how she thinks, or doesn't sometimes, and I thought you deserved advanced warning."

"Karen, you are a gem." Harry squeezed her shoulders in a grateful hug. "We'd best board. You can fill us in during the flight."

With the flight to Chicago full, Karen's seat was nowhere near ours. Harry offered to change seats so Karen and I could talk.

"Okay, when you say everyone knows, how everyone are we talking?" I had become remarkably calm. The vodka tonic Harry had pressed into my hand as we boarded had some small part in my altered attitude. The tiny vodka bottles Karen had pulled from her carry-on finished the job.

Karen waited until I had poured another bottle of clear

liquid over the melting ice in my airport cup. "I may have exaggerated about *everyone* knowing; I don't think they telegrammed your father's family in Naples."

I burst into laughter and knew she was trying to help.

"Your father's great aunt, the one in Villa Scalabrini?"

"Zia Assunta? She knows? God, she's ninety-seven." I shook my head in amazement at the Morelli grapevine.

"She knows but she doesn't understand. She told your Aunt Edna to start cranking out the pizelles for the baby shower."

The hoot that escaped my lips caused heads to turn and the cabin attendant to look at me with concern. I smiled assuredly with what I hoped wasn't a lopsided grin.

"It's like when your niece Katie thought I was her aunt, too, because she always saw us together at your house."

I smiled as I remembered all the time Karen had spent at my house while we attended college. Her mother had died the summer before we met at Regina. The Morelli family had embraced her like one of their own.

"It's like we were sisters; the ones we never had."

I leaned toward Karen like only the tipsy can when they think they're telling a secret. "If Ric marries Lily then he'd be a step-dad and Harry would be related by marriage and Hannah would be an aunt and you'd be a step-aunt and we still wouldn't be sisters."

My face must have reflected my failure to plot a familial connection. Karen's outburst of laughter sent me into a fit of giggles that escalated into hiccups.

The plane touched down and the realization that I would be facing my family, reality, and a new life in a few minutes snapped the fuzzy edge right off my vodka high.

Once again, we waited until most of the passengers had deplaned, leaving the aisles easier to travel.

I spotted Mike immediately. My sister-in-law, Carolyn, and Marty's daughter, Katie, stood next to him. How much

I'd missed my family became apparent as tears sprang to my eyes. Thoughts of ever living anywhere else evaporated like July rain on Chicago asphalt.

Mike hugged me, especially robustly it seemed, probably trying to reinforce me for what lay ahead. I kissed Carolyn and Katie and kept my arm around my niece's shoulder. I looked past them into the crowd.

"Just us, kiddo. You were expecting a band?" Mike laughed at his own joke.

"Just cousin Lou with his concertina. I thought Dad would be here."

"He wanted to come but he had too much to do for your party."

"Party?"

Harry and I echoed the question.

"Oh, yeah, Aunt Grace. Grandpa has been cooking for days. Everybody's coming." Katie's eyes gleamed with anticipation. "Dad and Uncle Glen are putting up a tent, the boys are in charge of the karaoke, and Chris is bringing his garage band, *None of the Above,* to play."

The boys were Mike and Carolyn's sons, Jeff and Joe. Chris was Lou's son. He played keyboard in a garage band with three friends from high school. I think Katie's interest extended beyond their style of music and directly to the blond lead guitarist.

"Sounds great," I said with some enthusiasm, not wanting to disappoint the look on her face. My stomach churned; the vodka trying to retrace its recent path. I grabbed Karen by the hand. "Where's the closest bathroom? You're in the airport all the time."

"This way. C'mon." Karen tugged me toward the bathroom. "We'll meet you at the luggage carousel," she called over her shoulder.

Throwing up always made me feel better. This time was

no exception. I splashed cold water on my face while Karen rolled down paper towels for me. She wet several, squeezed out the excess water, and clamped them on the back of my neck. I shivered and shrugged out from under them.

"I threw up; I didn't faint."

The lady at the next sink smirked at my comment, quickly dried her hands, and left.

Karen balled up the wet towels and tossed them into the receptacle. "Two points!" She rolled down a few more towels. "Gracie, you have to get over this. Your entire family is waiting under a tent in your dad's backyard. The guest list is boundless."

"You're enjoying this, aren't you?" I questioned her mirror image. She moved next to me and put her arms around my shoulders. Her eyes reflected in the glass filled with warmth.

"You can do this. They want to be there for you, to let you know they love you no matter what. So what if everyone knows about the boy? It's in the open and over with."

"Will."

"Will what?" Karen's eyebrows lifted.

"His name. The boy's name is Will."

"Oh. Okay. Let's get out there. You and Harry can stay for an hour or so and then plead exhaustion. I arranged for your cousin Nick to drive you home when you give him the signal."

I turned and hugged Karen. "Okay, let's do it." I let go of her and straightened up to my full 5'4" stature and moved toward the door. Almost at the door I spotted the double switch plate on the wall. *Oh, no. Not now. Fifty? No. Ten. I'll do ten. Okay, twenty. Only twenty.*

Karen recognized the silent struggle I held with myself. She had seen enough of my OCD behaviors to know one at its onslaught. "I'll get the door."

Karen stood outside ready to direct people elsewhere. She waited as I clicked the lights on and off twenty times counting, *one, one thousand, two, one thousand,* in my head between clicks. I sheepishly opened the door when I finished. "Sorry."

Karen took my arm and we walked down to the luggage area. "Don't be silly. Remember sophomore year when I stood outside the john on the fourth floor of Power Hall so you could tap dance across the tiled floor because the acoustics were 'perfect'? That was dicey. This is a piece of cake."

"Did I ever thank you for that?"

"Probably, or not. Who's keeping count, anyway?"

"Not me." I grinned and squeezed her arm.

We rounded the corner and spotted the pack mules. Mike and Harry worked at stacking suitcases, boxes, and garment bags on two airport handcarts. A summer abroad could add up to a lot of stuff, especially since we had arrived in England with practically nothing in tow. No longer true.

I walked over to the convoy and picked up a small box tied with twine and looped to a plastic handle.

"Gee, thanks, Sis. That makes all the difference."

I smiled at my brother and heard giggles from Katie.

Harry laughed and told Mike, "I don't think we'll get all this in one vehicle. Did you and Carolyn drive separate cars by any chance?"

"No, we didn't, but I know my sister and I borrowed my neighbor's Suburban. We'll fit fine. If not, Gracie can ride on the roof rack."

I responded like the bratty little sister of long ago. "I'll tell Dad."

"Who do you think suggested that seating arrangement?"

We laughed at Mike's quick wit and left the airport in fine humor. The thirty-minute drive from O'Hare to Berkeley would give me scant time to prepare for the questions, stares, hushed voices, pitying glances, and quick whispers waiting for me.

FOUR

THE BILLOWING STRIPED tent visible from a block away announced the event. The pulsating bass audible from half that distance engulfed the van like a beam pulling us closer. *Celebration time, come on, boom, boom, boom.*

The words were clear as we parked in a spot obviously left open for us since cars were already three deep on the dead-end street between my dad's house and the Byrds' house. My brother hadn't called from the car so either an advance scout, in the form of some cousin loitering in a bush at the corner of Taft and Bohlander or the Chopper Five News, was in on it. I prayed it was the cousin.

"She's here, she's here," the cry went up. People rushed from the house, from the backyard, even from next door where some of the overflow guests chatted with the Shedd family. In one surreal moment I envisioned the stampede of familial enthusiasm causing a shift in the earth by their sudden and pointed movement.

Real time kicked in and I leaped forward to hug my dad.

"Welcome home, honey. I missed you."

"Thanks, Dad. I missed you, too. I know I stayed too long."

"You did what you had to do and now you're home." I stayed in my dad's embrace, feeling the unconditional love that had always sustained me. I watched family and friends edging closer, waiting for their cue.

"I'd better let you say hello. I don't know how much longer I can hog my little girl."

"'Til the cows come home." I smiled and took a deep breath. I grinned, raised my hand and said, "Hi."

I tried to relax while moving among my friends and family, hugging and kissing my way to the house. Somewhere between the sidewalk and the front porch a glass of wine materialized in my hand. I briefly wished that Scotty from the *Enterprise* would *beam me up.* Instead, I allowed myself to be led around the far side of the house.

The backyard stood transformed; I stood transfixed. Yards of purple and yellow striped canvas rose above groupings of white tables and chairs. A dozen aluminum poles held up the canopy at the corners and sides around a large center post that looked like a mast. A striped pouch, filled with purple shades of lobelia, wave petunias, and alyssum hung from each corner. Each table center held a cachepot filled with pansies.

My father moved next to me as I took in the view. I linked my arm in his. "Dad, it's fabulous. Thank you so much." I was in danger of bursting into tears.

"Okay, everybody. Time to eat." His strong voice turned the tide of people from me to the long table set up at the far end of the tent.

I looked around for Harry, realizing that I hadn't seen him since we left the peacefulness of the van. He stood near my dad's grape arbor talking to my brother, Joe. Rather more like Joe was talking to him. Harry's hands were stuffed into his pockets; his posture looked tense. Joe, who doesn't wear his Roman Catholic collar when he isn't on duty, placed his hand on Harry's shoulder while he spoke. I considered walking over; I hadn't yet greeted my oldest brother, but I suspected that Joe might be recounting his surprise at finding out years earlier that he had a ten-year-old child he'd never known about. I turned away from the scene and the thought. This was my party and I didn't want to think about Harry and Lily's son.

It's my party and I'll cry if I want to, cry if I want to, cry if I want to...ran through my head until I laughed out loud. I never even liked Leslie Gore.

"Happy to see your sense of humor is alive and well," Tracy said. She handed me a bottle of water and took my glass. "You need to hydrate. Karen told me what happened at the airport."

Tracy was the third side of the triangle from Regina College and an excellent nurse at Elmhurst Memorial Hospital. Every bit as tall as Karen's 5'10" and similar in body style, Tracy wore her light brown, blond-streaked hair long and curly. Her gray eyes scanned my face with professional concern.

"Drink. You look beat. Let's sit down under the big top. Better yet, let's go inside and you can be comfortable."

"I can't leave."

"Now that the eating lamp is lit no one will miss you." Tracy smiled at her evaluation. She'd been to enough Morelli parties to know the procedure. "We have at least until cake and coffee before anyone will come looking for you."

THE INSIDE OF my father's house was cool and quiet. We moved into the living room and sat side by side on the loveseat.

"Take another drink," she ordered. "I know all about the boy."

I looked at her about to ask and then shook my head. "Who doesn't know?"

Tracy smiled and patted my knee. "Gracie, you know your family. To them he's another child to cherish and raise in the tradition of the Morelli *Familia*. Your cousins are already setting up outings to Cubs games for him with the Fragasso, Scala, and Anderson kids. By the time your family is finished with him, he'll be more yours than hers. Not that it's a contest or anything," she added quickly.

I felt a sense of release at her words. Discovering Will wouldn't be a disaster but rather a catalyst to continuing our plan to adopt. I realized that having Harry's son in our home on whatever terms would leave an ache when he wasn't there. An ache we would fill with a child of our own.

Tracy stood up and looked at her watch. "I can't believe how long we've been in here. I'd better find my husband and kids. We're supposed to be at my cousin's anniversary party right about now."

"They're here? I didn't see them. I have to say hello to those guys." Tracy's sons, Benjamin and Matthew, were the sweetest kids. They were all-boy and charming as all get-out, while they wriggled in and out of mischief.

"Stay. Relax. You need that more. You see them all the time. Anyway, I told them we'd come out to your place next week. They can't wait to use the hot tub."

"We don't have a…"

Tracy arched an eyebrow and grinned. "You do now." She leaned down and kissed my cheek. "I'll call you next week." Tracy took a few steps then stopped. She turned with what appeared to be the air of an afterthought. "Oh, by the way, the hospital posted a great job. They need someone who can—"

"Stop." I interrupted with my hand flung forward *à la* Diana Ross in her signature song. "What is it with all these jobs? I can't go two days without someone telling me about a 'great job,' 'made-for-you job,' 'can't-pass-it-up job.'" I stopped talking and pinned Tracy with the best angry look I could muster.

She laughed and shook her head. "You are such an exaggerator. A job at Trinity and a job at Elmhurst shouldn't evoke that response."

Before I could enlighten her as to the rising toll of job offers, Harry, my dad, and cousin Nick walked in. Nick pantomimed sweeping a cap from his head. "Car for 'ire, milady."

The cockney accent was a cute touch coming from a young kid with a surname that used more vowels than consonants. Harry smiled and rolled his eyes.

I stepped into a bear hug with my dad. "Thanks for everything, Dad. The party was great. I'll call you tomorrow when I'm back on USA time."

He patted my back. A small gesture but so comforting. He turned to Nick. "Take that box on the counter out to the car with you." He turned back to me. "You two hardly ate. There's some of everything in there."

"Thanks, Mike." Harry shook hands with my dad, who was a two-handed shaker, when he liked you. Harry followed suit and the two of them looked like a huddle ready to break.

A final wave and we headed to the home we hadn't seen since it had been damaged by an explosion and fire. Nick talked all the way down Taft Avenue to Butterfield Road, to York Road until he merged onto I-88. He stopped talking at the tollbooth.

I had leaned my head back and closed my eyes. I heard Harry caution Nick. "I think she's out." His voice was low. Nick got the message and stayed silent until we left the toll way. I could tell by the change in speed that we were on residential streets. I knew we'd be home soon. I opened my eyes as I felt the car turn onto the main drive into Pine Marsh. Our corner of the world consisted of six homes nestled in a pine forest surrounded by a semi-reclaimed marsh. Our home, the Atwater home, and now the DeFreest home were on the north side of the compound. Three other families shared the south side of the beautiful development.

Ours was the furthest away from the fork in the road. We passed Lily's house; no way to tell if anyone was home. Barb's house came next. I knew she and her husband and son were still at the party. A slight curve in the road and I leaned forward, anticipating the first look at my house since the bombing. I had walked away from it that day thinking that Harry lay dead inside the rubble.

Nick pulled into the driveway and immediately made himself busy with the care package from my dad and two small suitcases that Mike must have transferred from the Suburban to Nick's car. Harry and Nick headed for the front door before I could make myself move. The house looked exactly as it did before the explosion. At least from the front. Most of the damage had been on the side and back of the house. Harry stood at the threshold waiting for me.

I hesitated so long Harry must have thought he'd need to come get me and he started back. I slid across the seat and stepped out of the car. Both Harry and Nick looked relieved. My movement surprised me; it felt disconnected from my reality, as though I was watching someone else who looked an awful lot like me, or maybe I was sleepwalking. A cardinal's shrill cry penetrated my slow-motion brain function and I immediately stepped into the moment.

The tableau changed and I viewed my husband, the house, the entire day with a new focus. Two people had lost their lives in the explosion that day. I was the lucky one. Harry and I survived. My family worked all summer to restore *my* home.

My spine straightened and my step lightened. I covered the last few yards to the front porch in a fast walk. Harry slipped his arm around my shoulders and we mounted the steps to the front door. For the briefest moment I thought Harry was going to swoop me up in his arms and carry me over the threshold. It felt as if we were starting a new life in this home. Instead, he pushed the oak door wide open with a *ta-da* flourish and gently steered me into the foyer.

The lingering scent of fresh paint and room freshener vied for dominance in the still air of the empty house. The furniture was all there, but the sense of life and daily routine, the smells of recent meals and fabric softener was missing. I knew the entire house had been repainted after structural and cosmetic repairs were made. The hardwood floors shone with the newness of their restoration. Gone were the worn spots of countless treks of shoed, slippered, and stocking feet from room to room, walking the paths of the house. The patina of the house was gone; the years of lived-in air, emotions captured in oxygen and layered on the walls, gone. I shook my head and straightened my shoulders to dislodge the mantle of nostalgia settling around me. We would put new air, new life into our house.

"It's wonderful." I slowly turned in a circle and put out my arms. "I can't believe it looks the same. It's wonderful."

Harry's eyes gleamed with happiness. I realized in that moment that he'd been worried about my reaction. My smile and words assured him. Nick took that as his cue to leave, undoubtedly to return to the party and report on our reactions. I caught at his hand as he walked toward me. "Thank you. All of you. I can't believe how much you did for us." I smiled up into his eyes and pulled him into a hug.

Nick's smile broadened and he gave me a quick return squeeze before he stepped back. "We all pitched in after the contractor finished the major work. It was the same guy that developed Pine Marsh. He matched the brick and found the same roofing. We took pictures of everything; first for insurance but then we wanted to show you how the clean-up and rehab went. I even put them in an album."

Nick warmed to his subject. "You can't believe what it looked like the next morning. I've got the album in my trunk. I'll get it."

"No, Nick. Not now," Harry said. He tried to keep the anger out of his tone but I recognized the edge.

Nick immediately became contrite. "Oh, man. How stupid of me. I'm sorry, Gracie. Guess I got carried away. I've been looking at it all summer. Sorry. Didn't think how you'd feel. Didn't think period." He looked so deflated, like a child whose toothpick-bridge project had collapsed before the teacher could see it. I couldn't help but smile.

"It's okay. I know you meant well. And I'm sure we'll want to see them some day, just not today." I reached up on tiptoe and kissed him on the cheek. Nick grinned then glanced at Harry to see if they were okay. Harry put out his hand.

"I can't, we can't thank you enough for all you've done. You know that, don't you?" Harry put his left hand on Nick's shoulder. "I'm a little tightly wound when it comes to that one," he smiled as he nodded toward me.

"Yeah, you and her dad. Okay, gotta go. Anything you need, you call, okay?"

"Okay."

Nick hurried down the front steps and across the lawn to his car.

"Nice kid, but a tad intense," Harry muttered as he closed the door.

I smiled at Harry's assessment and linked my arm through his. "Well, we're home now. Guess we should unpack or inspect or something." I couldn't help feeling uneasy about this house, mine yet strange to me. I walked down the hallway to the kitchen. Harry followed me and immediately busied himself by putting on the kettle. That felt right. I walked into the living room and then the dining room. "This is so strange. I would have picked this furniture, this fabric, this color; but I didn't." I spoke more to myself than to Harry, not realizing I'd spoken out aloud until Harry answered.

"Karen, Eve, and Carolyn did all the shopping. Your brothers said their wives were living out every woman's fantasy: a *carte blanche* shopping spree."

"Apparently, you've kept in touch with this whole project. Why didn't you tell me?"

"I started to the first week we were there. Mike had called

to tell me the estimates were in and the insurance company had approved the entire list. When I mentioned that I'd had word about the insurance claim you became agitated. I didn't want to spoil our holiday."

"I guess I wasn't interested in equating our home with impersonal claim forms and red tape. I am interested in seeing the rest of the house."

A shrill whistle from the kitchen announced tea. We walked back to the kitchen. That's when I noticed the fresh flowers on the sideboard in the dining room. The sparkling jewel tones of freesia, gladiola, zinnia, and phlox filled my mother's Capodimonte vase. I cherished that vase as one of her favorite pieces. It never really went with the decor but it always belonged.

"Harry, look." I swooped it up in my hands and turned to hold out my prize. My eyes filled with tears.

Harry had stopped walking when he heard me call. He beamed, grinning from ear to ear at my joy. He inclined his head toward the china cabinet. I followed his line of sight and spotted my grandmother's china gleaming in the artificial light.

"How? My last view of this room was chaos and rubble."

"Me, too. I only remember smoke so thick you couldn't breathe, and Kramer trapped in the flames under—" Harry stopped abruptly and looked back at me. He continued in a brisk tone. "I was amazed at what your nieces and nephews pulled out of the rubble. Once the soundness of the structure was confirmed they were in there like a pack of toddlers on an Easter-egg hunt. They scoured the rooms for anything intact and pieces large enough to be glued. They took all the pieces to 'Mr. Chips' on Ogden Avenue and they repaired what they could."

I grinned as I noticed more and more of the mementos that make a house a home. "I can live with this." I walked into Harry's open arms. "Time to move on," I murmured against his chest.

Harry took that in the literal sense and turned us toward the staircase to the upstairs. "Let's see what's up there." Harry released me and took my hand as he started up to the second floor.

Our bedroom, swathed in twilight from the bay window, glowed invitingly in shades of purple, lilac, and periwinkle. The window seat teemed with similarly hued flowers set in vases and pots across its length.

"Oh my gosh, this is fabulous." I executed a slow twirl away from Harry, crossing to the window, plucking a lavender rose from a vase, and moving back into his arms.

Harry lifted me off my feet and continued the twirl. "Happy, darling?"

"Extremely." I smiled and lifted my face to his.

Our kisses tasted all the sweeter for the heady bouquet from both the wine we'd consumed and the flowers packed into the room

"Mmm." Harry broke off the kiss. "Oh, look. A mint on the pillow."

I left his side and walked over to the bed. "Really? You're joking, right?"

"Yes, I'm joking. But now I've got you right where I want you." He pushed against my shoulder and I landed in a cloud of sea-green comforter. His eyes gleamed with his intention.

"All you had to do was ask." I smiled as I kicked off my shoes and swung my legs onto the bed.

"May I?"

I slipped my hand in his waistband and pulled him down beside me.

"I guess that's a *yes*."

FIVE

"I DON'T UNDERSTAND why you feel you need to jump into a new career. We've only just returned home. You've barely unpacked."

Harry had been stewing about my decision to accept the job offer from the public relations firm Barb told me about. Not the job per se, but the timing. He stopped haranguing to sip at his tea. The Earl Grey brew seemed to give him a second wind.

"You've not done any PR work since you handled the reunion for Regina College five years ago. Times change, things change."

The look on my face must have registered with Harry as he quickly added, "Not to say you wouldn't be smashing at the job. You've got that innate sense of what people like, finger-on-the-pulse type of sense."

"Please." One word and he stopped. "Please support me on this. I haven't been able to write a word all summer. I've blown whatever credibility and second chances I had with my publisher. I've barely managed to complete the edits on other people's dreams. I need to get a job where I can report daily for work, complete projects that aren't mine, not personalize or internalize everything. I need a commercial kind of job that stays outside when I come home. Trust me, this is perfect for me."

"Of course I trust you. I love you. I'm a little worried that you're moving too fast, grabbing at the first thing—"

"This is hardly the first thing. Karen wanted me to teach

children's writing at Trinity. Sister Jeanette wanted me to be her assistant archivist. Janet Henry wanted me to work in the alumni department. Tracy had a job lined up at the hospital in the marketing department."

Harry put up his hands in a signal of surrender. "Okay. I will agree that you've had more offers than Elizabeth Taylor has had husbands, but why choose Schwarze and Krieg? Do you know what that name means?"

Since I spoke only Italian as a second language, I raised my eyebrows at my quad-lingual husband to enlighten me.

"Schwarze and Krieg means 'black one and war.' I find that combination unusual. Don't you?"

"What do you mean, like an omen or something? So they have strange names in German. I think it would have been equally strange if they had been 'war and peace.' Would that have made them literary giants? All I know is Barb said they're doing the PR for some local events and the interview I had with Lizabeth Krieg went well. Her family practically settled this area in the 1800s. We clicked. This isn't Regina, isn't Trinity, isn't anything connected to…before."

I hadn't meant to say "before." I hadn't thought in those terms but there it was. The traumas of this last year seemed connected to people and places from the past. Accepting a job in Naperville moved me far from those people and places. Harry seemed to understand or maybe he realized he wasn't winning his point.

The entire conversation took place while I paced between our closet and the bed, repeatedly throwing down outfits as I tried to determine what a public relations person wore on her first day on the job. Harry must have realized my dilemma as the pile of rejected clothes grew.

"Darling. The blue suit with the lavender blouse."

"What?" I was deep in the closet wrangling more hangers off the pole. Harry held up the two articles of clothing in question. "It's perfect for you. Anything you wear will be fine but I think this makes the statement you want for your first day."

I threw my arms around his neck, crumpling the blouse between us. "He does fashion consulting, too," I gushed in mock praise. "How did I get so lucky?" I kept my arms around his neck and let him pull me closer.

"Ditto."

It is now 7:30 a.m. You requested to be awakened at this time.

We both started at the voice of our "roommate," a talking Betty Boop alarm clock, a wedding present from his side of the family. If one of us didn't slap her molded plastic derriere and turn off her alarm the next sound would be a loud buzzing that could shake loose the fillings in your teeth.

"Sorry, I forgot she was on. Didn't want to oversleep." I walked over to the nightstand and shut her down.

Harry held out the ensemble to me. I took the clothes and rewarded his choice with a light kiss. "Gotta go. I'll fill you in on my first day over dinner tonight."

"Dinner?"

"You were going to suggest dinner out for my first day of work, weren't you?"

"Absolutely. I'll meet you at Sweet Basil at five-fifteen. Unless you want Mexican; we can go to Potter's Place."

"Sweet Basil is fine. I feel like Italian."

"Yes, you do." Harry smirked as he reached for me.

"You're going to make me late for work." I moved quickly into the bathroom.

"Tell them you got lost."

I smiled as I turned on the shower. Schwarze and Krieg. Prestigious company to land a job with. *Black and War,* that was sort of creepy. I wondered if they knew what their names meant in German. They *had* to. I wished Harry hadn't told me.

Shake it off Gracie. This is Yuppyville West. No shadows, no secrets. My brain admonished me to think clearly. I reached for the length of yarn tied to the medicine cabinet door and tied fifteen bowlines before I stepped into the shower.

SIX

THE AUCTIONEER BANGED his gavel.

"Ladies and gentlemen, we will begin the bidding in section two with offer number sixteen in your program…"

I tried to count heads from where I stood. I had judiciously ordered the largest tent available through Outdoor Events, a local party store. It peaked in five spots, center and corners, which gave the attendees a good deal of room to move around and enjoy the bar and hors d'oeuvres set up on one side. A stage took up only a quarter of the tent leaving space for 200 rented white folding chairs. The grass had been mowed that morning and the pleasant scent of nature mingled with the food, perfume and tobacco odors filling the tent. The clear plastic side panels had been tied up since the evening was mild and the light breeze felt refreshing.

The set up was directly in front of the depot and across from the Beaubien Tavern and the Netzley/Yender House, two other historical properties that had been moved to the park after the depot. Events ran in both buildings throughout the day: apple coring, pie making, biscuit baking in Netzley/Yender; booths with homemade soap and homemade honey, the Abner Doubleday batting cages, and tours of the station master's home.

The volunteers from the society, dressed in period costumes, conducted the demonstrations and tours. One gentleman dressed as the original station master of the depot who according to legend haunted the depot and his home. He had been killed by a band of men traveling the rails, plundering the depots along the way. The story goes that the station master surprised them and was overcome. He'd been knocked unconscious and locked in one of the trunks waiting for shipment. His assistant found the body the next day when he noticed a bit of cloth sticking out of the lid. The station master had suffocated in the airtight compartment.

His gravesite, in the Lisle Cemetery, teemed with flowers during Depot Days which was when most "sightings" of him occurred.

The society member playing the part wore great makeup, pasty white skin, and dark sunken eyes. I shivered and hoped he wasn't scaring the children.

Our goal—to raise twenty-five thousand dollars for the Lisle Heritage Society for maintenance and further restoration of two historical buildings—seemed within reach with the crowd that night. The society did a great job securing donations of wonderful nostalgic memorabilia and expensive antiques for the auction. But the *pièce de résistance* had been discovered by me, doing my usual obsessive-compulsive research.

I had explained the plans to Harry that first night at Sweet Basil. Barb Atwater had joined us to hear about my first day on the job she'd recommended. Halfway through cocktails I had Harry and Barb excited about the event.

"My job is to market, promote, advertise, and pull off an extraordinary auction and English Tea that will net the Heritage Society, our client, twenty-five thousand dollars. Lizabeth Krieg is doing the job at-cost since her great-great-uncle settled this area. She's to be honored for her contribution. Her partner's husband's family are also early settlers, so both women have a personal interest in the success of the campaign. In fact, Ava Deutsch, granddaughter of the original Johann and Marta Deutsch, is hosting the English Tea at the Jefferson Hill Tea Room. She lived there as a kid before it was

converted to the tearoom and shops. The top floor is supposedly haunted by a sobbing woman."

Barb's eyes positively gleamed. "Oh, this gets better and
better."

"I'd best let Hannah know," Harry said. "You know how
she goes on about hauntings. Could barely get her out of the
roadhouse on 55th Street. Kept insisting on going upstairs
to have a look."

Hannah made a practice of tracking down those places.
Harry was referring to The Country House in Clarendon Hills
supposedly haunted by the spirit of a young woman tragically
killed in a car crash.

Harry continued, "I blame that book you gave her about
Chicago area ghosts. I think her goal is to investigate each
one in the index."

Barb and I laughed at his pretended chagrin. We both
knew he'd accompanied his sister on many of her "jaunts to
the haunts," as they called their outings.

"Then I shouldn't tell her about the supposed haunting of
the depot by the original station master? They say he died in
one of the trunks in his keeping, murdered by marauders." I
couldn't resist the drama.

"Please don't tell my sister, she'll want to move into the
place."

We laughed at Harry's assessment.

"Maybe the sobbing woman ghost is the station master's
widow."

"No, she lived in the depot and moved back east after his
death."

"Maybe the legend is wrong. Maybe he was playing *choo-
choo* with Jefferson Hill Dolly, and Mrs. Station Master found
out and derailed him into the trunk. And Dolly is sobbing
because she missed her train."

Barb and I dissolved into giggles.

"Ladies, I am appalled that you would so malign a legend of Lisle."

We all burst into laughter and chatted easily about what would appeal to the upscale crowd Schwarze and Krieg hoped to attract. I listened to their ideas and advice about what to do and even committed a few of them to memory.

A VOICE AT my elbow brought me back to the auction.

"Did they get to them yet?" She pointed to an open page in the auction brochure. My sister-in-law, Hannah Marsden, stood next me. Her easy smile, a family trait she shared with her brother, lit up her face. She was excited about auction block 66.

"Not yet. The auctioneer is only in section two and the trunks are in section six. It should go quickly though, maybe another thirty minutes."

"Perfect. Karen drove on her own." I nodded in understanding. Karen Kramer, my best friend and Hannah's life partner, had a terrible sense of direction. She rarely arrived on time even when she left herself time to get lost, stop for directions and retrace her route.

"She should be here before then. I'm going to wait near the door, which is also near the bar. Clever girl to camouflage the bar in the old smithy shop. Shall I bring you a tonic?"

My English sister-in-law possessed the same dry humor as her brother did and even now I wasn't sure if her comments were genuine or tinged with light sarcasm. I kept reminding myself that Hannah came from a country whose smithies were hundreds of years old. I sensed her humor with *colonists* who were so excited about a centennial celebration. And I wasn't sure if tonic meant a specific drink like vodka tonic or if she meant a generic something to pick me up. *How could English be so difficult to understand?* Hannah stood looking back at me.

"No, thanks. I need to keep a clear head."

"Fine. I'll be back with Karen. Soon, I hope."

I smiled as I thought of the excitement and speculation my find had generated at Schwarze and Krieg. My compulsive attention to detail uncovered the receipt and record for off-site storage during the moving of the depot to its current location. The original depot had burned, but had been rebuilt in 1874. The edifice that had controlled transportation from then until 1978 had been carefully lifted and moved to its permanent home at the Lisle Station Park. The Lisle depot was unique along the Burlington line in the sense that it provided a residency for the station master. The depot remained operational with a station master in residence up until the day they moved it.

In doing the research to bring me up to speed on the event I ran across receipts and had to dig deeper. One storage facility was a lower-level basement in one of the antique stores on Ogden Avenue, a converted gristmill. That strip of old Plank Road had three antique stores in less than a mile: Antique Affaire, Antique Bazaar, and Antiques on Plank. The owner had been part of the preservation committee and volunteered to store the contents of the depot during the move.

The other storage area was in the basement of the Book Nook on Main Street. The Waskelis family offered to store some of the trunks.

The find of eleven railroad trunks, circa 1890 to 1920, generated all the excitement. The owner of the store, Ava Deutsch, was traveling in Europe. Her son, Karl, hadn't been much help at first. He had been a teenager when the trunks were moved and wasn't interested in finding them. He didn't want to be bothered to look up records or search through storage. He insisted, as everyone assumed, that they had been returned once the depot was in place. I thought my search over until one of the ladies in the store reminded him of the cement room on the lower level that opened to the back of the property. He had glared at her, seemingly angry that he had to put himself out any more than necessary. The trunks were found in a small separate room that Karl grudgingly opened.

In its day as an active mill, farmers would back their wagons into that room to unload the wheat harvest. The area had filled in with debris blown in under the uneven double-wide doors. Time and weather and lack of use had taken its toll. The floor was dark with bygone stains and current animal droppings. The trunks were sound and had not suffered much for their neglect over the last two decades.

Three trunks had been stored in the basement of the Book Nook back in a corner that reached under the sidewalk. Through the years, old displays and furniture blocked the trunks from view and memory.

We researched the tags on the trunks and were able to find descendants of the owners. The Godshalk family was thrilled to get the two trunks belonging to their great-aunt Alice. Three other trunks were also reunited with family. The remaining six trunks had no tags or obvious ownership; they were deemed abandoned.

The idea to offer them at auction came to me immediately. I thought of the big splash over Geraldo's attempt to open Al Capone's safe. People loved that kind of shtick. I sold Lizabeth on the idea and tonight's high bid would prove me right, or not. I scanned the room again, certain that at least another fifty people had entered; I hoped with the sole intent of bidding on the trunks.

"There you are. I thought you'd be up front ready to turn the key, as it were." Harry slipped his arm around my shoulders and kissed my cheek. His foot pushed against my tote bag on the ground. "Shopping?"

"Huh? Oh. I didn't set up all day in this," I put my arms out to display my Jones New York periwinkle-blue suit, "or these," pointing down to three-inch heels. "I put my clothes and some of the set-up stuff in here when I changed. Forgot to put it in my car before Barb drove it back to our house so she could come back with her husband and we could drive home in one car. See what a great planner I am?" I smiled sweetly at my husband.

"I'll take it out to my car."

"Don't bother, it's not a problem. I planned to watch from back here. I'm too nervous to be up there," I admitted.

"No bother, I'll be back in a bit." He lifted the bag with a mock grimace at its weight.

Hannah and Karen arrived as volunteers wheeled the trunks out on an old-fashioned luggage dolly. I motioned them forward. "Go on, get your seats. Barb's saving three up front. She has numbers for each of you."

"Did I see Harry leaving?"

"He's putting something in his car; he'll be right back. How full is the parking lot?"

Hannah smiled and signaled thumbs up. "Jammed."

I smiled as I watched them scurry to the front to claim their seats. People continued to pour in. Where was Harry?

On cue, he stood next to me. "Darling, you've got a winner here. At ten dollars a head to get in you're going to make a lot of money for the heritage society."

"Did you pay again? I forgot to give you your pass." I rummaged in my stylish but too-small purse for a plastic badge. I held it out to him. "Sorry."

"It's a worthy cause and it makes your bottom line look better. Although your bottom line looks fine to me." He smiled and slid his hand around my waist letting his fingers graze a little lower.

"Stop that!" I said, half-serious in my protest. "Later."

"How about we buy the whole lot and go home now." I

made a face at him and turned my attention to the stage. The auction was starting.

"Who is that woman walking up the far aisle? I saw her in the car park when I was putting your sack in the boot. She pulled in next to me, seemed in a huff when I didn't move out of her way quickly enough for her to park. My boot was jammed; forgot I had Walter's clubs. Had to pull everything out to fit your ditty bag. My clubs were in the grass blocking her. Tossed it all in while she glared at me. Hope I didn't leave anything lying about. Had to fidget with the locks again. Darling, remind me to have them repaired."

I followed Harry's glance.

"That's Ava Deutsch, the force behind most things in Lisle and a relative of my boss. You didn't say anything to her, did you?"

"Darling, I'm the soul of discretion. She was the one behaving rudely. I wondered is all. She looked familiar to me."

"She's involved in everything. You've probably seen her picture in the paper."

"Possibly. Familiar yet different. It'll come to me."

The sharp bark of the gavel cut off further conversation. Harry rushed to take his seat. The auctioneer began his description of the trunks. Each was to be auctioned and then each owner would open the trunk in view of the audience. None of the trunks had a key. A specialty locksmith, John Schoebel, had been hired to be on hand with his ring of metal shapes. The wizened seventy-something gentleman was actually related to Lizabeth by some twist on the family tree. His thinning gray hair matched the stubble on his face. He stood off to the side waiting for his time to take the stage.

The bidding was brisk for the three small bridal chests and the one domed steamer trunk. The excitement increased with each auctioned chest; drawing closer to turning the key on hidden secrets. At least that's how I had publicized the event.

The ploy had worked. People squeezed into the tent even after the bidding began. I suspected that most were spectators, come to enjoy the drama. Several of the costumed individuals from the heritage society were present. Gertrude, a new member, had convinced Walter to take the part of the smithy. I spotted her now across the room. Her brown hair tucked up under an attractive wide-brimmed feathered red hat gave her the look of a Victorian lady, further enhanced by the period costume in tones of red, purple, and black. She nodded graciously to onlookers and fanned herself with a beaded red and black fan attached by a loop to her wrist. I wondered if the fanning was scripted or menopausal. Three loud raps brought me back to the auction.

The last two items looked identical. "This is a Humpback wardrobe trunk circa 1890, made locally by the Chas. T. Wilt Co. of Chicago. The trunks were designed to ship upright with the peaked top to prevent crushing from other luggage. The pyramid top held a telescoping rod used for hanging garments. One of the more expensive designs for rail travel. The bidding will begin at $1550."

I spotted Hannah's card in the air, then Lizabeth's. I wondered if she was trying to run up the bid to insure success. Harry's hand shot up. Barb's hand made its debut, then Hannah signaled again. A flutter of white caught my eye. Ava Deutsch, the owner of Antiques on Plank, raised her card. Hannah reacted in kind.

Ava was a taller-than-average woman, maybe five feet eight inches, with short stylish blond hair. Her build was sturdy, but in no way stodgy. She wore a knee-length coatdress, a shade of deep peach. The patterned peach and tan silk scarf set the tone of high style, but her camel hued matching gloves and shoes polished her look of sophistication, outshining the jeans and Dockers in the crowd.

Ava's hand moved up again. Fabulous. This bidding was

almost higher than the other trunks combined. I knew Hannah had her heart set on one of those peaked trunks. Ava still had the high bid. Hannah backed down and Ava's bid stuck through the gavel's third rap.

"The last trunk, ladies and gentlemen, is an exact duplicate. Probably manufactured in the same lot. This case has slight damage around the base. Nonetheless a charming piece. The bidding will start at $1375."

He'd barely brought the gavel down to open the bidding when Ava Deutsch's hand lifted her white card in the air. I could see Hannah's shoulders tense. Her hand rose. A quick acknowledgment of her bid and the auctioneer nodded in Ava's direction. Then Hannah's, once more to Ava. This was becoming a horse race. I knew Hannah was stubborn. I suspected that she felt Ava Deutsch was being greedy. I also suspected that Ava, a shrewd businesswoman, knew she could triple her profit by selling the trunks as a set. Ava doubled her bid. The crowd got involved, swiveling their heads from one side of the room to the other, like a tennis match with the white cards passing back and forth across their vision. Hannah leaned over and said something to Harry. He nodded and her hand shot up and flapped her card twice signifying a match and raise on her bid.

"Wow, they're really going at it. I can't believe how much money this is raising. You were right, Grace. Nice call."

High praise from Lizabeth Krieg. I was about to reply with a modest "thank you" when I noticed a police officer moving toward Ava Deutsch. He motioned her out of her aisle. She acted reluctant to leave and tried to sidestep toward him while still keeping an eye on Hannah's card. When she was close enough to insure some privacy, the officer leaned toward her and spoke quickly, gesturing back toward the door. His news must have been important.

She leaned down to her son, handing him the card and

imparting what could have been some bidding instructions. It was apparent by his reaction that he hadn't planned on an active part. He looked as though he'd come from unloading one of their trunks: jeans, sweatshirt, gym shoes; work gloves stuffed in his back pocket and a small cooler at his feet. She left him looking angry and baffled.

The auctioneer had paused in his patter giving the young man a chance to answer Hannah's bid. His hand raised slowly.

Another white flash from behind Hannah. I couldn't see who it was. She turned in her seat to view the competition. Ava's son raised his hand again, this time more quickly. I still couldn't identify the newcomer. The chairs in that area had been curved to accommodate the public address speakers and the people were seated closer to each other. The new bidder signaled again. Hannah marked her next tier. She had moved the price to over three thousand dollars. She looked at the son whose hand was still down and then behind her; her eyes sent a message: *back off.* I held my breath as the gavel sounded and the auctioneer declared, "Sold to the persistent lady in the third row."

Three thousand one hundred and seventy-five dollars. I surely hoped Hannah thought it was worth the price once the adrenaline left her system. All smiles, she went up on stage to stand next to her property.

I noticed the last-minute bidder leaving the tent. I could see now that it was a woman as she hurried out. Her sturdy shoes carried her across the grass. I thought she looked overdressed, not in a fashion sense, but with a flowered scarf wrapped around her neck and chin and a pale green floppy hat enveloping the top half of her head. The rest of her outfit looked oversized like generous hand-me-downs. She certainly didn't look like anyone who could have afforded that trunk. I turned my attention to Lizabeth as she joined the new owners and the locksmith on stage.

"Ladies and gentlemen, thank you for your generous support of the Legends of Lisle campaign to promote the preservation of Lisle's historical treasures. The auction concludes our program for tonight but the excitement continues as we ask each person to open their trunk. The owner of the trunk with the most interesting contents will receive a $200 gift certificate from Village Vendors, redeemable at any store in Lisle."

I had taken Hannah's empty seat. "I feel like I'm waiting for a drum roll," I whispered to Harry. The first trunk opened easily from one of the keys dangling from the locksmith's ring. The trunk yielded a set of china with a bright floral pattern and two teapots. My throat tightened as I remembered another set of china that had been left behind. I shook off the memory and focused on the next chest.

Since the styles were similar, the locks opened quickly with the same key. *No china in this one.* This trunk must have belonged to a student or teacher. It was filled with textbooks, journals, and notebooks. The smaller of the two remaining chests revealed more books, two revolvers, and a dozen bottles of *Dr. Goodhealth's Elixir* and a partially used tin of rat poison. The audience chuckled at the combination. So far, this one seemed to be the winner. The other chest gave up maps, charts, and climbing equipment complete with ropes, crampons, and carabiners. *Interesting, but not a winner.*

At last, the matched trunks. Hannah practically vibrated with excitement as she waited her turn. Karl Deutsch, Ava's son, seemed uncomfortable standing in for his mother. He leaned over to speak to Lizabeth when the locksmith moved toward the trunk. Lizabeth shook her head and waved Mr. Schoebel toward them. He hesitated and looked out over the crowd as if waiting for Ava to rejoin them. Several heads turned to follow his gaze. She wasn't there. He turned back to Lizabeth. More discussion followed. She finally seemed to relent and turned to Hannah. Apparently they were going to give Ava more time to get back before they opened her trunk. Hannah looked thrilled to be next. I leaned forward in anticipation, hoping for vintage clothes or maybe a musical instrument.

Mr. Schoebel seemed to be having trouble with the lock. He stood back and shook his head. The entire audience sighed. It didn't seem to me that he'd tried all the keys he had on that ring. I heard Hannah ask him to try another. He backed away and shrugged his shoulders.

Lizabeth stepped forward to the microphone. "Some secrets must be kept," she said with a crafty smile.

I'm sure she was trying to "spin" this unexpected curve to the benefit of Schwarze and Krieg. "Some locksmith," I whispered to Harry. "He didn't try very hard."

"If he knows locks, he'd know if he had the right key. Odd, though. The trunk isn't that old, should still have keys."

Lizabeth moved toward the first trunk. "We'll start our judging with this trunk."

"Wait. I know someone who can open my trunk." Hannah's voice rang out over the audience. Harry grinned and started to get up.

"My brother, Harry Marsden, can pick locks." People started murmuring and turning their heads to stare at Harry who had stood, but now looked as though he'd rather sit down.

Hannah must have realized her gaffe. "I mean, he did when we were children in England and we found Grandmother's old trunks in the attic and when we were older, the wine cellar at Mum's brother's country house. Uncle Edward never did realize he was a bottle or two light after we visited."

I knew my husband's skill, but I hardly thought he wanted the entire assembly to know that the lock picking he practiced had become a valuable skill when he worked for British Intelligence. Who knew what Hannah would blurt out next?

Her stumbling brought laughter from the crowd and a sprinkling of applause. She stopped squirming and babbling, and motioned toward her brother. "Harry, do come up here." The clapping increased. My husband walked onto the stage and approached the trunk. I knew he hadn't brought the slim leather case containing various steel picks that I had seen him use only once before.

Harry turned toward the audience. "Perhaps someone has a metal fingernail file or a hatpin or hairpin?" Barb Atwater immediately began a hurried search in her purse. My neighbor adored Harry and would love nothing more than to come to his aid. She loved anything English, a true anglophile, and would be doubly pleased to be up on stage with two Englishmen.

"I've got one, I've got one," Barb announced. She quickly left her seat and made for the stage. Several women were ahead of her, converging on the stage and my husband with various offerings in their hands.

Harry, always the charmer, made a big deal of each item offered until he had at least three files, an assortment of hairpins, another key ring and one lethal-looking hatpin. Hannah had both hands out palm up to hold the items for Harry's use. The seven women who had charged the stage moved to the side, but not off the platform. They apparently thought they had a vested interest in the outcome.

The keys did not work, nor the hatpin or the files. Harry was down to the hairpins. The pressure mounted; with each attempt the audience leaned in closer. You couldn't buy this kind of publicity. I noticed that almost half of the audience had made their way back to the cash bar at some point during the suspense. *Good. More profits for the Lisle Heritage Society.* Actually, all profit. One of Liz's partner's relatives, a distant relative of the Godshalk family of Arboretum fame, had donated the bar. These German families were almost as entwined as the Italian families from Taylor Street.

Harry made a show of searching through the hairpins in his sister's hand and choosing one. I felt certain he could have opened the lock on his first attempt but he knew the value of showmanship and he was giving us our money's worth. He knelt on one knee in front of the lock with his head close to the trunk and cocked at an angle as though he were listening to internal directions.

My fingers reached for the length of yarn tied to the handle of my Dooney & Bourke purse. I looped three patterns as I waited for Harry's success.

Karen leaned toward me. "Do you think he can get it?"

"No doubt about it. Absolutely." She smiled at my loyalty.

Harry shifted his weight and stood. He gestured for Hannah to open the trunk. She eagerly flipped the metal bars and pulled at the handle. The collective curiosity of the entire assembly tugged with her. My three loops expanded to seven.

The metal seam parted and the front half of the tall wardrobe swung open. Hannah's gasp silenced the murmurs. Her scream started a cacophony of voices and a rush for the exit.

SEVEN

KAREN AND I SIDESTEPPED two women and worked our way toward the stage.

Three people, two men, one woman, moved in the same direction as we did. I noticed they wore dark suits, and earphones with a curled cable disappearing into their starched collars. Lizabeth's security from a private agency in Naperville, recommended by Pine Marsh's own Sergeant Peterson, moved ahead of us; they were unencumbered by high heels. Karen and I reached the stage in time to hear them ask everyone milling and craning near the stage to stand back. They positioned themselves to control the area in front of the trunk and the small steps to the left that led on to the stage. Lizabeth waved me over.

"She's with me. It's okay."

I moved toward the steps. Karen hadn't moved. Her tall, athletic frame stood rooted to the spot. She stared up at Hannah, who looked ready to scream again. Harry stood next to her with his arm around her shoulder blocking her view of the trunk.

"She's with me." I grabbed Karen's slack arm and pulled her along. "C'mon, before they change their minds." Karen climbed up the steps behind me but her long legs got her to the small knot of people before me. Harry let go of his sister when Karen approached.

"Hannah, what is it?" Karen put her arm around her partner and held her close. Hannah Marsden swallowed hard and pointed her head toward the trunk. Rotted material that looked to have been bright red moiré crammed the trunk. The awful stench from the fabric oozed from the interior.

"Harry, shut that thing. The smell is awful." I moved toward him. Only from a few feet away did I see what Hannah and Harry had seen. Behind the folds of the tattered material was the unmistakable form of a skeleton. My vision blurred. I squinted to focus and regretted the attempt. The people on stage around the trunk faded, but the contents floated forward without sense of purpose except to escape confinement. I felt my arms raise and open to embrace the moiré-draped skeleton. I stretched out my hand, my mind remembering another time when I had touched the skeleton of a long-dead woman.

"Grace." His voice slowed my steps. Harry's face filled my line of vision. *When did he move there?*

"Everyone stay where you are and don't touch that trunk." A demanding tone; I knew that voice. Sergeant Peterson moved toward us from the last row of seats. Only he wasn't wearing his Pine Marsh uniform. His clothes matched the dark suits standing at the stage, right down to the earpiece with the curly cable snaking down his shirt. Sergeant Peterson was *moonlighting*. Now I understood his referral for this particular security firm.

Harry stepped forward and put out his hand to the sergeant to shake hands but to also give him a lift up. Peterson mounted the low stage and finished his handshake.

"The Lisle Police will be here any minute." He nodded at me and smiled. "Hello, Mrs. Marsden. It seems you're on the scene again."

"Sergeant, I just stepped up here. My sister-in-law actually opened the trunk. It's hers." I don't know why I felt compelled to let him know I wasn't involved. Maybe because the last two times he'd spent significant time with me people were trying to kill me. Well, this time was not the third time, nor the charm.

"So now it's a family affair?" He chuckled at his rhetorical question. "It doesn't matter. The police will want to question anyone on stage at the crime scene."

Crime scene. How had this happened to me? Again.

"Crime scene?" Hannah's head came up from Karen's shoulder. "I only bid on the trunk. It's not… I mean he, she isn't, I mean…" Hannah stopped and looked from Harry to Peterson.

"Hanns, don't worry about it. No one thinks you or any of us for that matter is involved. Right, Peterson?"

"It would seem coincidence that a trunk you bid on would contain a body. Yes, strange."

"Of course it's coincidence. Would anyone who hid the body be stupid enough to open it in front of two hundred people? Would anyone who hid the body still be alive? These trunks are from the twenties or thirties. Some belonged to long-time Lisle residents. Others were unclaimed."

"That's a lot of information for someone who isn't involved. How did you know that?"

Before I had to answer, two police officers arrived. The older of the two, a solidly built man with close-cropped dull blond hair, immediately buttonholed Sergeant Peterson. The other officer, a petite woman with pinned back reddish-colored hair, stepped onto the stage and asked all of us to move toward the stairs she had used.

"My name is Sergeant Royal and I need to take your names and any information you have. First, who are the organizers of this event and who are the owners of the trunks?"

Once she had us separated, with a third category for friend or relative of someone, she began her information-gathering process. She talked to the auctioneer and dismissed him after a brief conversation. Sergeant Royal moved to the locksmith next. I figured she was eliminating the least involved people first to save the best...*best what?* My mind filled in with *suspect*. Is she looking for suspects? Why?

She finished talking to the locksmith and sent him on his way. *Funny, he seems to want to hang around. He looked so jittery before when he couldn't open the trunk I thought he'd be jumping off the stage to leave.*

Harry looked directly at Schoebel and the look that passed between them wasn't cordial. *Now what is that all about?* I turned to ask Harry if he'd ever met the locksmith before. The policewoman's voice, low-toned and firm, carried across the stage.

"Ms. Kramer? I understand you are not an organizer, nor a participant of this event. Why are you up here?"

"Because she makes poor choices in friends." Ric Kramer, Karen's brother, spoke the words matter-of-factly.

I turned toward the voice that had once spoken to me of love and watched as he made his way closer. I hadn't seen Ric since the day a nutcase launched a bazooka into the window of my living room. I stood mesmerized by his approach, absorbing every element of his appearance. His close-cropped black hair looked shot with more gray than I remembered. I could see even at this distance the puckered skin at his left jaw line. My heart lurched in my chest and my throat tightened painfully as I watched his slow progress. He used two canes to support his stiff-legged movement. I knew he'd had several surgeries on his legs and was scheduled for more. My eyes filled with tears and I hated myself for the feeling of pity that welled up inside me. I squeezed my eyes shut to stem the flow and bowed my head to hide the attempt. When I opened my eyes I stared down at my feet. I sensed rather than saw that he stood directly in front of me at floor level.

"Hello, Grace. You look great."

I raised my eyes and looked down into dark eyes that gleamed with tenderness. Then he smiled a dazzling grin that transported me to before the explosion, before the craziness of last year to a time, years before, when I had planned a life with him.

I felt myself drawn to him and in an instant I leaned on my hand, hopped off the stage, and walked into his surprised arms. *He's alive. He's here. He's real.* I slipped my arms around his chest and hugged him like a long-lost friend. I heard the canes hit the floor and felt his arms hold me as tightly as they ever had.

I could only mumble, "Ric, I'm sorry." The tears came quietly, slipping down my cheeks, absorbed by his shirt.

"Shh, it's okay, I'm okay." He held me as small sobs moved my shoulders.

I turned a tear-stained face up to his. "I should have come to see you. I just left."

"You did what you needed to do, for you. I did the same." He brushed a strand of hair away from my face, guided it behind my ear, and kissed my cheek. He tucked my head against his chest and gave me a final squeeze before he slowly lowered his arms to his side.

I stood still, not wanting to let go. Then I realized that it would be easiest for me to step away. I dropped my arms and took one step back, turning to look on the ground for the canes. Sergeant Peterson had already handed them to Ric who was now in conversation with Sergeant Royal who apparently had stepped off the stage.

"I'll have to ask you to leave, sir. We've enough collateral people here already."

Sergeant Peterson spoke up. "He's not collateral, he's part of the team, actually the other half of *P.K. Security and Investigative Services.* Sergeant Royal, this is Ric Kramer, Ric I'd like you to meet Nancy Royal, five-year veteran, crackerjack investigator, specialty in interrogations, former FBI. Nancy, Ric is—"

"I know who Ric Kramer is. Youngest cop to make Inspector at RWPD, former Special Forces Ranger, and the guy who broke my kid sister's heart. I heard all about your specialty."

The hand Ric offered stopped halfway to its target, suspended in uncertainty whether to move forward or beat a hasty retreat to his side and the cane held in his left hand.

Sergeant Royal's smile removed the doubt. She shook his hand and offered a further comment. "My kid sister was always the heart-breaker. She didn't like how it felt. Went back to the best, nicest guy she'd ever met and married him. I'm due to be an aunt next spring." Her smile broadened and the dimple that had been under wraps accentuated her grin.

I'd bet that many a criminal had been lulled into a false sense of security during a session with her. Karen and I looked at each other. I knew she was thinking the same thing as I was. Sergeant Royal's sister must have been the young woman with the copper tresses we saw with Ric last spring at the Braxton. When Karen smiled I knew she'd made the same connection.

Her partner had broken off his conversation with Sergeant Peterson when Ric had arrived. He had moved onto the stage and must have assisted and continued questioning the people because only Karen and Hannah were still standing up there. Liz and the other winners were gone. The lab team had arrived and was preparing to remove the trunk. The officer finished with Hannah and Karen, closed the notebook he'd been writing in, and motioned for them to leave.

I realized Harry wasn't up there, nor was he on the floor with the rest of us. I turned to look for him, to go to him. How could I explain what had happened? Why I had reacted that way? Every time Ric Kramer came into our lives the line between a painful past and current feelings blurred to the point of confusion.

Hannah sidled up next to me and whispered, "Harry said

to tell you not to worry. He thought of something and went after the locksmith. He said he'd meet you at home."

I was grateful that his reason for leaving wasn't disgust with my behavior. I hadn't given my statement but I had nothing to say that would shed light on anything. I thought I should ask to leave. I had left my shoulder bag on the stage and climbed up to retrieve it. I noticed that the last trunk, the one Ms. Deutsch had purchased, stood slightly opened. You couldn't see it from the floor or even from midstage. *That's odd. I didn't think they had opened this trunk. Everything went pretty crazy after Hannah's trunk gave up its ghost.*

"Excuse me. Don't touch anything." A male officer standing on the stage moved toward me. "This area is off limits."

"I know. I'm sorry; I wanted to get my bag." I pointed to the floor.

"Okay fine, let's go." He picked up my purse. From that angle he noticed the slightly opened trunk. He looked at me and then back at the trunk. I didn't like that look. He straightened and handed me my purse. "Royal," he called. "Was this trunk open when you arrived on scene?"

Nancy Royal thought for a minute before she answered. "I didn't see it open, Zaile. Wait." She opened her notebook and flipped through a few pages before she answered. "Witnesses say it was closed. Mr. Marsden had only opened the first of the two identical trunks."

"Well, it's open now." Zaile pointed to the trunk. "This locksmith, Marsden, he's got the only keys?"

"The locksmith is Schoebel. His keys didn't work. Marsden picked the lock with a hairpin."

"A hairpin? That takes talent. Where is this Marsden? I'd like to talk to him."

"So would I." Sergeant Royal looked at me.

The sinking feeling in the pit of my stomach hit my toes

when I heard Ric. "Let me fill you in. Marsden has a history, shall we say. It's on a need-to-know basis."

"Yeah, well, I need to know." Nancy Royal motioned for Ric to take a seat. Her partner escorted me off the stage and gave the lab team instructions to check the remaining trunk. I had seen enough through the partially opened panel to know there was no horrible surprise to be found. It looked like it was filled with books and papers and some clothes. The clothes were still hanging on a bar across the top of the trunk. There was only a scent of mustiness escaping from the interior. *Old books, old clothes, but no old murder. Poor Hannah. What a shock*. Shock? What about Harry? If he opened the trunk, and I don't know who else could have, is that the reason he left? I was about to find out.

"Grace, I'm pretty sure you know where Harry is or at least where he'll be. How about a lift home and we'll stop at your place first?" Ric's smugness annoyed me. I knew how he felt about Harry.

Nancy Royal raised a questioning eyebrow at him.

"It's okay, Officer. We're neighbors." Ric flashed his megawatt smile.

"How convenient."

EIGHT

HARRY WASN'T HOME. Ric insisted on walking me into the house from the garage.

"This isn't necessary," I said.

"I know it's not. It's good to see you again."

I couldn't argue that. It was good to see him. One cup of coffee couldn't hurt.

"Would you like a cup of coffee?"

"Thought you'd never ask." Ric smiled and moved ahead of me, confident of his route. It bothered me that he knew this house so well. He stopped at the entrance to the dining room. I imagined Ric's last memory of this room—being trapped under the collapsed china cabinet, flames devouring his legs and back—caused the muscles in his back to bunch and tighten. I stood quietly behind him and put my hand on his shoulder. He relaxed and turned to face me. The reaction was immediate. He caught me up in his arms, bracing his back against the wall. His lips found mine willing and aching. I felt my body respond. I leaned into him feeling the heat from his chest burn through his shirt to warm my skin.

My mind recoiled at the contact and the traitorous moment passed. I pulled my lips away from his hungry mouth and pushed against his arms. "Ric, stop. This isn't right. Stop."

"It's always right with us, Gracie." He spoke the words softly but released his grip. The corners of his mouth lifted slowly until his grin punctuated his statement. He didn't need to say another word.

"It's not right and you know it. We've been through this.

Now, if you want coffee, fine. That's the only thing on this menu." My mind raced with the thought that I should ask him to leave. *After all, he didn't have far to go. Now that we were neighbors. Oh, God. Maybe Harry was right in suggesting we move.*

"Coffee is fine, for now." He pushed away from the wall and continued moving toward the kitchen as though nothing had happened.

I waited until we were seated at the table with three feet of oak between us before I brought up our recent indiscretion. "Ric, that mustn't ever happen again. Ric?"

He fiddled with the pager clipped to his belt. I'd never seen him wear one before. I guessed high-tech security companies had high-tech toys.

"Ric?"

"Um, yes. Sorry. Gracie, relax. It was an event of the moment. Don't get all knotted up over it." He smiled at his little joke. I had braided a length of orange yarn while I waited for the coffee to brew. He hadn't missed my lapse. "I swear, you Regina girls examine and worry every detail of human sexuality to death. It must be those nuns from early on. Karen is exactly the same; it's that St. Luke, Trinity, Regina trilogy." His smug smile infuriated me.

"The only part of that trilogy for me was Regina. I went to Proviso West High School. What about your current *bead*, Lily? Does she fit your eschatological profile?" I had used the nickname given to Regina girls because of the school's devotion to praying with the rosary.

"Oh, Lily doesn't count. She went to boarding school in Europe somewhere and ended up at Regina as an exchange student. She liked the area and transferred. Anyway, she's not Catholic. No hang-ups."

"She took you in fast enough when Harry went out of reach." The words were out of my impulsive mouth before I knew it. I instantly regretted the barb. It sounded as though I cared.

"Meaning that she settled for me since she couldn't get your husband?"

"Ric. I'm sorry, I'm tired. I didn't mean anything. I was surprised to find out you were living with her. When I left, you two couldn't stand to be in the same room. Now this turnabout; seems unnatural."

"I got to know Lily, see another side of her; the talented, driven, natural side of her. She is an amazing person with a fabulous gift. It happened."

Great. Now two men in my life are her cheerleaders. Hold on there, Gracie girl, you sound unflatteringly jealous. Get a grip. Harry loves you and, well, Ric just put the moves on you. Make up your mind. Fast!

My thoughts must have painted a picture across my face, a face heating up with a blush.

"Grace, you look embarrassed. What's sliding around in that beautiful head?" Ric moved his fingers down his chin as though stroking a goatee. He mimicked a German accent, "A little jealous, perhaps?"

Instead of an answer, I refilled our cups. I stalled by arranging slices of pound cake on a platter and bringing it to the table.

"I kind of thought you'd be pumping me for information on the kid." Ric's voice went soft. The dish skidded across the table as I lost my grip on it. Ric steadied the cake plate as it wobbled on its base.

I sat down and sipped my coffee before picking up the orange braid. I felt the compulsion to braid and tears of frustration welled in my eyes.

"Sorry, Grace. Stupid of me to blurt it out. I really don't know that much about him. I met him once early in the summer. He spent a few weeks here. Seemed like a nice kid. I was still on a lot of meds. Kid probably thinks I'm some kind of weirdo. Lily's been in Europe on photographic assignments. She took him with her. He attends the same school she went to as a kid. She always arranged for him to spend time with her while she worked."

I braided quickly, trying to assuage that part of my brain wired differently from most. Questions twirled through my head as quickly as my fingers worked the yarn.

"Does he look… I mean, is he fair?" I knew the answer. What made me ask?

"Exactly like him, Grace. Same build, same face, the eyes are different; her eyes, that incredible shade of green. You can't confuse his lineage."

Confuse his lineage. Their son.

I jostled my cup and spilled the contents across the table. Ric quickly used his napkin to mop up the liquid. He moved the pound cake out of the way.

"I could use some help, here."

His voice brought me back to the moment. I raised my napkin from my lap and finished absorbing the coffee from the wood.

"Don't be this way, Grace. I know this must be a shock but you have to accept him. Unless you want DeFreest's comment about *a common bond* to pull them together."

"How did you know? You weren't there." I had been alone with that madman fighting for my life.

"The police wrote down everything you said while you were semi-conscious; standard procedure. You kept repeating, 'He said they have a common bond that will bring them together.' I read the report weeks later and asked Lily what she thought that meant. I was curious to know if there was such a thing that could turn Harry from you." Ric stopped and reached across the table to take my hand. I let him. He continued, "Anyway, that's when she told me about the boy—"

"His name is Nicholas William," I said quietly. It seemed impersonal to refer to Harry's son as "kid" or "boy," even if his name tugged at my heart every time I heard it.

Ric must have sensed my mood. He stood up and limped over to the doorway where he had left his canes. He turned back to me. "Grace, Lily will be back in a few weeks, with Nicholas. She couldn't get his paperwork completed in time once she made the decision. He'll be starting school in mid-term. She's going to raise him in the States and she wants him to know his father."

I stood up and walked to face Ric.

"Thousands of couples deal with blended families. We will, too."

Ric towered above me. He stared down at me with a softness in his eyes that seldom appeared. "Of course you will."

Did he believe that or was he placating me because he'd realized how upset I'd become? I walked him to the door and watched him make his way to his car. More importantly, did I believe we could?

NINE

ONCE RIC LEFT, my thoughts turned to what Harry might be up to. I had half-expected him to come home while Ric was here. He had come home once before to witness a scene that wasn't what he thought but sure looked like it. Tonight would have been impossible to explain or excuse.

My guilty mind shifted back to wondering where my husband had gone. The pealing of the door chimes interrupted my thoughts.

I swung open the door expecting to see Ric on the doorstep. Sergeant Royal smiled and nodded her head in greeting. "Mrs. Marsden, good evening, again. May I come in?"

I opened the door wider and stepped aside. "Yes, come in." She stopped at the entrance to the living room and waited for me to take the lead. I walked down the hall to the kitchen. "Please sit down. I've coffee on. Would you like a cup?"

"I'd love some. I'm sorry to stop in so late but we've been looking for your husband and thought he might be home. Is he?"

Seemed like she'd taken a long time to get to that question. She could have asked me that while she was on the doorstep. She wanted to come in and look around. I didn't like the uneasy feeling settling on me like a lead cape. I rolled my neck and shoulders to shake the sensation.

"Stiff neck?"

I brought the mugs to the table and placed one in front of her. "*Mmm,* no, I mean, I guess. Just tired. This evening was the culmination of an entire weekend of Depot Days events.

I'm glad it's over, just not the way it ended. I thought you'd come by about the trunks. Why are you looking for Harry?"

"Earlier this evening, your husband was seen arguing with the locksmith, Schoebel, near the smithy shop. The witness said the encounter looked heated, lots of gesticulating from both men." Sergeant Royal consulted her notebook before continuing. "'The taller one took a step toward the other guy and the small guy put up his hands like he thought he was going to be punched.'"

She closed her notebook, picked up the mug, and took a sip. "This is delicious. A blend?"

For a moment I brightened. I loved talking coffee with real drinkers. Then I remembered I wasn't sipping java with Martha Stewart. "I can't imagine why Harry would even be talking to that man unless it was to ask him why he wouldn't open the last two trunks."

"What do you mean *wouldn't?* I thought he didn't have the right keys."

"Harry seemed to think he did. Schoebel had been shown the trunks beforehand; he'd seen the locks. There were keys on his ring he didn't even try. It seemed to me that he didn't want to open the trunks; not that that would make any sense. We hired him to open the trunks. And another thing, he looked upset, almost angry when Harry was able to open it so easily. At the time I thought he was upset and embarrassed because Harry had shown him up. Maybe there was something else. Maybe you should ask him."

"That would be the normal course of action, Mrs. Marsden, but Mr. Schoebel was the victim of a hit and run accident. He died at the scene."

I drew in a sharp breath; startled, no, *shocked* by her implication. "And you think Harry did it? You are so off base. Talk to Peterson. He knows us."

"I did talk to Peterson. He told us about the events of the

last six months. About your husband's jail time for attacking Inspector Kramer."

"He didn't attack; he hit him. And Ric Kramer knew it was coming. They'd planned it."

"That's not what the report says."

"Ask Ric. He'll tell you."

"Actually, I did have the opportunity to talk to Mr. Kramer earlier when he left your home."

"So there. He told you. Right?" I felt my hand creeping toward the length of yarn I'd stuffed in my pocket. The knot in my stomach dictated action to my fingers.

"He told me to read the report. He was uncooperative in that respect. He did tell me about some run-ins with your husband years before. Threats were made?" Her voiced stopped. She waited for my response.

"I don't believe this. Harry saves his life and this is how he repays him."

"Excuse me?"

I took a sip of coffee before I enlightened her. "Sergeant Royal, you might say we have a history together, the three of us."

"Really?"

"It's a long story."

Royal made a show of checking her watch. "I've got twenty minutes."

"I'll try to give you the *Reader's Digest* version." I proceeded to explain, as succinctly as possible, the incredible web of our lives: Ric's successful attempt to free Harry from a South American prison; my earlier romantic involvement with Ric; Lily's arrival in town; Harry's heroic effort in saving Ric from the inferno that was our house a few months ago, and finally the shocking news about Harry's son. I finished in the allotted time. I didn't know if it made any sense.

"A history together? I'd say so. Mrs. Marsden, do you have

any idea where your husband is? This really would be easier all around if he cooperated."

"How do you know he won't? He has no idea this man is dead."

"We think he does." She stated it quietly and matter-of-factly.

"Because he was seen arguing with him? Because—"

"Because, Mrs. Marsden," her voiced raised slightly, "Your husband's Jaguar was seen at the Citgo on Ogden and Main at approximately the same time the 9-1-1 call came in from that phone booth." She held up her hand to silence my comment. "Mr. Schoebel was struck on the street in front of Antiques on Plank, less than a mile from that gas station."

As if to punctuate her last comment, her pager went off. She looked down at her belt and pressed the off button. "Mrs. Marsden, may I use your phone?"

I pointed toward the wall. While she dialed what I presumed was the police station number, I thought about this crazy night. The moment Hannah's trunk gave up its gruesome secret, it seemed as though twisted facts manipulated the bizarre events that followed. *How do I make this woman believe that Harry couldn't have done this? If Harry did call 9-1-1, then where was he?*

"At the station?" Sergeant Royal's voice rose in inflection. She glanced at me and then turned her body to insure more privacy.

This was my house. Let her go home if she wanted privacy. I moved toward the sink to position myself next to her. She hung up before I could hear anything else.

"Thank you, Mrs. Marsden. I won't need to ask you any more questions. Your husband is at the station. It seems he called 9-1-1 and then picked up his attorney before turning himself in for hitting Schoebel. His car has been impounded. Would you like to follow me to the station?"

I shook my head slowly. The last thing I wanted to do was get behind the wheel of a car. I felt queasy and light-headed. I managed to croak, "I'll get there."

"Fine. I'll see myself out." She started to leave then stopped and turned. "Mrs. Marsden, I noticed when I rang the bell tonight you opened the door immediately without checking who was out there. I looked for a peephole in the door and didn't see one. You really shouldn't open your door without checking. You never know."

I nodded again. I didn't feel the need to explain that I thought she was Ric. I heard the heavy door close behind her. The sound of her leaving signaled my particular form of compulsiveness. *One hundred slipknots—tie and pull. That's crazy,* I argued with myself. *I have to call Walter. I have to get to Harry.*

I negotiated twenty-five and then I could stop and call Walter to drive me to the station. Twenty-five more and I could call Hannah. The last fifty while I waited for Walter. Sometimes I was a pain in my *own* arse. I smiled as I thought of how I had adopted that word after meeting Harry. I tied and pulled knots; the smile replaced by a sterner mouth.

THE POLICE STATION, a short walk from the historical center down Burlington Street, overflowed with people, officers, and news reporters. The latter had finished gathering details about the macabre discovery in the trunk when the news came of a hit and run of one of the people involved in the trunk exposé.

They grouped around me as Walter and I entered. The two-story building was the original schoolhouse for the town of Lisle. The current use for city hall and police department had necessitated creative rehabbing to make it work. The reporters crowded the tight hallway. They moved toward me asking questions, asking for comments. I knew enough to walk fast and keep quiet.

The officer on duty showed me into an office. Walter held the door for me, but said he'd stay outside. His fireplug stature and grizzled brown hair above thick slashes of eyebrows stopped most people from approaching him. I thought I saw a look of relief on the desk officer's face as the door closed. You definitely want Walter on your side.

Harry, David Katernak, and the policeman, Zaile, occupied the small office. A gunmetal-gray desk and filing cabinet filled one side of the room. The desk chair had been pulled from behind the desk. Two metal chairs and a sagging leather couch covered the remaining floor space.

Harry stood and moved toward me. He took both of my hands and held them together. "Don't worry, Grace. Everything is fine."

Everything didn't seem fine. "Oh, thank God. You didn't hit him?"

Harry hadn't let go of my hands. "No, unfortunately, I hit him. It was an accident. He ran into the street from between two cars. I didn't see him until it was too late." Harry let go of my hands and rubbed his forehead with his fingers. "He never knew. He didn't even turn toward the car. Just jumped."

The door opened and Sergeant Royal came in. She walked confidently to the desk and accepted the report Zaile handed her. She picked up another folder from the top of one pile and by her familiarity with the paperwork I assumed this was her office.

I could tell that Harry was extremely upset and exhausted. The abuse he had suffered years before at the hand of his captors had caused a slight stroke affecting his left side. Months of intense rehab had brought him back to his earlier vigor but severe tension or exhaustion caused slight tremors in his arm and hand. I noticed how his left hand shook slightly as he rubbed his forehead. I didn't think anyone else saw it; I looked for the subtle signs.

"Mr. Marsden, in your sworn statement you never said 'jumped,' only that he ran out from between two parked cars." Sergeant Royal looked down at the document in her hands.

"Ran. Jumped. What difference does it make? I killed a man." Harry's voice and demeanor surprised everyone. They hadn't seen the signs. He sat down abruptly and lowered his head to his hands. I saw his broad shoulders move in a slow upward movement and I knew he was trying to relax. No one spoke. A few breaths accomplished his goal. Harry raised his head. "He seemed to leap across the space like he was focused on the far side of the street. He never saw me."

"Did you notice anyone or anything on the other side of the street?"

"I wasn't looking there; I was looking straight ahead. I had no chance to avoid him."

David Katernak placed a hand on Harry's shoulder. "No need to say any more. You've given your statement."

"Okay, Mr. Marsden. The technicians verify there were no skid marks until after contact with the body. You didn't appear to be speeding. It seems to have happened the way you say it did."

"*Seems* to have happened the way I say. What exactly are you implying?"

"Not implying, only wondering what you two argued about not more than an hour before you ran him down."

"My conversation had nothing to do with this. Are you crazy? Why would I kill a man I met tonight?"

"That was my next question." Sergeant Royal stared at Harry.

Harry's response came slowly, but when he spoke I shivered at the intense anger in his low, calm voice. "Charge me or release me. I'd be careful what you say next, Sergeant Royal." The slowly drawn-out sentence moved through the room like a curtain being drawn across a stage.

Katernak rushed to stand between them. I don't think he was confident that Harry wouldn't say more. To Royal's credit, she stared right back at Harry.

"Sergeant Royal. My client has nothing more to say." David tried to guide Harry to the door. Royal spoke to Harry as though David Katernak had been part of the wallpaper.

"You're free to leave, for now. Don't take any unexpected trips, Mr. Marsden. We'll be back in touch."

Harry never answered. He took me by the arm and led me out. Walter was waiting in the hallway. He said nothing to Harry but moved toward the exit. Harry placed me in front of him, effectively sandwiching me between them as we moved through the people still gathered at the front door.

WALTER DROPPED US at our door, apologizing. "I am sorry I am not staying, Mr. Harry. Gertrude will be waiting for me to take her back to Oak Park."

Apparently, Walter had left her at the depot when he received my call; his bond to Harry, still unclear to me but as strong as ever. I knew it had started with the elder Marsden when Walter, a young German flyer, was shot down over the tiny town of Arundel. Nothing could move his devotion to Harry off center.

"Not another word. You take your lady home and thank you for taking care of mine tonight." Harry smiled at Walter and accepted a bear hug from him.

"*Danke.* I *vil kommen furst* thing in morning for your back. I see you need *gut* rub."

Walter's almost daily massages had helped Harry immensely after his release from the hospital. Walter took over from the physical therapist after watching the process a few times. He never let Harry quit. I had watched a few sessions until my emotional distress at seeing Harry in pain caused him to become upset. Walter had barred me from the room at those times. I had seen Walter's eyes squeeze shut in his own pain because he knew he had to hurt Harry to help him. After Harry was pronounced healed, Walter still came. The daily massages kept Harry's damaged muscles limber and sound.

"See you in the morning." Harry spoke to Walter's retreating figure hurrying down the walkway to his car. Harry put his arm around my shoulder and guided me toward the stairs. "I'm beat, darling. Please, no questions now. I promise to answer everything in the morning. I do have a question for you, though. Sergeant Royal mentioned to one of the detectives that she talked briefly with Kramer at our house. Seems he took you home; spent some time here, if her notes were correct." Harry's raised eyebrows asked the question.

"She met him on the lawn as he was leaving. He dropped me off. His pager went off, had to leave. Peterson, I think." I knew I was babbling. I felt my face flush; I could only imagine how purple my eyes looked.

Harry stared hard at the lie. I couldn't bear his silent accusation.

"Let me make you some tea. I'll bring it up." I was hoping to avoid a confrontation and to wash up the *three* mugs on the kitchen table.

"No tea, Grace. Good night." He turned toward the stairs and moved slowly across the room. My breath caught in my throat. I hadn't meant to hurt him.

"Harry, wait." I started toward him but he kept walking.

"In the morning."

I turned back to the kitchen. I needed morning to come quickly.

TEN

A RESTLESS NIGHT filled with disjointed dreams of trunks and bodies, both dead and alive, drove me into a scared sweat. I couldn't remember exactly what had frightened me into wakefulness. *5:30* gleamed in the darkness from our Betty Boop clock. I couldn't stay in bed. I had to move, to fidget, to get some fresh air. My "clear the cobwebs" routine involved April Showers, my Tennessee Walker. She lived in a small barn at the rear of the property. I owed my sanity and mostly sunny disposition to her. A brisk ride atop April balanced most my moods and cleared my mind. I always joked that she was cheaper than a shrink. Since the craziness of six months ago, I owed her my life.

I snaked out of bed, mindful not to let cold air under the covers to disturb Harry, and quietly left the room. I always kept riding clothes in the mudroom to avoid having to ransack drawers in the early hours. I pulled on socks and worn jeans under my sleep shirt. Our furnace was set to kick up the heat at six o'clock. The mudroom was chilly enough for me to consider layering over my Winnie the Pooh sleep shirt. I reluctantly pulled the still-warm shirt over my head and tossed it toward a peg. Thermal top, denim shirt, black plaid wool jacket. I fingered the mended hole in the fabric; a hole made by a bullet meant for me.

April heard my approach and whinnied her greeting. Her head nodded in excitement. I kept her treats in a larder box in the mudroom. My offering of baby carrots and apple wedges was gratefully and messily accepted. She snuffled with approval at my choice. I wiped my hand down my jeans before rubbing her muzzle. "Hey, girl, ready for a ride?" She never said no.

I saddled her quickly and led her out. Once I climbed on her back her body quivered with anticipation. I turned her head and tapped her sides with my heels. Our walk was a slow, stretching pace until we reached the outside perimeter of the backyard. I signaled a canter and her stride lengthened to my favorite gait.

Our route took us to the top of the knoll overlooking a man-made lake. This was our spot. The sun had lifted over the horizon while we were working our way to meet it. I sat with my eyes closed, facing east, letting the warmth cover my face and create sunspots on the inside of my eyelids. "It doesn't get much better than this." April whinnied her version of an affirmative response. I leaned down and slipped both arms around her neck and rubbed under her chinstrap. April would stand for this all morning. I knew I had to get back and deal with explanations. At least my mind felt clear; the jangle mode of last night dissipated like the stream of breath from April's nostrils. I chuckled to myself at the odd comparison. *That would make a great line in a children's story.* Maybe I wasn't finished yet. *Mick the Monster isn't PC anymore but maybe zoo animals.* I had enjoyed the time I'd spent with my niece Jolene at Brookfield zoo. Almost all of the time. The *Whirl,* the zoo's gala fundraiser, had turned deadly. Those thoughts filled my mind and April sensed the tension in my body immediately. She tossed her head and pawed at the ground. "Sorry, girl. Let's go back." I turned her toward home and she did the rest.

HARRY WAS STILL upstairs when I got in. I filled his electric kettle and plugged it into the outlet on the side of the island. As I measured the coffee for my percolator I practiced what

I would say. Before I could fine-tune my explanation, I heard a truck outside. Harry appeared in the doorway and motioned for me to follow him out to the backyard.

A black pickup truck with the name HorseSense Farms stenciled on the door, carefully pulled a small horse trailer up the driveway.

I looked questioningly at Harry. "What's going on? Who's this?"

A snort and whinny responded from the back of the trailer. A corresponding whinny echoed from the barn. April was curious too. The truck stopped; my niece Jolene and another woman got out.

"Hi, Aunt Grace." Jolene hugged me and kissed my cheek. "How are you? Hi, Uncle Harry."

Harry stepped forward claiming his hug and kiss. He kept his arm around Jolene's shoulders while she continued.

"Aunt Grace, this is Kay Stec. We work together at the zoo. She is the docent who took care of April while you were away."

Kay stepped forward to shake my hand. She stood about my height, 5 feet 4 inches, and my build. Her blond hair was cut chin-length and layered around her face. She smiled as she took my hand, but her blue eyes looked troubled.

"I can never thank you enough for what you did. Knowing that April was in good hands made such a difference in my being able to relax and enjoy my stay. Thank you. If there's ever anything I can do for you, let me know."

"It's nice to meet you, Mrs. Marsden. April is a sweetheart. I loved having her at the barn."

"Call me Grace." I had guessed her age at late thirties, early forties. "Mrs. Marsden" wouldn't do.

"Grace, I hope our being here is okay with you. I mean, Jolene said it was all discussed but then she said it was to be a surprise." Kay paused and looked uncomfortable. "What I mean is if you're not ready or interested in Cash then I need to know."

"Cash? What cash? Did I sell you something?"

Harry and Jolene burst into laughter. Kay's smile wasn't as robust. A series of equine snorts erased her tentative smile.

"If you're not sure about taking Cash, I'd rather not bring him out to have to load him in again. He doesn't travel as well as other horses." A hoof to the metal bottom of the trailer punctuated her statement.

I walked to the back of the trailer. A swishing black tail and dark brown rump met my view.

Harry and Jolene flanked me on each side. Harry put his hand on my shoulder and flourished his other arm toward the occupant. "Darling, meet Cash Cow, April's new barn mate."

My grin must have set everyone at ease. "Let's not stand around. I'm sure Cash wants to stretch his legs."

Within minutes Cash was on the driveway stepping and prancing at the end of his lead, happy to be out of the metal box. I could tell in a minute that he had a sweet disposition. He stood about sixteen hands tall, definitely taller than April. His mane was as black as his tail but the rest of him was dark chocolate. If I didn't know how expensive it was to keep a horse I would have named him *Black Cow* after the ice cream creation. He accepted all of our praise and pats and especially enjoyed the baby carrots Kay had slipped us for him as we approached Cash. His black lips gently rolled the treat from our open palms into his mouth.

"He's wonderful. But tell me again why he's here?"

"I thought April might need company since you're back to work and can't spend as much time with her." Harry's grin was insufferable.

"She's not a cat, for heaven's sake."

Harry shrugged his shoulders. "I bought him for me. I re-alized that I've missed riding these past years. My leg seldom acts up so I thought it time to get 'back in the saddle,' as you Americans say."

Jolene and Kay laughed at his comments. They were funny to those who didn't know the real reason he stopped riding. Only close friends and family knew the rehabilitation it took for him to walk again after his rescue from a South American prison.

I suspected another reason. Harry never liked that I rode alone. I loved a solitary ride in the early morning. I did my best thinking, "cleared the cobwebs" on those rides. Unfortunately my well-known habit was almost my undoing a few months back. I felt certain that event had prompted my husband's renewed interest in riding.

CASH AND APRIL met and made *nice nice*. Since Cash was a gelding we didn't need to worry about how nice they made. I latched the door and walked back to the house. The morning's activities had delayed my confrontation with Harry. He had acted so carefree with Jolene and her docent friend. I felt like a little kid that wanted her friends to stay because her father wouldn't yell at her in front of them. Then I remembered that my dad, Mike Morelli, used to yell at me whenever he thought he needed to. I picked up my pace and went into the house. I could hear Harry in the kitchen. I turned to hurry up the back steps to change my riding shirt and freshen up a little. Feminine wiles couldn't hurt about now. At least it might help if I didn't smell like a stable. Harry's suitcase stood at the bottom of the stairs. Suddenly, perfume didn't seem to be enough.

ELEVEN

"Hullo, Grace. I was coming out to get you."

Harry stood in the doorway holding his travel mug in his hand. I smelled the pungent scent of his newest tea, Moonlight Mango.

"Coming to get me," I repeated. "Are we going somewhere?"

"I am, Grace. I'm flying out of Milwaukee. Walter should be here any minute."

"Where, what? Where are you going?"

"Grace, I wanted to tell you last night. The timing was wrong. I'd arranged this last week. With your schedule getting Depot Days completed I never found the opportunity to tell you."

"Harry, I know you were upset about Ric, but I can explain. This is no way to…" I stopped talking as his words finally sunk in. "Last week?"

"Grace, this has nothing to do with you and our newest neighbor; although I'm not pleased at his close proximity to you. But, we're all adults. Except for one of us. And that's the person I'm concerned with now."

The light bulb went on. Harry planned to meet his son. I wasn't sure if I was relieved because he wasn't mad at me, or if I was upset because he hadn't included me.

"Lily sent me a wire letting me know where they are. We both thought it best if I met him on his turf, where he can be comfortable. I've got to do this, Grace. You see that, don't you, darling?"

What could I say? *No, I don't want you to meet your son.* Of course, I did. But why did they have to discuss what was best for Will? *Because he's their son. The common bond that will bring them together.* Lily's father's words echoed in my head. *Of course this is a common bond, a genetic bond, a human bond.* I stopped "bonding" before my head twirled off my neck. Harry had said something that apparently required an answer. He looked at me expectantly.

"Uh, I didn't hear you."

"No doubt. Your eyes are pansy-purple. When you hit purple your brain is usually on overdrive and not much else gets in." He smiled and put his arms around me. He knew only too well my quirky physiology; normally lavender-hued eyes turned dark at the onset of fear or excitement. "Darling, this is about Will, not Lily. I want you to meet him as soon as possible. I want us to be a big part of his life. I've so much lost time to make up."

The sound of a horn from the driveway interrupted us. "There's Walter. I'll call you when I arrive." Harry's kiss took me by surprise. Delighted me, in fact. The perfunctory peck I'd been expecting was instead deep and lingering as he pulled his mouth and arms away. "I love you. Always."

My eyes brimmed with tears. He leaned toward me again, kissed the tip of my nose, and tapped the bottom of my chin with his thumb. I smiled and nodded my head. Harry lifted his suitcase and walked to the back door. He stopped in the doorway. "Be back before you miss me."

"Too late, I miss you already." We played this game when we had to be apart. He grinned and waved goodbye.

I watched Walter's Rover back out of the driveway and move down the street, taking Harry to Lily in… *Oh, cripes. Where? Taking him where? I forgot to ask where. How totally stupid. And he didn't volunteer that information. Or did he, when I wasn't listening?* Now that his face and mouth weren't vying for my brain cells, why Milwaukee?

I picked up the phone to call Harry on his car phone and put it down, remembering Walter was driving. Maybe Hannah knew where Lily and Will were. I picked up the phone to call Hannah but put it down. I didn't want to admit I didn't know where my husband went. I'm a terrible liar, even over the phone. Maybe Ric? I didn't want to make that call. I stared at the phone turning over my options in my head. My fingers began braiding the lengths of yarn attached to the cord so I didn't braid that into uselessness when I talked on the phone.

The phone rang. I was on top of it and answered before the ring ended.

"Hello."

"Mrs. Marsden? Good morning. This is Sergeant Royal. I'm sorry to be calling so early on a Sunday but I need to speak to your husband. Is he there?"

Oh, my God. The police. Harry wasn't supposed to leave town. He knew that, he knows better. Now what?

"Mrs. Marsden? Are you there?"

"Yes, of course, why wouldn't I be?" *Great, now I sound like an idiot.* "I mean it's early, but not that early. We've been up and about already. In fact, I've been out riding already and we had another horse delivered this morning. Beautiful horse. Do you ride, Sergeant Royal?" *Lord, I'm babbling and braiding at breakneck speed.* The yarn twisted and looped like my convoluted thoughts.

"Uh, yes, I ride, but..."

"Maybe you'd like to come out and ride sometime when you're not on duty?"

"Mrs. Marsden, is your husband home?"

She wasn't buying the chitchat. I gripped the phone harder and squeezed my eyes shut. I always shut my eyes when I lied—psychological, I guess—but stupid since if you saw my eye color change you'd know I was lying and if you saw me close my eyes you'd know I was lying. *This not-in-person lie might work.*

"He's not here right now. Stepped out to get some things for the new horse and to get some breakfast to bring back and some office supplies for work he'll be doing later." *Even I don't believe me.*

"He certainly sounds busy today. Mrs. Marsden, it's important that I talk with him. Can you reach him by phone?"

"I thought of that but he's not in his car," blurted out before I could stop myself.

"You thought of calling him before I asked?"

"I, uh, thought of something else he could pick up but I remembered he didn't take his car."

"Is he in your car? Can you call him on that phone?"

"No, he took, I mean he left with Walter." I felt a little better. This wasn't a bald-faced lie but now I had involved Walter.

"The man who brought you to the station last night?"

"Yes. And Walter doesn't have a car phone. I'll tell Harry to call you as soon as he returns." Once again, not a total lie; I would tell him. I was feeling better about this call. I hated it when I got over-confident.

"Mrs. Marsden, some new information about the hit and run has come to light and I need to speak to Mr. Marsden. If he doesn't call me by 2:00 p.m., I am issuing a warrant for his arrest. And Mrs. Marsden, so you know, if you are withholding information, you will be charged with obstruction."

"I'll give him the message." My tone sounded dull to my ears.

"See that you do, Mrs. Marsden." She hung up and I stood there holding the phone to my ear. The off-hook signal sounded and I almost dropped the receiver.

How long would it take to get to Milwaukee and was his flight leaving soon? Had I stalled enough to give him time to get away? *Get away? I'm making him sound like a criminal. If he'd known there was new evidence he'd have stayed. I think. Too late now.*

I knew I had to stop thinking and start acting. I refilled my coffee cup to the top with Cinnamon Nut Swirl and pulled out our address book from the drawer.

David Katernak, our attorney, answered on the third ring.

"Hi, David, this is Grace Marsden. I'm sorry to be calling so early on a Sunday." *Déjà vu with Sergeant Royal's opening line.* "There's been a development in the hit and run case and the police want to talk to Harry."

"When do they want to see him? I can be there by early afternoon. D.J. has a soccer game at noon and I'm a sideline coach."

"She said she wanted to talk to him but the problem is Harry's not here. I mean he won't be home for a while. I mean, David, I think he left the country to go meet Lily and his son."

"What! Is he crazy? He's involved in a hit and run. He can't leave the state let alone the country in the middle of the investigation. What is he thinking?"

"David, it's not like he did it on purpose. He made his plans last week. How could he know he'd run over someone? He didn't hit that man intentionally. Meeting his son is important to him. They can certainly understand that. Can't they?"

"Grace, the law doesn't work that way. When did he leave? What flight is he on and where is he going?"

"I don't know his flight or carrier and I don't know his destination."

"Grace, this is not the time to stonewall me. Whatever you tell me is confidential but we have to stop him and get him back here."

My mouth dried up and my throat tightened and I heard the frustration and tears in my voice. "I don't know where he's going. He left with Walter for the airport." I prayed he wouldn't ask me which airport.

"Okay, Grace. I believe you. There was something not right about Harry last night. He probably didn't tell you so you couldn't be charged with obstruction. I'm sure Harry wasn't going to sit around O'Hare long. He's probably already in the air. Do you at least have a guess as to which country he was headed for?"

I really felt stupid now. "I know she was on a photographic shoot in Europe. I think maybe France, maybe England." How could I not know where Harry was meeting Lily? "I'm sorry, David, I don't know. Is he going to be in a lot of trouble?"

"He's going to be arrested. Since he's proven to be a flight risk the Judge will either set a bond so high you won't be able to make it or no bond. I'd say that's trouble."

My soft gasp must have caused him to rethink his tone.

"Grace, take it easy. Can you think of anyone who might know where he's going?"

"Maybe Hannah, or…Ric." The last name I gave hesitantly. David heard it.

"Well, try Hannah and get hold of Walter as soon as you can. Not that he'd give him up. Harry probably didn't give him any information either. God, Grace, he makes it damn near impossible to defend him. I wish he'd stop playing secret agent; it's going to backfire on him one of these days."

David was referring to Harry's earlier career in the service of British Intelligence. I thought David's reference to *playing* unjust, but it didn't seem the time to tell him.

David promised to call me if he could find out what the new development was and I promised to call if I found out Harry's destination. I had more confidence in David's promise than in mine. I wondered if he felt the same.

TWELVE

Walter wasn't home; he'd probably gone straight to Gertrude's in Oak Park after dropping off Harry. Hannah wasn't home either. That left Ric. He'd said something about Will going to the same school Lily had attended. Would that have been in South Africa, France, or England?

I dialed reluctantly, pressing each button slowly and with concern. *Maybe he won't be home. No one else is.*

"Hello."

His voice sounded awake and eager. I wondered if he had caller I.D.

"Ric, its Grace."

"Well, good morning. I didn't expect this call."

"Yeah, well, I didn't expect to have to make it." My voice caught.

"*Have to?* Grace, what's wrong?"

"Harry left this morning to meet Lily and William. Sergeant Royal called wanting to talk to him. She said that if he didn't call by this afternoon she would get a warrant. I don't know where he's meeting her. Do you? David Katernak says he'll be in trouble if we don't get him back soon."

"He's right about that, but he's in trouble as soon as they figure out he skipped."

"Ric, he didn't skip. He made these plans last week. I need to know where he went."

"He really didn't tell you? I'm not surprised. You can't divulge what you don't know and that keeps you safe. Up to his old agency tricks again."

That was the second person today to mention Harry's previous profession. When would *retired from active duty* mean just that in people's minds? I missed most of Ric's next comment but got the gist of it: he was coming over. The line went dead and my mind went numb.

I didn't want to be alone with Ric. I could refuse to open the door. But I needed to know if he knew. I didn't have much time; even with canes it wouldn't take long for him to arrive. Thank goodness I still smelled like a stable.

I OPENED THE DOOR immediately when he rang and walked quickly toward the kitchen, ignoring his slower pace. I sat at the table with my hands wrapped around a large steaming mug of Jamaican Blue Magic, which I had quickly brewed before he arrived. I nodded to the other mug at the place across from me. Good, three feet of oak between us.

"You didn't need to come over. You could have told me over the phone."

"I wanted to see you again. I know we didn't leave on the best of terms last night."

"Last night we agreed it wouldn't happen again—an 'event of the moment,' I believe you called it. We also agreed not to mention it. See, there was no need to come over." I thought my logic impeccable. But in the emotional gambit of *rock, paper, scissors,* logic never wins.

"I love you, Gracie. That's never changed. You know that. Living this close to you now and not taking every chance to see you, won't work for me."

"Ric, don't. You know I don't—"

"You don't what? Feel the chemistry between us? You don't see how we keep coming together, like fate? You need me."

I gripped the edge of the table to keep my hands from straying to the cord tied to my belt loop. The last thing I needed was to become distracted. I leaned toward Ric and used what I hoped sounded like a serious tone. "What I need is for you to tell me where my husband is."

"Sure, Gracie, I'll tell you. He's with another woman and their child."

He couldn't have hurt me more if he'd punched me in the stomach. I lost my grip on the table and sat back in a slump.

"Dammit. Gracie, I'm sorry." Ric moved around the table and tried to comfort me.

"You're not sorry," I yelled at him. "You wanted to hurt me. Humiliate me."

"No, Grace. I never want that." He looked wide-eyed at me and tried again to put his arm around my shoulders. I shrugged him away. "God, Grace, I'd never hurt you. I want you to see we belong together."

"I don't belong with you. We've been through this. When they found Harry alive, what we had stopped. I told you. I've been telling you."

"Everything is different now, Grace. You know Harry would have married Lily if he had known about the pregnancy. They're his family now. He might not even realize that, but he will when he meets his son."

I tucked my chin against my chest and put my hands over my ears in a childish gesture to block out his voice. My voice sounded far away when I spoke. "You're wrong. Harry, Will, and me. That's the family he wants." *Why didn't I sound more confident? Could Ric be right?*

"I'm sure he believes it can be that easy. Can it, Grace? Living down the street from them? Where will he spend all his time? Ten years to make up. Tucking him in, having a catch on the lawn, checking his homework. Where do you think that will happen? Your house or hers?"

"Ric, please. Why are you saying these things?" I realized he'd been rubbing my back much like I imagined Harry would rub Will's back to comfort him, or maybe Lily's. The tears flowed before I could control my feelings. "Harry and I are planning to adopt," came out in small sobs.

"I know, Gracie. Hannah and Karen told me you would all fly to Europe together when the agency approved the adoptions. They've already submitted the paperwork and are waiting for approval. Where is your application?"

Ric's words chilled me and stopped a sob forming in my throat. He seemed to sense he'd scored a hit. His arm moved around me; his hand lifted my chin and gently turned it toward him. "Mmm, *eau de April*." He sniffed my hair and tucked one side behind my ear and pushed some tears from my cheek with his thumb.

"*We* could have children together, lots of them."

I came undone. I buried my head in his chest and cried like someone I loved had died. Maybe in a sense, I thought they had, or at least the relationship.

Ric coaxed me from the chair so that he held me full against his body, wrapping his arms tightly as though to keep me from unraveling. "Shh, Gracie. It's okay. I'm here. I won't leave you. Never, angel. Never."

Ric's pet name for me, not spoken for almost eight years, ratcheted up the emotional upheaval. The barrier of fresh memories with Harry, renewed vows, the exhilaration I felt when they found him alive, began to slip like layers of photos sliding from a pile to scatter across the table leaving the finish exposed. *Photos, like Lily takes. Lily, William...layers of Harry's new life.*

I don't know how long we stood together; Ric never moved a muscle. Thoughts, snippets of conversations and juxtaposed events swirled through my mind, further dispersing the photos of my life. I breathed slower, deeper. As the photos settled in disarray, I realized that nothing is coincidence; just luck of the draw. The images lay in different relationships, not an impenetrable barrier, more like a robe drawn around me. I was part of Harry's life, whatever changes William brought to it. I would make those changes favorable. I lifted my head from his chest and in my mind tightened the belt of that robe.

He must have sensed the shift. His eyes dimmed as he looked into mine. "He's a lucky bastard."

"Luck has nothing to do with it." I turned away from him and leaned my forearms on the table. "Will you tell me where they are meeting?"

Ric kept his arms around me. He leaned his lips close to my ear. I felt his warm breath and something else. I had to get that table between us again. As he ducked his head closer, I quickly turned mine as though to comment. He pulled back and I sidestepped against his right arm pushing it open like a garden gate and stepped out from his proximity. I circled to the other side, effectively trading places with where we started.

"Where, Ric?"

His slow smile never reached his eyes. "I don't know."

My hand went around the mug, flinging the lukewarm contents at his face before the words exploded from my mouth. "You son of a bitch. You don't know?"

Ric wiped liquid from his face with the napkin at my setting and pulled my coffee mug closer to him. He put one hand up to ward off more missiles. "I don't know for sure. Lily was on the Normandy coast, shooting some sea birds. I don't know if he was meeting her there or on the other side. People in Europe hop back and forth across the channel like we drive to Crown Point and back."

"Ric, you lied to me." I put up my hand to stop his speech. "You led me to believe you knew. That's still lying." He didn't look remorseful. He ran his left hand through his hair, a nervous habit. *Good. Let him stew.*

"Grace, I didn't lie about still loving you, always loving you."

I picked up his canes from where he had leaned them against the table. A brief look of concern crossed his face.

"I should, but I'm not. I'm finished flinging." I thought about what I had said; I hoped he understood the double meaning.

Ric gripped the canes and moved toward the hallway. I walked ahead and opened the door. He stopped in the doorway. "I was always there for you, Grace. Now I'm closer." No smile, no brag, just fact. He *would* always be there. I watched him hobble down the sidewalk to his car. I closed the door and leaned heavily against the paneled surface. *God, Harry. Please hurry home.*

THIRTEEN

THE PHONE RANG several times before the meaning of the noise penetrated the funk I had fallen into. I still leaned against the door; only I had slid to the floor and subconsciously started braiding the yarn on my belt loop.

I let the answering machine take the call. A click, no message. *Maybe it was Ric. Glad I didn't answer. Maybe it was Harry, not wanting to talk if he didn't know who might be listening. Maybe it was Sergeant Royal, again.*

I needed to get out of the house and away from the phone. Harry was probably still in the air going to...who knows where. Ric or Royal was a better bet.

I climbed the stairs to my bedroom and turned the spigots in the Jacuzzi. I needed a hot soak to soothe my brain and dispel the aroma of stable that still lingered. *Hadn't stopped Ric. That's what I get for teaching him to ride.* I unwrapped two cubes of bath salts labeled "Lavender Stress-Relief" and crushed them under the running water. *If two is good, four has to be better and eight would be best.* I quickly depleted my "Lavender Stress-Relief" stash. I heaped my riding clothes on the floor and slipped into blissful bubbles.

The hot soothing water pulled the tension from my muscles and I felt my shoulders loosening, allowing my arms to lift and float. My mind drifted from point A from the night before through to this moment. There was no horror, no fear, only a calm viewing of a tape rolling in my head.

As the water cooled, my thoughts began to swirl, increasingly pushed aside by one stark image after another like frozen faces on a flashing loop: Hannah's terror, Harry's glare, Schoebel's fear. My gentle introspection roiled inside my head. I pulled the plug on my bath and wrapped myself in a huge white towel embroidered with pink flamingoes on the edges. Sitting on the edge of the tub, waiting for the water to drain I stared at the whirlpool rushing to find escape.

Schoebel's fear; rushing to find escape. My thoughts were revisiting every move that locksmith made last night. *He did look nervous about not opening the trunk.* I thought he was embarrassed that he couldn't. *He looked absolutely panicked after Hannah's trunk was opened.* Why? What business was it of his? And why on earth did Harry follow him? If only he hadn't gone after him. If only he were here.

He did and he's not, so stop going there. Think of what you do know. What do you know? Slowly, while I absent-mindedly picked apart the stitching on two flamingoes, the part of my brain that doesn't go AWOL on me started to form a plan.

I had all the information on the event in my files at the office. It would take forty-five minutes round trip. I thought about the contents of three bulging folders in my credenza while I dressed. If I timed it right I could make the last seating for tea at the Jefferson Tea Room. That ruled out jeans and a sweatshirt. Must be the nun influence, but I couldn't imagine sitting down to tea in jeans or sweats. A brown suede boot-top skirt with a butternut sweater set would be perfect. My hair, always the issue, fell smooth on one side and slid out in a wave on the other. I couldn't undo one side or redo the other. With a high-brim bowler type hat covering my hair down to my ears, I looked less lopsided. The skirt had a short, matching cape and that would be heavy enough for the pleasant early autumn weather.

The phone rang while I was backing out of the garage. Still too early for Harry. Ric or Royal again? I didn't want to talk to either of them. I thought myself pretty slick skipping out on further confrontation. I turned onto the iron bridge that spanned the marsh that surrounded most of the compound. This was the only way in or out of Pine Marsh. A sheriff's squad passed me coming in. It turned right. Only three houses were on that side. Lily's, Atwater's, and ours. The compound was patrolled by private security. I could think of only one reason a sheriff's car would be coming to visit. I needed to get some answers that didn't spell *Harry Marsden*.

I didn't feel so slick anymore.

FOURTEEN

THE OFFICES OF Schwarze and Krieg occupied a portion of a converted building on the outskirts of downtown. I loved going to work surrounded by antique stores, candle shops, and wonderful restaurants. I planned on doing all my Christmas shopping downtown; The Stamp Shack, The Mole Hole, Jan's Hallmark and The Cranberry Moose.

I found parking a short distance from the building. My keys would open the street door and the suite door to our offices on the second floor. It was obvious this had been someone's home in the early settlement of Naperville. The stairs had been refurbished and covered with deep pile carpeting to eliminate noise. I climbed quickly, lost in thought about the squad car and reached the landing before I realized I wasn't alone. The door to the office stood ajar and I could hear Liz talking to someone. Suddenly, I felt foolish, poised on the threshold of my office on a Sunday afternoon, attempting to be *Nancy Drew.* I hesitated and the voices grew louder. Liz must have moved closer to the door.

"Aunt Ava, why are you so upset? So you didn't get the other trunk. Be glad. Who'd want it after what they found? I don't understand why you're so upset."

"I'm upset because all this was done without my knowledge or permission. Your girl snoop went through business records and bullied Karl into turning over my property."

Girl snoop? Was she referring to me? Bullied? I don't bully...nag, maybe, but never bully.

"Grace Marsden did not bully Karl. The trunks were not

your property. The agreement Grace found in the old files was for you and Aunt Eva to store them."

Ava Deutsch's voice grew louder. I couldn't tell if she was shouting or moving closer to the door. I certainly didn't want to be caught flat-footed eavesdropping. I moved across from the office door and carefully opened the door to the bathroom, praying that neither one of them decided to use it before they left. I didn't push the door totally closed; I wanted to hear what else they had to say. Only seconds passed before I heard Liz's voice uncomfortably close to the bathroom door.

"I'm more concerned with the pall that Schoebel's death has thrown over the event."

"Don't be silly, Liz. That's what people love." Ava Deutsch's voice snapped with harshness I hadn't experienced in the brief conversations I'd had with her a few days prior to the auction. "On my way here I drove by the depot. The vendors are doing 'blue ribbon' business with all the thrill-seekers rubber necking and trampling the ground. They should have a murder every year."

Liz's voice sounded strained. "I can't believe you said that. Wasn't that poor man a cousin of yours? What's gotten into you? You don't sound like yourself. You sound like—"

"Like who?" Ava's voice insisted.

"Nothing, never mind. I'm tired; I've been up most of the night. I'm going home."

I heard the office door being locked. Soon, I could leave my hiding spot.

"Oh, look at this. They never lock this door."

The door pulled shut with a firm yank from the other side. I could smell Liz's perfume.

"I keep telling the cleaning people to keep this locked. The tenants from downstairs are always using our bathroom. They have their own."

"You should use my cleaning lady, Jan Pauli. She does an adequate job, better than most."

I could hear the sniff of dismissal in her voice.

"You should know, Aunt. Since Irene left you haven't been able to keep one. What number is this? You go through cleaning ladies like toddlers go through training pants."

I clamped a hand over my mouth to squelch the chuckle. Ava Deutsch was no one to confront. My heart pounded in my ears as I realized too late what was happening. I heard the click of the lock engaging from the other side, followed by the scraping sound of Liz hanging the key on a nail in a niche behind the door molding.

I froze to the spot. *Say something,* my mind shouted. My brain skipped out. I could only respond by pattern. *Click the light switch twenty times on, twenty times off.* I didn't want to; I had to. I clicked *on, off, on, off,* for twenty repetitions before my voice would call out.

"Hello. Hello! Help. I'm locked in. Hello!"

I pounded and called out but I knew they had left the building. I hadn't been fast enough to get their attention. *Oh, man, how did this happen? Okay, okay. Take it easy.* I rolled my shoulders to relax and took a deep breath. *How would Agatha Christie write me out of this locked room?* I smiled to myself as I realized that my reading habits might be the means of my escape. I knew you could never read too much, and now I would prove it. I stood in the middle of the tiny room and began the scrutiny of each wall. The original claw-foot bathtub stood in a small alcove. It brimmed with gewgaws of another era. Puffy quilts, crewel pillows, hat boxes, dresser scarves, colorful silk nosegays hanging over the edge on wrought iron hooks, and a stuffed ring-necked pheasant perched on one end of the tub. A small concrete gargoyle stood guard at the base. A potpourri of interesting stuff, but no way out.

I shifted to my right and looked at the short wall opposite the door. *The window. Of course.* I stepped around the toilet, gripped the handles on the sash, and yanked. The window moved three inches up the track and stopped. My shoulders jolted at the sudden stop. I tried again. It wouldn't lift beyond that point. I saw why. A small piece of wood was nailed to each side of the track on the outside of the window. The building owners probably didn't want people leaving the window open in case of rain or pigeons.

I chuckled as I pictured someone answering the call and being surprised by a pigeon perching on the toilet paper roll. I still had my sense of humor and two walls left. The toilet and pedestal sink were just that. I noticed a small door, about two feet square on the wall close to the floor. *A laundry chute.*

I bent down to open the door. I could easily fit through there. My excitement mounted faster than my common sense. I rummaged inside my purse for my keys. A small penlight hung from the key ring. The light reached forward into the void about six inches. That was enough. I had expected a wooden slide of some sort. I found a shaft with two deteriorated ropes hanging from a pulley. The movement of air caused them to sway on the metal track. *A dumbwaiter. Why would anyone want a dumbwaiter to the bathroom?*

I'd seen the one at Regina College used to bring stored food items from the basement up to the kitchen behind the dining hall. Maybe the original owner enjoyed breakfast in bed or dinner in the tub.

Interesting architectural innovation from the 1800s but I was still trapped in a bathroom. By now, I'd been in here for fifteen minutes.

I lowered the lid on the toilet and sat down to think. No one would be here until tomorrow morning. This was fast becoming a nightmare. I stared at the door. My golf instructor used to stress that trees were ninety-percent air. Whenever I sliced into one, it seemed solid to me. Like this door.

The hinges! My brain embraced the idea before I left my seat. I inspected the hinges. They looked like the originals and they hadn't been painted over. The head of the pin stood a tiny bit up from the top of the hinge. *I can do this. I saw this in a movie. Pop the pin up. I need a metal file, or a strip of metal, or a screwdriver, or a...* My thoughts slowed, then stopped. I didn't have any of those. *Now what? The movie. What did she use in that show?*

In that episode of *Moonlighting,* Cybill Shepherd happened to have a butter knife that she'd stolen from a suspect to check for prints, in her purse. She quickly popped the pins up and escaped before the commercial. Didn't matter that she'd smudged the prints because she recognized the murderer's voice when she got locked in the room.

Just like me. Oh, cripes, Grace. No one wants to kill you and this isn't a TV show. I shook off the eerie sensation and regretted not carrying cutlery in my purse. Maybe it wasn't a movie, but I'd watched enough television that something should come to mind. *Macmillan and Wife, Hart to Hart, Remington Steele,* I scrolled through programs. *Magnum P.I., Jake and the Fat Man, MacGyver.* That was it. *MacGyver.* He could use anything to do anything. I had to think like MacGyver.

I spun around and looked at everything with a different perspective. I needed a piece of metal. I looked back at my recently occupied seat. A tissue box and a can of Glade sat on the top of the tank. I removed those and then the top to look into the water tank. I recognized all the working parts. The toilet in my first apartment sometimes ran even when you jiggled the handle. I'd have to fiddle with the chain that connected the float to the flap.

I used a thin dime to unscrew the float apparatus from the

vertical pipe and lifted it out of the tank. The metal arm un-screwed easily from the bulbous float and I had half of my equipment. I had already identified the stone gargoyle as my hammer. Thank God the pins had not been tapped all the way down the channel.

I started by tapping from the bottom up and managed to push the metal pin up a quarter of an inch. The gargoyle was heavy and I worried that the metal would bend under the force. Several minutes later, I had the top pin halfway out. The bottom one proved more difficult since I couldn't get the same leverage to swing my "hammer."

Thirty minutes later the pins were out, but I was still trapped. I couldn't budge the door. I had no way to pull the door toward me and I couldn't push it out against the lip of the doorjamb. *Maddie Hayes didn't have this problem; her door swung in off the hinges. Cheap door. More like no one ever really tried it.*

My frustration overtook me and my hands sought the com-fort of the light switch. *Click, click, click.* I lost track of the sequence. My hand stopped; my head re-engaged. I searched through the bathtub for anything I could use. This was an old door and there was a small gap between the door and the frame. Removing the pins had increased the gap by a skosh.

My search zeroed in on the iron hooks holding the silk flowers. Two were thick braided metal, the third piece simply curved at both ends. I pushed the iron through the gap and then turned it to the left to position the hook against the door. The curve at my end was a perfect handhold. All I needed was enough clearance to get my hands around the edge.

Crack! Something had happened. I pulled harder. *Pop!* That did it. The lock lost its internal grip and the door shifted in toward me on an angle.

I grabbed my purse and shimmied through the open space. Halfway down the stairs I thought of why I had come there in the first place. Reluctantly, I retraced my steps and stood before the office door pretending not to see the wreck behind me.

My desk wasn't locked. I never kept anything of value in there or the credenza. Anyone was welcome to my Altoids, Baby Ruths, or Midol. I opened the credenza and ran my fingers over the file tabs. *Expenses, Interviews, Photographs, Releases, Research;* the Depot Days file was bulky. I tried to separate items as they accumulated but I intended to thoroughly catalog the contents when I closed the file with my final rundown of the event.

Run down. I cringed as I remembered my reason for this visit. When I opened the research folder I knew someone had looked at the contents; the papers were slightly skewed, not squared off. If you are "blessed" with an obsessive personality, little things matter a lot.

I couldn't find the sheet on Schoebel. The smaller folder with notes on vendors wasn't inside the larger manila jacket. Who would take this? Had the police been here? I returned the folder to the credenza and opened my bottom desk drawer. I never could compose on a computer. Even when I wrote children's books I wrote them longhand and then copied them into the computer.

Please be here. Tell me I kept you. Yes!

I pulled a composition notebook from the drawer. The title on the white block on the cover read, *Depot Days.* Now, I could leave. I locked the door behind me and looked at the shambles across the hallway. *Fingerprints. Geez, Louise. My prints are all over everything. They're bound to call the police.*

I pulled a handkerchief from my purse and climbed back through the gap. *Okay, wipe stuff you touched. Window pulls, dumbwaiter door, toilet top, hinges, float arm, hook, pins, door edge.* I looked around, satisfied that I'd wiped off everything I'd touched that I'd have no reason to touch in normal use.

I'd been here for almost two hours. I looked at the commode, realizing I needed to use the facility. I weighed the need and the risk of using a toilet I had tinkered with and decided I could wait.

FIFTEEN

ELEVEN MESSAGES. Three from Hannah, three from David Katernak, two from Ric, and one each from Sergeant Royal, Walter, and Liz.

"Hallo." Walter's deep voice answered.

"Walter, its Grace. Where's Harry? It's important, Walter. The police are looking for him."

"Ya, I know. That sergeant lady called me. She wanted to know where Mr. Harry is going. I tell her what I know. Noth-ink."

Part of me smiled at the Sergeant Schultz response but more of me worried. "Walter, Harry tells you everything. You must know where he's meeting them."

"No, missus. Mr. Harry don't want me to lie or be in trouble. He says not where he is meeting Miss Lily."

Miss Lily. Before he referred to her as "that woman." That's changed now. She is the mother of Harry's son and that certainly raised her status with Walter. I'm only the wife.

Stop it!

"Missus Grace? Are you hearing me?"

"Yes, Walter. I hear you fine."

"Everything will be good. Mr. Harry must do this for his son. You call me if you are needing something. *Tschuess.*"

I hung up with Walter and dialed Liz before I could dwell on Walter's comments.

"Hi, Grace. Thanks for calling back."

That still spooked me when people used caller I.D. to answer that way. We had it but still I answered "hello." People couldn't wait an extra minute?

"Hi, Liz. It's Grace," I said slowly to get my minute. "You asked me to call?"

"Yes. I stopped in the office earlier to look at your file on Depot Days. My aunt wants to find out about poor Mr. Schoebel. She knew him years ago; wants to contact next of kin."

I felt a huge sigh of relief. I realized I'd been holding my breath. "Uh, that's nice of her."

"My Aunt Ava is like that. She's the sweetest person."

She didn't sound sweet to me earlier today. Seemed kind of stuck up to me. Liz had asked me a question that I missed. I could tell by the way her voice had ended on an up note.

"Sorry, Liz. I floated away for a second. You asked?"

"I said I couldn't find the folder on Depot Days. Where did you put it? And the disk for the event is not in the box."

"The folder is in my credenza."

"Grace, it's not there. I looked." Liz's voice crept up the scale.

"Of course it's there. I just saw it." *Damn. Too stupid for my own good.*

"You saw it; when? Were you in the office today?"

I squeezed my eyes shut. "I mean as in the last time I was there. At work. I don't work on Sunday." *Okay, Grace. Just sell it, don't buy it back.* I put my hand over my mouth to stop any errant sentences from tumbling out. I must have looked like two-thirds of those "no evil" monkeys.

"I guess I missed it. My aunt was rushing me. Sorry to bother you at home. I'll go take another look." *Great! What I thought wouldn't be discovered until tomorrow will be on the police blotter within the hour.*

"Liz, why don't you check with the police? They must have that information. I'm sure someone knew him and came forth. Why drag yourself all the way to the office again?" *Again.*

Oh, man. Just cuff me. I held my breath, waiting for a comment, but Liz must have been focused on saving a trip and missed my slipup.

"That's a good idea. Thanks, Grace, see you tomorrow."

I mumbled a hasty goodbye. I needed a strong cup of Blue Mountain Brew if I was going to get through the rest of these calls, especially the one from Sergeant Royal. In the time it took me to brew that pot my next return call beat me to the punch. I recognized the police number when the phone rang.

"Hello."

"Good afternoon, Mrs. Marsden. This is Sergeant Royal."

"Yes?"

"Mrs. Marsden, have you talked with your husband since our last conversation?"

"No. I have not." I was determined to keep my answers short and to the point.

"Mrs. Marsden, why didn't you tell me your husband was leaving the country when I spoke with you this morning?"

Again, with my eyes shut tight, "I didn't know he was leaving the country. He said he was going to meet his son. That meeting could be in Chicago for all I know." I felt smug with my answer.

"And would that meeting have taken place before or after he completed his errands to the hardware store? Or after Walter Stahl dropped him off at the airport in Milwaukee?"

My eyes flew open; my mouth stayed shut.

"Mrs. Marsden, you are being charged as an accessory to his flight. I'm sending a squad for you; should be there in twenty minutes. Stay put, Mrs. Marsden. You're in enough trouble."

Neither of us said goodbye.

David Katernak answered the phone on the first ring. "David?"

"Hi, Grace. I heard about the charge. That's why I've been

trying to reach you. They called me as your attorney of record to see if I knew Harry's whereabouts and they told me
they would be charging you. I'll meet you at the station. This
is a ploy, pressure to get you to disclose Harry's location."

"Then I don't have to worry?"

"I didn't say that, Grace. You're still in trouble. It's Harry
they want, and I'm assuming that they're assuming that as
soon as he hears you've been charged he'll be turning himself in."

"What if he doesn't find out?"

"Grace, if there's one thing I know about Harry it's that he
can track practically at will what's happening to each special
person in his life. And no one is more special to him than you.
Once he's on the ground and he finds out, he'll be in touch."

Tears filled my eyes. Would I be more special than meeting his son? I cleared my throat. "Thank you. I'll see you at
the station."

THE POLICE PARKING LOT seemed crowded. Attendance seemed
high for a Sunday. I guess I considered it a day of rest for
crime too. Before I walked in I spotted Walter's Land Rover
and David's BMW. The squad slipped into a spot a few cars
away.

"Grace, over here. We saved a chair for you."

Saved a chair? Karen was waving at me from a bank of
chairs at the left end of the corridor. Hannah was seated next
to her and Walter beyond her. If not for Walter's presence I
felt as though I'd walked back in time into Sister Cyrille's
lecture and my chums were saving a choice spot for me. The
notebook each held on their lap supported the illusion.

Before I took a step, David called out my name. A glance
to the right showed me David, Sergeant Peterson, and Ric.

"Grace, I need a quick word with you before we go in."
David walked toward me and indicated we should step out-

side. Ric followed him at a slower pace. David stopped walking and addressed Ric. "Mr. Kramer, this is a private conversation between me and my client."

"Mrs. Marsden happens to be my client, also." Ric looked at me and then inclined his head behind me toward my chums. "They hired me to investigate the hit and run."

I swiveled on the balls of my feet. "What in God's name is going on here? How you could do this without asking me?"

Karen answered first. "I told her you'd go nuts. I didn't want to involve him, Grace. Hannah said—"

"I can speak for myself." Her clipped tone told me they had discussed this already. "I don't want my brother hunted down. This business has to be handled quickly and efficiently. I know you want that too, Grace. You're too close to the, ah," Hannah's voice sputtered and continued at a faster pace, "the, um, core; the core of the case. Much like the forest and the trees analogy."

"This isn't the Arboretum, Hannah. This is Harry's and my decision. He will not be amused." I felt guilty about referencing her Queen's line but I knew I had to undo this mess. I wished life had an "undo" button.

"Deal with this later. I need to talk to you now." David placed his hand under my elbow and guided me outside. We walked into the park in front of the building and sat down on a bench. "Grace, you need to stay focused in there and above all you need to keep quiet. Let me do the talking. It may seem that I'll put the burden of guilt on Harry. I don't want you to jump up and defend him. I know what I'm doing. Right now, Harry is free and you may not be. So do it my way, okay?"

What could he say about Harry that would be so bad? He's supposed to be his lawyer.

"Grace? Agreed? Trust me on this."

That was a line I'd heard a few times in my life. The girlfriend in junior high who swore no one would notice the

turquoise-colored tissues I'd used to fill out my B-cup bra...
Ah, yes. All eyes were on me at the Elm Skating Rink. My co-
editor on *The Mural,* the yearbook for Proviso West High...
"No one cares if good students take one senior ditch day."
Pearl Broderick, our counselor, cared to the tune of a week
of detention.

David shook my shoulder. "Grace, where the hell do you
go in there?" My eyes focused on his tight lips and tense
shoulders.

"Don't yell at her." Ric had followed us outside. "And take
your hand off her."

David moved his hand. "Grace, I didn't mean to yell. I'm
sorry." He stood up.

"I'm the one who's sorry. I wasn't concentrating. I'm nervous. It's okay."

Ric hadn't moved. He faced David. "It's not okay. You
want to yell at someone, you yell at me. You want to shake
someone..."

"Ric, stop it."

David put his hands up chest high and palms out signal-
ing truce. "You're not my concern. She is. Grace, remember
what I said. I'll see you inside."

I watched him enter the building and started to follow. I
thought my best defense against Ric would be to ignore him.

"What did he tell you, Grace? Hannah wanted to hire another attorney, too. She doesn't like him. What's his plan?
Don't say anything you don't want to."

Tears itched at the back of my throat. My head pounded
with each step I took. "He wants me to keep my mouth shut
while he lays the whole thing on Harry. Satisfied?" I increased
my pace and yanked open the door but not before I heard a
low whistle and Ric's comment, "Maybe I underestimated
him. Do it, Grace, keep—" the door closed on his words.

SIXTEEN

TWO HOURS AT the police station exhausted me beyond belief. Time would have passed faster if everyone in the hallway hadn't insisted that they be allowed to be character witnesses for Harry. The officer pressed for facts, not hearsay fluff.

Walter, who I thought would be in trouble, had a perfect out. He hadn't been in the room with Sergeant Royal when she told Harry not to leave town. I vouched that neither Harry nor I shared that information with Walter on the way home.

Walter had driven Karen and Hannah here, so once they released him they all left. Peterson had already left when I re-entered the building and Ric never came back.

That left me, David, Sergeant Royal, and a short man with thick black hair, who she introduced as Detective Garza. I felt like a ping-pong ball as the police and David argued my culpability. He insisted that I had no knowledge that my husband was fleeing. I only knew he was leaving the house to run errands and that Walter picked him up.

I had decided to follow David's warning to not offer any information to the police. Nothing, no conversation with Harry except that he was going out with Walter, no observation (especially not that he had a suitcase), and no speculation on his motives.

At one point, Sergeant Royal asked me a question and she asked that I look directly at her. I had been staring down at my lap into the handkerchief I had knotted in my hands. I'm sure she wanted to see the color of my eyes. Someone must have

clued her in. Before I could lift my head, David announced
that my particular physiology produced that change in eye
color for a number of reasons, all documented by a physician,
and extreme fatigue was a definite factor in that phenomenon.
He effectively cut off that argument.

I was released with the admonition to stay put. Exactly
what I had in mind. David drove me home. All I wanted was
to soak in a hot tub and curl up with my pillow.

I checked the machine for new messages. Nothing from
Harry. He should be on the ground somewhere by now. I filled
the Jacuzzi with medium hot water and added crushed dried
rosemary. My body needed to relax and my mind needed to
unwind. Before I climbed in, I placed my tub tray across the
edges and pulled the black marble design notebook on Depot
Days from my purse. Settled in with a shell-shaped bath pillow supporting my shoulders, I re-read my notes.

Schoebel had lived in the condominiums on Ogden Avenue near St. Joseph Creek. *Nice place for such a scruffy-
looking fellow.* I remembered he mentioned he'd be moving
soon, somewhere over in Green Trails. *Even nicer place.
Locksmithing must be lucrative.* I started to drift off. *Where
did he get his money? Great investments? Inheritance? Un-
locking secrets?*

I sat up quickly and bumped the tray. The notebook slid toward the bubbles; I grabbed the edge and shrieked as the book
went under. I pushed aside the foam and flung the soaked
cardboard out of the tub onto the floor. I got out quickly, not
bothering to dry off, quickly wrapping the bath towel around
my soapy body. I carried the book to the bathroom and laid
it on the counter.

For the next thirty minutes the hum of my blow dryer provided the background to my thoughts about Schoebel. *What if
he knew the contents of that trunk? He plainly didn't want to*

open it. What if he killed the person in the trunk? I wished for the hundredth time that Harry were home so I could bounce these ideas off him. His mind processed and analyzed information much better than mine did. I seemed to fly off on tangents and go with my intuition. Harry's training didn't work that way. Neither did Ric's. *Don't call him, Grace. Of course I won't call him Grace.*

"I'M SURPRISED TO hear from you so soon. Since you're calling I imagine you followed your attorney's excellent advice." Ric sounded too cheerful. "The girls are here. Why don't you come over." I heard Karen's voice raised in protest, "Girls? Honestly, Ric."

"Excuse me, Ms. Marsden and Ms. Pain in the—"

"I get it," I interrupted. I smiled as I heard more protest. That they were there was serendipitous. I could hash out my idea with Ric but not be alone with him. He was talking about ordering Chinese from King Choy in Lisle when I cut him off again.

"Okay, give me twenty minutes. I just got out of the tub."

"In that case, give me five minutes."

"Ric."

"Okay. See you in twenty. If you meet the delivery guy on the porch, take care of the tab, will you?"

I hung up on his laughter before he could hear me chuckle. I felt better when I sneered at Ric Kramer. *Not really.* I loved his sense of humor; just didn't love him. *Not really.*

I MISSED THE deliveryman by minutes. Ric accused me of idling down the street until I knew the coast to be clear. We settled in the great room with our assortment of white containers, chopsticks, (forks for the chopstick-challenged or the starving) and paper plates. Hannah served green tea.

The conversation ranged from my new horse, to Hannah's fast-breaking news that in two weeks she would be an innkeeper.

"I've been talking about it forever. Karen is sick to death of listening to me patter on about it and now I've done it. The property was right under our noses. Gertrude is moving out here to be with Walter. I'm buying her house and opening a B and B for business people from England. I'm calling it *Brit Haven*."

"Buying her house?"

"Walter found an apartment for her in his complex. I predict it won't be long before they move in together."

"I don't think so, Hannah. Walter and Gertrude are pretty old-fashioned about those things." I smiled as I thought about how concerned he'd been about what I thought of her when he spent the night on her couch last year. I said as much.

"Gracie, that was almost a year ago. They're not getting any younger."

We laughed at her implication. Hannah continued. "I'm scouring the antique stores for authentic early twentieth century pieces to decorate the house. My theme is the twenties and thirties, you know, Roaring Twenties, prohibition, Al Capone."

"I thought this was a haven for Brits. Shouldn't you be decorating it like an English Country home?"

"Absolutely not! We *have* all the bloody country homes we can stand. You Yanks are the ones who love to visit those drafty, boring halls. This will be fun and something they can't get on the other side."

It did make sense. At least she didn't call us *colonists*. Her eyes sparkled like bright blue crystals. It was clever. With her connections in England and her marketing sense I had no doubt it would be successful.

"I'm learning the trade from a lovely woman Karen met

through the 19th Century Club in Oak Park. Her name is Gloria and she owns and operates a beautiful B and B called Under the Gingko Tree. We stayed there two months ago and approached Gloria then. She's been ever so helpful with advice and contacts. We're going to refer our overflow to each other."

"And this is why you fought for those trunks?"

"Yes. They'd be absolutely perfect."

At the mention of the trunks the mood shifted quickly. I hadn't meant to curtail the fun. The time seemed right to bring up my theory. A theory that resembled a motive as closely as the swollen pages in my purse resembled a notebook.

I waited a moment to make sure Hannah was finished speaking. "I have an idea about Schoebel and the trunks." Three pairs of eyes focused on me. I touched the length of yarn tied to my belt loop; no urge to braid surged through my fingers. "What if Schoebel knew about the body in the trunk? What if he knew because he was the killer?"

Ric recovered first. "Why would he leave the body in the trunk? More to the point, why would he have used the trunk to hide the body?"

"Ric's right, Grace." Karen seldom agreed with her brother. "Why wouldn't he drive a few miles and dump the body in a river?"

"Karen, you've been watching too many movies." Ric grinned at her. "It's not that simple to carry a body down to the riverbank and toss it in. Most rivers run through forest preserves and under bridges; places that aren't easy to negotiate at night."

"Last time I agree with you," Karen muttered.

"Maybe we'll have some answers when we get the results from the tests on the trunk and its contents. It'll take a few weeks but we have some information already."

"I must have missed the memo; who is 'we'? I thought you were on disability and working with Pine Marsh security from here." I waved my hand to indicate Lily's house.

"I guess you are out of the loop. I am on disability. That's a nice phrase for *out to pasture* from the RWPD. Peterson's crew does security for several communities and I convinced him he should do security for events as well. There is a high demand to outsource security costs for some villages. We're cheaper than police OT and we're on our own if injured on the job."

"Tell her the rest," urged Hannah.

Ric looked down at the chopsticks in his hand. He balanced a piece of Governor's Chicken between the slender wooden tips.

I sensed embarrassment. Odd reaction from Ric, the most confident man I'd ever met. I wondered at the mental toll he'd suffered.

"I wasn't sure what I'd do. Knew I couldn't sit around with nothing on my plate." He smiled and put down the chicken bit and his chopsticks. "I applied for a Private Investigator's license. As of this month, Peterson Security Services is now PK Security and Investigative Services." He picked up his chopsticks and popped the spicy morsel into his mouth.

Now I understood the embarrassment. I recalled many times in the past when Ric would mock a P.I. that he'd meet on a case he was working. He used to lament, "Another wannabe messing up my investigation." To Ric, a P.I. was a loser who couldn't make the force so he became a *private dick,* a *gumshoe,* and other not-so-nice monikers. I didn't know how to respond. I hated to see him look so crestfallen at his admission.

"Now at least you won't have your hands tied by bureaucratic red tape. How many times have you said you could have caught the 'perp' sooner if you didn't have to stop and fill out paperwork?"

I must have caught the brass ring with that one. Ric's face brightened and his smile reached across the table and touched my heart. For once, I hadn't put my foot in my mouth.

"So, if you're *Spenser,* who's *Hawk?*" The second I said it I tasted shoe leather. I'd identified him as Spenser, an ex-boxer in great shape. There he sat, a near cripple. I caught myself looking at the canes next to his chair. He followed my gaze and probably my thoughts.

Ric's face darkened. He mumbled something into his tea-cup. I didn't ask for clarification. *How to redeem myself?*

I lifted my purse from the floor next to my chair and removed the notebook. I had their attention. "These are the notes I compiled for Depot Days. I took the original notes in longhand before I typed up the file which is, uh, at the of-fice." I'd almost said *missing.*

"What happened to it?" Hannah, who was seated next to me, fingered the pages.

"It fell in the water while I soaked in the Jacuzzi."

"Better that than a radio." Hannah's humor was a tad dark, but her smile beamed genuine.

"I can't believe you said that." Karen looked horrified.

"What's in the book, Grace?" Ric's question brought us back on track.

"Schoebel lived in this area since the early seventies. He's somehow related to the Deutsch family, fourth or fifth cousin, if you can get that distant and still be related. During this twenty-year period he moved five times but always within Lisle. Isn't that odd? He was moving from the condos at St. Joseph Creek to a house in Green Trails. He didn't seem to have a thriving business, so how could he afford those resi-dences? That's why I suspect that he made money from kill-ing that person in the trunk."

"Maybe he followed the victim home from the bank. A robbery gone wrong." Karen's dark eyes sparkled with her theory. She really did watch too many movies.

Hannah wasn't about to be left out. "I think it's what you call a *hit*. Someone paid him to do it. Maybe your gangsters."

The Italian side of my heritage bristled. "The mob? That's ridiculous. And they are not *my* gangsters." Hannah's being an aficionado for everything from that unfortunate era of Chicago's past clouded her common sense.

"Sorry, Grace. I meant that someone hired him to kill. Or maybe it was a robbery that went awry." She looked truly contrite.

"Sorry I snapped at you. My Nonna Santa always cringed when the radio or television ran a story about the Mafia. She didn't speak much English but she understood the news content. Guess it's in the genes." I smiled at Hannah.

Ric pulled a small notebook from the pocket of his denim shirt. He flipped a few pages. "Our preliminary report on Schoebel has one interesting fact that your notes don't cover. He was a registered sex offender."

Silence curtained the table. Ric continued, "That may be the reason he moved so many times."

"You mean people found out and forced him to move?" I didn't think that could be done, but then I didn't think I'd hired a pervert to participate in Depot Days."

"A sex offender has to register with the local police department when he moves into a city. By law he cannot reside within 500 feet of a school, day care center, park, anywhere that children would be present. It might even cover school bus stops."

"He wouldn't be able to get a job working in close proximity to kids, either. The school does background checks on all employees from teachers to custodians."

Karen referred to Trinity High School where she taught English.

"Grace, do you have his old addresses?" Ric asked.

"Only the one before St. Joseph Creek. He was somewhere near the library. That puts him near the Catholic School, St. Joan of Arc."

"The school has probably been there longer than the seventies. Why would he move there if he knew he shouldn't?" Hannah's question made sense.

"Maybe when he moved there he wasn't too close." Karen pushed her Chinese dinner aside and leaned forward. "Several years ago, Trinity expanded. Some of the neighbors on the street adjacent to the build-out weren't happy. They had enjoyed the green view of a manicured lawn for years and now they were practically sitting in a classroom."

"Good point," Ric praised his sister. "If a build-out or expansion moved the school closer to him then he might have felt the need to relocate. Grace, what about the condominiums?"

"About six months ago, a new day care/pre-school opened up across the creek from them. The parking for the condos is in the back. You can walk out the front door, cross the creek via a pedestrian bridge and be in the pre-school's playground."

"It seems to me that Mr. Schoebel is the possible victim here." Hannah's politics rose closer to the surface. My sister-in-law seemed a socialist at times in her view of law, order, and justice. "It isn't his fault that a school expanded or someone built a pre-school outside his front door. I don't approve of his crime but I think it was unfair to make him move."

"There is no record in my notes indicating a court order forcing him to move," Ric said.

"Then why would he?"

I nearly jumped out of my chair with the answer. "Because he is the killer and he didn't want to give the police any reason to look at him."

Ric sat up straighter. "A distinct possibility."

"Do they know yet if the skeleton is female or male?"

"Should have more information tomorrow. Peterson got a better look when the coroner removed the body. He guessed female because of the size. Could be a young female or a young male."

The thought that a child may have been molested and then murdered changed the atmosphere in the room. What for me had been an exercise in solving a puzzle now became too real and disturbing. I sensed the same mood from the others, even Ric who I thought would be immune to those feelings. It was different with a child.

Ric stood up from the table. He hobbled across the room to a corner away from the windows and the fireplace; the living room area of the great room. I noticed a computer desk and daybed set up discreetly behind a three-panel screen. The muted tones of blue, cream, and gold from the main area repeated in the fabric in the panels and on the coverlet.

He motioned us over with a flourish of one cane toward the area. "Be it ever so humble," he joked. I realized in that instant that he wouldn't be able to climb the stairs. He slept down here, not up there. My face must have shouted my thoughts to Ric. His smug smile and lifted eyebrows gave me an "Aren't you sorry you rushed to judgment?" look. I didn't know what to think. *Was he or wasn't he sleeping with Lily? If he wasn't, was Lily still focused on Harry?* A nudge from Karen broke a train of thought that was headed for derailment.

"Watch this. Ric took his first disability check and bought a new computer with Internet access."

"Harry talked about getting the Internet but we never pursued it. We don't have cable, either. I guess we're boring."

"Extremely. All you have is a secret room, a seven-hundred-year-old sarcophagus used as a planter, and a horse barn in your backyard." Karen grinned.

I smiled back. I hoped she wouldn't notice the smile only

moved my lips. I fervently hoped that I'd have a husband with whom to share those things and more by the end of this week.

Noise from the computer focused my attention on Ric's progress. The series of beeps and boops apparently connected him to the Internet. He looked up and explained. "There are government sites, state-wide mainly, that have databases of missing persons reports. Since the Lisle Police aren't likely to give me any information, I'll see if I can search these sites for any children reported missing in the last twenty years."

"Why twenty years?" Hannah asked the question on my lips.

"Seems like a good starting place. I don't know how far back the data goes. Maybe they don't have even that recent a time in their database yet."

"I can narrow the time period for you." Everyone looked at me. I went back to the table to retrieve my notebook. After flipping a few pages I read from my notes. "The city moved the original train depot in 1978 to its current location in the Lisle Station Park.'" I stopped reading and closed the book. "That should narrow it down. The trunks didn't move with the building at the time. Whoever moved them would prob-ably have noticed a smell or something, don't you think?"

Hannah and Karen both looked squeamish. Ric reached for the notebook. "What else have you got in there? Maybe I don't need the Internet, only the Gracenet." He grinned as I relinquished the book. His comment eased the tension.

"How long does that take?" I motioned toward the com-puter that displayed little boxes blinking on across the bottom of the screen until the line was complete. An official look-ing page appeared on the screen. Ric guided the mouse to a small box marked "records" and clicked. The little boxes began their journey across the bottom again.

"What's this about Ava Deutsch?" Ric had returned to reading my notes.

"What about her?"

"Is that the woman I bid against? Notice, I didn't say 'lady.'" Hannah leaned toward Ric to read over his shoulder.

"Yes. What about her?"

"Your notes say the trunks were in her basement."

"Not the basement of her home. The cellar of the antique store she owns. She offered to store them there until the depot was moved. Three trunks were stored in the basement of the Book Nook. The store had changed owners during that time. I guess everyone forgot about them until I found receipts for their delivery. I'm not sure which trunks were where."

"No wonder she bid so high. A matched set would sell for more. I had no idea she owned an antique store. Where is it?"

My sister-in-law couldn't resist haunted places and antique shops. "It's on Ogden Avenue in Lisle."

"We've been. Remember? We went there twice. That's where you bought the boot bench and that thirties-style liquor cart."

"Oh, lovely place. Wonderful pieces. I never saw her. I thought that young man owned the shop."

Ric's voice broke in. "According to this," he lifted the book, "that young man is Ava Deutsch's son. She turned over day-to-day operations to him after he returned from college. Business major, boarding school as a child..." Ric looked at me. "Why would you have notes on this?"

"I don't know. I was reading the old newspaper accounts of the relocation of the depot. Ava and her sister kept coming up in all the news items. The Deutsch family is big-time money in this area. Their story intrigued me."

"She has a sister?"

"An identical twin, Eva. Like two peas in a pod. Actually, there was a third girl, but I think she died at birth or days after."

"I didn't see Eva at the auction. Does she live around here?"

"Not anymore." The screen changed on the computer and Ric turned his attention to manipulating the mouse to the correct boxes.

Karen touched my arm. "Where does she live?"

"Europe, according to the newspapers. The sisters got into a big snit when their grandfather died. Johann Deutsch was an old-time German who immigrated here as a child with his parents. His father built the grain mill that the antique store sits on and became quite wealthy in the process. All the farmers came to him since his was the closest mill. When Johann took over he expanded the business to include brickmaking using the limestone from the local area. Johann developed into an incredibly astute businessman but he overlooked a legal point in his will. He used the same wording as his father's before him, namely that the family fortune would pass to the oldest child.

"Here's the strange part. The will further charged that the inheritor could not will or give away more than fifteen percent of the total amount without forfeiting the inheritance and causing the monies to revert to the oldest surviving Deutsch male in the family. I think he added that clause to prevent an opportunist from marrying a Deutsch female and squandering the family fortune. Ava Deutsch won the privilege by being born first, by one minute, thirteen seconds."

"I'd be in a bloody snit for sure if Mum and Dad had concocted that stupid of a will." Hannah's vehement outburst was understandable; she was two minutes younger than Harry.

"Exactly. When he died, the will went to probate and the terms came to light. That's when it hit the fan. Eva Deutsch went nuts according to the accounts. She threatened to sue her sister, the attorney, anyone who could matter. She even went so far as to try and declare her father mentally incompetent posthumously."

"How awful. Their father should have realized the problem when he had twins." Hannah still brooded about the injustice.

"Luckily for Eva, her sister was the nice one. Eva was the witch."

"It said that in the newspaper?" Ric grinned. "I've got to subscribe."

"No. I got that from Liz. She's their niece, remember? Liz told me that her Aunt Eva screamed and bitched about the unfairness of it all until the family was sick to death of her. They all thought it was unfair, but Eva's ploys and shenanigans were turning family against each other. Liz said it came to a head at a family party where both Ava and Eva showed up with their attorneys. Ava had a document drawn up that would reallocate fifteen percent of her inheritance to Eva. She would also buy out Eva's half of the shop so she could funnel more money to her."

"That was decent of her." Hannah seemed to be calming down.

"Eva didn't think so. Her attorney had papers prepared to tie up the shop, the inheritance, everything they owned in a nuisance suit."

"Who won?"

"If you can call it winning, I guess Ava did. She took out a huge loan against the business and her home, signed over the fifteen percent, and paid for her sister's new home, a villa, somewhere in France or Italy."

"Wow, and she won?"

"Liz says she won peace of mind. She's not hurting for money, but all the things she would have done with the funds have taken longer to do."

"Such as?"

"She donated quite heavily to Illinois Benedictine, Benet Academy, the Lisle Heritage Society, the Lisle Garden Club, Willowbrook Wildlife Haven, Brookfield Zoo—"

"Okay, I get it. What about Eva, 'the evil twin'?" We smiled at Karen's assessment.

"I can't believe twins wouldn't reconcile after all this time. It's like being mad or not speaking to yourself." Hannah shrugged her thin shoulders.

"You say that because you and Harry are so close." Karen looked back at me.

"Liz doesn't talk much about that aunt. Liz remembers her mother throwing out the few postcards the family received from Eva. Every now and then someone from the antiques industry would run into her in Europe. They'd be sure to let the gossip of Eva's '*dolce vita*' make the rounds while Ava struggled with the business. She is definitely '*persona non grata*.'" I turned to Ric. "Do you think the forensic people can—"

"Got it." Ric cut off my question. He tapped the screen with his finger. "Look, here. Two people were reported missing; a thirteen-year-old girl in August of 1978 and a seventy-two-year-old woman three months later."

"How can we find out more about them? Does that report tell you if they were found?" Hannah asked.

"No, that's another report. I'm not sure how to access that. Let me play with this and see what I can come up with by tomorrow."

"I know someone who might help. Dr. John Weber is a retired ob-gyn who happens to be on the historical society board, sort of the town historian. He loaned us some of the photos and documents we used in the displays. He's in his eighties but as sharp as a tack. Lived here all his life; probably delivered most of the town. I'll call him tomorrow."

The phone rang and Ric gestured across the room. Hannah went to answer it. "DeFreest residence, may I help you?" She listened and then looked toward Ric, who by this time had started walking toward her. "He's here, hold a moment, please." She covered the mouthpiece. "It's Peterson." Ric accepted the phone and waited for Hannah to move away.

"This is Kramer." Ric listened, but for a lot longer. He turned his back to us. "Uh, huh. That's nuts. I'm not a fan, but he wouldn't do that. Okay. Thanks for the call, I'll let her know."

The high ceilings and wood floors didn't muffle Ric's voice. Everyone looked at me. We all knew who the "her" referred to.

"Grace, Peterson went out on a limb to alert us because he and I work together but more so because he likes you. The Lisle Police have a search warrant for your garage and they're on their way to execute the warrant."

"The garage? Why? They have Harry's car."

"They're looking for anything that may have concealed a body long enough to transport it to the scene of the accident, ah, homicide."

"Homicide?" Three voices sounded as one. Ric held up his hand to stop further questions. "After further investigation of the accident scene they determined that Schoebel didn't die there. That's all Peterson knows. The autopsy was moved up to today."

"Did you mean what you said to Peterson about Harry not doing it?" Ric hesitated for too long. "Ric?"

"Yeah, I meant it. Working at cross-purposes with him this past year, I learned about his particular code of ethics. If someone threatened his family or friends he'd find a way to make them disappear." Ric held up his hand to stop my protest. "I don't doubt for a moment he still has connections to people who do that sort of favor. Technically, I'm even in that category, I mean as far as owing him my life."

"Then repay him." I moved so that I stood directly in front of Ric and lifted my head to lock eyes with his. "I don't know where Harry is. He purposely didn't tell anyone so no one could get in trouble with the police. He's meeting his son, for God's sake. He won't know what's happening. This crime isn't national news; checking the Chicago Tribune for news on a crime that he didn't commit wouldn't enter his head. Not in his current state of mind."

Ric narrowed his eyes. I read his expression as anger at being reminded of his debt. He shrugged his shoulders. "At least I'll be able to keep an eye on you. C'mon, the police are on their way." He turned to Karen. "Let yourselves out when you've finished the dishes." His grin lightened the mood. Hannah stuck out her tongue at him in a childish response. Laughter connected us for a few moments.

I hugged Karen and Hannah goodbye and promised to call them later. Ric used the three-minute door-to-door drive to remind me to stay calm and keep quiet. Not necessary. I had no intention of talking to Sergeant Royal or whoever would be there.

SEVENTEEN

THE DOUBLE-SIZED DOOR lifted smoothly. I wasn't going to be confrontational so why not open the door for them. I pulled into my spot and stepped out of the car. Headlights illuminated the garage from behind. I recognized Peterson once he got out of the car. I walked out to greet him.

"I'm a minute or so ahead of them," he said, quickly cutting off any salutations. "Mrs. Marsden, I want to go over a few things with you."

"I already gave her the drill." Ric moved slowly from the shadow of the garage.

Peterson looked surprised to see him. I wondered at that. After all, he had talked to Ric less than twenty minutes ago. Wouldn't he expect him to be here? I didn't like the look that passed between them; it didn't seem *partner-like*.

"Good, 'cause here's John Law." He sounded like the police version of the old Carson show—*here's Johnny*.

Detective Sam Garza handed me a folded document. Peterson took it from me and read it. Detective Garza directed an accompanying technician to begin her process of evidence collection. She opened the trunk of the detective's car and lifted out several cases. Ric turned toward me and whispered, "Start moving slowly to your car. When I distract Garza, pull your car out of the garage all the way onto the driveway." He turned away and walked toward the detective. His voice had been urgent. I knew better than to question that tone. I sidled over to my car. Ric walked beyond Garza and then turned to him as though an afterthought. Garza turned to answer Ric's question and in that moment, Ric "lost his grip" on his right cane, sending it a foot to Garza's left.

I opened the door, turned the ignition, and backed out in the space of seconds. I looked in the rearview mirror as I moved. The evidence technician looked up in surprise. Garza, occupied with the process of bending over to retrieve Ric's cane, stopped and whirled from his crouched position. He stood quickly and shouted at me to stop.

I already had. He loomed at my window in a heartbeat, gesturing for me to get out of the car. He stopped short of grabbing the handle and jerking the door open, which is what he looked like he wanted to do. I opened the door and slid out of the car. "What's wrong?"

"Why did you do that, Mrs. Kramer?" He had confused our names but didn't realize it. Ric and I locked eyes. I knew his thoughts as I knew mine; it almost had been "Mrs. Kramer." The detective saw the exchange and realized his error.

"Excuse me, Mrs. Marsden." He emphasized the name. "Why did you back your car out of the garage? Did he suggest it?"

I looked at Ric again. "Why would he? I wanted to make room for your technician. I thought this way she wouldn't have to keep walking around my car." I heard the note of innocence in my voice. I would believe me. I hoped no one had told Detective Garza about my peculiar "sincerity barometer." He looked hard into my eyes I think not to gauge color but determine by his own methods if I lied. He must have decided I told the truth.

The evidence technician looked at him. Her head tilted slightly and her eyebrows raised. He shook his head and motioned her toward the garage.

The garage. If my car had been in the garage they could have searched it. The warrant must be for only the contents of the garage. They already had Harry's car so whoever drew up the warrant didn't think to include my vehicle. *Boy, is that person going to be in trouble. Trouble? There's nothing in my car they couldn't see. Is there?*

I stepped toward my car.

"Don't." His authoritative voice again. He reached his left cane out in front of me more as a gesture than an impediment.

I felt distracted by the evening's events. My fingers felt for the length of yarn tied to my belt loop. It wasn't there. *Damn! I must have left it at Lily's house.* I still held my car keys in my hand. The lanyard attached to the ring teased my brain. I slipped my middle finger through the ring and ran my thumb across the rough plastic. My fingers twitched with the need to braid or knot something. I looked down at my loafers, over to Ric's shoes, also loafers, and across the driveway to Peterson's shoes…sneakers with long laces. I practically salivated.

How could I ask him to untie his laces and give me one? *I can't ask him. Can I?* In my focused state of mind I walked toward Sergeant Peterson, forgetting about Ric's cane. I stumbled and knocked the cane from his lax grip. Ric caught his balance and tried to hold me from falling. He couldn't move fast enough and we both tumbled into the side of my Jeep. He managed to twist around me at the last moment and his back absorbed most of the shock when we hit the car. I saw the spike of pain in his eyes right before they rolled up into his head.

I tried to ease his body to the ground. "Call an ambulance. Hurry!"

Peterson reached me and helped me lay him flat on the driveway. He felt his neck for a pulse. "He's breathing, knocked himself out."

"He's unconscious? Do something!" My panicked voice drew the technician from the garage.

"I'm a paramedic, too. Let me take a look at him. The

cement is cold. He could go into shock. Does anyone have a blanket?"

"I do." I lurched to my feet pressing the back door release on my keypad. I heard Ric groan. He was regaining consciousness. The back latch clicked and I pulled open the door. I always kept a blanket, extra jacket, and emergency gear like flares, candles, and even a pair of hiking boots in a plastic crate. My hands touched rough fabric of the blanket before I could pull the crate out. I pulled it free from under the crate and turned to give it to the paramedic.

"Hold it right there, Mrs. Marsden. I'll take the blanket." Detective Garza stepped forward holding a large plastic bag. "Put it in here."

I stood dumbfounded and rooted to the spot. My hands instinctively tightened around the blanket. Garza saw the movement and interpreted it as obstruction.

"Mrs. Marsden, that blanket is evidence in a homicide investigation. I was briefed about you and so far your actions have skated on the line of obstruction. This will land you on the wrong side." He took a step toward me with the open evidence bag.

Peterson spoke up. "This warrant doesn't say anything about her vehicle or its contents."

"A technicality. Do you have reason to withhold the blanket, Mrs. Marsden? Did your husband tell you to hide the blanket?" His voice grew louder with each question.

My head pounded with confusion. I needed to braid, I couldn't think.

"Don't badger her. She doesn't have to turn it over."

"She doesn't, unless she's covering for her husband. Unless she knows that blanket will incriminate him."

Harry is innocent. This blanket could prove it. Give him the blanket.

"Don't give it to him, Grace." Ric's voice sounded groggy.

I wanted to look at him, but my eyes were locked on the detective moving toward me.

He stopped two feet away from me and extended the bag under the blanket so that all I needed to do was let it drop. I did.

"Thank you, Mrs. Marsden. I will note in my report that you cooperated with our search." He wasn't smug, just matter-of-fact.

I knelt down next to Ric who struggled to get up. The evidence tech/paramedic held a hand against his shoulder. "I don't advise getting up. Wait for the ambulance."

"Help me up or get out of my way." Ric's voice regained its timbre. "I don't need an ambulance." He turned to me. "Help me up, Gracie. Get me inside."

Peterson had returned from his car with a blanket. He leaned over and put his arm out for Ric to use. I put my hands under his armpit and slowly stood up, pulling him with me. I found his canes and held them out to him. Peterson and I were silent as we watched for any sign that Ric would topple. He stood rock solid. His eyes looked clear.

"It's over out here. Let's get inside." He walked toward the garage to take a shortcut into the house. Apparently he thought better of that idea and swerved toward the front door; a longer walk with steps. Garza must have seen his choice. He called out to him, "We're finished in there."

Ric ignored him and kept moving toward the front. The sound of a siren grew louder. He didn't stop for that either. I needed to open the door. Peterson patted my shoulder. "Go ahead. I'll keep an eye on everything."

"Thank you. Please come inside after they leave. I'll leave the door unlocked."

"Bad habit of yours, Gra—Mrs. Marsden. Lock the door. I'll knock."

He looked embarrassed at his lapse in protocol. I reached

the front door at the same time as Ric. We both turned to view the tableau of my driveway; two squad cars, Peterson's vehicle, an ambulance, and my Jeep, still standing open, exposed to official eyes. *At least the neighbors don't live close enough to see this. Not like in Berkeley where the houses sat a narrow driveway apart.* With that thought barely out of my head, Barb Atwater drove slowly by the house. I knew I'd have some explaining to do when we went for our standing six o'clock walk in the morning. I waved cheerfully as though everything was hunky dory. "Let's get inside."

EIGHTEEN

I SETTLED RIC in the dining room in a straight-backed chair with the promise of ibuprofen, an ice pack, and coffee. Now that his "I'm okay get me inside" show had played out, he looked to be in a lot of pain. His face lacked color except for flushed cheeks. I suspected fever. I wondered about his decision to decline further attention. He shook out six tablets, popped them in his mouth, and downed them in a large gulp. "Thanks, Gracie. That should help."

"What would have helped is a trip to the hospital. You might have a concussion. Why didn't you at least let them look you over, take some vitals, whatever it is they do."

"You wouldn't understand, Grace. Let it go. How about that ice pack?"

I knew he wanted to change the subject. *Fine. I have enough to worry about with one man. Ric's someone else's problem. Or is he?* "Okay. Ice pack coming up." I spoke with as much disregard as I could and turned away before he could search my eyes for the truth.

"Coffee, too," he shouted to my back. "Please," he added quietly.

A smile curved my lips; a smile I dared not let him see. I stayed in the kitchen while the coffee brewed. The Cinnamon Nut Swirl scented the room and made me feel safe and cozy. *I must be nuts! My husband is a fugitive, my ex-lover is in the dining room, and the police are in the garage. Safe and cozy?* Maybe safe and cozy wasn't the operative phrase— maybe "less intimidated" fit better.

I pulled a notepad across the counter toward me and listed "Things To Do" at the top. After I wrote down "Call Dr. John Weber" I stopped writing. I didn't have additional entries. In fact, I didn't think I had Dr. Weber's home phone to make an appointment. I knew who would.

Liz's phone rang three times and then the machine picked up.

"Liz, this is Grace. I wanted to talk to Dr. Weber. I thought I could ask him some questions about his recall on when the trunks were last on display and get his thoughts on the skeleton. Might make interesting copy for the tie up of Depot Days. Please call me as soon as possible. Thanks."

Why did I make up that bit about "interesting copy" instead of telling the truth? Harry's "need to know," cloak-and-dagger training must be rubbing off on me. My mind shifted to a Bogie accent. *If I tell you that, sweetheart, I'll have to kill you.* I giggled out loud but sobered as the last *tee hee* passed my lips. *What if Schoebel knew something that Harry didn't want made public? If I tell you...*

I pushed away from the counter and started filling a tray with cups, teaspoons, sugar, and the ice pack. The banging that accompanied my movements made welcome noise in my traitorous brain. *How could I suspect Harry? He had better luck with strangers.*

I was angry at my lapse of faith. I entered the dining room, ready to hash out a plan with Ric to help Harry. Ric had tried to keep my car from police eyes. Did he suspect Harry? That would be my first question. The chair was empty.

I hadn't heard the door. Had he gone to the bathroom? I put the tray on the table and walked into the hallway to check the bathroom; the door stood open. I turned around and walked across the foyer to the living room.

Ric had moved to the couch. His slow deep breathing indicated that he was comfortably asleep. His six-foot-plus length fit the space with a spare inch. He'd aligned his shoes neatly on the floor; ready at a moment's notice. It was obvious from his movements on the driveway that he wouldn't be leaping up "to the rescue" if needed. Maybe that's what he meant when he said I wouldn't understand. Before his accident, he could have caught me in time.

I lifted a chenille throw from the back of the loveseat and carefully covered him, opting to stretch the less-than-six-feet-long fabric from his feet up. I retrieved the tray from the dining room and settled again in the kitchen. Wistfully, I raised my full cup to my lips then inhaled deeply, trying to regain my earlier sense of safe and cozy.

The doorbell and phone rang at the same time. My knee-jerk reaction was to reach for the phone. "Hello."

"Hi, Grace, it's Liz. Is something wrong? You sound different."

The doorbell sounded again.

"I'm fine. Someone's at the door. Can you hold on a second?"

I put down the phone without waiting for a response and rushed to open the door as Peterson's hand raised to ring again.

"Sorry, Sergeant. I'm on the phone. Ric is in the living room asleep. I've got coffee in the kitchen. Help yourself." I turned the corner into the kitchen, not sure if Peterson followed. I picked up the receiver. "Thanks for holding, Liz."

"No problem. Your message said you wanted to talk to Dr. Weber? He's retired."

"Actually, according to my notes, he's sort of semi-retired. He does some training at Good Sam for their home nurse program for new mothers. He is still an assistant coroner for the county. Don't think he gets much action there, though."

"Grace, I'm impressed. You've done excellent research on someone who didn't figure into our campaign."

"That's how I tick. Once I get a piece of information, I like to see where it fits into the whole. I'm a little obsessive sometimes." I chuckled at my understatement. Liz didn't laugh.

"Obsessive. I guess that's the word for you. You probably don't let go once you catch the scent."

"I'm not a Labrador, Liz. I just like things to fit."

"I wasn't being dismissive of your talent. On the contrary, I admire your ability to ferret out information. And I know you're not a ferret." We both laughed. "I may hire you to figure out some puzzles for me. Wait a minute, you're already hired." She laughed at her joke. "Here's Dr. Weber's number, 555-2342. Hope he doesn't have anything to hide. It's a good thing you're honest—you'd make a great blackmailer."

Now her laughter irritated me. I forced myself to remain cheery and stretched my lips into a grimace of goodwill. "Thanks, Liz. See you at the office." My fake smile dropped from my lips like an algebra book from a teenager's hands.

"I used to feel that way about my boss. That's why I started my own security company."

I'd forgotten about Peterson. He stood leaning against the island with a cup of coffee in his hand.

"That was how you resolved your problems?"

"It seemed wiser than killing him." He smiled and raised his cup to me. "Excellent coffee. Of all the calls we answered this year, me and my crew agree that you have the best coffee and Danish." He looked toward the cake plate in the center of the island.

I waved at it. "Help yourself, there are napkins on the tray. Please, sit down." I waited until he settled in. "Have they finished?"

"They packed up and left right before I rang the bell. They took the blanket and a length of wood they found in the garage. Looked like a scrap piece, maybe left over from the construction, and a metal baseball bat. I signed for the receipt and—"

"A baseball bat? Harry doesn't own a baseball bat. That's not his. You shouldn't have signed anything." I didn't know if that made a difference but in my mind it did.

"Mrs. Marsden, it's okay. I signed that what they took was spelled out on the receipt. You'll be able to tell them it's not his. Are you sure, though? Most guys have bats, gloves, you know, sports equipment in their garage."

"Maybe most guys that are born here. My husband was born and raised in England. He played rugby and soccer in school. He played keeper for Manchester United for two seasons. Does he sound like a man who would have a baseball bat in his garage?" The question left my mouth as a roar.

"Grace, stop." Ric's low tone snuffed out my lit fuse like two wet fingers on a candlewick. "Pete's right. It doesn't matter who signed. It doesn't mean anything." Ric leaned against the doorjamb. His face wore that flushed and vulnerable look left over from a deep sleep. "Geez, Louise. Can't a guy get a little shut-eye?" He motioned toward the tray on the island. "Got an extra cup for me?"

"Sure. When you conked out, the sergeant…" Ric's words finally settled in. "Your first name is *Peter?* Why would your parents do that?"

Peterson turned a little pink around the ears. "Lack of creativity after the ninth baby. I'm number ten. I feel lucky I didn't just get a number." He smiled.

I grabbed a mug from the cabinet and poured Ric his coffee. He looked a little wobbly so I spooned in a tiny bit of sugar. He raised his eyebrow but didn't complain. Peterson shifted to his right to give Ric the closest stool to the door. He shuffled across the remaining tile and sat down.

I had forgiven Peterson for any imagined gaffe in handling the police. Peterson caught my look of concern. He seemed to understand. I think he noticed how much difficulty Ric had walking.

"I noticed you're without wheels. How about I drive you home?"

Ric nodded. He swallowed his remaining coffee before I could offer a Styrofoam cup to go.

"Go out through the garage, it's shorter."

Peterson moved ahead to open the door. Ric stopped in front of me and transferred his canes to one hand. He tipped my chin up with his forefinger and thumb. "Don't worry. We'll figure this out." He leaned forward and brushed his lips against my forehead.

I stepped back and turned to make room for him to move past me. His new partner waited at the door. I leaned against the closed door and wondered how more confusing this could become.

While I washed the dishes, I thought about the last twenty-four hours. Nothing made sense. At first, Harry was accused of running down Schoebel, and now he was being accused of killing Schoebel then running over him to disguise the murder. I thought long and hard about circumstances that might cause Harry to commit murder. All I could resolve with absolute certainty was that if my husband had killed Schoebel there wouldn't be a body.

I climbed the stairs to our bedroom. I had to find another plausible suspect to hand the police. And I'd probably be doing it on my own, with Harry incommunicado and Ric incapacitated. That left me in deep without a shovel.

I hoped things would look better in the morning. Sleep eluded me. I tried to remember the saying, "Only the guilty sleep well, or only the innocent sleep well." Was Harry sleeping well half a world away? Was he sleeping alone? The tears came unbidden, slipping down my cheeks.

NINETEEN

THE PHONE RANG several times before the shrill tone permeated my sleep-sodden brain. I rolled toward the nightstand and opened my eyes. Instantly, my body snapped awake; it was two o'clock in the morning and the light on our personal line blinked at me.

It had to be Harry. I snatched at the phone, worried he might hang up. "Harry?"

"Good morning, darling. It's wonderful to hear your voice. I'm sorry to call you in the middle of the night."

"Where are you? You don't know what's happening here. You have to come back."

"Grace, calm down. It was an accident. When they finish their investigation they'll know I'm innocent."

He sounded so calm; more like "not a care in the world" in tone. Before I could contradict him he confirmed his frame of mind. "Grace, he's fantastic." Harry's voice had a quality I'd never heard before: immeasurable pride.

He continued, "He's better-looking than in that photo, he's bright, honors courses, and he's well-spoken and polite. Lily's done a marvelous job with Will. We're still finding our way together; it will take some time. That's why I have to stay. I can't leave him after just meeting him; can't tell him how important it is for me to be part of his life and then fly off to America. You see that don't you, Gracie?"

All I "saw" is what I heard; high praise for Lily's parenting skills and higher praise for a tow-headed replica of Harry.

The lump forming in my throat prevented an immediate answer. I swallowed hard.

"Gracie?"

"It doesn't matter what I see, it's what the police don't see. You." I thought that answered his question.

"I don't give a fig what the police think. I'm asking you to understand why I can't come home. I care enormously about what you think and feel and I know you must be feeling left out. It won't be for long. I promise. Will you trust me, darling?"

The lump was back. I knew I had to answer. My brain blocked my words until my fingers performed its demand. *Ten crossovers.* I knew better than to argue. I scrunched the phone between my ear and shoulder and grabbed the blue cording on the nightstand.

"Gracie?"

Can't talk. One loop, crossover...

"Gracie, are you okay?"

God, Harry, you know me. Four loop, crossover...

"Okay, darling. If you need time, I'll give it to you. Don't be angry. I love you both. I'll call when I can. Love you."

No! Wait. Eight loop, crossover, nine loop, crossover, ten loop, crossover.

"Harry, wait!" The disconnect tone sounded in my ear.

"Dammit! Dammit!" Hot tears blurred my vision as I stared at my offending fingers tangled in blue loops. I knew I wouldn't fall asleep now. I needed to do something; too dark to ride, which was always my first choice.

I threw off the covers, stripped the bedding, and carried it all to the laundry room, which our builder had the good sense to put on the second floor. Within minutes, the washer hummed and the scent of Tide wafted from the machine. I inhaled the familiar smell and felt a little more in control. When my obsessive disorder was diagnosed my mother tried various ways to channel "the jitters," as we called them. She encouraged my Boy Scout brothers to teach me to braid and tie knots and she instructed me on the finer points of house-cleaning to refocus my nervous energy. I think she was a genius; she made the boys practice their knots and she made me *want* to clean my room.

We'd lost rotation in our cleaning service's schedule since the explosion and re-build. I hadn't found anyone to come in. Really hadn't looked. Maybe I'd make that call today, too.

The next hour flew by as I remade the bed, dusted, vacu-umed, cleaned the vanity, shower, and toilet. I stopped to ad-mire the now sparkling mirrors on the sliding doors in our bathroom. *Mirrors. Something about mirrors, mirror image.* Whatever tugged at my brain couldn't get a good hold.

Three-thirty. At least two hours to dawn. I'd promised my-self a break and coffee when I finished the bedroom. I hur-ried down the stairs to enjoy my treat. The familiar noise and putter involved with grinding beans and brewing a mango Jamaican Blue blend served to further calm me. I sat at the island and chose a Danish from the cake plate. I found my notepad where I'd left it; blank except for "Call Dr. Weber." I pulled the pad closer and sipped at my coffee. I picked up the pencil and tapped the eraser against my bottom lip. "Cleaning lady" appeared on the next line. *Tap, tap, tap.* "Ric about more missing people from database" took third place, quickly followed by "Gertrude about historical society," "Ava Deutsch about trunks," and finally, "Sergeant Royal about Schoebel's record."

I couldn't call these people until at least eight o'clock; maybe Gertrude at seven. She was an early riser. I lingered over a second cup of coffee. Was I missing something? How would this help Harry?

I jumped when the phone rang. *Four-thirty! Harry!*

"Harry?"

"No, it's Pete, ah, Peterson. Sorry to disappoint you."

"It's okay. Is anything wrong?"

"I apologize for the early call. When I took Kramer home last night he didn't look good. I talked him into letting me take him to Edwards. He wouldn't go until we went inside and checked his fax machine and email for that missing person database he searched for you. I think he knew they'd admit him."

"Ric's in the hospital? Is he okay?"

"Moderate concussion. He's in for at least two days. He wanted me to give you the information he gathered. I have an early appointment downtown so I wondered if I could swing by and drop off this envelope."

"Ric's going to be okay, isn't he? Have you told his sister?"

"He'll be fine, needs bed rest. He asked me to call his sister at a reasonable time."

"I'll call Karen. You can drop off the envelope anytime. I don't leave for work until eight-thirty." Still too early to call anyone, so I reviewed my list. I crossed Ric off the list since I would be receiving his information shortly. I would call Karen at six o'clock; she liked to get to Trinity by seven-thirty to be available to the students before the school day began.

Peterson arrived within twenty minutes, still apologetic about the early hour. He stepped into the foyer with the folder outstretched like a peace offering. "Thanks for letting me drop this off. Kramer wouldn't settle down until I promised to deliver this to you ASAP." He grinned. He looked so different in the "civvies" he wore today. Creased gray slacks with a crisp white shirt and a tie with gray, navy, and yellow stripes. I thought the yellow a bit exotic for the sergeant, but it softened the navy sports jacket. He shifted from one highly polished black shoe to the other and fingered his tie nervously.

I must have been obvious in my assessment. I looked down at the envelope I had accepted.

"No problem," I assured him. "I've been up for a while."

"I figured as much when I smelled the coffee." He grinned again.

He wasn't too subtle. "I know you're headed downtown but how about a cup to go?" He nodded. "I'll be right back." I filled a travel mug and snugged down the top. As an afterthought, I wrapped a raspberry Danish in a few napkins.

"Here you go, coffee and raspberry, okay?"

"Thank you. Yes, great."

"Sergeant, where does someone go to look up a will?" I figured he could trade info for food.

"Depends where it's filed. If it's in DuPage it'd be in Records at the county building. If its in Cook it'd be downtown in the building I'll be in this morning. You need something looked up?"

This was better than info—it was legwork. "I do. I'm trying to find the will of Johann Deutsch. I think he died in the late seventies. Could you spare some time to see if it is on file there?"

"I'm on it. If it's not there, I'll check in Wheaton this afternoon. Ric mentioned the same thing last night. I guess I'll be working on this eventually, might as well get a head start." He left with his usual admonition to lock the door.

I looked at the clock. More than three hours had passed. It seemed as though the surreal float time of the wee hours of the morning surged into real time as the day crept closer to an official start for most people. I realized that time passed too quickly now.

I threw on a jacket, grabbed some treats, and went out the mudroom to the backyard. Soft whinnies greeted me. "Good morning, girl." I patted April's extended muzzle and palmed some baby carrots for her. Her gentle snuffle tickled my open hand. "Good girl, good girl. Hey, Cash, how's it going?" I moved over to his stall. He didn't greet me as readily but the lure of those sugary carrots won him over. I patted his muzzle as he chewed his treat. "Good boy, nice boy. You are a pretty one."

My routine with two horses would have to change. I quickly led April out of her stall and clipped a short lead to her chinstrap and clipped the other end to a ring set in a post, horse-head high. As an efficient "mucker," it took only a few minutes for me to pitch the soiled hay in her stall into the wheelbarrow destined for Harry's compost pile and lay down fresh, sweet hay. Since Cash just arrived, his stall looked clean.

I always talked to April in the morning. "I'll give both you guys a good brush this afternoon. I promise. Maybe Devon will come over and meet you, Cash. He'll love you, don't you think so, April?"

"Most definitely he will."

I jumped and spun around at the voice behind me. My neighbor, Barb Atwater, stood in the doorway."

"You scared the chickens out of me!" I smiled and shook my head. "How long have you been standing there?"

"Long enough to hope you'd think April descended from Mr. Ed." Barb laughed and stepped up to Cash's stall. "He is a beauty. I'll tell Devon he's got a new neighbor." April snorted and tossed her head. "Hey there. You're still my pretty girl."

We both laughed at the "sibling rivalry" and offered the last of the carrots. "Barb, I'm not going to be able to walk this morning. I have a ton of calls to make before I go to work."

"This job of yours is getting in the way of your life." Her voice sounded stern, but she smiled as she shrugged her shoulders. "Oh well, another day of bonbon sans exercise." Barb Atwater hardly needed the exercise. She stood my height but with a different body style. Whereas most considered me "curvaceous," but possibly closing in on that euphemism towards "chunky," Barb's slender frame would never be described as either. We both wore shoulder-length hair, hers a light brown, mine sable.

"Yeah, right." I also knew the bonbon bit to be bogus. Barb had been recently diagnosed with high blood sugar. Our bakery treats after our walks had changed to granola bars, rice cakes, or something equally tasteless.

"Are we on for tomorrow?"

"Absolutely."

"Will you tell me then what an ambulance and police car were doing on your drive last night?"

I'd forgotten she'd driven by. What a friend to not jump me for answers.

"Definitely. In fact, meet me for lunch at Sweet Basil and I'll fill you in."

"Perfect. I'm headed over to Antique Bazaar later. I'll come downtown after that."

I still chuckled when I heard people born and raised in the suburbs refer to any district other than State and Madison as "downtown." Living my early years on Taylor Street and then living in Berkeley, a scant nine miles from the loop, there was only one downtown.

"How's twelve-thirty?"

"Perfect."

"And you'll fill me in on how you're involved in another murder?" She responded to my look of surprise. "It's all over the news, Grace. Didn't you watch any of it? They went all the way back. The thing with Harry in prison and Ric's involvement, the Rosary Bride murder, the body in the woods last Spring, the whole enchilada." Barb's eyes had been gleaming, but now clouded. "They even had a short piece about me, you know."

Her enthusiasm waned, as I suspected she had trouble saying: *when I was shot because someone mistook me for you.*

"Anyway." Her tone picked up. "You had your fifteen minutes of fame again last night."

"Thanks for telling me. I didn't watch TV last night; there's never anything good on." I smiled at my weak joke. "See you at Sweet Basil."

TWENTY

KAREN ALREADY KNEW about Ric. He had called her himself to assure her that he was fine. For all their head butting about politics, religion, civil rights, and most other controversial subjects, they were close and cared genuinely about each other. Ric had been looking out for his sister since their mother, Elizabeth Kramer, died in a boating accident on Lake Michigan almost fifteen years ago. Karen had watched the tube last night. Her only comment had been concerning the old picture they used of me. That's my Karen.

My subsequent phone calls took longer since each person I called, including Dr. Weber's wife, made a point of telling me they saw the newscast. Mrs. Weber wanted to chat about "those murders I solved." *Solved? I'd been damn near killed both times!* She spent five minutes talking to me before she told me her husband wasn't home yet. "The police wanted the autopsy done immediately and the usual coroner is on vacation. They sometimes call John for special needs. He was a pathologist before he switched to ob-gyn. Said he'd grown tired of the end process. Wanted to be in at the beginning." She spoke with such pride and devotion. I envied her. "I thought he'd be home by now. He called late last night to tell me he was too tired to drive and catch a few hours in one of the offices. I teased him that he'd best be careful not to fall asleep on one of those tables; he's such a sound sleeper they're liable to slide him into a cooler." She laughed.

I found her dark humor unsettling from someone her age. I expected a "blue rinse" lady who waited up for her country doctor. Doctor humor must be like cop humor—a way to get you through the night.

She took my number at the office and promised to have him call me when he got home.

I only had time for a quick shower as my long morning had disappeared. Traffic crawled and my right turn onto Washington Street coincided with when I was supposed to be at my desk. As I approached the building, I saw the squad car. *Gee. How could I have forgotten?* I drove past the building and found a spot a block away. I took my time knowing my tardiness would hardly be an issue while the police milled about underfoot. I was a terrible liar. How could I fake surprise?

Liz stood at the top of the stairs talking to a policeman. She broke off when she saw me. "Grace, it's terrible. We've had a break in. Must have happened yesterday. I'm glad you're here. We're checking to see if anything is missing."

Break in? More like a break out. What did they expect to be missing from the bathroom? I started to turn to the right to look in the bathroom. Liz stopped me. She leaned toward me and whispered, "You can't use the bathroom. The door's broken. Can you wait until you check your desk and then go downstairs and use theirs? You're the last one to arrive."

I mumbled something about parking. She nodded her head and waved me toward the office. I had not left it this way yesterday afternoon. The three potted plants on the window ledge had been smashed, scattering dirt, vermiculite, and shriveled African violets across the floor. The desktop waterfall in the reception area lay overturned and the water formed a large puddle on the almost-certainly ruined wood floor next to that desk. The contents of the feng shui sand tray with the smooth river rocks and tiny rake piled next to the puddle like a miniscule tidal wave had come and gone. Filing cabinet drawers stood open exposing folders in disarray. Other folders were strewn across desks as though they had been checked, found wanting, and discarded.

How could anyone tell what was missing? I already knew what was missing from my files. I picked up some folders from the floor and desktop. I figured I'd tidy up some and go through the motions and then announce the disappearance of my Depot Days file. As I shuffled the folders into a neat pile, I noticed the edge of one. *This can't be. It wasn't here yesterday. I know it wasn't.* The sticker of a steam locomotive that I had placed on the file tab caught my eye. When I needed the folder I could spot it easily. *Who would break in to replace something?*

"Grace, are you okay? You look odd. I mean, you look upset. I mean, more upset than this." Liz waved her hand at the office.

"I'm fine. Just surprised." She nodded and walked back to the officer. I looked more carefully through my desk and files and couldn't find a single thing missing; things out of place but nothing missing. It appeared as though someone wanted us to think we had something important to...*what?*

That question was answered with another question from a newly arrived source. I recognized Detective Garza's voice before he entered the office. He looked surprised to see me. Surely he knew where I worked? His eyes held mine for the briefest moment and then dropped to the file I still held in my hand.

"Is that your file on the Depot Days campaign?" *Is this guy psychic?* I followed his gaze and realized he had spotted the sticker. *Still a big leap.*

"Yes." He held out his hand; I unconsciously tightened my grip on the folder.

"Mrs. Marsden, I'm impounding everything connected with that event. The folder?" His fingers closed on the end of the file and slowly I released my grip.

What difference does it make? I already know every scrap of paper in there, have the original notes back home. Oh, no.

I snatched at the folder, but he had switched it to his other hand.

"Grace, what is wrong with you?" Liz's face turned beet red. She turned to Garza. "I apologize for my employee, Detective." They both glared at me.

"Don't you need a warrant or something since there is some personal information in there about people? Maybe we'd be in a legal loophole if we handed it over." I made up stuff as fast as I could remember it from TV. I wanted to put some doubt in Liz's mind.

I wanted that file back to make sure my suspicion was wrong. Why would someone ransack the office to put something back that they could have done without the hoopla? Because they added something to the one file that the police could possibly want for their investigation. My heart pounded while I waited for Liz to decide.

"Maybe I should call my attorney, Detective. I'll only be a moment." Now she held out her hand. Detective Garza fixed me with none too nice an expression as he handed the file to Liz.

I moved to follow Liz to her office. Detective Garza had other ideas. "Mrs. Marsden, I have no doubt you are suppressing some information on this case."

I interrupted with my best bluster. "Detective, I assure you I am cooperating with your—"

He waved a hand at me to stop. "We both know what you're doing and as soon as I can prove it, you're going to jail." His voice had been low but anyone looking at us could have guessed we weren't exchanging pleasantries.

Liz walked quickly toward us. The look of abject embarrassment on her face told the outcome of her conversation.

She passed the folder right by my nose as she returned it to Detective Garza. "I apologize for the inconvenience."

"So, it's okay with your attorney if you cooperate with a homicide investigation?" His tone dripped with sarcasm.

Liz flushed deep red. "Yes. He told me whoever suggested that concern has been watching too much TV." She locked her blue eyes on mine as she continued. "Schwarze and Krieg has no problem cooperating with the police."

"Fine. Then if I have all the materials concerning your campaign, I'll let the officer continue with his report."

"It's all right there. Grace, uh, Mrs. Marsden handled all the details."

Mrs. Marsden. Distancing herself; that can't be good.

Detective Garza left, triumph plastered across his face. I skulked back to my desk wondering what *had* been *added* to that file. That must be the reason for this mess. "I'd like to see you in my office."

There was no "please."

Liz closed the door, motioning for me to take a seat. She sat behind her desk and folded her hands on the blotter. I looked up at the clock behind her on the wall. Eight-thirty. I'd been here only twenty-five minutes.

"This isn't working out, Grace." She rushed on before I could open my mouth. "You're not a good fit. You're a loner, never joining us after work, you stop in the middle of things to tie knots, you talk to yourself quite a bit; I mean, your strategies are brilliant and you've done a fabulous job with this campaign, but you don't fit in the big picture of Schwarze and Krieg. Maybe a more solitary job, like a research person or an analyst of some sort. Anyway, I'm going to pay you through the month. I think that's fair, actually generous. Let's gather your things and get on with our lives." She had spoken her piece in less than thirty seconds.

I'd never been fired from a job before; people loved me,

thought me clever, witty; a nice person. I wanted to defend myself, explain. I didn't know what to say.

Liz moved out from behind her desk. *Two days ago she thought I was the greatest thing since sliced bread, now I am* persona non grata. *No, worse, I am* persona non jobba. I smiled at my twisted Latin.

"That's better. Let's get your things. I'd be happy to supply a reference for you. And we'll do lunch soon and keep in touch." She had taken my smile as acceptance. What the heck, I'd only been here three months.

I stood up and followed her to the main office. My co-workers, two twenty-something recent grads with marketing degrees, averted their eyes as we passed their desks. The office manager, still involved with the police officer, glanced up at us. The only person not present was Liz's partner, Lucy. She seldom came in; worked from home to be with her three-year-old daughter.

I really hadn't settled into Schwarze and Krieg. The few items that I lifted from my desk—a photo of Harry, a stuffed horse, three pieces of yarn in various stages of knots, and a plaque with the saying, *It might be insane to live in a dream, but it's madness to live without one*—testified to my lack of connection. I wondered whether to say goodbye but Liz saved me the trouble by turning me toward the door and mumbling something about "lunch, real soon."

I felt like braiding one of those pieces, but I didn't want to give her the satisfaction of showing her my "weird" side. I walked down the stairs.

"Are they about finished up there?"

I hadn't noticed the woman in the foyer area of the main floor. Her voice was soft but firm as though accustomed to answers. She sat in one of the highback chairs and waved her hand up toward Schwarze and Krieg. "She called me to come in as soon as possible but he told me to wait down here." By "he" I guessed she meant the policeman. "I'm on the clock; eight-thirty."

I liked her immediately. Her chin-length, curly blond hair framed her face and softened a short straight nose and heart-shaped face. Frank blue eyes looked back at me from a tanned fiftyish face. Her petite stature—I guessed 105 pounds and 5'2" tops—looked toned from golf or swimming or aerobics. She had that kind of light muscle tone that thin people in good shape have.

"Hi, I'm Grace Marsden." I put out my hand. I don't know why I introduced myself. She stood up and extended her hand. I expected the light, firm handshake.

"Nice to meet you. I'm Jan Pauli. You know anything about what's going on up there?"

"Nothing. I just got fired." I couldn't believe I'd shared that with this stranger. What was it with her?

"First time, huh?"

I looked at her in surprise.

"In another galaxy a lifetime ago, I used to fire people all the time. You've got that 'first time ever' look."

I wondered about her now. *Another galaxy; A Shirley McClaine groupie?* My brain kicked in and I understood her usage. I smiled at her. "Yep. First time. It still hasn't sunk in." I realized that it hadn't.

"Sit down." She motioned at the other chair as she resumed her original position. I noticed the small cooler at her feet. She slid the top open and pulled out a plastic container. "Have some; you need a little sugar boost to get over the shock." She lifted the lid and exposed a collection of malted milk balls. "Go ahead, take a few. I keep a supply when I'm working. Sometimes need an energy boost. Beats that dry granola crap."

Who was this delightful creature? I grinned and lifted two from the canister.

"Thanks. This is exactly what I need." I popped one in my

mouth and enjoyed the sweetness as I sucked the chocolate off the tiny orb then crunched until it became a sweet memory. *"Hmm."* I did the other one the same way. She hadn't said a word. I liked that. Neither one of us felt obligated to chitchat.

I broke the amiable silence. "You mentioned work. What do you do?"

She pulled a card from the pocket of her jean jacket and handed it to me.

Clean Sweep Service, Have Broom Will Travel

Her name and contact number were listed at the bottom. Plain cardstock with purple raised printing.

"That's an interesting slogan," I said. I wondered if she'd thought about the double meaning.

"I like it. In my corporate life some called me worse, but not for long." She grinned and winked. "I think it intimidates some of my clients. They don't nag me about little things."

I wondered what she meant, but an idea pushed into my head that demanded center stage. Out it came.

"I desperately need a cleaning service. The last woman left after the explosion." *Way to go, Grace. Why don't I jump up and down and babble at her like the crazy person she must think I am?*

She raised an inquiring eyebrow, then grinned. Her small white teeth glowed against her tan skin. "I'm your gal. Write down your number and address and I'll stop by this afternoon, say two-thirty, to work up an evaluation." She whipped out her day timer and made a note. "Better yet, give me your info and I'll jot it down."

She carefully noted my information and then beamed at me. "I've never worked in Pine Marsh. I'm in a social group with a woman who knows someone in your compound. Wait a minute. Is your husband English?"

"He is, but I don't think…"

She clapped her hands together like a child on Christmas

morning and her blue eyes sparkled. "Now I know why your name rings a bell. You're 'Missus Grace,' aren't you?"

"Only Gertrude calls me that. You know Gertrude?"

"Sure do. We're Hessian Hunnies." She smiled and touched a small pin on her jacket lapel. It was a circa Kaiser Wilhelm helmet with a banner that read "Hunnies" through the pointed top. The red pin stood out against the blue denim. I had been too preoccupied to notice.

"Excuse me?" I was doubting my judgment in blurting out my offer of employment.

"We're in a chapter in the Red Hat Society."

I must have looked confused.

She explained further. "It's a social club for women over fifty. They're springing up everywhere. It's for women who've done the PTA, Boy Scouts, Girl Scouts, school board, all that, and now want to kick back and have fun. Kind of matronly 'material girls.'"

I laughed out loud at the visual that description brought to mind; Gertrude and Madonna. "Is this club in Naperville?"

"No, this one is a little different. Each club has a Queen." She stopped and smiled a dazzling display of perfect teeth. I wasn't surprised she was the Queen.

She continued. "Our club is not geographical but rather ancestral. The Hessian Hunnies are woman over fifty who were born in Germany or who are first-generation German. Our group is comprised of women from all over the Western suburbs. We even have some Hunnies in waiting; usually daughters of Hessian Hunnies."

"Hunnies in waiting?"

"Those are woman under the magic age of fifty. They wear pastel shades of our colors because until you're fifty you're not entitled to the vibrant, royal colors of purple and red."

I wondered now if the beautiful chapeau Gertrude wore to the auction had been her club hat.

"Gertrude thinks the world of you, Mrs. Marsden."

"The feeling is mutual. Your club isn't an investment-type club, like Beardstown Ladies, is it? I mean, Gertrude isn't on the hook for an endowment or anything?" I hoped I sounded casual about my concerns.

Jan Pauli stared at me for a good thirty seconds before she answered. I think she was assessing my motive behind the questions. Her lake-blue eye color seemed a shade darker as she composed her answer.

She spoke slowly and distinctly as if to make sure of no misunderstanding. "There are dues and outing costs but no automatic withdrawal from checking accounts or automatic charge to their credit cards. I am responsible for paying the chapter dues, and the Hunnies know when I mail my check." She smiled now, apparently comfortable with my concern. "See you this afternoon. I'm going up there and find out if they want a cleaning service or not. One way or another I'm submitting a bill for thirty minutes." She pushed her small cooler behind the chair out of sight and took the stairs at a brisk pace.

I had no doubt she'd get her answer and her wages. Jan Pauli seemed like that kind of woman. I looked forward to turning over my domain to *Clean Sweep Service;* only wished she could clean sweep the entire Depot Days mess.

With unexpected time on my hands, I reverted to errand mode. I picked up Harry's shirts at Leo's Cleaners; light starch on a hanger, and stopped across the street at the Coffee Depot for a tall *Pine Marsh Madness.* The owner named coffees after the local subdivisions. Clever idea. I had already tried *Meadows Mocha* and *Woodridge Estates Espresso,* but usually chose *Madness.* I ordered a cup to go. With the morning rush customers behind desks and counters by now, the café's quiet murmurs and delicious scents lured me to stay. I cancelled the to-go and added a Bavarian apple slice to the order.

I draped Harry's shirts over the empty chair across from me and settled in to sip, munch, and think.

Who would break in to replace the folder they'd removed? What did they add to the information? If they only wanted to add something, why remove the folder in the first place? Who removed the folder? It was there Friday morning because I'd copied down a phone number I needed. Between Friday and Sunday afternoon, someone removed that folder. We were all chasing in ten different directions trying to get set for the auction. Any number of people moved in and out all day. But who would have an interest in that folder?

My apple slice a sweet memory and my coffee a tasty chaser, I gave up thinking about the folder and drove home wondering about the trunks instead. Schoebel had balked at opening them, Ava had been desperate to get them, and Ava's son Karl had them in the basement of the old mill for years. Was he hiding their secret? Why? According to Liz, her cousin had been away at boarding school, then college for the last fifteen years. Ava was a shrewd businesswoman whose interest in the trunks translated to her bottom line. Schoebel, on the other hand, could have had the best reason to want the trunks to remain sealed.

I pulled into my driveway and pressed the opener. The door moved up slowly. My eyes wandered over the contents of the garage as I waited. *The baseball bat!* I'd forgotten to call the police about the bat.

Previous scenarios drained from my brain like water through a colander, leaving only the residue of my thoughts. One thought clung to my brain like the one strand of pasta that sticks to the colander. *Schoebel. If a child were missing... Dr. Weber. I'll give his wife my office number.*

I entered the kitchen with my plan to make those two important calls. They say, "God laughs when men make plans." He must have been doubled over.

TWENTY-ONE

I GASPED AND stepped back instinctively. Crockery and flowerpots lay broken, their contents strewn across the ceramic floor. Bosc pears and California oranges dotted the tile in a wobble and roll pattern from where their bowl had landed. Pieces of newly started oregano, cilantro, and basil plants clung to shards of the terra-cotta pots smashed in front of the sink.

I felt a sense of *déjà vu* from the scene at the office. A different thought entered my head; whoever had trashed my kitchen could have moved on to another room. I stood still and listened; my pounding heart and sketchy breathing filled my ears.

Then I turned stupid and mad. "Dammit," I shouted at no one and everyone. "I've had it." I brought both fists down on the counter and caused one of the mugs that hadn't been smashed on the floor to tumble over the edge and join the set. My mini catharsis cleared my mind enough for me to know I should get out of there.

I got behind the wheel and backed out of the driveway. I looked around for another car. I didn't see one, but I wasn't going back in without someone armed or at least big. I sat in my locked vehicle in front of my house and called the police from my car phone. The instrument was still a novelty to me, and I refused to use it while I driving. After I dialed 9-1-1, I thought about making those two calls, but I didn't know the numbers by heart. I knew Karen's so I called her.

"Hello."

"Hi, Karen, it's me. How's Ric? Have you talked to him?"

"He's bored. I'm on my way out there now."

"No school today?"

"Teacher's institute. I had a two-hour workshop, but nothing else. I planned on visiting Ric and then surprising you at your office."

I could hear God chuckling. "Yeah, well. I'm home today, too."

"Ah, a little R & R after your spectacular debut as a PR guru?"

"No, more like I got fired for being weird and not a good fit at Schwarze and Krieg."

"Gracie, are you joking?"

"I wouldn't joke about this. I've never been fired before. Even when I got my yarn caught in the meat slicer at the Butterfly Delicatessen and broke the machine I didn't get fired."

"I'm sorry, Grace. Gee, fired. Want me to come over? I could stop before I go to Edwards. Ric's not going anywhere." She chuckled.

I heard the siren getting closer. I didn't want to explain this right now. "Come by later, after Ric. I mean, I have a little cleaning to do." The sound grew louder.

"What's that noise, a siren?"

I quickly rolled down the window; I hated lying to Karen. "My window is open, must be going by; probably trying to get to the golf course." The squad stopped and a Sheriff's policeman approached my car.

"Karen, I've got to go now. Stop by later, after Ric. Bye." I cut off her answer and replaced the phone in its holder. The officer walked slowly toward me.

"I'm Grace Marsden. I called."

"Can I see some identification, Mrs. Marsden?" I had put both hands on the steering wheel. He watched my hands now as he requested my ID.

"I don't have any with me. It's in the house. I went in, put down my purse, saw the kitchen, and came back out. I didn't bring it with me."

He stepped closer and looked into the backseat. He motioned for me to get out of the Jeep. I opened the door and noticed the cleaning hanging from the hook in the back. "Officer, I have my husband's shirts I can identify, I mean the markings, and the light starch on a hanger notation on the ticket."

He must have decided I wasn't the bad guy. He smiled and introduced himself. "I'm Patrolman Jeffers, Mrs. Marsden. Wait here and I'll check the house. Your keys?"

"Oh. I always go in through the garage. My house keys are in my purse."

I hadn't lowered the garage door. He walked up the driveway and I followed him. Before he entered the garage he turned and motioned for me to stay. I felt like I should thump my tail on the driveway. He entered the kitchen from there.

Why was this happening to me? Who wanted anything I had? Minutes clicked by in my head and I felt the undeniable urge to do the same. I looked down at my outfit, no snaps, no zippers; I shopped with an eye for avoidable noise rather than pure fashion. I returned to my car and happily manipulated my turn signal lever. *Click, click...click, click...click.*

A soft rap on the window startled me. Patrolman Jeffers stood at the driver's side window, slightly bent at the waist, peering in at me. What he must have seen. He'd broken my pattern. I had to fix it. *Click, click...click, click...click, click.*

He had stepped around to the front of the Jeep and turned when he heard my door open. "There's no one inside. Let's go in and you can tell me what happened."

He didn't mention a word about my behavior. *Probably thinks I'm a nutcase. Can't wait to leave.* He stepped aside at the kitchen door and I preceded him into the room. It still looked as trashed as before but I was prepared for the sight this time.

"Can I make you some coffee?" I craved a cup.

"No thank you, ma'am."

Afraid to drink anything.

"Raspberry Bavarian? It's from Joyful's Café."

He hesitated but resisted. "No, thank you."

Food too, eh?

I decided to wait to brew coffee. I wanted to finish this business and let him be on his way. "Patrolman Jeffers, I came home less than twenty minutes ago and found the kitchen like this. I didn't go anywhere else in the house so I don't know if anything else is damaged or if anything is missing."

"The rest of the house is in order, ma'am. The rage seems to have been contained in this room. They may have heard you pull in and left through the front door or out the back and circled to the front. Did you see a car on the street when you arrived?"

"No, and there was no car when I came out; I checked."

"The person could have been gone by then. This road dead-ends around a slight curve toward the woods. You may not have noticed a car parked there. Did you hear a car start up?"

"No. Nothing. You think the person that did this was still here when I arrived?" An icy finger poked at the base of my neck. My shoulders twitched and I clasped my hands together. Another thought entered my brain. "You said, 'rage' earlier. Why?"

"Unless the break in was to search for something small, it looks as though whoever did this was angry; trashing may have eased their anger, almost a cleansing." He closed the notebook he'd been writing in and looked me full in the face. "Mrs. Marsden, is there anyone you know who is extremely upset with you or would wish you harm?"

"No."

"Think carefully. Someone at work? A disgruntled employee? Someone from a past disagreement or lawsuit? Anything?"

This is the second time this year that a police officer is standing in my kitchen and asking if I know of anyone who'd want to hurt me.

"Mrs. Marsden?"

"Oh. Uh, I don't have a job, I've never been anyone's boss, and the people who meant me harm from my past are all dead." I hadn't meant to say that.

"What?" His head snapped up like a cheap shade on a bedroom window.

"They didn't both hate me. Only one. The other hated Harry, but was hired by the first one to kill me." I stopped talking when he flipped to a new page and clicked his pen.

"I know this sounds bizarre; this entire year has been bizarre. Do you know Officer Manelli?"

"Yes." His answer came slowly, as though he feared his brother officer's connection to me.

"He knows all about the explosion and can fill…"

"What explosion?" He stood up quickly. I think he was weighing whether this might become a *fight or flight* scenario.

The phone rang and I don't know which of us breathed a bigger sigh of relief.

"Hello."

"Hi, honey. I called your office and they said you didn't work there anymore. What's going on?"

"Hi, Dad. It's a long story and I'm kind of busy right now. Can I call you back?"

"I'll bet you're busy. Do I have to hear about Harry's trouble from my cleaning lady?"

"Dad, Harry's not in too much trouble. It will… Cleaning lady? You don't have a cleaning lady."

"If you'd come visit more you'd know I have a cleaning

lady." His smirky tone infuriated me. My four brothers had inherited that tone, even my oldest brother, Joe, the priest.

"Okay, Dad. I should visit more. I can't talk now. Let me call you back."

"No need. Now that I know you're home I'll be right out."

"Dad, you can't drive. Unless you have a chauffeur I don't know about." I put as much smirkyness into my voice as I could. It came out sassy; I instantly regretted the lapse in respect. My father had flunked the vision part of his driver's test. He couldn't drive until he had long overdue cataract surgery. "Sorry, Dad."

"It's okay, honey. Your cousin Nick stopped by. We're on our way." He hung up before I could argue, an exercise in futility when Mike Morelli made up his mind.

"About Manelli?" Patrolman Jeffers had regained control of his emotions.

"He can tell you all about the explosion and the shooting on the golf course." *Geez, Louise. Open your mouth wider, dummy.* My silent chastisement kept me quiet.

"Mrs. Marsden, I have everything I need. I'll file this report. Keep the door from the garage locked and start using your house key to get in. It's not that difficult for someone to access your overhead door, especially if the houses had the same builder. They tend to use the same products in construction."

"You think a neighbor did this?" The thought was ridiculous, especially with Lily out of the country.

"Mrs. Marsden, there are no signs of forced entry. This was the only door not locked." He pushed in the button under the knob. "If you think of anything else, let me know." He handed me a card with his name and number.

"You're going? What if they come back?"

"Mrs. Marsden, I don't think you need to worry. If that person had wanted to hurt you they would have stayed to confront you."

"You're a profiler, now?" I heard the Morelli smirk in my voice.

"Actually, a profiler in training, ma'am. I'll be receiving my master's in Criminal Behavioral Psychology in December."

My slack-jaw appearance must have softened him. He smiled gently. "I really don't think you're in any danger."

A thought occurred to me. "Is that why you didn't say, I mean in the car, when I couldn't…didn't get out?"

"No. My little brother has a slight degree of autism. I'm used to compulsive, repetitive behavior." He stepped into the garage. "I'll wait until you pull in your Jeep."

"Thank you." I pulled the door behind me and followed him out of the garage.

He stopped and turned quickly. "Mrs. Marsden, I locked that door."

I turned the knob frantically. "Dammit! What next?"

Jeffers walked toward me. "I'm sorry. I thought you saw me do it."

"I did. It's not your fault. It's a habit."

"Can I give you a ride to somewhere, someone with a key?"

"My dad will be here in a few minutes. He has a key."

We continued walking out of the garage and down the driveway.

"Do you want me to wait until he arrives?"

"Thank you for the offer, but it might be better if a police car isn't here when he arrives. He worries a lot."

"I'll bet and how," he mumbled.

"Excuse me?"

"I said, 'I'll get going now.'" He lied worse than I did.

He did wait until I pulled the Jeep into the garage and emerged with the remote in my hand. I sat on the top step of my front porch idly opening and closing the garage door.

My father's blue Oldsmobile, with Nick at the wheel, pulled

up at the front. I waved nonchalantly like I always sat on my concrete steps in a business suit, nylons, and heels.

My dad and Nick walked across the lawn to me. No "hello," no "how are you?"

"We passed a squad coming from your side. What was he doing here?" My dad stood with his hands on his hips; his lean stature puffed out by his akimbo posture. I knew better than to stand up and be taller.

My cousin stood behind him. "Why are you out here?" Nick asked.

Before I could answer, Karen pulled up. She hurried across the lawn to join us.

"Hi. Why is everyone on the porch?"

"We just asked that question," Nick answered.

"No big deal. I locked myself out of the house. Karen, how's Ric?" I stalled for time.

"What's wrong with Ric?" My dad turned to Karen.

"He has a concussion from last night when Grace tripped over him."

Gee, Karen. Make me sound like a moron.

"Tripped over him?" My dad's full eyebrows were some-where in his hairline. He looked at me with his "what in the name of Santa Lucia is going on?" look.

Karen continued, oblivious to the yawning hole at my feet that she enlarged with each comment. "Sergeant Peterson took him to the ER last night."

"He was here?"

"Uh-huh, with the other police."

My father exploded. "What other police?" He whirled on me. "Graciella Elena Morelli, what in the name of *Santa Lucia* is going on here?"

Oh, man. The entire moniker meant big trouble; the Ital-ian version meant really big trouble! "Could we relax and talk about this? How about we grab some lunch?" I made a show of checking my watch. "Look at the time. No wonder I'm so hungry. What do you guys feel like eating? We could go to Clara's. You love that place, Dad. Or The Country House for sandwiches? Maybe the clubhouse at…"

"Gracie, stop." My dad's voice was gentle but firm. He dipped his head toward my left side and only then did I realize I had been twirling my hair as I spoke. He knew the signs. "What is it, honey?"

"Okay, let's go inside. Do you have my house key?" I asked the question as I turned to climb the steps. Three voices answered in the affirmative. I turned to stare down at them. "You all have my house key?"

"I got one when they were rebuilding so I could come over and help." My dad shrugged his shoulders. He looked at Nick.

"Me too, Uncle Mike. I helped with the cabinets."

"I helped with the decorating." Karen smiled up at me.

Maybe Jeffers is right. All the residents of Pine Marsh and points East and West could have keys to my house.

"Do you want it back?" Nick held out his key ring. He looked embarrassed. *These people love me, in spite of me.* I felt ungrateful for all they had done for Harry and me. "No, of course not. How about using it to let us in?"

He grinned as he stepped around me to open the impressive oak door. It didn't budge. He looked down at his key and then at me. "You've got the deadbolt on and this key is for only the lock."

Karen and my dad both nodded, confirming their keys had the same function.

"Gracie, use the opener and we can go in through the kitchen. That's never locked." Karen brightened at her suggestion.

"Right," confirmed Nick. "You never lock that door."

Point two for Jeffers on that count. I had to ask. "If someone had the same garage door opener installed could some-one else use their remote to open the overhead?"

Nick answered. "Not necessarily; the codes are different. It's more likely that someone flying a radio-controlled air-plane or an actual airplane flying low might addle the signal and open it. Of course, it they don't pay attention to how they program the unit, it could happen. Why?"

"Just wondering. You know, questions pop into my head all the time." I cleared my throat as we waited for the over-head to stop at the top. "I may have locked that door today, so we may need that key." I motioned to Nick, who had re-turned his key ring to his pocket.

"What's going on? You never lock that door?" Karen asked.

I ignored her question and tried to prepare them for what was behind door number one. "The kitchen is a little messy. A lot of things got broken…" The explanation died on my lips as Nick pushed the door open and stepped in.

"Holy shit!" He didn't even apologize for his language. My dad hurried in after him, followed closely by Karen. I wondered about the possibility of skulking away before they noticed.

TWENTY-TWO

IN A RARE MOMENT of courage I swept in and faced them. "It's not as bad as it looks. Nothing is missing and this is the only room affected. Someone got a little nuts in here."

Karen and Nick turned slowly in their places surveying the damage. My father locked his gaze on my surely pansy-purple eyes. I didn't look away, but what I saw disturbed me. His expression was one of deep concern and a little bit of fear. I didn't understand until he spoke softly to me.

"Honey, did you do this?"

The fact that he asked me shouldn't have come as a surprise; as a child when "the jitters" would overwhelm me I would fly into a rage and destroy my room; the destruction was the only way I could deal with the obsessive demon I hadn't yet learned to control. Rage wasn't what I used anymore; hadn't used for years. I felt my eyes filling with tears.

He opened his arms and I stepped into a bear hug of epic proportion. "Sorry, I had to know."

I managed to limit my emotions to teary eyes. Karen and Nick had stood silent during that display. I smiled at them and cleared my throat.

"The police officer you saw leaving responded to my call. He searched the house. In his opinion, someone angry with me did this. He doesn't think they wanted to hurt me, only scare me."

"Why? Who'd be this mad at you?"

"Maybe this person is upset with Harry and doesn't know he's out of town."

I hadn't thought of that possibility. I don't know why; it had been Harry's dark past that produced the person who had blown up our house.

"I don't know what to think, Dad. Right now I want to change out of these clothes, clean up this mess, and make some phone calls to try and clean up another mess."

"I told you before, you need a dog here for protection. Look at you out here in no man's land. No sidewalks, no curbs, no streetlights... On a cloudy night you can't see your hand in front of your face."

Three heads nodded agreement. My father continued. "Remember your 'gypsy' apartment in Bellwood?"

I nodded. He always referred to my first apartment, one the owner had built in the basement of his home, when he talked about home security. It had a flimsy door, only one entrance, and small basement windows high on the painted cement wall. My father had insisted I keep a baseball bat near the door in case of intruders and a chair under the bedroom window in case of fire. My dad had mentioned bats again since our return because of the problems we'd had in the last year; not that a bat would have stopped a bazooka. I wasn't sure if he was joking but I didn't want to hear it.

"So, thank you for stopping by but I've a lot of work to do." I waved at the room. I didn't want to sound ungrateful for their concern; I wanted to get on with my list. A sidebar problem with obsessive-compulsive personalities is that once they commit to tasks, they have to complete or at least attempt completion on a certain timetable. In other words, it makes us *anxious* if we can't work our timetable.

"We're not going to leave you with this mess," Karen said. "Go up and change and make your calls. I'll make us some coffee, your dad can put together some lunch, and Nick," she smiled sweetly at my cousin, "can pick up the pieces."

We laughed at her delegation. I did feel better having them

in the house. My bedroom seemed a calm haven compared to the chaos of the kitchen. The hands on the Betty Boop clock on Harry's nightstand reminded me it was only noon. *Noon! Cripes... Barb.* I'd totally forgotten our lunch date. Add another phone call to my list. I could leave word for her at Sweet Basil. I checked the clock again. The clock had been a wedding present from one of Harry's eccentric English clients. Of all the things destroyed in the explosion, *she* survived. I'd never liked the piece and had tried unsuccessfully to donate it to anything more than once. Harry is a creature of habit; he always pats the exaggerated ceramic behind before he gets into bed. He jokingly bids us both sweet dreams.

My heart lurched in my chest. Unbidden thoughts like vipers through the grass flowed through my brain. *Whose behind does he pat good-night? To whom does he wish "sweet dreams"? Not you, Gracie girl.*

"Not no one," I yelled at the air. Boy, I needed to unwind. I stripped off the rest of my clothes and headed for a hot shower. The water didn't heat up immediately, but the cool stream felt good until the water worked up to the steamy temp I enjoyed. Harry marveled at how I could enjoy such hot showers. I had to turn down the heat if I invited Harry in to share. *Who is he sharing a shower with today?*

"Stop!" I screamed in the confined space and slapped at the tiled wall in frustration. Both sounds reverberated. I pushed the center knob shut and jumped out, suddenly claustrophobic in the small space. My breathing grew uneven. I felt like I was unraveling.

I dressed and headed downstairs within minutes. I smelled the French Vanilla roasted blend before I entered the kitchen. If I'd been asked which coffee Karen would make, I would have said that one. We are creatures of habit.

Everyone stopped and looked at me when I entered the room. The cleanup had progressed nicely; Nick had swept

up all the broken crockery. Some larger pieces lay on the island; maybe he thought they could be repaired. The breakfast
nook table had four settings, with place mats and silverware.
I noticed my angel mug had survived and sat waiting on the
table. Someone knew me pretty well, too.

"Did you make your calls already, honey?"

"I made one. I feel restless. I want to take April for a ride,
you know, *clear the cobwebs*." My family did know. Everyone knew riding calmed me; another predictable point. "If
lunch is ready, though…" I let the sentence hang.

"Nothing that can't wait a half hour or so." My dad looked
at Nick and Karen for confirmation. They both nodded.

I remembered they didn't know about Cash. I looked at
them. "Either of you want to come along?"

Karen giggled, "Should I jog next to you?"

"You jog, I'll ride Cash." Nick smiled broadly at me.

"Does everyone know everything in this family? Can't a
girl keep a secret about anything?" I smiled at the thought
that any Morelli could keep quiet about anything.

Karen looked confused. "And Cash would be?"

"A horse Harry bought for Grace from the lady who kept
April at her horse farm this summer." Nick laughed at my
surprised look.

"Any other questions?" I asked Karen as though I had
answered her first one.

Karen looked down at her dress slacks and pumps. "I'm
not exactly outfitted for a ride. You go, Nick. Besides, I'm
going to use the time to go over to Lily's and get some things
for Ric. How about we all meet back here at one-thirty?"

"Dad, that leaves you odd man out. What are you going
to do?"

"Don't worry about me, I brought along some homework."
He pulled a small booklet from his back pocket. *Rules of*

Soccer. "Some of my baseball kids want to play soccer in the fall league. They need an assistant coach."

I shook my head in amazement. My father had organized the local boys and girls in the neighborhood to play baseball in the Park District league. Now this. I marveled at his energy and commitment to the kids. The ethnic mix in my old neighborhood had changed but one thing remained constant: kids playing ball.

WE SAT DOWN to lunch at the pre-agreed time. Dad had prepared a mixed salad of arugula, endive, tomato, cucumber and chives, followed by thick lentil soup topped with chopped onions and sour cream and accompanied by warm crusty rolls. He had grilled a piece of salmon to perfection and quartered it with a precision King Solomon would have envied.

"Mr. Morelli, this is fabulous. If you give up managing ball clubs would you consider cooking for Hannah and me?"

We laughed at her comments. My dad waved his fork above his plate to stop the laughter. "If it weren't for the well-stocked pantry my son-in-law keeps, our fare today would have been Yo Ho potato chips, Oreo cookies, and celery sticks."

Nick laughed so hard he sprayed the sip of water he'd taken across his side of the table. He dabbed at the table with his napkin. "Sorry." His shoulders shook with continued laughter.

"I'm serious." Karen's voice cut through the waning giggles. "Hannah's going to open this boarding house and she's looking for an Italian chef to do Sunday afternoon dinner. Her idea is to play off what most Europeans and especially Englishmen connect with Chicago, Al Capone, gangsters, Italian food, etc."

"I thought this was a bed-and-breakfast? You know, stylish, Victorian, like Under the Gingko Tree in Oak Park."

"Hannah says everybody in England knows one of those, because when older couples can't make it on their pensions and their children have gone off to the big cities, they list themselves as a bed-and-breakfast for the tourists. Hannah wants a 'Roaring Twenties' feel."

"This could be fun. I could serve family-style and carry 'heat' so they wouldn't complain about the service or the food."

"Uncle Mike, I could be the waiter and make comments like I'm checking out their jewelry, uh, 'ice.'"

"You two are over the top. Why don't you plan a shoot out and have Ness crash through the front door with his Untouchables." I twirled my pointer fingers in small circles on both sides of my head.

The fact that they seemed to be thinking about that scenario worried me. Then an unfamiliar voice spoke.

"After all that you might need a good cleaning service, what with the *pasta e fagioli* all over the walls."

We turned toward the voice.

"Hi. The garage was open," she explained.

"Hi, no, that's fine. Come in." I glanced at my watch.

"We did agree on two-thirty, didn't we?"

"Yes, we did. And you're right on time."

"Amazing," my dad muttered.

"Actually, I was early. I took a stroll around the house. Your gardens are lovely. Hope you don't mind." Jan walked into the room and I made quick introductions. Everyone started making noises about having to leave; except my dad. He would have stayed but Nick had driven and he had to get to work. My cousin worked for the town of Elgin as an EMT.

Jan offered Karen one of her cards. "Please consider me for the cleaning service at your B and B."

"It's not mine and we already have the job filled." Karen turned to me. "Hannah's hired Gertrude."

Now it clicked. I looked at my dad. "Is she the cleaning lady you mentioned?"

My dad grinned. "We're bartering. I'm teaching her to cook Italian and she's cleaning the house. She drives a hard bargain. I have to clean up the kitchen after our cooking lesson."

We laughed at his mock protest. Jan fixed her sparkling eyes on my dad. "Gee, she gets all the interesting jobs."

I didn't like the way she said "interesting." My dad apparently loved it. His ears turned pinkish. Jan's laugh sounded light and airy and for a moment reminded me of the laugh I'd grown up hearing from my mother. I wondered if my dad heard it that way.

I promised each of them I'd call if I needed anything. I leaned against the closed door for a moment to collect my thoughts; the wits had long since left the building.

"Sorry, about the delay. I know you probably have a tight schedule."

"No apology necessary. I'm off until tomorrow afternoon; tidying up a house in Green Trails before a dinner party. The hostess is an old friend of mine from college, a million years ago." I laughed at her hyperbole; it was lighthearted, not self-depreciating.

I took her through each room and explained what I wanted her to do and what I planned to continue doing. I'd never asked my former cleaning lady to clean up the mudroom, as it could likely have wayward clumps of nasty hay and the occasional piece of horse patty.... It happened.

She took some notes and asked a few clarifying questions on the tour. When we returned to the kitchen, I offered her some coffee.

"You have a lovely home. Without kids running amok it stays picked up longer." My eyes narrowed and my lower lip found its way between my teeth. She shifted gears immediately. "I'm also available to help out with gardening and I'd be happy to trade stall mucking for riding time."

We agreed on the next morning at eight. I let her out the front door and made sure to turn the deadbolt in place; a new action I needed to do until it became a habit. I sat at the counter and pulled my notepad closer. I still hadn't made that call to Dr. Weber to give him my home phone. I doubted Liz would be forwarding calls to me. At least I could cross off *cleaning lady.* A sensation akin to light pin pricks on the surface of my skin swept over me. My list had been altered. A line crossed through Dr. Weber's name and a phone number was printed next to Ava Deutsch's name. Not by my hand.

TWENTY-THREE

WHY WOULD ANYONE alter my notes? I couldn't imagine that my father, Karen or Nick would have done so. That left only the person who'd smashed up my kitchen. *They broke in to leave me something?* A repeat of the mess at the office; whatever they put in the folder.

I should have seen the connection sooner. I picked up the phone to dial the number on Officer Jeffers's business card. I wondered how many times he'd said, "If you think of anything else give me a call at this number," and people actually called. The first three numbers were punched in when I hung up.

What would I tell him? The same person who trashed Schwarze and Krieg and left a piece of paper in my folder, trashed my kitchen and left me a phone number? Instead, I dialed the crossed-through phone number for Dr. Weber.

"Hello, Weber residence." This was a different voice, younger.

"Hello. May I speak with Dr. Weber? This is Grace Marsden."

"Mrs. Marsden?" The voice translated into a face—Sergeant Royal's.

"Sergeant Royal?"

"Why are you calling Dr. Weber? Do you have particular business with him?"

I felt like telling her to mind her own business, but the little hairs on the back of my neck alerted me to the possibility that it may be her business. I answered slowly. "I wanted to follow up on some historical details to finish the Depot Days file."

"Odd that you'd continue to work on a project when you are no longer employed by that company."

Damn! She knows everything. I scrambled for a reason and came up with the truth. "I called this morning and left a message for him to call at my office. I didn't know then I'd be fired, uh, down-sized. I called to apologize for any confusion in case he tried to reach me."

"How nice of you." Her praise seemed shallow. "Unfortunately, it won't be necessary. Dr. Weber was the victim of a hit and run this morning. He died about two hours ago."

"Oh, my God. That's awful." My next breath caught in my throat and I felt a tingle at the back of my throat that signaled tears. I swallowed hard. This day had unnerved me and here was the proverbial last straw.

"Mrs. Marsden?" Her voice sounded firm. "I didn't realize you knew him well."

"I didn't. I've spent most of today feeling sorry for myself because I lost a job. Sometimes we don't know how lucky we are. I met with him twice to get some historical details for the promo material. He seemed so full of life, reminiscing about the early days of the town. It's so unfair." My tiny voice catches accompanied by sniffles were on the verge of escalating into full-blown sobs. I didn't care if she thought me weak; by the same token, I didn't want to burst into tears.

"You're right about that, so unfair." The timbre of her voice softened.

"Did you know him, Sergeant Royal?"

"I'd say so. He delivered me and got me through every childhood disease and broken bone until I left for college." Her voice spoke of her pain.

"I'm sorry. I should have thought that being from here you might have…" I took a breath. "I'm sorry for your loss."

"Thank you, Mrs. Marsden. If you'll excuse me, some friends of the family have arrived."

"Of course. Again, my condolences. Goodbye."

The connection broken, I stood leaning against the wall with the receiver against my chest. *Two hit-and-run deaths in two days; that can't be coincidence.* My spirits lifted as I thought that with Harry out of the picture it would hardly seem likely that there were two deadly drivers loose in Lisle. I looked at the receiver in my hand as though to recall the conversation and felt a twinge of guilt that this second death might exonerate my husband. I replaced the phone in its stand and looked down at my list. The enormity of what I saw hit me. I couldn't keep this from the police.

I hit the redial button and waited.

"Hello, the Weber residence."

"Sergeant Royal, this is Grace Marsden again. I know you're busy, but when you have a chance, I think I should talk to you. Could you come to my house?"

"Do you know something about this, Mrs. Marsden?" The gentle voice I had hung up with two minutes ago was gone.

"No, not the hit and run, at least I don't think so. Something weird happened here and I don't know if it's connected. I'm sorry. It's probably nothing. I'll call Officer Jeffers back. Sorry to bother you."

"Jeffers? Sheriff's guy? How do you know him?"

"He was here earlier. Someone broke into my house and smashed up the kitchen."

"Mrs. Marsden, I'll be there in ten minutes." Again she broke the connection with no "goodbye."

I wanted to relax and gather my thoughts but ten minutes didn't give me much time. I glanced at the clock. Only four o'clock. I was starting to fade having been up earlier than usual. I envisioned a glass of wine and an early turn-in around eight. I could handle another four hours. *Should I brew coffee or decant wine? Cinnamon Nut Swirl or pinot grigio?*

The phone rang. "Hello."

"Hi, darling."

"Harry!" My thoughts jumped back to this morning. "Harry, I had to braid. I do understand, I do." I was frantic to make sure he knew why I hadn't answered.

"Gracie, it's alright. I know. I should have realized. So much has been happening with Will, I haven't been thinking straight. That's why I wanted to call at a decent time so we could talk. Will and I and his—well, some friends—we've been boating all day. You'd love her, Grace; a thirty-six-foot yawl. Will's a natural sailor."

I knew he had stopped himself from saying "Mom" when referring to Lily. He had to know that would hurt. He sounded so proud of his son. He chatted about their day. I tried to stay focused.

"We were out much too late for the little chap. I carried him up to his room and tucked him up in his cot. Gracie, wait 'til you meet him. You'll love him as much as I do. I know you will, darling."

I wished I could muster as much confidence of my impending motherhood as he seemed to. Now, however, I was worried about Sergeant Royal on my doorstep any minute. I didn't want to spoil Harry's joy by telling him the latest news. Cutting him short on the phone now would seem like I didn't want to hear about Will. Maybe I didn't.

The doorbell sounded and I had my excuse. *Excuse? An odd word choice. I'm on overload, aren't I? Don't answer that.* I shook my head to clear it.

"Harry," I interrupted. "Someone's at the door."

"I'll hold on. Tell them you're on long distance; have them take a seat." His voice boomed with exuberance.

"I can't. I have to talk to them."

"Who's coming over that you can't talk to your husband? A neighbor, perhaps?" An icy tone, like a hard frost freezing over a pond crept across the phone line.

A neighbor? Oh, damn!

The bell sounded again. *He means Ric.*

"Don't be ridiculous." Tears stung my eyes and I wanted to say something witty and sharp. The doorbell rang twice more. She must be leaning on the button. My head filled with noise. "You're there with Lily. Has she come ringing your bell?" That wasn't witty or sharp, only shrewish.

"Grace, this is entirely different. Lily is the mother of my son. Ric is… Dammit, Grace, you know what Ric is."

I know what he could be: the father of my child. Somewhere inside me I knew if I threw down that gauntlet our future together would be over. And through the grace of God I kept my mouth shut.

"It's not what you think and you'll have to trust me. Goodbye, Harry." I hung up and raced to the door.

Sergeant Royal was walking down the sidewalk when I opened the door. She heard the noise and turned back. "I was about to call for backup. Thought something might be wrong."

"Sorry, I was on the phone." I moved my fingers and thumb together and apart to indicate a real talker.

She entered the house and waited until I closed the door to drop her bombshell. "Mr. Marsden checking in for the night?"

I flushed like an eighth-grade girl who'd pulled a tampon instead of a pen out of her purse. I knew I couldn't lie. I stammered instead. "He, uh, c-called. Yes." I took a deep breath and released it slowly. "I don't know where he is. Honest. He said he'd been out on a boat all day with his son. They could be anywhere in England or France," I added quickly.

"How about Chicago?"

TWENTY-FOUR

"CHICAGO?" MY VOICE carried a combination of disdain, confusion, and fear. Disdain for her apparent lack of logic; confusion about why she said "Chicago"; fear because the hairs on the back of my neck were tingling.

"The phone call you were on came in from a location in Chicago, on the lakefront." The noise in my head increased and I heard only snatches of "phone tap" and "tracing." "Mrs. Marsden, you need to give me his location or I have no choice but to arrest you."

How could he lie to me? Why? All this time he'd been here? No, I won't believe it. "I don't care what your trace tells you, my husband is not in Chicago. He left Sunday for somewhere in Europe or England. You're wrong." Only righteous indignation sounded like righteous indignation, and I felt it.

She shook her head slowly and muttered something about "having it bad."

"Excuse me?" I asked. My voice sounded higher than normal, but then, nothing had been normal all day.

She must have decided on another course of action; she would now become the "good cop" to her previous "bad cop." Sergeant Royal shifted her weight to one foot and the tiny slouch softened her demeanor. "Look, Mrs. Marsden, sometimes we want to believe the people we love. I'm sorry you've been pulled into all of this and now have to go it alone. I had hoped your husband would turn himself in for your sake as well as for justice's sake. He must have panicked and now you feel his fear and you want to help him any way you can.

This isn't the way." Her eyes filled with a calm light that reached out to me.

I found myself nodding my head in agreement with her. *Wow, she's good! She must already have whatever Jeffers is studying for.* I shook my head to break the spell. "You're wrong. Harry isn't in Chicago and he isn't even worried. He's enjoying his son, the son he didn't know he had. The furthest thought from his mind is what's happening to me." I hadn't meant to say that. Sergeant Royal straightened up and looked at me with surprise. I had surprised myself. "I mean, he's not concerned with the investigation because he's innocent."

Sergeant Royal reverted to "bad cop" again. "He'd better worry. The bat we removed from your garage turns out to match the indentation on the back of Schoebel's head."

"I told those people that Harry doesn't own a bat. That wasn't his."

She continued as though I hadn't spoken. "It's being tested now for any trace of the victim's blood. We already have your husband's fingerprints on the bat. It was easy to run his prints; they're on file right here in DuPage. And since he's in the area we can't rule out his being the driver of the vehicle that killed John Weber."

I exploded. "Are you crazy? Now you think Harry ran over a man he didn't even know? What other cases can't you solve? Maybe you should pin them on Harry, too." I was furious and knew as I spoke I was probably going to regret my words. I couldn't help it. I had to defend Harry. He wasn't in the frame of mind to defend himself.

"Mrs. Marsden, calm down." Sergeant Royal stood her ground, but shifted her hands to the stick she carried at her hip. At least it wasn't her gun.

"I called you to tell you someone broke in this morning and crossed off Dr. Weber's name on my list. I called to try and help. Do you think Harry stopped by and did this, too?"

She held out her hand. "Give me the list."

I picked it up from the counter and explained that when I left in the morning his name was clear. She asked about the other names and who had been in the house. It seemed curious to her as well that someone would go to the risk of entering a home in daylight to leave some kind of damning clue.

"I should tell you something else." I felt that as much as I hated to confide in her, I had no choice. I wanted her to see that someone was planning against Harry or me or both of us.

"And what would that be?"

"Let's sit down." I sat on one stool at the counter; she mirrored my choice. I picked up a piece of blue cording. Its weight and texture felt comforting against my fingers. Fortified, in a sense, I explained the entire Sunday afternoon fiasco, skimming over the bathroom escape, and ending with the revelation that the folder that had been missing Sunday afternoon appeared in the disheveled pile Monday morning with an addition that I didn't put there.

"Did you see what it was?"

"No. I can't imagine what anyone would add to my notes. Or why."

"How about to further incriminate your husband in Schoebel's death?"

"What are you talking about?"

"I've seen the Depot Days file you compiled. You are thorough, incredibly detailed and precise in your information and notes."

I didn't think a "thank you" seemed appropriate under the circumstances.

"One half page of paper, appears to be from the same stock as other half pages in your file, has notations about a possible connection between your husband and Schoebel. Something to the effect of," she looked up at the ceiling as though reciting a memorized piece, "'Harry seemed upset that we hired Schoebel; wanted to know who suggested him, where he lived. He might know him from before.'" She continued, "You underlined 'before.' What does that mean?"

"It doesn't mean anything because I didn't write that."

"Actually, it's typed…on your word processor. Your files are filled with half pages that you've written and others that you've typed. I figure you type up some notes and when you're finished if the information doesn't fill the page, you cut the page in half and use those sheets for handwritten notes. Admirable thriftiness."

"I'm telling you I didn't write or type any such thing. Anyone could have used my machine." I rattled off the names of everyone connected with Schwarze and Krieg.

"Ava Deutsch? How does she fit in at Schwarze and Krieg?"

"She's Liz's aunt. I thought you grew up here."

"I did grow up in Lisle, just not that Lisle." Her tone said the rest; it wasn't pining, but rather, defiant. I instinctively understood her meaning. I had grown up in Berkeley in the shadow of Elmhurst, a more affluent suburb. Only a four-lane tollway separated the two, but the fancier homes there were a lifestyle away from the small ranch homes in my neighborhood.

She seemed to take my silence as acceptance of her explanation. Somehow in her statement she had leveled the playing field and I understood her and her approach better than I had ten minutes ago.

"Then you wouldn't know much about that crazy will that caused trouble between Ava and her sister." I stated it as fact, throwing down the glove, hoping there was a remnant of the teenager whose life may have included "her nose pressed against the window of *the other half's* life." I wondered how much of that teenager I still carried.

The cop seemed to retreat as she started her "I'll show you" narrative. She repeated most of what I had already heard up to the point that the sisters split. After that point the story became sketchy but bizarre. Ava, who was the sweet one, suffered from depression after her twin, Eva, split in such an acrimonious manner.

I used a memory tool I'd learned in a Dale Carnegie course to keep the two straight in my mind. Ava was the "angel" and Eva was "evil." Probably not fair to Eva but at least I could follow the story easier. Nancy Royal paused and asked for a glass of water, which I quickly poured hoping the break wouldn't stall the story. She sipped at the water and continued.

"Her depression grew so severe, she sent her son to boarding school. While Eva sent postcards home flaunting her trips to Venice, Singapore, and Stockholm, Ava struggled with depression and a failing business. Eva had been the buyer for their antique store; Ava handled the day-to-day affairs of the store.

"Dr. Weber tried to treat her depression, but she shut out everyone. The rest of her family tried to rally around her but she wanted no part of anyone."

Royal stopped talking to drink. I used her break to comment. "She looked pretty feisty to me at the auction."

"Oh, well after a few years I guess she snapped out of it. She'd been seeing a doctor in Chicago—Michigan Avenue type—and apparently the treatment took. Ava started traveling abroad to buy her own pieces. Cutting out the middleman she had used really helped her bottom line. The business did an incredible turn around practically overnight. Her rise from the ashes was written up in the DuPage Ledger and the Lisle Chamber of Commerce made her Businesswoman of the Year. Nice piece about local founding family's granddaughter continuing the Deutsch tradition of success. Good German stock."

"Sounds like something Gertrude would say."

"Gertrude?"

"Friend of mine. Came here from Germany as a child, always going on about German stock. Joined a group of like-minded older women. Hessian Hunnies."

"Ava Deutsch is a Hessian Hunnie."

"Really. Who else belongs?"

"It's my understanding you have to be a German immigrant or first generation German, or more than half German in ancestry. That would mean a lot of women in Lisle and Naperville would qualify. Both towns were settled by Germans in the early 1800s."

"I remember reading in my research that Lisle is the oldest town in DuPage County. I thought at the time perhaps that fact would have aggravated Naperville."

Nancy and I laughed the coconspirators' laugh of the "have-nots" taking a potshot at the "haves." I refilled her glass and poured one for myself.

"Why did you want to see Dr. Weber?" Her question caught me off guard. I'd almost forgotten that I'd wanted to talk with him. I'd already confessed so much to her I thought I could tell her the theories concocted at Lily's house last night. I didn't trust her enough to name names.

"I found out from a reliable source that John Schoebel was a convicted child molester." Her raised eyebrows led me to think that she knew the information, but seemed surprised that I knew.

"Was this reliable source Ric Kramer?" Her mouth pursed in an "I knew it" smile.

"Ric's in the hospital. Concussion." I looked down into my glass.

"Right. Go on, your reason." She didn't sound convinced. I wouldn't have believed me, either.

"I wanted to ask the doctor about two missing persons cases from about fifteen years ago. I didn't think I could ask the police since they were so single-mindedly fixated on

Harry. I thought Dr. Weber would know about any children that may have disappeared from around here."

"So you think Schoebel molested and killed a girl about fifteen years ago and then hid her body in a trunk that ended up and stayed hidden in the Gotschalk mill until—"

"The Gotschalk mill?"

"Oh yeah, when I was a kid that property was the old mill. The Deutsch sisters didn't open their antique store until the early seventies."

"That's right. I didn't connect the name. I think it's a possibility. That's why he wouldn't open the trunks. Maybe a relative of the missing person was there, saw his hesitation, and put two and two together. Wouldn't there have been an investigation fifteen years ago and wouldn't he have been the first person the police contacted?"

"That was before my time, but that would be the process. This is all speculative. Our case against your husband has evidentiary aspects that make him our only suspect at this time."

Her about-face stunned me. I thought we had bonded. *What a fool I am. She probably gave me that wrong-side-of-the-tracks baloney to lower my guard. She probably went to Benet and grew up in Green Trails.*

"I've enjoyed our time together, but in about two minutes my sergeant will be calling to tell me who they found at the number your husband called from earlier. He may already be in custody. If he's not, then you will be." She stood up and carried her glass to the sink. "Thanks for your hospitality."

Witch! She'd kept me occupied and under her eye so I couldn't warn Harry. The phone rang before I could comment. Royal turned toward the wall. I rushed to the phone. "It's still my house and my phone." She stepped back and dipped her head in agreement.

"Hello? Yes, she's here." I handed her the phone with greater reluctance than I thought possible.

Had he been arrested? That would mean he never left town. Impossible!

I watched her face as she listened. The gloat I feared never came. Her replies were curt. She hung up with a graceless gesture.

If he wasn't there, which he wouldn't be, does that mean the cuffs are coming out for me? I admit, I've been accused of being a drama queen.

"Mrs. Marsden, it appears I owe you an apology."

Sure, another ploy to disarm me.

"Your husband used an overseas connection to a landline in Chicago to contact to you. Not everyone has access to that kind of technology. I find that interesting. What is it you said your husband does for a living?"

I knew her tricks. "Are you arresting me?" I held my breath.

"Since I can't determine that you know any more about his location than you did yesterday, I will not be placing you under arrest."

I let my breath out slowly. "If you want to ask me any questions, you can ask them through my attorney."

"I'm sorry you feel that way. I suppose I'd feel the same. Good night, Mrs. Marsden."

I followed her through the hallway and opened the door. She stopped on the porch and turned, lifting a hand as though to prevent the door from closing. "Since your husband had no opportunity to run down Dr. Weber, I will look into your idea about Schoebel. It would seem coincidental that Lisle would have two different killers using the same M.O."

Once again she surprised me. I watched her walk to her car and pull away. Maybe she really was considering people other than Harry? Yeah, and maybe she was setting me up, again.

TWENTY-FIVE

I WAS TOO TIRED to eat and too hungry to sleep. I compromised with a large glass of icy cold milk and a small plate of Oreo cookies. I added half of one of the recovered pears for balance; I should try to eat healthy.

Ten minutes after I cleansed, toned, and moisturized according to the *Mary Kay* rigors, I plumped up mine and Harry's pillows and sat up with my snack to watch the early news. I hoped it would mention Dr. Weber's death in the local segment.

According to the news account, after finishing the autopsy last night he had called his wife to tell her he intended to sleep in an office there rather than drive home. A car struck him as he walked through the county parking lot to his car early this morning at approximately five-thirty.

I had learned several things from the newscast. First, the doctor was doing an autopsy on the skeleton and not Schoebel's body as I had assumed. Second, he was already dead when I spoke with his wife this morning. Remembering how she referred to him in the present tense, not knowing what fate had decreed brought tears to my eyes. I swallowed hard and reminded myself of the third thing I'd learned. I didn't have an alibi for that time. I wondered if, at the rate things were going, I would need one.

I had more milk than cookies left. Usually I'd get more cookies, but I was too tired to go downstairs. I ate my pear and finished the milk. Sleep came sooner than I thought possible; I never saw the ten o'clock news.

I awakened briefly and looked at the hands pointing out two in the morning; work of my subconscious waiting for a call from Harry, perhaps. I let my mind slide back under the quilt of deep slumber until shortly before six o'clock, my walking time.

Barb always met me at my back door. She stopped a few yards away when I stepped out. Her bright orange Patagonia jacket stood in sharp contrast to the greenery, but would soon match the leaves that would turn and fall within a month.

"Good morning. Hope this is a better day for you." Her cheery greeting inspired me to keep my complaining to a minimum.

"You're mighty chipper this morning. Does that mean we're still friends even after I no-showed for lunch?"

"Of course we're still friends. I got your message and the complimentary glass of wine. Excellent Pinot Grigio. However, if you don't start filling me in on the trunks and the police on your driveway, that could jeopardize our friendship." She kept her tone light, but her eyes gleamed with intense curiosity.

We were three-quarters through our route before I finished explaining the police presence and the search warrant. I'd left Schwarze and Krieg for last. "I'm sort of out of the loop now about the trunks. With the project over, Liz didn't feel she needed the added expense of me."

"I'm sorry, Grace. I can't believe she wouldn't value your talent for other projects. She raved about you; I thought you had a job for life the way she went on."

"Yeah, what a difference a braid makes," I mumbled.

"Pardon me?"

I didn't have the energy to go into explanations. My head still swam when I tried to make any sense of all this. Since this job had been a lead from Barb I didn't want her to feel bad. "Really, it's okay. I'm not sure if PR and event planning is what I want to do with the rest of my life. I've been writing a little, again." I hadn't meant to let that out but Barb looked so concerned at my loss of work.

"Talk about great news. I'm thrilled to hear it." Her mood lightened and she continued. "This is perfect timing because now you can come to the Garden Club Last Fling Spa Day and Luncheon this Friday at Jefferson Hill Tea Room." Her easy grin reached across to me.

"I don't know that I'm that committed to gardening; maybe if Harry were home he'd jump at it."

"Ladies only, I'm afraid. Though for Harry I think they'd roll out the red carpet."

I smiled at my neighbor's unabashed crush on my husband. "Barb, I don't know a crocus from a cucumber."

"You know massage, don't you?"

She knew my weak spot. "What does massage have to do with the garden club?"

"This event is the culmination of the season. Last fling? The program starts at eight o'clock with speakers from The Growing Place and Hidden Gardens instructing us on how to prepare our gardens for winter. At nine-thirty we'll have two shorter presentations by Fran Ledbetter on attracting birds to the winter garden and by Ava Deutsch on medicinal plants in our local gardens."

"Ava Deutsch is in the garden club?"

"In it? She's on the board. Past president, too. It'll be fun, Grace. After the speakers, we're all booked for facials and mini massages. The idea is how to prepare our faces for the winter weather and colors. Then we finish up, with our marvelous new looks, for afternoon light luncheon and tea. Admit it, doesn't that sound like a great day?"

The chance to talk to Ava Deutsch in a natural way sounded great. My curiosity about this woman kept growing. She'd been through so much. I admired her strength of character, which made me more than a bit curious about her bizarre family: a pervert cousin, a jet-setting sister, and a son who grew up in boarding schools.

"Will Liz be attending? It might be awkward."

"I have it on good authority she won't be there—I'm the program person for this year. She never responded. You can sit at my table. You'll like everyone; nice people." She counted the names off one by one. "Fran Ledbetter, Joan Shuster, Mary Jean Gotschalk, Jan Pauli and June Weber."

The last two names intrigued me. "Jan Pauli? I hired her to clean my house. She's in the garden club, too?"

"Past president. Jan's a character. She retired from her company, J.P. Enterprise, at the height of an impressive career. Said she reviewed her life and decided she wasn't where she wanted to be. Said *adios* to corporate and the next thing we knew she started her cleaning service. Has cleaning people all over the suburbs, many of them like her, women who decided to chuck the grind and go back to basics."

I smiled at Barb's description. She sounded like Helen Reddy promoting *I Am Woman*. "She's starting for me today. Interesting. I bet she knows some secrets."

"Secrets? Oh no, she's discreet. What secrets are you interested in? Anything to do with the trunks?"

I hadn't meant to think out loud. Now we were back to the trunks. I moved on like I hadn't heard that she heard me. "I'm surprised to hear that June Weber will be there."

"We were too, but that's June. She's the president this year and feels she should be there. Her daughter and son-in-law have been in town all week. Jennifer came in early to attend the Last Fling with her mom. Lucky, in view of what happened. They've had each other."

"It would be nice to have your family under the same roof at a time of crisis."

"Oh, Jennifer's not staying with her. John and Jennifer's

husband, Lloyd, never saw eye to eye. John and June did everything they could to help Lloyd with career opportunities. John got him a great job selling pharmaceuticals but he blew that when he came up short on his consignments once too often. He served jail time somewhere in Ohio. John had no use for him after that, especially when Lloyd apparently decided to live off Jennifer's excellent salary as a stock analyst. Jennifer defends him, ex-con, no one willing to give him a break. She's an extremely intelligent woman, but has a blind spot the size of New Jersey when it comes to Lloyd."

"Yeah, well, she wouldn't be the first woman to think with her heart and not with her head." I wondered what drove my life choices.

The cast of characters intrigued me too much to decline the invitation. "Okay, you convinced me. I'll be there. Dress code?"

"Tea attire, of course. Most likely all the ladies are wearing hats."

"Oh, the hat-society ladies? Gertrude's a member in one of those."

"Some of the garden-club ladies are Red Hat members, so chances are you'll see several extravagant designs. If you don't have an appropriate hat, I can loan you one."

"Thanks. I'll come up with something." We had reached the back of Barb's property. She started up the path to her backyard. "See you tomorrow morning."

I waved and continued to my house. April and Cash heard my approach and whinnied their greeting. April knew by my pattern that in a few minutes I'd be back with treats.

I hesitated as I approached the back door. The window curtain on the door looked like it had been stretched across. I normally bunched it together to look fuller and pleated. I could go back to Barb's and ask her to come in with me.

Great idea, Grace. Maybe someone will shoot her again.

Barb had been mistaken for me this spring during one of our walks and the bullet intended for me struck her. I couldn't ask Barb. Ric wasn't home. I didn't have a phone out here.

I heard April and Cash reminding me about our schedule. I could hide in the barn. Maybe bring April out on a lead; not exactly a guard dog.

Get a grip. It's a curtain. Harry could have moved it before he left. Nick might have moved it yesterday. That's it. He went out the back to dump the trash.

I felt instantly better and continued to chide myself as I walked briskly toward the door. I looked at the curtain and mentally dared it to move.

It did!

TWENTY-SIX

Jan Pauli's sunny face smiled at me from the window. She opened the door and stepped out. "Good morning. No answer at the front so I came around. The door was open and I called out. I found these," she held up some baby carrots, "and decided I could meet your horses. Hope you don't mind."

I'd been speechless during her entire Mary Poppinesque explanation, mainly because my throat froze and my breath stalled a split second before I thought I should scream. Even now, as she walked toward me, my heart continued to bang against my ribs. *She must hear the racket.*

"I thought you were coming at eight o'clock," I managed to say.

"Eight? I thought we said seven. You mentioned how you walk in the morning and then take care of the horses."

"I did?" *Since when did I start spilling my guts and my routine to strangers?*

"Yes. If I'm too early I can come back in an hour. I'll pop over to Starbucks on Rt. 53. I've got a great book I'm reading. I don't mind."

I knew the coffee shop she referred to; it was ten minutes away. Seemed silly to send her off for forty-five minutes. "Don't go. I probably confused the time. It's been a rough week." It was only Tuesday. "As long as you have a handful of treats, let's put them to good use." I smiled and turned back to the barn.

Excited whinnies greeted our arrival. Jan stepped up to

April and offered her the delicious goodies. "Ladies first, Cash."

I laughed at her ease with the horses. It hit me, then, that I hadn't confused the times. She wanted to be here when I fed and groomed the horses. I couldn't blame her. It didn't get any better than brushing down a horse on a beautiful crisp morning. I handed her Cash's brush.

Thirty minutes later, April and Cash were fed, watered, and turned out into the small pasture connected to the barn. Jan and I were washing up in the mudroom when I noticed the time; eight o'clock. I smiled again and decided to let her think she'd snookered me. It was an acceptable snooker.

Jan wiped her hands on the towel I handed her. She looked at me and grinned. "You did say eight o'clock."

"I know."

I opened the door to the kitchen and froze. The view from this end of the kitchen today looked as bad as it had from the other end yesterday.

I felt Jan lean forward to look over my shoulder. "I guess I'll start in here." Her tongue-in-cheek comment wasn't funny.

"Don't touch anything. I'm calling the police." I walked across the room, careful to avoid the fruit, coffee grounds, and pieces of pottery strewn on the floor. On closer look it wasn't as bad as yesterday, only because I hadn't repotted the herbs yet or replenished the fruit bowl. This trashing seemed superficial.

What? A copycat trashing?

I realized that my cleaning lady hadn't followed me into the room; she still stood in the doorway. Good. She didn't look scared. Actually, she looked pensive.

"I hope you don't mind my saying, but your kitchen looks remarkably like the mess I cleaned up yesterday at Schwarze and Krieg."

"No, yesterday's mess in here had plants. That was more like the office."

"*Hmm.* You're right. Yesterday?" She asked after my comment must have sunk in.

I nodded as I finished pressing those three little numbers, 9-1-1. I gave my name and address to the operator and explained the emergency. I hung up and turned to Jan.

"He suggests we wait outside—just in case."

"Just in case?" Jan's eyes traveled upward to the ceiling. "Oh, just in *case*."

We went outside and walked to the enclosure around the pasture. April immediately trotted up to meet us, certain we had more treats.

"You are a piggy not a horse," I said as I scratched her muzzle.

"You seem pretty calm for someone who called 9-1-1." Jan's voice sounded a twitch higher than earlier.

"I went through this yesterday. No one was in the house yesterday; the police called it a crime of anger, maybe teens being destructive."

"I hear a siren." Jan pushed away from the fence.

I put a hand on her arm. "Stay here. He'll probably check the house." I walked around to the front of the house in time to meet the police officer.

I thought of a "we've got to stop meeting this way" comment to lighten the scene, but Officer Jeffers's look stopped me cold.

"Who does this car belong to?"

"My cleaning lady. Why?"

"We received a report about two hours ago from a resident that claims the same car had been driving back and forth by her home in south Pine Marsh. The squad that investigated didn't find the car but the woman who called in, Mrs. Divine, described it as a dark blue or dark gray sports car. And she remembers seeing it yesterday, too."

We both looked at Jan's classic dark green two-seater SL 450.

Jeffers spoke. "Cleaning lady who drives a Mercedes?"

I shrugged. Let him figure out Jan Pauli. She knew how to get here so she shouldn't have been cruising in the other half of Pine Marsh. She *said* my door was open?

She was early; earlier than seven; she could have messed up the kitchen. Why? She had been in the kitchen yesterday. Maybe she crossed off the doctor's name.

Jeffers broke my train of thought. "Where is this cleaning lady? I'd like to talk to her."

"She's in the back. We came outside when we discovered the break-in."

"Break-in?"

"More like unauthorized entry." Officer Jeffers tried to hide the smile tugging at the corner of his mouth. I continued quickly. "My back door must have been unlocked. Jan said open but I don't know if she meant unlocked or standing open. She scared me to death when she looked out at me."

Jeffers stopped walking. "Looked *out* at you? Where were you?"

"Coming back from my walk with my neighbor. As I got closer to the door I noticed the curtain on the window was stretched too tightly across the rod. I stopped and was deciding if I should go in or—" *wasn't going to tell him I thought about hiding in the barn* "—walk back to my neighbor's house, when the curtain moved and Jan looked out at me."

He started walking again. "How long have you known her?"

"I met her yesterday morning. My employer hired her to clean up the mess in our office. Someone had smashed pots and strewn folders and papers all over the room."

"Who handled that?"

"Naperville police."

He nodded his head. "I'll check it out." He slowed his pace to write in his spiral notebook.

I turned the corner of the house a step ahead of him. Jan was gone.

TWENTY-SEVEN

"WHERE IS SHE?"

"She was standing at that fence." I pointed toward the horses. "Maybe she came to the front round the other side of the house; there's a flagstone path down the side."

He started in that direction. I noticed he'd put away his notebook and moved with a different sense than when we walked back here.

"Maybe she's inside. I'd like to make sure she isn't."

Officer Jeffers nodded and walked toward the back door and entered the house with that same heightened movement.

I followed him in, staying a few paces behind. From the mudroom I heard the seductive tones of Yanni coming from the kitchen. Jan Pauli nodded her head in sync with the music from a small boom box plugged into the wall.

She had cleaned the floor, at least picked up the mess; piled the big pieces on the counter and swept the smaller bits and dirt into a dustpan. My previous cleaning lady wore yellow latex gloves when she cleaned; Jan wore surgical gloves.

She looked down at something in her hand, noticed Jeffers, then me. "Grace said you thought it was kids being stupid. I thought I'd get started. I found this under the edge of the cabinet."

Jeffers unfolded his handkerchief and took the prescription bottle. "Warfarin sodium," he read from the label. The top half of the label was missing.

"It's a blood thinner," Jan said.

Jeffers and I both looked at her.

"I cleaned house for an elderly gentleman last year. He took that medication. Tricky stuff. Too much and you can bleed internally."

Jan seemed nervous, her voice climbing in pitch. I wouldn't blame her if she decided not to work for me.

"Ms. Pauli, I'd like to ask you a few questions. Let's move into another room. Mrs. Marsden, would you please check to see if there is anything missing or added?"

He motioned Jan ahead of him into the mudroom, inclined his head for her to sit on the boot bench, and positioned himself at the back door. His large body nearly blocked the light coming in from the open curtain but he stood enough off center to allow the light to shine directly into Jan Pauli's eyes when she looked at him. I wondered if that was part of his training, to use what he had to take the upper hand in his interrogation.

I roamed the kitchen, checking for anything missing. Was this connected with the trunks?

Still deep in thought, I didn't hear them come into the room. When Jeffers cleared his throat I jumped and banged my elbow on the counter. "Ouch!"

"Sorry, I didn't mean to startle you. I'm finished talking with Ms. Pauli. Apparently, she drove up and down the compound to write down the addresses of the other homes, her intent to send them a brochure about her service."

I looked at Jan. "It's true," she said. "I was going to ask you after I cleaned if I could use your name in a note to each of your neighbors." Her eyes pleaded her case with sincerity.

I felt uncomfortable with her in the house; too many coincidences. But she'd been so good with the horses. April had approved. April knew people.

I shrugged my shoulders. "I can't give you a recommendation if I don't see your work." I smiled at her. Her face filled with relief, so much so that I wondered if the facade of "bored retiree looking for pin money and gossip" was just that. Maybe Jan Pauli needed to work, had to work. An accusation of vandalism would sink her career in Pine Marsh and beyond. I decided to call David later and ask if he could find out about her financial situation.

Officer Jeffers motioned for me to join him in the mud-room. We stood away from the window and the glaring sun. I guessed he wasn't interrogating me.

"I'll take this bottle in. You're sure it's not anything you or your husband might have had filled?"

"Positive."

"Are you okay with her?" He nodded toward the kitchen.

"Absolutely. Thank you for your help. After we finish cleaning I may pack a bag and spend a few days with a friend."

He smiled. "I was about to suggest that. The intensity of the vandalism seems lessened but you can't figure what goes on in someone's head. I'll think we'll find out that teenagers are pulling pranks for rush week or some other nonsense. The same woman who saw your cleaning lady also reported four teens in the area earlier this week. She said they came out of the woods and up between her house and the neighbor."

"From that direction they had to come in off the golf course. A foursome of prankster golfers?" I skrinched up my nose in skepticism.

"Easy enough to check; the course would have a record of a tee time and I think you have to surrender your driver's license to rent a cart. Maybe they recorded the number or made a copy."

I let him out the back door and watched him turn the corner. The mutant teenage prank sounded like a plausible bet. Maybe they just wanted to play with my head; crossed off Dr. Weber's name and wrote in Ava's number. *Ava's number. That may not be her number.*

I rushed into the kitchen and searched through the extraneous stuff on the counter for my pad.

I ran through to the living room in time to see the sheriff's squad pulling away from the curb. I returned to the kitchen and threw my notepad on the counter.

"This kitchen is cursed. People break in, no, make that walk in; nothing's removed but things are left behind. Notes I never wrote, medication I don't take, phone numbers I didn't have—"

"Phone numbers?" Jan's voice squeaked.

I stared at her with renewed suspicion.

"I am so sorry. When I was here yesterday I saw your pad of paper and the notation next to Ava's name. I figured I'd be helpful and jot down her number. I meant to tell you but I got sidetracked. I didn't mean to alarm you."

She looked down at the floor. The sight of her curly blond bowed head to her bright white gym shoes triggered a childhood memory of me as a little girl waiting for Sister Mary Evangeline to pronounce sentence for the infraction *du jour*.

I realized that Jan had raised her head and looked expectantly at me.

I wondered if this is how Sister Evangeline felt, unsure of the course to take. No. She enjoyed meting out corporeal punishment. Jan wasn't off the hook. "How did you know I wanted her phone number; it could have been an invitation list?"

"You wrote 630 next to her name. I figured you were after her number."

I felt sheepish as I looked at the pad. It was my 630 next to her name. I hadn't noticed the next seven digits were different. My face felt warm. Then I remembered the other name. "Why did you line out Dr. Weber's name?" I showed her the pad. "Did you know he was already dead and I needn't bother calling him?" My voice rang out with accusation.

"Look, Mrs. Marsden, maybe my working for you isn't such a good idea. I wrote the number down but I didn't cross off his name. If someone did then I'd be wondering how that person knew, too. I thought working for you would be exciting; you solved that old murder at the zoo. For Pete's sake, this day has been too creepy; people sneaking in, my being questioned by the cops and now you looking at me like *I'm* the nutcase."

Her emphasis made it plain who she thought owned that title. I'd been fired by my employer because of the weirdness that surrounded me, and now my "employee" was quitting for the same reason.

"I'm sorry. I'm just a little jumpy."

Jan swung her purse strap over her shoulder.

"Wait, don't go. I really don't think you did any of this. I'm just too confused to think straight. Let me make some coffee. I think better with coffee."

"You sit, I'll make the coffee. I've the exact coffeemaker at home. Do you keep your coffee in the fridge?"

I shook my head. "The cabinet to your right. I keep a few days' supply of ground coffees in glass jars. They're labeled."

I sat down at the breakfast nook and tried to calm my frazzled thinking. Jan pulled one of the jars from the shelf. In a moment, the aroma of Cinnamon Nut Swirl teased my nostrils. I heard her fill the kettle. *Another tea drinker.*

"The tea box is in the drawer to the left of the sink."

"Thanks. Coffee's almost ready."

I decided to assume there must be a logical reason why someone would try to frame Harry for Schoebel's death. Was I looking for someone from Harry's past? Was his connection to the locksmith more recent? Was there a connection?

Jan placed a cup on the table and slid in across from me. I noticed she curled one leg under her as she sat down. I stared out the window at the empty Yankee Droll feeder and wondered when the birds had finished the seed. Harry always kept them full.

"You've had two visitors already," Jan said pointing to the feeder. "A black-capped chickadee and a purple house wren; they didn't look happy. I swear they looked in here."

I smiled as I thought of the reproachful look on their feathered faces. Harry sat in the nook each morning drinking his tea and reading the paper. He enjoyed watching the birds; kept a tablet handy so he could record any new visitors. Sunday was the last time he filled this feeder or any of the others scattered around the house. *They'll have to wait for him to come home; just like me.*

"Why did you want to call Ava Deutsch?"

The question startled me. I froze a little. I raised the mug to my lips and took five tiny sips and lowered the mug to the table. Again, I raised the mug and took five tiny sips. This time when I put the mug down I felt no compulsion to repeat the process.

Jan's eyes widened as she watched me.

I'll give her nutcase.

"When I listed her name I planned to ask her if she had any information about the locksmith who was killed. He was some kind of cousin, but I wanted to know more. I found out that he was a convicted sex offender."

Her eyebrows shot up into her hairline. She squirmed and shifted then sat upright, both feet on the floor. "Is that what you were going to ask Dr. Weber?"

"I had a question about a missing person. He lived here for so long and knew most of the local people; delivered a lot of them."

"He delivered the *Gabor Girls.*" She laughed at my surprised look. "That's what the town called them, according to June Weber. She assisted her husband in their births. Dr. Weber had strongly advised that Mrs. Deutsch have her babies in the hospital but Johann, her father-in-law, insisted she give birth at home like all the Deutsch women. The husband, Karl, didn't object. According to the grapevine, his concern boiled down to keeping the patriarch happy, staying in his will, and producing grandsons."

"Didn't the youngest die?"

"That would be Eva; she's alive and well somewhere in Europe. It was actually the first little girl born that died."

"Odd that the first would die at birth but the second and third would make it."

Jan looked at me in surprise. "Who told you she died at birth?"

"Someone mentioned there were three but one died. I thought they meant at birth. She didn't?"

"No, she died a few years later. Her birth went smoothly, but there was an accident afterwards. June would know the details; I'm guessing she's lived with them all these years. The investigation resulted in a negligence verdict against June. She never worked as a nurse again."

"What happened?"

"The doctor wasn't expecting triplets; he hadn't picked up a third heartbeat in the exams. They had set up for two babies. As soon as the second girl was delivered, two things happened: they realized a third baby was crowning and the mother's vitals dropped through the cellar. June worked on delivering the baby and he worked on saving the mother. He called the hospital for an ambulance; he knew the mother needed more help than he could provide.

"June delivered the baby even though the mother's uterus had gone hard; she had to use forceps. The baby took too long to start breathing on her own. June wanted to get her on oxygen. She made the decision to remove the first baby's cannula, since she had breathed heartily on her own and was the biggest of the three, and use it for the tiny one."

Jan paused at this point. She shook her head slowly and took a sip of her tea. "You know how sometimes you set something in motion and you see the results a split second after the irreversible process begins? That's how June described it the one and only time I heard her speak of it. She cried when she explained.

"She was racing against the clock to help the last baby breathe easier. June switched the cannula before she moved the first baby. She tried to nestle the little one between her sisters on the card table they'd set up for them next to the bed. And in that moment, the unthinkable happened."

TWENTY-EIGHT

I LEANED FORWARD, both hands around the mug.

Jan sipped her tea and continued. "The table leg gave way and one side collapsed. June still had her hand on the last baby and was able to stop the slide of the baby on the high end of the table. The firstborn toppled from table along with the tray of instruments and various bottles Dr. Weber had used during the labor and delivery."

I stifled a gasp. "Oh, my God. How terrible."

Jan nodded her head. "The baby suffered broken bones and deep gashes in her face. One of the bottles broke and splashed her face and upper body, leaving ugly spots and pits on her skin. She breathed in too much of the ether the doctor had used sparingly on his patient. The paramedics arrived in time to resuscitate her but some lung damage occurred. The mother died in the ambulance."

"What about the baby? You said she made it."

"She made it, but maybe she'd have been better off if she hadn't."

My outrage died on my lips as Jan continued.

"Her father couldn't stand to look at her, the grandfather had no use for a damaged child; only her nurse cared about her and for her. The nursery had been set up for two children and that never changed. Ava and Eva spent their first two years in constant companionship while their sister languished in a room on the floor above them."

"That's terrible. How could people let that happen?"

"June told me that she and John tried to adopt the little girl so they could raise her and give her a normal life. They were willing to take over all her care including the breathing treatments she needed to help heal her scarred lungs. June said that if you spent just a little time with her you didn't notice the disfigurement; just a delightful child. Johann turned her down cold. He didn't want people to think he wouldn't raise his own granddaughter, but he didn't want people to stare at her or pity him."

"Nice guy. Does Ava take after him?"

"No, not Ava. That's more Eva's style from what I hear."

"You seem to hear quite a bit."

She shrugged her shoulders. "I'm like the postman."

"You always ring twice?" I joked.

Jan smiled. "No, I become part of the furniture. People talk around me, even about me like I'm not there; in person, on the phone. It's like I'm invisible."

I made a mental note to keep my conversations private. Yet, I understood what she meant. When Royal had asked me who had been in the house, I named my dad, Karen and Nick. I never even thought of the cleaning lady.

"The girls were getting older and Johann feared he couldn't keep his *perfect pair* from wanting to know their sister. He gave the nanny, who by this time loved her little charge like a daughter, the money and the means to adopt her and move back to Germany."

"What a prince."

Jan nodded. "June and John gave the nanny money and more medication for the toddler's nebulizer. June included stationery and airmail envelopes with postage. I think she desperately needed to know that there might be a happy ending after all."

"But there wasn't?"

Jan shook her head. "They sailed in 1939. June received two letters; war broke out, and she never received another word. After the war, she tried to find the nanny. She knew her surname was Hochwasser. With the help of the German community living in Lisle, she contacted another Hochwasser from the same town, a cousin, and discovered that Hilda's house had been destroyed in a bombing raid. The cousin told her that everyone in the house, including her own brother who had been visiting, Hilda, her parents and several children perished."

"Who knows all of this?"

"All the old-timers. Johann Deutsch was a powerful man in this town. Nobody talked about it; except among themselves."

"So bringing all this out wouldn't hurt anyone now?"

"Hurt anyone? How?"

"I don't know, but every time I try to figure out why someone would kill Schoebel I come back to that trunk and that takes me to Ava Deutsch. When I think about who would kill Dr. Weber, I get to the skeleton in the trunk and that brings me back to Ava Deutsch."

"That's impossible. You're accusing a middle-aged pillar of the community with tons of good works to her credit of killing two people? You're way off base."

"I'm not accusing anyone of murder. I just said my line of thought keeps taking me to her."

"Then, lady, your line is terribly skewed!" Jan stood up and looped her bag over her shoulder. "I can't clean for you. Sorry. You're just wound the wrong way for me."

I sat stunned. Jan Pauli's steps were quick and sure as she left through the back entrance. She'd seemed incensed that I accused Ava Deutsch; but I didn't accuse her, I only said she seemed involved at every turn. I absentmindedly tapped the bowl of the spoon on the table. *Tap, tap, tap.* Of course, Harry appeared to be involved at every turn and I knew that wasn't true. *Tap, tap, tap.* My brain registered another sound:

footsteps in the mudroom. *Maybe Jan has had a change of heart.* I got up from the table. The footsteps were slow and tentative, almost stealthy. *I don't think it's Jan.*

TWENTY-NINE

I FELT LIKE a deer in the headlights; my mind froze. I couldn't decide whether to move or hide or scream. My shoulders lifted and my lungs filled with air. I hit a high note that startled me. My normally midrange tone climbed to a shriek of epic proportion.

I heard the crash of metal hitting the floor and then hurried steps moving away from the kitchen. The back door banged against the wall, then silence. I'd have run, too, certain a banshee haunted the kitchen.

It took more courage than I thought I had to go into the mudroom and lock the door. Whoever had been in there knocked over the treat bin. Horse chow nuggets, baby carrots, and apples dotted the floor. I bent to the task of retrieving and restoring my horses' goodies. In a cluster of chow I spotted a flat, shiny object.

I picked up the key by the grooved end and looked for markings. The numbers engraved on the wide top meant nothing to me. It looked old. It wasn't ours, unless Harry had a secret safe deposit box. If that were the case, putting the key in a bin I reach into every day wouldn't be too smart.

Jan Pauli had reached into this bin today. Why would she leave this key? *No more questions without answers. Start with answers.*

I pulled a plastic sandwich bag from the recyclable pile and sealed the key inside. I decided to call Royal and fill her in on my morning.

Never willing to leave coffee to waste, I poured the quarter

pot into the thermal butler and toasted four slices of bread;
two slathered with butter and two covered with crunchy pea-
nut butter. So armed, and in my locked house, I sat down in
the nook with my notepad and wrote *Answers* across the top,
underscored three times.

This worked like jeopardy; I put down an answer then I
made up questions. Karen used this exercise in her writing
class at Trinity to jump-start ideas. She'd have a list of answers and the students would suggest corresponding questions and *voilà!*

I sat for several minutes thinking back to Saturday night at
the auction. I let the smooth warm taste of the ground beans
roll over my tongue and touch the back of my throat before
I swallowed. A few deep breaths, I opened my eyes, ready
to write down all the answers on the left side of the tablet:
*missing girl, Schoebel killed her, 1978, Harry knew him, rel-
ative of dead girl attended auction, Harry suspected him of
something, knew his mother was upset, wanted those trunks,
knew the contents of the trunk, John Weber found out something from the autopsy, Liz knew about Schoebel, Ava recommended Schoebel.*

I stopped writing answers when I reached the bottom of
the first page. If these were the answers, I would really have
to stretch for the questions. I munched at my toast and looked
at the names that had popped up. Maybe that was the starting
point. Schoebel and Weber were dead. I could stop by Antiques on Plank and talk to Ava's son, Karl Deutsch. On Friday, I'd be sitting with June Weber and Ava Deutsch. That left
only Liz and Harry. I could visit Schwarze and Krieg under
the pretense of confirming my final paycheck and expense
report. That left Harry. Why did he follow Schoebel out of
the tent? What did they argue about? *There you go with the
cockamamy questions again.*

A frustrated sigh escaped me and I shoved the last piece

of toast into my mouth. I washed up the few dishes and idly thought about what to ask Karl Deutsch. *Hi, your mother thinks I'm a snoop. By the way, did you kill the girl in the trunk?* My heart started pounding in my chest. What if he knew the girl? They would have been about the same age. What if some horrible accident happened and he panicked and hid her body in the trunk in his mother's storage room? They could have been down there.

Two kids; cool place to meet. Maybe he tried too hard to get her to go all the way. Maybe she said she would and then wouldn't. Maybe he raped her. She said she'd tell. He panicked and killed her. That would explain being sent to boarding school at such a young age.

That meant Ava knew and had protected her son. Was she still protecting him? Would she kill to keep his secret? Why did she keep the trunk? Why did he let me take it? Why didn't he bid through the ceiling to get it back? My perfect candidate for murder looked less guilty as I worked through the logic. *Guilty is as guilty does.* He didn't act guilty. He could be a sociopath—no guilt, no conscience. I needed to talk to him in person.

THIRTY

ANTIQUES ON PLANK was located between Antique Bazaar and An Antique Affaire. One of my favorite restaurants, Del Debbio's, was east of the shops on the same side of the street. I had introduced Karen and Hannah to the eatery's wonderful Northern Italian cuisine and they'd been back several times in conjunction with Hannah's obsessive antique hunts. It suited both of them; fabulous food and three antique stores to wander through.

I pulled into the lot and had my "cover" story prepared. I would be looking for small trunks to accessorize Hannah's new B and B. Hopefully, I could swing the conversation to the auction and get a feel for his reaction.

He stood behind the large glass front counter close to the entrance. "Good morning, may I help you?" His smile slipped a little as he stared at me.

"Good morning. I'm hoping to find something for my sister-in-law's new home."

"Looking for more trunks, Mrs. Marsden?"

Now what? My face flushed. "That certainly was an unfortunate outcome," I said slowly, hoping he'd comment.

"Unfortunate? We've sold every trunk in every size, shape and color that we had in the store, and, in storage." He drew out the last word, I was sure, for my benefit.

"Uh, that's good then, right?"

"Yes, it's been great for business. Too bad your husband isn't around to pick the locks on the ones without keys; we could charge extra and build the suspense." His tone matched his phony smile.

"How do you know my husband 'isn't around,' Mr. Deutsch?"

"My cousin is with the police. You hear things when you're family."

I don't like this. Who else knows I'm home alone? I looked at Karl Deutsch. Over six feet tall, thick blond hair, clear hazel eyes, strong features. He could easily pick up a small man like Schoebel and toss him at Harry's car. Why kill Schoebel? He didn't open the trunk. If Schoebel killed the girl why would Deutsch care?

The questions swirling through my head must have reflected some confusion on my face.

"What's the matter, Mrs. Marsden? You look ill." Again his tone sounded flat, no concern, just comment and the briefest glimpse of a nasty smile.

I realized there were no customers or staff in the store. Maybe they were down the many aisles that stretched from the front area, but I didn't want to chance it. I felt threatened. I'm certain my lavender eyes had turned a deep shade of purple.

"If you're out of trunks I'll be on my way." I tried for a breezy kind of tone; it came out squeaky. His thin smile told me he was happy to have upset me. I left and didn't look back.

I turned south on Main Street and pulled into a diagonal spot close to the Book Nook. My heart still thumped against my ribcage, but my breathing had slowed to an acceptable rate for conversation. That's what I needed: conversation with a normal person whom I didn't suspect of murder.

Book Nook News, an old-fashioned establishment, carried the best selection of newspapers, magazines, and candy. The site, originally a diner, had been converted to the store after World War II. It had four owners throughout its history. The Waskelis family owned it for twenty years. The previous owner had been a blind man who successfully ran the store,

amazing children and adults alike with his uncanny ability
to use his other senses to function. His store had been the
destination of choice for all the current baby boomers when
they were children.

John Reeder had purchased the store from the Waskelis
family. He had been one of those children rushing in to buy
penny candy and comic books every chance he had.

It remained a popular stop on Main Street; the best place
to get your magazines, newspapers, and lottery tickets.

You couldn't ignore John. He wasn't tall—maybe six
foot—but his broad, usually flannel-covered chest implied
strength. His full beard and plain speaking manner reminded
me of the pioneer spirit that must have settled the area. I liked
his open, friendly demeanor.

"Hi, Grace. I hear you started some commotion with your
action at Depot Days?"

"*Et tu*, John? And it was auction not action."

"You had more action than auction. People haven't stopped
talking about the trunks. The festival coordinators are considering substituting trains and trunks for hot air balloons."

John referred to the annual Eyes to the Skies Festival held
over the Fourth of July holiday.

"Auction, action, potato, patato, whatever."

John poked fun at the English language, twisting it *à la*
Gallagher. His reading list would overwhelm most people and
his command of the language, knowledge of archaic words
and rules made him a sought after partner in Scrabble and
Trivial Pursuit.

My degree in English served me poorly when tilting with
John. He earned the title of "Wordsmith" from Harry after
the two of them waged a Scrabble tournament last year.

He laughed and reached below the counter and brought
up a bag. "I've got Harry's *PW* and *Midwest Gardener* and

your *Writer's Digest*." He placed the bulging brown bag on the counter. "I've mailed out your in-laws' paper, too."

Dorothy and William Marsden subscribed to the *Lisle* and *Naperville Sun* newspapers so they could keep up with our local events. We paid for their subscription as well as for one from Arundel for us. When we spoke or wrote letters we had a common knowledge of each other's current events.

Damn. They were going to read all about Harry. I made a mental note to call them as soon as I got home.

"Thanks, John." I opened my wallet to pay for the magazines.

"I've been meaning to ask Harry how close Baulfield is to Arundel. The store has another customer in that area; last name Highwater, Headwaters, something waters. Perhaps sparkling, or rising, or troubled." John grinned. "Thought maybe Harry knew them."

"John, that's like me letting someone in Europe know I'm from Chicago and being asked if I know a gangster or if my grandmother knew Al Capone."

"She didn't?"

"Don't push it."

The small space next to the register overflowed with flyers announcing community events. I had left hundreds of Depot Days Auction bookmarks with him at the beginning of the month. I didn't see any in the plastic holder.

He followed my glance. "I gave out more of those bookmarks since the auction than before. Everybody wanted one because it had a picture of the trunk. Business picked up, too; I think they felt they should buy something. Too bad Harry's not in town. They'd have loved the autograph of the man who opened the trunk." John's laugh boomed genuine and hearty.

Does everyone know Harry is out of town?

"John, how do you know Harry is out of town?" My tone sounded sharper than I intended.

His smile stalled. "It's a small town, Grace. Everyone knows Harry argued with the dead locksmith and the police talked to him. Someone who came in told me he was out of town."

"Who, John? Can you remember?" I heard the panic in my voice.

"What's wrong, Grace?"

My entire visit with Karl Deutsch tumbled out in short staccato sentences. I omitted my reason for the visit; just hit the highlights of our conversation.

"He's an odd one. It's always harder for a kid with no father around. Kids from divorced or deceased parents have memories or occasional contact and visits with their dad to fill in the gaps. For Karl, it was like he never had one.

"Old man Deutsch was furious that Ava got pregnant. Surprised everyone. Eva was the boy-crazy twin. Ava and her boyfriend, can't remember his name, not a local boy, had planned to get married all along. He was the only young man she ever dated. He was drafted a few weeks after they found out Ava was pregnant. Never made it back.

"Instead of celebrating Karl's father as a hero the old man had his grandson legally named Deutsch and listed the father as 'unknown' on his birth certificate."

"Was this guy crazy? Why would he do that and why would she let him?" My anger with this family was building to a point of contempt.

"He wanted an heir to carry on his name. His last shot had been his son Karl, the girls' father, but after his wife died in childbirth he was pretty removed from the picture. Drank himself off a road one night. The girls were raised by an aunt, their grandfather, and a series of German nannies."

"He was named after his grandfather, not his own father, who died?"

"Ava didn't have much say and like I said she was the quiet

one. Eva would have put up a fuss. But then, Eva wouldn't have gotten pregnant."

I raised my eyebrows. John continued quickly, anticipating my question. "My older sister, Mary, hung around with Eva one summer. They acted in some local summer stock theater in Glen Ellyn. Mary would tell the family about things Eva said and did. It didn't take much to reach the conclusion that Eva Deutsch was the savvy, thrill seeker in that pair of siblings."

"She helped raise Karl?"

"No. By an aunt I meant the old man's sister, Wiltrude. She was your boss's grandmother."

Aha! He doesn't know everything. Apparently the grapevine hasn't dripped the news of my lost employment into his ear yet.

"Eva left when he was about thirteen, right after Johann's will set off the battle between the girls. In my opinion, that's when the boy really turned. Never normal, it seemed, after they sent him packing. If you ask me, he takes after his aunt more than his mother. Got a mean streak."

John had inadvertently confirmed my own thoughts. Maybe his mean streak started the night he killed that little girl.

"John, you've been around here a long time. Do you remember a girl reported missing about fifteen years ago?" It was a long shot.

"That would be fourteen years ago, the summer of 1978. Amanda Jhanson. Her family owned a couple of those farm stands, flowers, fruits, veggies, and pumpkins for Halloween, that kind of thing. She disappeared one evening after getting an ice cream right over there on Ogden." He pointed in the direction I had just come from. "As far as I heard, they never found a trace of her. Listed as a possible runaway. The family sold the stands and moved. Bad time." A grim look of sadness darkened John's eyes and replaced his normally jovial expression.

"Did Karl Deutsch and Amanda Jhanson know each other?" It wouldn't prove anything, but I was curious.

"The town was even smaller then. I worked here summers. They were junior high sweethearts. Puppy love kind of thing. He was a year or two older; used to come in together and he'd pay for a candy bar for her. She always picked a Nestlé Crunch. She'd unwrap it real careful and break it in half and pop one half in his mouth. She'd nibble at her half while they looked at the magazines. Sometimes they stood holding hands and looking at the rows of covers. Puppy love stuff."

Maybe their puppy love had turned vicious.

"He sounded like a nice kid. Why'd you say he had a mean streak?"

John waited to answer. I looked around thinking he didn't want to be overheard; we were alone.

"He seemed to change right before he left for that fancy boarding school. Maybe he thought he was better than the other kids. I didn't understand why Ava sent him. She didn't strike me as the type. I know the old man had been pushing for his great-grandson to follow in his footsteps at that school; some elite academy in Germany. The kid seemed too tightly wound the few times I saw him after that summer. He never had a chance to grow up like the other kids. Everybody else in town went to Lisle High School or Benet."

I said goodbye to John and drove away deep in thought about a girl who never had a chance at high school. I intended to take Main out to Rt. 53 and head for home. At Front Street I made an unplanned left and drove past the train station and St. Joan of Arc Catholic Church on my way to the Lisle Library. Having spent several years as a college librarian at Regina, I knew how to use a library. Poor, uninformed masses that thought of only Dewey Decimal when they entered a library;

if you knew how, you could gather amazing information and uncover secrets without leaving the reference area.

Lisle Library's reference area was organized in fiche, film, and print. The microfilm machines sat on the right hand side in a small alcove beyond the reference desk. The reference librarian looked up as I approached. I didn't know her. The tag on her lapel said "Abby." I knew Irene, the other librarian who worked more evenings than days. She had helped me with research on the trunks.

"Hi, I'm looking for back issues of the *Lisle Sun* from 1978, August or September. Would you have those on microfilm?"

Abby checked a binder and indicated that they had them. "Please take a seat at one of the machines. The Chicago papers are in those cabinets but I need to go into the back room for the *Lisle Sun*."

I sat down at one of the cubicles next to a group of orange cabinets. Abby brought out two thin, flat boxes labeled, *L. Sun 8/78* and *L. Sun 9/78*.

The story played out over two weeks of issues and then faded from the news. I had the information I needed to approach Officer Royal with my bizarre accusation. Only who was it? Schoebel, the pedophile, or Deutsch, the hormone-crazed kid? The police would sort it out once I gave them an explanation other than Harry.

THIRTY-ONE

I KICKED OFF MY SHOES and dumped my purse and folder on the counter. The meeting with Royal hadn't gone off as I expected. When I arrived and presented my theories she immediately brought in Detective Garza who sat quietly and apparently disinterested throughout my explanation. I offered the printouts from the research I'd just completed. They politely thanked me for my time and firmly suggested that I let them handle the investigation. I had the key in the baggie in my purse but decided to withhold it from them; they hadn't appreciated the printouts, didn't even take them.

Harry still ranked as their prime suspect. They didn't say it; they didn't have to. At least they couldn't tag him with Dr. Weber's murder. By their own admission his call to me had been routed through Chicago but originated overseas.

The phone and the doorbell rang at the same time. I grabbed the phone. "Hello?"

"Grace, it's me. We've got the best news…"

"Karen, hold on, someone's at the door."

I turned the doorknob and yanked. My elbow jolted; the deadbolt held. "Just a minute," I shouted through the plane of solid oak. I fumbled with the knob; left, right, it didn't release. *Oh, no, not now.* I sighed and resigned myself and shouted again, "It'll be a minute, the lock is stuck."

Stuck in my head. Left, one thousand two thousand three thousand, right, one thousand two thousand three thousand, left, one thousand two thousand three thousand, right, one thousand two thousand three thousand and left, one thousand two thousand three thousand.

"Okay, I've got…"

"Grace, I'm here."

I screamed in spite of recognizing the soft voice behind me. "Geez, Ric. You scared me to death."

"I'm sorry, Grace. I figured you were having trouble with the door."

"How did you get in here? I know we didn't give Lily a key."

Ric's smile touched his eyes. He shook his head. "I got the key from Karen when…"

"Karen! I left her on the phone." I rushed by Ric through the living room and whipped around the corner into the kitchen. "Karen, hi, sorry. Your brother's here." I panted from the dash to the kitchen.

"Slow down. What's he doing, chasing you around the house?" She laughed.

I took a deep breath. "Very funny. Why did you give him your key? He used it just now and scared me half to death."

"I thought you said he was at your door?"

"Never mind. What's your news?" Ric had made his way to the kitchen. I motioned for him to sit down.

"Hannah and I got the call. The agency has a little girl for us. We're leaving this afternoon."

Distinctly different, but equally powerful emotions of joy and envy welled up inside me. I couldn't be happier for Karen and Hannah. They deserved my enthusiastic support. The basic goodness that God blessed me with won the toss.

"Oh, my God, Karen, that's great. I'm so excited for you. When do you get her? When will you be home? Call me from there, okay? I want to meet my niece as soon as you land."

"I will, we will. We're so excited. Hannah's got all the arrangements made and I just packed some stuff for us. We should be back on Sunday. Sunday, Grace, and we'll have our little girl home."

My eyes filled with tears. I could hear the tears in her voice.

"Grace, gotta go. The cab will be here soon. You know how Hannah is."

I laughed at her reference to my sister-in-law's obsession with timeliness. "Okay, hug Hannah for me. Take care, be careful with my niece. Call me."

"You got it. I love you, Grace."

"Me too, bye."

I swiped at the tears rolling down my face with the back of my hands. Ric extended his handkerchief into my blurred vision.

"Thanks."

"I know how hard that was for you to hear. You were wonderful, Gracie." He stood close to me; so close I smelled the Gray Flannel cologne he always wore. I had given him his first bottle over seven years ago when, for a time, I thought I'd be sharing my life with him.

I closed my eyes and tried to find that calm space in my head. I heard his voice through a fog.

"Karen picked me up this morning at Edwards. She got the call from Hannah while she was still out here. She tried to call you then. She told me she'd try you again after she got home and packed. I wanted to be with you when she told you." His low, gentle voice and the slight pressure of his arm against mine welcomed me into his embrace.

I burst into tears and sobbed against his shoulder. To his credit, he held me like a sister, which made me cling to him even more. I could sense, though, that with more contact his resolve might crumble. His shoulders tensed a little and the soothing sounds he made stopped when he gently kissed the top of my head.

I reluctantly pulled away from his comfort. "Thank you. I'm going to wash my face. Sit down. I'll make us some coffee."

"Take your time. I'll make it. Any preference?"

"No, you choose." I used the powder room and spent extra time composing myself as well as removing the evidence of heavy crying. Some people cry dainty, I cry ugly; red splotches on my face and neck, running nose with enough mucous to rival a day care center during cold season, and eyes shrunken to the size of peas. Not a pretty picture. I splashed my face with cold water and pressed a wet finger-towel against my face until the cloth felt warm. After the third "toweling," the splotches retreated and my eyes widened to almost normal. With the edge of the towel I gently removed the smeared mascara and eyeliner; bare looked better than blotchy. The face that looked back at me appeared clean, calm, and collected. I could guarantee only the first.

THIRTY-TWO

Ric had set two places in the nook. My angel mug and a napkin waited for me. He had relocated the plate of sweet rolls to the table along with two dessert plates. The kitchen smelled of Honey Pecan Roast. I slid into the bench side, reasoning that maneuvering onto a bench might be too uncomfortable for Ric. I guessed right. His rueful smile as he pushed my mug across to me said he understood.

With some physical distance between us, I thanked him for his thoughtfulness. "How are you feeling?"

"I feel fine. They had me on forty-eight-hour observation. I had a lot of time to think about this whole case. I'm still on the case, aren't I?" His smile warmed me like the coffee couldn't.

I nodded my head.

"Good. So I'm thinking about all the angles and if I were investigating from the police point of view, Harry looks good for it."

"Ric, whose side are you on?"

"Hold on. I said from the police point of view. Now from my new perspective I'd look at the person who wanted that trunk so badly they'd forego common sense."

"Hannah?"

"No, not Hannah." He looked at me in surprise.

"I thought she lost hold of her senses. She bid over three thousand dollars for that trunk."

Now he looked surprised. "Really? That is extravagant for a trunk."

This comment from a man who purchased Armani suits

and drove a Porsche. He and Karen both had trust funds the size of Peoria.

"Not Hannah but Ava. Ava Deutsch would be my first stop."

I got up to bring the coffee pot to the table; this was definitely a multi-pot night. After I refilled both mugs, I took my seat and leaned forward across the table.

"Your eyes are positively purple. What's on your mind?"

I quickly filled in the events of the last two days, covering everything from the break-in at Schwarze and Krieg, to the break-ins at my house, to Harry's call, to the doctor's death, to my conversations with Karl Deutsch and with John at the Book Nook. I showed him the key and told him about the blood thinner. My down-and-dirty explanation lasted more than thirty minutes.

He had taken a small notebook from the inside pocket of his coat. Ric never interrupted me during the entire time. I saw him jot down notes but he kept his eyes on mine. It reminded me of the first time I sat with him over seven years ago and told him my husband had gone missing. His eyes never left my face but instead softened or questioned as if to give me encouragement to tell my story.

At the end of my epic narration he sipped at his coffee, staring at me across the rim of the cup. "How about I dump Peterson and make you my partner?" I felt giddy, like I'd aced a homework assignment.

"Harry's in the clear for the second homicide. It's too coincidental to have two homicidal maniacs loose in Lisle. It's bad, however, that his prints are on the bat. The blanket from your car hasn't been tested yet according to Peterson. I know Harry would never implicate you so I know he didn't do it. If we could find out how his prints got on the bat, we'd be closer to finding the murderer."

"Oh, my God. Ric. My dad."

"Grace, you're not making sense. What is it?"

I had already jumped up from the bench, bumping the table and sloshing coffee from my full cup onto the table. The phone was in my hand and my fingers flew across the pad. *Please be home. Please be home.*

"Hello."

"Dad, remember when you said if I wasn't going to accept a dog from you for protection you joked about putting a baseball bat in every room? Remember?"

"Gracie, what's wrong?"

"Did you, Dad? I mean did you bring baseball bats over here? Ever?"

"Grace, honey, I was joking. Why are you so upset? Harry stopped me from bringing them in."

"When? When did you do this?"

"Now stop right there. This isn't about a few baseball bats. What's going on? Straight answer or I'm coming out there and calling your brothers."

The last thing I wanted was the Morellis en masse on my doorstep; especially with Ric in my kitchen. I explained.

"Oh, Grace. Why didn't you tell me about this? You were at work when I brought them over. Harry nixed the idea and I shoved the bats back into the bag. When I stood it on end and lifted it, the bottom gave out, and bats spilled out all over the garage." My dad stopped talking and silence filled the wire.

"What is it, Dad?" The sensation of dread, when you ask a question you suddenly don't want an answer to, overwhelmed me now. I leaned against the wall.

"Honey, he never touched the bats. I put them back in the bag; Harry held it open."

"Are you sure, Dad?" My voice caught in my throat. I was nailing down evidence against Harry.

"I'm sure." He sounded flat.

"Dad, it's okay. There's an answer in all this. I just have to find it. Honest, it's okay. I'll call you in the morning."

I hung up the phone and turned to Ric. He had heard my side and guessed the rest. I filled him in on the details.

"This isn't good. We're working from the point that Harry is innocent. Someone wants to incriminate him. They see him arguing with Schoebel and in that moment decide to kill Schoebel and frame Harry. How does the bat that may have been in your garage end up being the murder weapon and then end up back in your garage? If this is a crime of opportunity, how would they know that Harry would be driving west on Ogden so they could toss the body in front of his car?"

"Schoebel wasn't near his apartment. If he was on foot, he was walking in the wrong direction. Maybe he arranged to meet Harry later. That's what the killer heard."

"Why? What could have been so important that he couldn't talk to Harry at the depot?"

"I don't know, Ric. Someone thought it important enough to kill Schoebel before he could talk to Harry again."

Ric stood up and stretched. "I need to move around a little." His first steps around the kitchen looked painful. His stride lengthened and steadied as he continued to walk.

"Is there a lot of pain?" I wasn't sure if refocusing the conversation on a personal level would be smart, but I couldn't think straight about the investigation.

Ric stopped a few feet away from me. His dark eyes glowed soft like charcoal smudges. I'd seen his eyes harden and glint with anger like anthracite coal or obsidian marbles. The eyes I looked at now were the eyes I had fallen into those many years ago.

"Sometimes more than other times. I can't sit too long. Being laid-up in the hospital took its toll. Fluid built up around the scarring. Gotta work that out or I run the risk of infection. I'm scheduled for three sessions tomorrow, hydrotherapy, massage therapy, and physical therapy, after which I'll be crankier than hell and not fit for human companionship." He smiled and shrugged. "So, let's think this out tonight because I won't be functioning until Friday."

I topped off our mugs while he continued his route through the kitchen and living room. I needed to stay focused and charged; I looked for the honey jar to boost my energy. *The honey! Oh, my God.* I'd forgotten about the honey for Ric. Harry and I had left England so quickly after Hannah's news we never had the chance to go back to the bee lady for her healing honey.

Since our return I'd been consumed with my new job and new house. I felt a pang of guilt as he shuffled into the kitchen. His smile seemed tighter and I saw the ring of pain in the fringes of his eyes.

"Whew. I know I have to stop when the pain from walking matches the pain from sitting. My life has become a balancing act." He sat down and rested his elbows on the table. "What's this?" He pointed to the honey jar. "I'm not sweet enough?"

"Drink your coffee. I'll be right back."

My mind had registered that Harry's hands had healed before he finished the last jar of honey he had received from Maeve's bees. I rushed up the stairs and into our bathroom. His side of our vanity wasn't as neat as I'd have liked it to be, but then I lined up my jars and bottles according to height within their usage category. Still, he was neater than my four brothers had been; a livable compromise between obsessive and philosophical. I looked behind daily use containers like shaving cream, which seemed logical to me. It wasn't there. I did a cursory search of my side.

Oh, gee. Grace, get a grip. I had moved the honey jar to the kitchen so I could use it on my hands after barn chores. If it worked that well for Harry, it could do wonders on my cuts and scratches.

Ric's head rested on his hands, his eyes closed. He opened them when he heard me. I checked the cabinet above the sink and pulled out the container. I put the large jar on his side of the table. He looked at the label.

"I thought I was kidding about being sweet enough. No, huh?"

"I'm not attesting to your sweetness or lack thereof." I sat up straight, prepared to spin a convincing argument for Maeve's bees. My rambling rendition stalled about the point where the recipient had to thank the bees or someone who loved the recipient had to thank them. I don't know why I included all the rigmarole of the legend except I felt compelled to tell the story as it had been told to me. Ric straightened in his seat and interrupted me.

"You thanked the bees for me?" The question implied the rest of his question.

"Ah, no. I never made it to see her. This is Harry's jar. He doesn't need it anymore and I want you to try it. It works; I don't know how but it does."

"According to the rules it won't work. Harry thanked the bees for himself and we know *he* doesn't love me." His smile wrapped around my heart. Ric pushed the jar toward me.

"Ric, forget the rules, the legend. It really works. Harry's hands are completely healed, no pain, no scar tissue. I don't believe the story; I believe what I see. Take it, try it. If it doesn't work you'll at least be as sweet on the outside as the inside." I grinned at him.

What I can only describe as a smirk came over his face. "Okay, Grace, I'll try Maeve's *woo-woo* on one condition. Tell the bees you love the man who will use their honey." He sat back in his chair and stared at me, his head cocked slightly as if daring me to jinx him and at the same time pleading with me not to.

"Don't be silly. I told you I didn't believe the story. Anyway, there aren't any bees here." I felt a flush creeping up my throat to my face.

"C'mon, Grace. What's the harm? Just to make sure it works. The bees will hear you. They need to know. I need to know." His voice lowered and I saw the hope in his eyes.

"Ric, stop it. You always twist it around to this. How can we ever hope to have any kind of a civil relationship if you keep doing this." I stood and paced the kitchen, flinging my arms about to accompany my comments. "It's never enough that we at least talk to each other now. You never let it go." I struggled for better words.

He sat patiently through my tirade. Maybe I'd gotten through. He reached his hand out and gently tapped the top of the jar.

"Dammit, Ric. You have to stop; let it go, let me go."

Tap, tap. He raised an eyebrow.

"All right. Because you were a part of my life at a painfully difficult time and because you were there for me when I needed you and because I thought we had a life to share, all right, I love you." I fumed and sputtered the last words.

He looked up to the corner of the kitchen. "Hear that, bees, she loves me." He placed his hand, palm out, behind his ear, as though listening. "What's that? I'll tell her."

I felt totally frustrated and wanted to scream at him but I couldn't stop the tug of a smile.

"The bees say 'it's about time.'"

"The bees are full of—"

"Honey," he finished for me. "A simple yes would have been enough, Grace, but as we're on the subject you are right about some things. I do hope for a *civil* relationship with you, my courthouse or yours? I won't ever let go of you because we do have a life to share."

"That's what I mean. You twist my words to suit you."

"No, maybe I untangle your words to get at the truth."

"The truth is that I don't want you here. Take the honey and go." I thought he would argue. He surprised me by getting up and slipping the jar into his pocket.

"Let me out the back. It's shorter through the woods."

"It's shorter but the ground's uneven and…"

"Careful, Gracie. I might get the impression you care." He lifted my chin with his thumb and before I could react, kissed me on the lips.

I pulled away and turned my back on him. "Fine, break your neck out there." I knew I'd over-reacted. I took a few deep breaths as I led the way through the mudroom and out the back door.

He walked out the door with a quiet, "Good night, angel."

I knew it would be useless to tell him not to call me that. I stood mute and watched his slow progress around the carriage house and back to the path that connected the properties. In the stillness of the night I listened to the crunch of the crushed pecan shells when he reached the path.

April whinnied a soft greeting. I stepped into the barn. She thrust her muzzle over the stall to search my hand for a treat. Cash mimicked her behavior. His dark head inched out.

"See what a bad habit I've instilled in you. You can't just be happy to see me? I always have to bring a treat." My gentle scolding brought a playful nod from April. "Not tonight. I came in to say good night and talk to someone who wouldn't talk back." April snorted and nodded. "I guess I won't get the last word here, either." I kissed her muzzle. Cash snorted. "Okay, okay." I moved to his stall and rubbed his soft hair. Satisfied that they were set for the night, I closed and latched the door behind me. *Latched! Oh, no, don't let it be locked.*

I ran to the back door and turned the knob. Nothing! *Great! Now what? Okay, relax. Barb has a key. Ric! Ric has a key. He can't have gotten far.*

I TURNED AND HEADED in the direction of the path. I knew the terrain better than he did and I could walk faster. Pine Marsh wasn't the boonies but it didn't have streetlights and mini-marts every fifty yards. I loved the way night *fell* out here, like in the cartoons where the dark sky crashed to the horizon complete with stars and a moon that popped up with a *thwop*.

Twenty yards into the woods, the light dimmed; the universal theater signal to return to your seat. Was the universe trying to signal me? *All right, Grace, don't get goofy. You like the dark, the quiet. You think best in the dark. No I don't! I think best in the sunshine on top of April out in the open. Who are you kidding?*

My internal struggle hadn't stopped me from walking, just from paying attention to the path. I missed a slight curve and plowed into a bush. The crackle of my contact sounded deafening. In the split moment between the dying rustle and the renewal of night noises I heard a soft grunt and a crunch of shells.

Someone was on the path ahead of me. I thought someone and then tried to put Ric's name in that sentence. It wouldn't go. I froze to the spot and strained to see anything on the path. I was looking for Ric, I expected to find Ric, but this didn't feel like Ric. I'd learned the hard way to follow my gut and the little hairs on my neck were standing out straight enough to hold a key-chain.

I moved around the back of the bush. I made negligible noise. You learn stealth when you're the only girl, playing hide and seek with four brothers and their friends. You had to be better.

I stared at the path, fearful that soon I'd be imagining movement and miss the real thing. My eyes felt gritty and I blinked several times to draw fluid across them. I knew if I moved I'd alert whoever was out there to my location. I couldn't stand here much longer. I leaned forward, focused on the path, and kept straining to hear something. I heard nothing. The slight movement of air behind me came too late.

THIRTY-THREE

THE HAND ACROSS my mouth and the arm clamped around my chest effectively disabled me. My brain froze, stuck on a frame from six months ago when someone had hurt me in these woods. I couldn't move and drew tiny gasps under the firm hand. My lungs started to tighten; I couldn't exhale.

I felt rather than saw someone move down the path. The artificial breeze pushed against my face and swirled around my head and brought relief from an unlikely sense. I caught a whiff of Gray Flannel. My body relaxed and I exhaled through my nose, which had been functioning but somehow disconnected from my brain. I nodded to let Ric know I recognized him. I'm sure my semi slump against him already told him I wasn't afraid. He removed his arm and waited for me to turn.

"Was that absolutely necessary?" My question came out as a hiss.

"I couldn't take the chance you wouldn't start walking again. What made you get off the path?"

"Dumb luck. I wasn't paying attention and I missed the curve."

"Dumb luck or divine intervention, you missed running smack into someone sneaking around out here. Why are you here, anyway?"

"I'm locked out. I need your key."

The soft chuckle didn't endear him to me at that moment. "You're not going back there tonight. I'm not sure who's out here, I'm not even sure if it was a man or woman, but they came down the hill from Lily's in stealth mode and passed up the Atwaters' property heading straight for yours."

My heart thumped against my chest with the thought that maybe Harry was home. "Ric, maybe it was Harry."

"No way. He wouldn't be skulking in his own neighborhood. Wrong feeling."

Right! I would have sensed if my husband had been out there. *Really? You didn't sense Ric, you had to smell him.*

"Come with me to the house. I want to see if anything's wrong up there. I'll take you home after I call Peterson out here and after I pick up a few things."

He walked out to the path and waited for me to join him. He spoke in quiet tones even though I assumed he felt any danger had passed.

"Why would anyone be at your—Lily's house?" I still didn't understand their relationship.

"Maybe the word is out that I've been hired to look into the homicide."

"How? We only decided Sunday and you've been in the hospital since then."

"I don't know, Gracie. Maybe I talk in my sleep and the floor nurse spilled her guts." He said this with a Bogart voice, not a good one.

"I'm serious."

"You're right. If I talked in my sleep it would be about you and that nurse would have been blushing." His soft laughter lightened the mood. "We talked about it at the police station. Any number of people could have heard. Police stations are the worst places to keep a lid on anything."

Right again. Karl Deutsch had said as much.

We reached Lily's back door and Ric took the precaution of having me wait until he checked the house. I'd seen this scene a hundred times in movies. I always wondered why they thought it safer to stay outside. What if the bad guy were out there waiting? I shifted from one foot to the other and tried to blend against the brick. I'd much rather be inside with Ric.

He stood at the door holding it open for me. "Can't see that they took anything. Peterson gave you the stuff I printed, right?"

I'd forgotten about the envelope that Ric had forced upon Peterson as a condition of Ric's admission to the hospital. I felt guilty telling him I hadn't looked at it yet. I nodded my head hoping he'd drop the subject.

"That's all I could think someone might want. And this." Ric lifted one side of his jacket to reveal a gun pushed in the waistband of his pants. "I guess I need to keep this with me. I'm calling Peterson; let him know what's happening. Why don't you go in the kitchen and wait. I hate these giant windows." Ric waved his arm at the half wall of windows that faced the backyard.

He moved to the back end of the room not exposed by windows where he had set up his living space. I followed him to the sitting area cum sleeping area.

"Do you think someone broke in looking for weapons because they know you're a cop?"

"It's always a possibility, but in this case I don't think it's a strong one. It's more likely that someone thought they might slow me down. Anyone who's seen me knows I'm not one hundred percent; a shove down that slope, a crack on the head; I could be out of commission for a few days, again."

"Why didn't they wait for you?"

"Don't know. Maybe he thought I was spending the night." His smile blazed and then faded. "And maybe he thought he'd get two birds with one stone if he went to your house."

I was glad he hadn't said "kill two birds" but my eyes still widened at the thought.

The knock on the door came as a welcome distraction. Sergeant Peterson's demeanor was brisk and focused; no chitchat. Something was wrong. Ric filled him in on the earlier events.

"You know something? What happened?"

He looked at me with an odd expression.

"She does that all the time, kind of creepy, you'll get used to it," Ric assured him.

"There's been another accident. The victim is at Good Sam. It doesn't look good."

"Oh, my God. Who is it?"

"A woman by the name of Jan Pauli."

"I know her. She's my cleaning lady, well, she was going to be, but it didn't work out. This is terrible."

"It gets worse. The police think Mr. Marsden is involved."

My head spun with the news. I closed my eyes to reorient my thoughts. "That's crazy! Harry's out of the country. We went through this before with the phone call he made." I looked from Peterson to Ric for some explanation.

Peterson cleared his throat. "They checked the information they had on that call and a more advanced tech showed them how the signal could bounce back and make the call appear to originate in Europe when it actually did come from Chicago. He called it a 'double helix' program."

"Sort of like doubling back. Even if he were in town, why do they think he's connected with this?" Ric asked.

"The speculation is that someone forced her car off the road near the entrance to Pine Marsh; luckily it didn't roll into the marsh."

He was referring to the main entrance to our compound that spanned the marshlands at the front end of the development. My heart raced as I remembered being forced off that narrow lane. Only the grace of God and Harry's determination to battle a two-thousand-pound car saved me from tumbling into the dense ooze.

"But why Harry?" My voice squeaked with frustration

and my fingers tingled. I felt the urge and succumbed. The length of yard tied to my belt loop lay between my fingers in a heartbeat.

"Because this Pauli woman was the witness that positively identified Harry as the man arguing with Schoebel. The others say they saw the two men but couldn't remember what either man looked like."

A familiar pattern of loops and twists grew in my hand as I struggled to stay calm. I couldn't speak until I looped two more. I could braid and tie knots in my sleep; I didn't need to look at the yarn. I kept my eyes glued to Peterson, imploring him to wait for me to answer.

"This is wrong. If Harry were here he could explain. I know he could."

"He's not here and without a feasible explanation..."

Peterson left the sentence hanging. Silence filled the space between us. Panic took hold of me. My nostrils flared like April's when something spooked her. *Spooked. That's it. No matter which way I turn everything points to Harry. I can't catch a breath to think straight.*

They'd have to think for me. I held out my hands, palms up. "You have to find out who did this, all of this. You know it wasn't Harry. Start with that. I have all the papers you printed; I have notes on my research for the event."

Peterson and Ric exchanged glances.

"Please help me." I felt the itch at the back of my throat and swallowed hard.

"We've got to check out your place anyway in case your visitor headed there."

Ric nodded his head and added, "Not to mention, you're locked out." He smiled and pulled a key from his pocket.

They exchanged looks again. Ric's face had a crooked grin. In the split second when Peterson saw the key, a narrowing of his eyes made him look angry. *Must be my imagination.* When he looked at Ric his expression looked neutral.

PETERSON DID THE SWEEP of the upstairs while Ric checked out the first floor. I made a pot of coffee. While that brewed, I pulled leftovers and first-timers out of the refrigerator. My hand stopped next to the pickle jar. I didn't own a blue container. *Now what? This weirdo is leaving me food?* I straightened up and called Ric.

I pointed to the container when he came into the kitchen. "That's not mine."

Ric leaned into the fridge and carefully pulled out the covered blue plastic bowl. He carried it over to the sink and removed the cover. The kitchen filled with the fabulous aroma of beef stew. We looked at each other. If I wasn't wound tighter than a top I would have laughed. I don't know what we expected to find.

Instead, I closed the refrigerator door and leaned against it, slowly letting a tired sigh escape my lips.

Ric turned the cover over in his hand and seemed to be trying to remember something. He replaced the cover, snapped it in place and lifted one end slightly to "burp" the container. Bachelors knew the art of maintaining leftovers. He held the bowl over the sink and turned it over.

"I thought this bowl looked familiar." He tilted the bowl toward me. On a piece of surgical tape was the word *Klops*.

"Gertrude?"

"She's been doing some cooking for Karen and Hannah and they've been sending some out to me. She makes a great beef stew."

"Karen must have brought some for you, but left it here when you weren't discharged from the hospital. Guess she forgot it."

"Or figured you'd eat it."

Peterson joined us and told me that he'd checked the top floor. "I'll check down here."

"It's done, no need," Ric said over his shoulder. He had decided to reopen the stew.

"I thought maybe you didn't get to it." His eyes narrowed on the back of Ric's head.

"Nope, it's done." This time Ric turned to emphasize his words. "All clear."

Tension seemed to float up between the partners. I physically stepped forward to interrupt the flow.

"I'm going to put out some cold ham and heat up this stew. I have wheat bread, American bread, and Italian bread. Pickles? Olives? Giardinera?" They nodded yes to everything.

Twenty minutes later, we were settled over bowls and plates filled with half the contents of my refrigerator. I felt like I was back on Victoria Avenue trying to defend my plate against four growing brothers. *You don't want your pork chop, Gracie, you'll get fat; take my spinach. We won't pick you for short center if you can't run for the ball.*

"Grace?" Ric looked at me.

"Sorry, zoning out is all." I realized they had finished eating and had pushed the plates to the side and cleared a spot for the files.

"Let us work on this; you look beat. Go on up to bed and we'll leave you a note if we come up with something important."

I was tempted. My eyelids felt like lead scraping over two gritty pebbles. "Let me splash some water on my face and I'll be fine."

I came back a few minutes later and noticed the dishes in the sink and the coffee butler on the table. Ric stood up and motioned for me to slide in on his side of the bench.

Ric started. "We tried this earlier. Let's fill in the blanks we know and take good guesses at what we don't know. Do we know the identity of the skeleton?"

"A good bet is Amanda Jhanson. She disappeared in the summer of 1978."

"Who killed her?"

Peterson answered. "Schoebel looks good to me for this one. Convicted pedophile, lived in the area at the time."

"I disagree. Karl Deutsch was Amanda's boyfriend at the time. He went a little strange that summer according to someone who knew both of the kids. That's the summer his mother and aunt kept the town entertained with their legal and moral battles over the grandfather's will.

"I think Karl and Amanda were fooling around in the lower level of Antiques on Plank and things went too far. Wouldn't be the first time a young girl changed her mind but couldn't change her fate."

Ric looked at both of us. "Okay, two suspects; one dead, one alive."

He continued. "Why did Harry follow Schoebel out of the tent and what were they arguing about?"

"I've been thinking about this all week. Until I heard that Harry had argued with him I thought he'd gone after him to, I don't know, maybe apologize for upstaging him. Hannah sort of forced Harry into opening the trunk."

"Now the woman who reported the argument is forced off the road, resulting in serious injury."

"Allegedly run off the road," Ric reminded him. "The M.O. has been hit and run. Why wouldn't this be the same? Which way was she headed? Does the report say?"

"West. She was headed into the compound."

"Why would she be coming back? She made it plain that she couldn't work for me." I quickly filled them in on how upset she had become when I suggested that Ava Deutsch might have any connection to the murder.

"Ava Deutsch? Mrs. Marsden, that's like trying to pin the tail on the donkey and you tag a thoroughbred. She's done more for this town, heck the entire DuPage area, than any three people with her means." He ticked off her accomplishments. "Town council, school board, Lisle Women's Club, Library Trustee, Lisle Heritage Society, Chamber of Commerce…" He slowed to a stop. "You get the picture. It's not just her money; she served on every committee, helped wherever she could. It wasn't until the battle over the will that she had to pull back and let go of the committee work. She still donates money, plenty of it, but can't free up her time since her sister left her with both sides of the business to run."

"You sure did your homework or let me guess. You grew up here?" I knew only years of proximity could produce all that casual information.

Peterson smiled. "Yep. Lisle High School, class of seventy-two."

"Did you know Karl as a kid?"

"Not really; he was younger and I went to public school, he went to St. Joan of Arc. Then he went off to that German school."

"Okay, so Mother Theresa Deutsch is out. Let's move on. I find it interesting that the only witness, such a good witness, is now in ICU. I can see why the police are looking at Harry again." Ric's voice wasn't accusing, just stating facts.

"What if someone asked her to do it?" I wanted to get their minds off Harry.

"You mean asked her to say she saw Harry?"

"No. We know Harry went after Schoebel and it's possible he talked to him. We have only her word that they were arguing. That's what makes Harry look guilty: the argument." I'd done it. I could almost hear the gears in their heads slow, stop, and shift.

"Excellent, Gracie. So who would benefit?" Ric threw out the question.

"Maybe she knew Schoebel and he asked her to implicate Harry if anything happened to him. Of course, that would suggest that he thought something might."

Peterson played his own devil's advocate. "If he killed that little girl that would certainly be reason to not want to open the trunk. If he hid the body in the trunk, he would have known long before that moment on stage. You said he saw the trunks earlier. Why would he even show up to the event? Doesn't make sense."

"Unless he's not the killer. If Karl killed Amanda, maybe he paid Schoebel not to open the trunk, especially if his mother didn't win the bid. The trunks were identical, except for a little damage on one. Fifteen years is a long time to remember exactly which trunk you stuffed your girlfriend's body into."

"Then why didn't he bid higher?"

That was a puzzle. "He seemed to be unsure after his mother left him in charge. Why did that policeman come and get her? What was that about?"

Peterson looked at his papers. He pulled a sheet from the middle of the pile. "Silent alarm went off. Protocol says you find the owner or designated caretaker. Safe bet that everyone knew she'd be at the auction."

"Anything stolen?"

"No. Seemed like an electrical fluke of some sort. Two other businesses on Ogden reported malfunctions around the same time. It's like something swept down the street and jammed the electronics."

"Sergeant, do you happen to know what Karl Deutsch studied at that academy? I mean, did he major in retail management or business?"

"Not sure. I do know it wasn't a 'fluff' school. The local

paper ran stories about Karl every now and then. They ran a large one when he graduated." He closed his eyes as if to dredge old newsprint to his consciousness. His eyes popped open. "Some kind of engineer." Peterson shrugged.

"Maybe electrical? My brother Mike is a graduate of ITT with a degree in electrical engineering. He's always fiddled with electronics."

Peterson smiled at my enthusiasm. "You're starting to convince me."

"Hold on." Ric picked a sheet from his papers. "My printout on Schoebel shows that he worked for several companies, one as a bench electrician and one as a garage door installer. He'd know about electronics, too."

"Where did he work last?"

"Company called Open Sesame. They fired him after they found out about his record. Wouldn't do to have a pedophile in someone's home."

"What about the other company?"

"J.P. Enterprise. He was there until a few years back. Up and left. No reason."

I leaned forward. The excitement I felt must have spread to them. Each looked at me. "J.P. Enterprise was Jan Pauli's company. She sold the company and retired a few years ago. Bet she knew him and kept his secret. When she left it wasn't safe for him to stay on."

"Why would she cover for him?" Ric sounded astonished.

"I don't know except that everyone in this town is related. Gee, go back one generation and they all came from the same town in Germany, probably the same house."

I realized how bitchy that sounded about the same time I remembered that Peterson had told us he grew up in Lisle. My face flamed and I quickly looked at him with an apology on my lips.

He held up a hand to stop me. "No problem, we're Swiss.

My ancestors populated Geneva first. My grandfather drifted down to Lisle when my dad was accepted at North Central College. The family couldn't afford for my dad to board and they didn't have an extra car so they moved to Lisle."

I smiled at his candor. Ric picked up the thin string we were pulling at. "Pauli knows his background because maybe they're related. So how has he been supporting himself since his golden goose retired? He doesn't have a business, no ad in the book, can't get bonded because of his conviction. No one would call a locksmith that isn't bonded and insured."

I thought about what Ric was saying. I probably wouldn't have thought twice about checking for insurance. I would have opened the yellow pages and picked a nice-looking ad or clever name. Is that what happened to Amanda's family? Is that how he met her?

"Ric, we can get copies of yellow pages from fifteen years ago when Amanda disappeared. Maybe he had an ad in the book then. Maybe her parents weren't as careful about checking credentials. It was a different time."

"Good idea. That's the reference librarian in you, isn't it?" He smiled at me and I felt silly about enjoying his praise. "Okay, that's for you to check tomorrow. Now, what about the physical evidence against Harry? The bat was found in your garage, the blanket in your car."

"The bat belongs to my dad. He remembers dropping several of them on the garage floor and maybe one rolled under the workbench. If Harry found it he might have put it in his car to return to my dad."

"That could explain the fingerprints and their location."

I looked at Peterson.

"According to what I saw, his prints were on the middle of the bat and not at either end where you'd expect them to be. The police aren't saying too much about that because it is possible to hold the bat by the middle like a baton and inflict that wound."

"Were the prints from his left or right hand? Could they tell?"

"Left hand. Why?"

I felt a sigh of relief wash over me. I knew we were on the right track. "Harry is right-handed. He probably discovered the bat under the bench while sweeping out the garage. He would have used his right hand to guide the broom to move the bat toward him and then bent down to pick it up with his left hand. He knew it was my dad's bat and he probably put down the broom and opened the trunk of his car and dropped it in for future delivery. His trunk! That's it." I wanted to jump up and high five someone. "His trunk doesn't lock. Don't you see? The mechanism broke months ago and with us gone, well, he never got around to having it repaired. Anyone could have opened the Jag's trunk." I was so excited I couldn't sit still. I didn't understand why they were so calm.

Ric put a hand on my shoulder. "Gracie, how would anyone know what he had in his trunk? If they wanted to frame him and leave the body in his trunk that would work, but that would mean that Schoebel was already dead and the killer wouldn't have used the bat or the blanket. I agree that this crime wasn't premeditated. Someone perceived a threat and used what was at hand to kill Schoebel and implicate Harry."

I sat back, deflated like a Mylar balloon three days after a party. My energy spent, I didn't know what I needed more, sugar or sleep.

"We've been at this long enough." Ric slid out from the table and stretched. "I have to move around. Let's go at this from another angle. We know Marsden didn't kill Schoebel. We think Schoebel killed Amanda Jhanson. We don't know who killed Schoebel. Or why." He ticked those statements off on his left hand. He raised his right hand and started again. "Is

Amanda Jhanson dead? Does she have family living around here who might have always suspected Schoebel and meted out their own justice? Why frame Harry? Did Schoebel know the killer? Could he have been blackmailing him?"

"I know from talking to John Reeder that Amanda's family moved after she disappeared. Maybe Schoebel didn't kill her but knew that Karl Deutsch had and he was blackmailing Ava to keep the secret. Maybe that's really why a mother would send her son across the world to a boarding school. Blackmail would explain why Schoebel could afford to live where he did without having steady employment."

Peterson and Ric nodded their heads.

"When I was doing my research for the event, I found out that Schoebel was moving to Green Trails. I thought at the time that locksmith work must be lucrative, but maybe he had upped the price and Ava didn't want to pay it any longer."

Peterson shook his head. "More likely that if Karl knew about the blackmail he wouldn't want to pay Schoebel. He's got a temper. He's got the size to overpower him."

"I could overpower him, especially with a baseball bat from behind. He was a skinny old man."

Ric looked at me and then asked Peterson, "Do we know he was hit from behind?"

"I haven't been able to get my hands on the autopsy report. I did get my hands on the contents of the trunk." He pulled a sheet from the middle of his notes. He turned it and slid it toward us. I scanned the list. One dress, a comb, some toiletries, a roll of Certs breath mints, three metal hangers, a pair of shoes, several large bundles of dried flowers, and an acrylic fingernail.

"The trunk should have had more in it. No one would have paid the charge for these few items. The killer had to have removed most everything so the body would fit," Peterson said.

"Why not take out everything?" I asked.

"Because I think whatever the killer removed he thought could be easily left behind or disguised."

Ric and I both waited for Peterson to continue.

"Think about it. If he took out all of the clothes except maybe the one to hang in front of the body, he could leave them in any of the boxes of estate purchases. They'd be vintage clothing. Toiletries might cause suspicion when someone went to catalog the contents."

Ric nodded his head. I couldn't picture Schoebel killing his young victim and then making those rational and fashion-conscious decisions.

"Flowers, bundles of flowers? A macabre funeral tribute? No one travels with flowers, unless…" I thought about drawer sachets. "What kind of flowers? Could they have been to keep the contents fresh-smelling over a long journey?"

"Or maybe keep the odor from alerting people to the crime," Ric offered.

"I'll try and find out." Peterson scribbled a note in the margin.

I looked at the list again. "What about the nail? They found only one? Wouldn't there be nine more in the trunk?"

Peterson shrugged. "Like I said, I haven't been able to get the autopsy. Maybe the other nails are still attached to the fingers. Maybe they fell off but were caught on the body. I overheard the techs who removed the body mention there was still some soft tissue on parts of the body. They'll send that, along with the teeth, to a forensics lab to try for a dental match and a DNA typing. That could take months, if ever. They'd need a sample from the missing girl to prove anything. It's unlikely the family would have kept any of her personal toiletries."

"See if your paper is still good with the coroner and get both autopsies. Make that all three."

"Three?" Peterson asked.

"Yeah. Three: Schoebel, the skeleton, and Dr. Weber."

I had forgotten about Dr. Weber. His funeral was the next day. "Why Dr. Weber?"

"It's too coincidental that two longtime residents somehow connected to the family that may or may not have murdered someone would both be killed two days apart. Somewhere they're connected." Ric stared off into space as though trying to make the connection. He shrugged his shoulders. "Something's not right."

"Dr. Weber was doing the autopsy of the skeleton. That's why he was out at the county building. Maybe he recognized something. You know, like a mended bone in a leg that maybe he set years before. He'd been the local doctor forever. He probably delivered most of the kids, including Amanda."

"That's an interesting point, Grace, but why would Schoebel's killer care if she were identified? People would assume Schoebel killed her. There would be no advantage to running the risk of another murder. In fact, they'd want him alive to announce his findings. The police would continue to look at Harry or maybe, like you said earlier, a family member. It might eventually be marked as 'person unknown.'"

That phrase jogged my memory. "Speaking of unknown, did either of you see a stranger that night in the tent, the one who'd been bidding against Hannah and Karl?"

"A stranger, at a tourist event that draws hundreds of people to the depot?" Ric's voice lifted in irony.

"I mean she looked strange; all bundled up in clothes too big for her and a scarf around her neck up to her ears topped by a floppy hat. She left the tent right after the bidding, but I saw her inside when the police first arrived. I didn't she her again after that. Maybe she's involved."

"Grace, we don't need more suspects. We can't nail down the ones we have."

"Hold on, Kramer." Peterson seemed interested in this

stranger. "Was there anything more about her? Could you get an idea of her height or build?"

"Well, she was bundled, but I'd put her height a little shorter than Karen, not as thin but not as big as the clothes made her look. As I think about it, she may have been wearing padding. I remember her hands and wrists stuck out beyond the sleeves, which were much too short. In hindsight her wrists seemed too slender for the rest of the body. Why are you so interested?"

"There's been a lot of activity from Pine Marsh. I scan the Sheriff's calls."

"Oh, that was Jan Pauli that someone saw in the compound," I interrupted.

"Not her. There was another call about a heavily clothed person, hat, scarf, exactly what you described."

Ric stood up straighter. "The person I saw tonight could have been a woman in bulky clothes. I caught a glimpse. Who the hell is this person?"

The rhetorical question hung in the air.

"Let's call it a night. We all have our assignments." Ric paused to make sure I was listening. An idea began to form at the back of my mind, shifting, moving out of reach. I looked at Ric and gave him my attention. "Grace, do more research on the Jhanson family, and Schoebel too, but be discreet. Only paper research, no face-to-face questions, especially with Karl Deutsch."

"I'm not stupid."

"No, but you are curious; too curious. If your pit bull persona takes over, you could get into trouble. Promise me." Ric stared until I conceded. "Good. Pete, you're going to get on those autopsies."

"Yeah. I heard the one on the doc almost didn't happen. Seems the daughter was hysterical about her dad being cut up. The wife resigned herself to it, being a doctor's wife. I guess the son-in-law really went to bat for his wife's side. They tried to get an injunction but the last call belonged to the wife."

"Odd that the son-in-law would be so helpful. I heard he didn't get along with the doctor. No love lost between them; I would have thought he'd love to have him cut up. Sort of revenge."

"Who told—"

"How did you—"

Both men started and stopped. I smiled the smile of the grapevine connoisseur.

"Before Jan Pauli decided she couldn't clean for me we had quite a conversation about the locals."

"Save us from loose lips."

Peterson chuckled. "Good thing we're not in the navy. What are you doing, partner? I didn't hear your assignment."

The question was good-natured. Ric smiled and shrugged. "I will be enjoying a three-fold therapy session with *Attila the Hun;* hurt him, hurt him some more and then do it again." His smile remained but the tightness around his mouth belied his good humor.

Peterson clapped him on the back. "There are worse things." His face clouded over. I knew he referred to the officer under his command killed in the explosion that injured Ric. The somber moment permeated the room and I wished we could turn back the comments. I felt uneasy about staying alone but could hardly ask either of these men to spend the night.

Peterson clapped his hands together and lifted the mood. "So, we meet back here Friday morning to compare notes?"

"This kind of rehab lays me pretty low. I think I could be here in the afternoon."

"Make that late afternoon and it works for me." I explained my Spa Day and Luncheon on Friday. "How about six o'clock and I'll make dinner?"

The two bachelors perked up.

"Sure."

"Great. I'll pick you up so you don't have to hoof it."

"Yeah, I don't move so well after I dance around with *Attila*."

When they were leaving, I reminded Ric to use the honey tonight and tomorrow after his therapy. I dutifully locked and bolted the door behind them and shuffled back to the kitchen to clean up.

I wouldn't be able to sleep if I left dishes on the table. The few plates were tucked into the dishwasher but I still roamed the room swiping the dishtowel at imaginary crumbs.

I knew my jitters were escalating. The sensation in my arms, as though each nerve ending were tingling, was as familiar to me as my face. Through the years, when this happened, there was almost always someone there with me. My mom would sing to me and soothe my spirit, Karen would joke with me until I laughed, and Harry would hold me until I fell asleep. When no one had been there, the night had stretched endless as my fingers twisted, turned, tied, knotted until by morning the tips ended up scraped and bleeding.

This would be such a night. I had learned some tricks from a therapist. One was to wear gloves to slow down my frantic braiding and keep my fingers whole. I went to the mudroom and picked up a pair of thin riding gloves.

I didn't want to change, didn't want to wash up. I felt less vulnerable staying clothed. I took an afghan from the end of the couch, collected my scattered yarn from various spots, kicked off my shoes, and curled up on the couch. I lay on my left side, braiding, sighing, and finally crying silent tears long into the night.

THIRTY-FOUR

I STARTED AWAKE, sitting up in a tangle of blanket and yarn. Something woke me. I looked around and remembered I'd slept on the couch and not in my bed. The dream had forced me to wakefulness; horrible dream. In it I, but not me, only my hands, was swinging the bat at John Schoebel's head. I felt the thud as it made contact. That's what woke me. I looked down at my hands and realized I had dreamed of my hands wearing these gloves. Thin gloves. *Oh, my God!*

My hands flew up to my mouth as I thought about the bundled woman. I had said it earlier but it hadn't registered. Her wrists looked slender because that's all I could see. She wore gloves. I was certain that the woman I saw at the auction was intimately involved with this murder. My dream showed me a bigger woman than I, only with my gloved hands, swinging the bat. She had killed Schoebel. *Who was she? Oh, God, why was she hanging around here? Everyone else knew Harry was gone, surely she knew. Then it's me she's after.*

The matter-of-fact statement moved me to action. I needed to be thinking and talking clearly when I took all this to the police. I had inadvertently held back information that could help them pin this on the real killer.

I took the stairs two at a time and rushed into the bathroom to start the shower. Stripped naked I waited for the water to heat up. I twirled my heavy hair into a loose French twist and held it off my neck with a banana clip.

Hot water pulsed over my shoulders, loosening my tight muscles and twisted thoughts. The rhythmic movement of the water soothed my brain until I could gather my thoughts into a coherent pattern suitable for presentation.

Once out of the shower, my thoughts turned to other needs like grocery shopping for the dinner I promised Peterson and Ric tomorrow night, house cleaning, and research at the library. I dressed quickly. The other tasks could wait; facing Detective Garza couldn't.

Detective Garza greeted me pleasantly. He guided me to the same small room in which I had been questioned.

"Can I get you something to drink?"

"No, thank you."

"Have you remembered something, Mrs. Marsden, or has your husband contacted you?"

I figured the latter is what he was interested in; I hoped I wasn't going to disappoint him too much. "I thought of someone I saw at the auction, a stranger acting suspiciously." I waited for him to question me.

"There were a lot of strangers at the auction. Why this one in particular?"

"She was dressed oddly, like in a disguise. And she bid on the last trunk, the one with the body. She left the tent right after Schoebel did."

"So did your husband," he reminded me.

"I'm not making this up. Other people must have seen her. She was tall and bulky-looking only she wasn't big; her wrists were small. She wore big clothes and a floppy hat and gloves, all too big for her. Someone had to have noticed her."

To his credit, he had jotted down a few lines of writing. "I'll re-interview some of the witnesses in the tent. Unfortunately our only witness to your husband's argument is in the hospital."

"How is she?" He looked at me in surprise. I squared my shoulders and decided not to involve Sergeant Peterson. Garza apparently thought it possible I'd heard the news already. He answered me.

"Her condition is stable. Looks better for her but she's still unconscious."

"That's good. I mean that she's stable not unconscious."

Garza smiled. "Relax, Mrs. Marsden. We only want to find out the truth."

"I know the truth. My husband did not kill Schoebel. I'm worried that you're not looking anywhere else."

"So you brought in someone for us to chase?"

"Yes. I mean, no. Not chase but at least consider. Have you considered that the body in the trunk is Amanda Jhanson, a local girl missing since 1978? Have you considered that John Schoebel who was a pedophile lived in this area when she disappeared?" I didn't want to add my theory about Karl Deutsch yet.

"It may seem to you that we are concentrating on your husband to the exclusion of other leads, but I assure you we don't work that way. If your husband would contact us, we could clear up some questions like, why did he follow Schoebel out there, what did they argue about, did he see anyone else near them, how long before he left in his car, and a half a page more." Garza's voice seemed genuinely frustrated. "Mrs. Marsden, look at it this way. We can't clear him if we can't talk to him."

I hadn't thought of it that way. The rest of my conversation with the detective was conducted with a little less hostility on my part. I explained about my dad, the bat, the lock on the trunk and that the unknown woman had been seen in my neighborhood. That last bit seemed like news to him. Other than a small blip on his radar my narration seemed bland and boring to him.

He stood when he determined I had stopped talking and

put out his hand. "Thank you for coming forward with this information. We'll look into it."

I remained seated and automatically reached for his hand. I knew a brush off when I got one. My slack-jawed expression and slumped shoulders must have moved him to add more than the standard issue statement.

"Mrs. Marsden, I will look into this. If you think of anything else, remember more about what she looked like. If her disguise is for everyone to remember a big woman in odd clothes once she changes those clothes she disappears into the crowd. You could pass her on the street and not know her."

I left the station feeling slightly better. The short ride to the library gave me barely enough time to change gears and put on my research hat. The Lisle Library was a gem in the community. The programs were diverse, from *Writers Live at the Library* to a *Young Authors* program, from readers groups to writers groups, from pre-school to seniors-plus programs; if you couldn't find it at Lisle Library you weren't looking.

I breezed by the reference desk and nodded to Irene, the librarian I'd badgered with countless questions when I was rushed and couldn't do my own research. She was assisting someone and waved hello.

I usually worked at a carrel near the windows. I slipped off my jacket and set up my pens and notebook on the table.

Irene had finished helping her patron. "Hi, Grace. You sure know how to run an auction." She smiled.

"Tell me about it. You know how they say, 'If I'd known then what I know now'? Well, I would have shredded that research on the trunks, which, if I remember correctly, you helped me gather." My grin was a tad smirky.

"Oh, no. Don't get me involved." She held up her hands in mock surprise. "Seriously, if you need help with anything else, let me know." Her eyes gleamed with a coconspiratorial light.

"I will." I spent the next two hours searching through additional articles for information on the Jhanson family. These covered Amanda's disappearance, the search, and the dismal results. There was a mention of Schoebel as a person of interest who had been questioned and released. His alibi— a business meeting at the Hilton in Naperville—held up. A few months later a follow-up article about the family moving made the news.

I returned the materials and waved goodbye to Irene who stood knee-deep in young children on a field trip from Scheisher elementary.

Next stop: the county building. A great source of information for births, deaths, marriages, all kinds of records at my disposal.

The records department counter was empty. A good omen? I put in my request and waited for the materials. Most of the time research is the framework into which a result or event is placed. It's not fast-paced or exciting. Every now and then research discloses a jewel. I realized as I stared at the names on the marriage record that I had stumbled on such a moment.

THIRTY-FIVE

I FELT PLEASED with my efforts of the morning and stopped to treat myself to a coffee from The Coffee Depot before I shopped for the next night's dinner. I parked in front of Marino's Butcher Shop. The smell of spices and herbs filled my nostrils as I pushed through the door. The aroma from my Rain Forest coffee mixed well with the more exotic smells.

I asked for six thin slices of veal and prosciutto each. I selected three types of olives and roasted peppers for the antipasto and a pound of angel hair pasta to accompany the veal. I finished my purchases with feta cheese and a chunk of Romano cheese.

I left Marino's with a swagger. I had information to share and a great dinner to share it over. I'd thought of one more detail I could nail down at the depot before I went home. My swagger turned to a stutter step as I caught a glimpse of a bundled person pulling back between two of the buildings.

I started to follow but stopped, realizing I couldn't chase someone down a gangway with a sack of groceries in my arms. I put the bag on the floor in the backseat. I listened to the sensible part of me that was shaken and I didn't pursue her. Had she followed me or had our almost meeting been a coincidence?

A car on the street with its directional blinking waited for me to back out. I left the space without another glance at the gangway.

I knew from my notes that Joe, one of the volunteers from

the heritage society, would be at the Lisle Station Park. He'd been helpful when I researched the train station.

I parked on the street by Beaubien Tavern. That building was closed. The kitchen door of the Netzley/Yender house was open. I called out. No one answered. That left the depot. I crossed the grassy area that separated the buildings.

The door stuck a little but I could tell the building was open from the light inside. I called out again. The station master's quarters were at the far end of the depot. I walked through the old waiting room and down the small hallway to the kitchen. Sometimes the volunteers sat there.

I knew someone had to be about because the doors wouldn't be unlocked. I was startled to hear the telegraph key kick into action. I heard the tapping of Morse code. I only knew the basics my brothers taught me from scouting. I walked toward the front of the depot and used my best De Niro accent.

"Joe, are you talking to *me?*"

I stopped in the doorway. No one sat at the desk in the depot's office. The tapping continued, the key sending its message, it appeared, unassisted by human hands. Except I knew I'd find the human hand in the basement of Netzley/Yender where the other telegraph key was set up.

During Depot Days you could send a message from the depot to the house and pick up your telegram from the operator.

Joe must have seen me come in here. I had no idea what message he was sending but at least I knew where to locate him. I retraced my steps across the park. From this angle, I noticed that one side of the cellar doors lay open, flat against the ground. This was shorter than going into the house and down the stairs.

I stepped down the short flight into the lower level of the old house. My eyes hadn't adjusted to the dim light but I could see across the room, beyond the model train exhibit to the small desk in the corner. Joe sat at the desk wearing one of the station master costumes.

"Smart thinking, Joe. I don't know what you said, but here I am." A few feet away from the desk I felt a draft of cold air move in front of me and smelled dank, stale air. I stopped.

THIRTY-SIX

THE FIGURE AT the desk leaped up swinging. The air around me turned icy; movement froze and the silence thickened. I saw the bar coming at my head and raised my arms to block the blow.

I turned and took the full brunt across the top of my shoulders. The force knocked me to the floor. I landed on my right shoulder and rolled under the high, skirted table.

A scream pierced the silence. I heard footsteps running and then the slamming of the cellar door. The minimal light that had penetrated under the heavy cloth blinked out. I lay still, groggy and hurt. The temperature rose and I could feel the stuffiness replacing the icy cold. The dust that had been raised with my arrival now settled in my nose and lungs as I gasped breaths to calm myself. I needed to get out.

I carefully lifted the edge of the cloth and felt cooler air against my face. I scooted out on my back and rolled free. My head pounded and the room spun as I made it to my knees. On the floor nearby lay the costume jacket, scarf, and hat my attacker had worn. I slowly stood, running my hand up the wall to steady myself. I leaned against the wall and felt a sharp poke in my side. My eyes could make out the big square-head nail in the wall. My fingers felt fabric on the head. I touched my side; my jacket was intact.

Suddenly light flooded the basement and my eyes squinted in protest.

"Mrs. Marsden, are you down there?" a frantic voice shouted. I heard and then saw Joe barreling down the inside stairs. He reached the bottom and swung his head from side to side surveying the room.

I must have looked worse than I felt.

His eyes widened and he rushed to me. "Are you all right? Should I call an ambulance?"

"I think I'm okay; just need to sit down. And maybe a glass of water?"

He pulled the chair away from the desk and brought it next to me. "Here, sit down. I'll get you some water."

I didn't want him to leave. "No, don't go. I'm fine sitting."

He seemed to understand. "I came as soon as I heard your call."

"I didn't scream. That wasn't me."

"I didn't hear a scream. I meant your call over the line." He nodded his head toward the desk.

"What are you talking about? I didn't touch the key. I don't know Morse code well enough to send anything except SOS."

"This is strange. Let's go upstairs and wait for the police."

"Police?"

"Yes. When I came rushing across the park I saw one of the volunteers who'd been working in the garden. I told her to call the police."

I stood and followed him. He stopped when he saw the costume on the floor.

"What's this doing here?"

"The person who attacked me had it on."

"We've been looking for this jacket and the hat. It's been missing from the costume closet. There's a rip in the sleeve." He looked at me for an answer.

I'd forgotten about the cloth in my hand that I'd pulled from the nail. "Here, I think it happened when the person ran out." I handed him the cloth. In the light it was easy to see it matched the tear.

We were upstairs when the police arrived.

"Mrs. Marsden, are you all right? Do you need medical attention?" Nancy Royal asked.

I shook my head. "I'll be fine."

"Can you tell me what happened?"

I explained that I went looking for Joe and thought he had seen me enter the depot and starting sending a message so I'd know he was in Netzley/Yender. I told them about the person at the desk, the temperature drop, the way the swing looked like slow motion.

"That's what gave me time to get my arms up. Otherwise that bar would have taken off my head."

Royal had written quickly to keep up with my narration. She looked up. "Who screamed? You said you heard a scream?"

"I don't know. I guess I'm the only one who heard it. I do know it wasn't me. I was gagging on the dust balls under the table." I sat back against the chair and shivered despite the warm room.

"What is it, Mrs. Marsden?"

"The scream didn't sound like surprise or hurt, more like terror."

Royal turned her attention to Joe and asked for his statement. He told her he had seen me enter the depot and went there looking for me. He had gone around to the back by the kitchen. By the time he came to the front, I was gone. He stayed in the depot and worked on a new logbook.

"What made you go to the Netzley/Yender House?" Nancy Royal asked him.

"The telegraph started up and the message sent was 'help me.'"

"Did you send that message?"

"No. I don't know Morse code."

Nancy Royal looked at both of us. Joe seemed comfortable

with the dilemma. "Okay, so you're telling me you heard the Morse code spell 'help me,'" she pointed at Joe, "and you're telling me you didn't send the message. Is that correct?"

We both nodded.

"Who called 9-1-1?"

"Eileen from the garden club. She's in the kitchen with some of the herbs she collected."

Eileen wasn't any more help than Joe or me. She hadn't heard a scream. "I was out front in the garden. The basement walls are thick. Ava may have heard a scream."

"Ava Deutsch?" both Royal and I asked.

Eileen seemed surprised. "Yes. She was picking herbs and plants for the presentation she's making at our luncheon. She was gone for a while, I was about to see if she needed help with the plants she was preparing when she came from around the back of the house. She said she'd finished."

"Did she seem anxious to leave? I mean, did she look upset?"

"She's a busy woman with a busy schedule. Wasn't on the list for today, she stopped to pick her herbs."

"What are you saying, she wasn't scheduled to garden?" Royal asked.

"That's exactly what I'm saying. She hadn't even brought her long gloves."

Royal looked lost. I knew Eileen meant the gauntlet-type gloves that gardeners wore to weed or prune thorny areas.

Eileen stared at Royal for a moment then spoke slowly. "I thought I saw Joe earlier in the house, in his costume. I looked up once while weeding and saw him walking through this room." She waved her hand around. "I have to get these herbs trimmed, tied, and hung. Did you want anything else?"

"No, we're finished." She looked at me and shrugged. "I'll

stop in and ask Ava Deutsch if she heard anything but she was probably already gone."

"It was him."

Royal immediately shifted her look to Joe. "You know who attacked Mrs. Marsden?"

"Not attacked her, protected her. The station master. I wasn't in this house in costume."

"C'mon, Joe. That's an old ghost story you guys at the Heritage Society started telling to get visitors." She put up her hand to stop his complaint. "If your group didn't start it then the Chamber did.

"Somebody was down there and for whatever reason miscalculated the speed of the swing. He may have bumped into the telegraph equipment and when it went off, he dropped his coat and ran out. Or maybe he heard you shouting. Or maybe you really did scream, Mrs. Marsden, and don't remember because you were so frightened."

"The equipment doesn't 'go off,'" Joe grumbled. "I'm telling you, he sent the message."

"I'm telling you not to start any stories. There is a logical explanation and until I find it, I don't want to hear any new ghost tales around town; I'll have local kids sneaking in to ghost hunt."

She dismissed him with her tone and turned to me. "Are you okay to drive home? I can get a squad to take you."

"I'm fine. I'm planning a long soak in a hot tub."

"You look like you can use it. I don't know what's going on here but you've upset someone. This doesn't make any sense. Please go straight home and don't do any more investigating. By the way, why did you come here?"

"I wanted to ask Joe who was working that night from the society."

"You didn't think we asked for that same list and questioned them?"

"I was going to ask if they'd seen that bundled person. I figured you only asked if they'd seen Harry and Schoebel."

Royal shook her head. "Please, Mrs. Marsden, leave this to me."

ALL THE WAY HOME I thought about the cold air and the bar slowing in its forward progress. Could there be a supernatural explanation for what happened?

When Shakespeare wrote, "There are more things in heaven and earth than are dreamt of in your philosophy," he must have had this in mind. I knew better than to scoff. My mother had told me exciting stories of the little people and the fairies in Ireland. My Italian grandmother, a devout Catholic, placed a small twisted horn trinket over every threshold to keep out evil. I grew up believing there were angels in our lives. Had my guardian angel stepped in to help me? The thought comforted me even though any of Royal's explanations made more sense.

The entrance to Pine Marsh is a narrow two-lane road that crosses the only bridge of the seven in the complex that can support car traffic. The others are meant for foot traffic or golf carts. I saw the tire marks in the soft shoulder and realized that Jan Pauli must have been coming into Pine Marsh when she went off the road. Why would she be coming back?

I crossed the bridge and turned right to reach my side. The garage door went up slowly, revealing the interior foot by foot. Tires, chrome, license plate, Jaguar. *Harry!*

The wait for the door to clear my antenna seemed forever. I drove in too wide, had to stop, back up, and pull in again. I slammed the car into park and jumped out. "Harry!" I shouted his name expecting him to materialize. *He can't hear me. He's probably upstairs. Why did I spend so much time farting around this morning?*

My recriminations and footsteps stopped at the door. I read

the note twice before I burst into tears. *Grace, Walter and I brought the Jag back this morning. Thought it best to get it out of impound since they were finished with it. Call me if you need anything. David.*

I needed my husband. My sobs turned to shouts of anger and I brought my fists down on the hood of the Jaguar. "Where are you? You should be here. I need you!" I didn't feel any better. I ripped the note off the door and crumpled it into a wad that I flung at the car. *Yeah, that'll show him. Try a brick.*

I retrieved my groceries and hurried inside before my inner voice convinced me to do its bidding.

There were three messages on the machine. Gertrude had left a message about planning a baby shower for Karen and Hannah's baby. The other message was from Karen letting me know that they had arrived safely and would be meeting the officials at the state orphanage later today. The third message was completely unexpected. The caller had whispered an entirely cryptic and totally creepy message: *The bones are talking, listen to the bones. Older than you think more alive than you know.*

I saved the message and turned off the machine. I'd be sure to play it tomorrow for Ric and Peterson's better-trained ears. Crackpot call. *How'd they get this number? Couldn't be anyone I know. Why whisper? To disguise their voice, his or hers.*

I shook my head to clear those nagging questions and tried to focus on the success of my research today. I was buoyed by the knowledge that I would be contributing a juicy piece to the puzzle at the confab tomorrow night. Or, maybe it was meaningless; nothing seemed to be what it appeared. I quickly wrote a dinner menu and jotted down cooking times next to the entries. I rinsed and ripped lettuce and stored it in the crisper; arranged the olives on a rectangular platter using them as buffers between strips of Genoa salami, bite-sized chunks of feta cheese and rolls of prosciutto and artichoke hearts. Instead of toothpicks to secure the roll-up, I tied a thin strand of raffia around each morsel.

My thoughts strayed back to the murders and I found myself eating as I prepared. A handful of olives, salami rolled around the feta, a few artichoke hearts. At this rate there'd be none left for dinner. I needed a distraction from current events. I cleaned the cutting board, rubbing it with a piece of leftover lemon to remove the cheese odor, and threw out the oily containers and deli wrappers. Culinary duty complete, I traded my loafers for boots, grabbed a handful of treats and went out to the barn.

April and Cash whinnied their salutations and eagerly accepted their goodies. "Hi, guys. Been good today? 'Course you have." I could scratch each extended nose by standing between the stalls and stretching out my arms. "You're a good girl. Yeah. Good boy, good boy." I enjoyed the contact as much as they did, maybe more.

I brought them out on their leads and turned them into the small corral. I'd ridden April bareback many times. I swung onto her back and gripped her with my thighs and knees. Her body quivered in anticipation. April was the sweetest horse I'd ever known. What I loved about her was that each time I rode her she acted as excited as the first time. Impossible to find in human relationships.

I concentrated on the paces and patterns we practiced to perfection. April had a rough gait for a Tennessee Walker, a fact that almost sent her to her death by her previous owner. Her owner and I weren't on speaking terms so a friend had brokered the deal for my purchase of April. I didn't want her as a show horse; I wanted a friend. April seemed to relish the workout of loops and turns and I loved being able to "braid" the ground from her back.

Cash eagerly moved with us but without my thigh pressure to guide him we kept turning into him. He seemed to think that was the game and moved closer to us. When our pattern turned us from him he spun around and moved to the other side. I wondered if I could choreograph an equine ballet.

I'd lost track of time. The afternoon sun began fading and dark got pitch-black out here. I felt rested and calm; an easy peace that I found whenever I rode. That's probably why I dallied in the barn with them, brushing them down, chatting them up. I gave them fresh water and a little feed for the evening. Grateful whinnies and soft snuffles accompanied me to the door as I wished them a good night.

As I switched off the inside barn light I realized I hadn't left the back-door lights on and more distressing, I hadn't locked the back door. Darkness surrounded me and I froze. I waited until my eyes became accustomed to the inky black. Little by little the terrain between the barn and house came into focus. A sliver of a moon, which wouldn't be full until weeks from now, provided minimal illumination.

A chill crept around my feet, up my legs, and out across my arms into my fingers. I stayed still. Someone was near the back door. The gender of the person was indistinguishable. I didn't care; I wasn't going to make a move. Whoever it was moved in a stealthy manner which told me he or she wasn't here to borrow a cup of sugar. I carefully lifted April's lead from the peg on the wall. The metal clip on the end of the braided length of rope could do some damage if I had to defend myself.

The figure peered in the back-door window but didn't try the door. Instead it bent over and seemed to slip something under the door. My visitor blended into the shadows on the side of the house and disappeared.

My heart rate continued at breakneck speed. *What if he saw me in the barn? What if it's a trap and he's waiting for me to step out into the open?* I wanted to bolt for the safety of the house, but my legs felt rooted to the spot. I stood for minutes and snapped and unsnapped the clip. Eventually my heart stopped racing and my mind assured me that whoever had been there had left.

I walked slowly toward the house with my "weapon" down at my side. I opened the door and slipped inside. My fingers fussed at the lock until I heard the *click*. Only then did I look down.

A white envelope lay on the floor. I stared at the stationery, deciding whether to immediately call the police in case of fingerprints, or to look inside in case it turned out to be another red herring about Harry. My desire to help Harry won the mental coin toss. I did pick it up by the corner trying to avoid adding my fingerprints to the mix. The envelope wasn't sealed and the contents—a sheet of newspaper, folded in thirds like a letter—slid out onto the tabletop with minimal prodding.

I used two wooden spoons to unfold the paper. The tabloid-sized sheet was dated from 1978. Several articles were on the page but the one that drew my attention was the article on Amanda Jhanson. A school photo showed a sweet-looking young girl, with shoulder-length hair framing a heart-shaped face. Her eyes looked out shyly from under her bangs and her smile, closed lips perhaps hiding braces. I read the article under the picture. I'd seen the same photograph in the other papers I'd researched. This paper, dated a week after her disappearance, rehashed the story and the people who had been questioned. A new name popped out at me. John Reeder. He was questioned because he lived three doors from Amanda and had driven her home from school several times. He was older than she and that brought out speculation about his motives for the rides.

John hadn't mentioned any of this to me. Then again, why would he? That had to be an awkward time for him. Why was this article brought to my attention? Had John been somehow responsible for Amanda's death? Maybe he'd been attracted to her and felt she should be flattered by his interest. He may have felt snubbed when she preferred wealthy, privileged Karl Deutsch rather than him. What junior high girl wouldn't go for the gold? Surely Karl would have been the prize.

I sat down and began to rework the events in my head. I'd seen John at the auction. He could have been outside with Harry and Schoebel and heard their conversation. He knew Harry was out of town. Maybe he'd seen Dr. Weber right after he killed Schoebel and thought the doctor had seen something. He knew Dr. Weber was doing the autopsy. His store put him in a position to hear and know most everything that went on in Lisle.

My shoulders sagged as I considered the possibility of his guilt. A new scenario pushed its way into my head. Maybe he hadn't killed her. When the trunk revealed the body he realized that after all this time it had been Schoebel and he went a little crazy. Maybe he killed Schoebel and used what was at hand to frame Harry.

Either way, my calculations had him possibly guilty of two or three murders. Someone else must have added it up the same way. Why didn't that person come forward? I was almost certain that my visitor had been the bundled stranger. She apparently wanted me to know the truth, or at the very least suspect it.

I added the news article to my research folder. Tomorrow night's meeting would be interesting indeed. I left one light on in the living room and climbed the stairs to the bedroom.

Laundry and ironing awaited me. I counted my blessings every time I dragged the bed linens a measly twelve feet to the upstairs laundry.

I looked at the basket of ironing and estimated it as at least a three-cup pile. My own creature comfort addition to the room was a Mr. Coffee set up on one of the shelves. Up here I kept coffee packets for convenience. I thought about that article again while I prepared my coffee. Mr. Coffee would need a little more time than my brand new Krups in the kitchen. My other indulgence hung on the wall near the ironing board. Many an ironing session breezed by chatting with Karen or Tracy.

I lowered the ironing board from the wall and plugged in my steam iron; it would take a few minutes to heat up. The iron had belonged to my mom. The same one I'd used as a teenager living at home. With eight people in the house we ironed a lot. While we ironed we talked a lot and discussed, disagreed, and decided issues from birth control to the *Beach Boys*. After she died, my dad offered me whatever I wanted of hers. Along with the expected choices of china, linens, and such, the iron came home with me. Two cords later it still worked.

I smelled the Mocha Madness and poured my first cup. My ritual began. One sip before I picked an item out of the basket. One sip before I sprinkled it with water. One sip before I began to iron. From that point I couldn't take another sip until I finished. This was the only way I could iron. As a child the treat had been a vanilla wafer. My mom found she could focus my attention if I followed a pattern. I ironed with a pattern too. Back first, and next the front; button side first, then in and around, shoulders, sleeves, cuffs and collar.

My mind relaxed and floated easily as I performed this routine, mindless task. Somewhere between the second and third blouse, a sequence of events began to form in my mind. I didn't force a point or push a direction. I knew if I let go of the part of my mind that demanded precision and repetition it would gather the facts and thoughts in my head and separate the grain from the chaff. My brain had to put everything in order. The strands of logic were emerging from the tangle and pulling together to weave a pattern that made some sense.

The phone rang and startled me. I ran the tip of the iron into my left thumb.

"Ouch. Damn!" The phone rang again. I turned to grab the phone but I realized the ringing was from my bedroom; the second line on our phone.

"Harry! Oh, God, don't let him hang up!" I ran out of the room down the short hall into the bedroom and lunged onto the bed to reach the phone on the nightstand. My hand knocked Betty Boop off the edge in my hurry to lift the receiver.

"Hello, hello!" I heard the strain in my voice and tried to catch my breath.

"Grace, are you all right?" Harry asked sharply.

I took a deep breath. Hearing his voice did wonders for me.

"Grace, answer me." His tone raised in concern.

"I'm fine. I ran in from the laundry room. I was afraid you'd hang up. Harry, where are you? You've got to come home. All sorts of things have been happening. The police have to talk to you."

"Grace, I'll be home tomorrow night. I've talked to the police. Detective Garza graciously insisted on meeting my flight and giving me a lift home. Well, not exactly home."

Harry's dry humor usually appealed to me. Not tonight. "What do you mean? Are you going to jail?" My throat swelled and I felt hot pinpricks of tears behind my eyes.

"Darling, it's only a formality. David will get me home as quickly as possible. I am relinquishing my passport. I won't be a flight risk; I contacted them to turn myself in. I've so much to tell you. I've missed you. I'm sorry I wasn't there with you this week."

He paused, waiting for me to tell him it was okay that he'd

been gone while my life twisted like a leaf slowly turning at the end of a spider's thread. It wasn't okay.

"I understand," I managed to say between hard swallows.

"Gracie girl, I know you don't. But understand that you are the love of my life, no matter what. Don't ever doubt that."

His words snatched away whatever control I'd held. Tears streamed down my cheeks, small sobs caught in my throat as I clenched my lips together and inhaled short, quick breaths through my nose.

"Please don't cry, darling. I know this has been difficult, that you deserve better. Please, Grace, hold on one more day."

I managed to stop sobbing and cleared my throat. I loved what I heard and that gave me solace. I cleared my throat again. "How's Will? Are you two getting along?" How could I not ask him about his son? Hurt as I was, I couldn't ignore his desire for this new relationship.

Harry's voice warmed. "We're getting on splendidly. I can't wait for the two of you to meet." He paused and I waited. His voice sounded a tad husky when he spoke.

"It means a lot to me that you asked." Another pause. I heard him cough. "If I'm going to arrive tomorrow evening I had best be getting to it. I'll call you when I land. I'm sure the good detective will allow me my one phone call."

His sense of humor was in play again. "Good night, Grace. I love you."

"Ditto," I whispered. I struggled to hold back tears as I hung up. Didn't work. I rolled over onto my back and sobbed at the ceiling, feeling renewed tears sliding down my face into my ears and onto my neck. I reached across to my nightstand for tissues to mop my face. I sat up to blow my nose and a burning smell reached my nostrils.

My blouse.

Wisps of smoke curled around the base of the iron, which had burned down through my blouse and the padded ironing-board cover. The yellow padding seemed to be what was causing the smoke.

I yanked the plug from the wall and lifted the iron. The Teflon coating on the pad had transferred to the bottom of the iron. I put the iron in the washtub. The singed area glowed with tiny threads of embers. I wondered how much longer it would have taken for the threads to ignite the rest of the fabric. I used my sprinkle bottle to douse the triangular imprint.

What else can go wrong? No, God, don't answer that question.

I removed the blouse and pad from the ironing board and lifted it back into its niche. I walked back into my room to decide what to wear tomorrow since I had destroyed the linen blouse that went with the suit I had chosen. I selected a burnt-orange-colored long-sleeved dress and hung it on a wardrobe hook to air for the night. I checked that my tan pumps were clean and pulled the matching tan purse off the shelf. I carried the purse to my bed to load it up for tomorrow.

I'd used it on Saturday night. It had my auction booklet and some other pamphlets I had picked up during the event. I pulled out the literature. One of the pamphlets had photos of founding families; the old settlers on one page and the modern-day descendants on the opposite. A black-and-white photo showed the patriarch of the Deutsch family scowling from one side of the page. He stood next to a tall woman who had her large knob-knuckled hands on the shoulders of a young boy standing in front of her.

A color photo on the facing page showed two identical women in face only. The caption gave their names and the date they opened their store. If you drew a circle around their faces right along the hairline and under the chin you'd swear they were carbon copies. Beyond the circle the difference showed day and night. I'd never seen a picture of them together. Ava gazed slightly off center of the lens as though she was unaccustomed to attention. Eva stared at the camera with her lips slightly parted and a confident look like she knew she was the pick of the litter. Eva's confidence extended beyond her gaze. The photo was taken outside Antiques on Plank on either side of a decorative hitching post. Eva posed with her hand atop the post while Ava's hand barely touched the side. I noticed they both wore gloves. If they had inherited their grandmother's knobby knuckles I didn't blame them. They wore similar styled dresses but Eva's accessories made the outfit while Ava's lack of extras made hers look plain. The Ava that I saw at the auction seemed to have taken a page from her sister's style. I remembered thinking how smart Ava looked. When this picture came out she probably decided to go to Eva's hair stylist and seamstress. She still didn't have her sister's panache but now she at least looked like a wealthy do-gooder. What a contrast of appearance from two identical people.

Even Hannah and Harry exhibited a similar sense of humor, sense of high esteem, and style of movement. Ava and Eva looked like personalities switched at birth. I reminded myself that they were two-thirds of triplets. I couldn't help wonder if the sister who died would have been a perfect blend of both.

I left the pamphlets on the dresser to include in my Depot Days file and filled my purse with minimal necessities for tomorrow's luncheon.

Talking to Harry had calmed me in a way no sedative could. I knew he loved me. I never really doubted he did. Too much had happened over the last year and my brain had struggled to organize and make sense of the chaos. Harry would be home tomorrow night and everything would be fine. *Hang on, Gracie girl.*

THIRTY-SEVEN

BARB AND I COMPLETED our walk and agreed to meet in ninety minutes. We were riding to the tearoom together. I showered and dressed in thirty minutes. Even my usually unruly hair cooperated this morning. I used the curling iron to turn under my ends then used the big round brush my hair dresser had recommended and sold to me to smooth it out and curl it slightly forward. It seemed a pity to cover the tame curls with a hat but Barb had insisted that everyone would be wearing one. The cloche I'd chosen for my suit ensemble wouldn't work with this dress. I retrieved my straw sun hat from the mudroom, tucked the ribbons under the band, and safety-pinned an orange-toned floral wall swag around the brim. *Voilà!* Instant chic and still ahead of schedule.

With extra time I checked tonight's menu. *Omigod. Tonight's dinner. I can't have Ric and Peterson here. Don't want them here.*

I had to cancel. I didn't know what time Harry would be home but I believed him when he said David would fix it so he would be. I had Peterson's card and left a message for him on his machine. I knew Ric's number at Lily's house. He answered on the fourth ring.

"Hello."

"Ric, it's Grace. You and Peterson can't come over here tonight. Harry's coming home." I said it fast and firm because I knew Ric.

"Probably just as well. I feel like crap. Every muscle in

my body aches." He didn't sound like himself. No zing in his voice.

"I'm sorry you don't feel well. Have you tried the honey yet?"

"Yeah, I used it Wednesday night and twice yesterday and this morning. Smells wicked. You sure it didn't go bad?"

"Honey doesn't go bad. It might crystallize. I don't understand. Harry's hands felt better hours after he used it." I thought about how the bees had to approve the person benefiting from their honey. Maybe if you tricked them it worked against the person.

Gee, Grace. It's herbal honey not black magic.

"Grace. Earth to Grace." Ric had said something I totally missed.

"Sorry. What did you say?"

"I said maybe the person who gives the honey has to apply the honey." His voice still sounded off, but the comment was more like Ric.

"It doesn't work that way. Ever. Now be serious and make yourself some tea. And eat something, too. Maybe the honey would work better that way. Sweeten your tea with it and put some on toast. You need to eat if you don't feel well."

"Why, Gracie, I almost think you care." He chuckled.

"Stop being a moron and take care of yourself."

"Yes, ma'am. Will you check on me later? Maybe tuck me in?"

"No. I'll be busy." I stressed *busy* for his benefit. "I'll have your partner check up on you. Bye." I hung up before he could answer and called Peterson again to leave the second message that he might want to check in on Ric. Maybe the two of them could at least share their notes.

THE JEFFERSON HILL TEA ROOM, a stylishly renovated farmhouse circa 1845, anchored the elegant Jefferson Hill Shops. A second floor, pillars, and fan window, in Greek Revival style were added in 1900 by the Kendall family, a founding family.

Barb and I enjoyed afternoon tea there when our schedules allowed. Barb knew Kris Guill, the current owner, from several committees they'd worked on together. Kris's parents, George and Shirley Olson, purchased the mansion in the early seventies as their home. George ran his architectural firm from the mansion. Shirley opened a yarn shop on the first floor. The tearoom opened in the mid-seventies in the lower level. In the mid-eighties Kris and her husband, John, purchased the building and enlarged the tearoom and adjacent area using a plan designed by her father.

I introduced Hannah and Karen to the classic Victorian house and they instantly loved it. Hannah especially liked it because, according to talk, the top floor of the house was rumored to be haunted.

George Olson never noticed anything unusual but the young architects working for him hated working late into the night because that's when they'd hear the soft sobbing, a woman's lament. They reported that the sound seemed to come from all around them as though the walls, permeated with years of sorrow and grief, released their burden little by little in the night.

Mr. Olson had assured them that what they heard no doubt was the settling of an old house or wind flowing through chinks to reverberate through old ductwork. Nothing more.

Hannah's eyes had practically bugged out of her head when she first heard the story from Barb. She dragged Karen out to tea and spent an hour roaming through the lower-level floors enjoying the shops that rented space and finally walking upstairs.

Karen had recounted how Hannah had been disappointed at not hearing or sensing anything. Hannah felt she had a heightened awareness of the supernatural. Harry assured me in private that Hannah was as sensitive to the beyond as a fence post. We always had the most difficult time keeping a straight face when Hanns would launch into one of her "encounters."

Today the tearoom sparkled with crystal and china. Shell-pink walls and white iron garden furniture evoked a sense of serenity. Ecru-colored linen lay softly across each table. Matching napkins were rolled into a crystal ring wrapped with an artificial sprig of fall leaves. Each table held a clear glass vase filled halfway with smooth pebbles that held the stems of multicolored mums; a lovely centerpiece.

I followed Barb to our table. She greeted a few women on the way and introduced me. Everyone seemed pleasant enough. I looked forward to a fun day.

Two women were seated at our table.

"Good morning, June, this is my neighbor, Grace Marsden."

I thought the one woman, the younger of the two, recognized my name. Her eyebrows lifted slightly. I nodded and greeted both of them.

"This is my daughter, Jennifer Buckner. She's visiting."

We offered our condolences to both women.

I sat down next to June and listened while she chatted with Barb about projected attendance for the day. June Weber didn't disappoint my idea of the country doctor's wife. Her small-boned build, spry movement and gold-rimmed half-glasses reminded me of Irene Ryan's role of Granny on the old *Beverly Hillbillies* television program; quick, clever, strong-willed with a lot of common sense. Her white hair wasn't pulled back in a bun, rather cut short and layered to create a full cap of waves under her black pillbox hat.

Her daughter must have favored the doctor. She had excused herself to find the ladies' room. I watched her graceful movement across the room. She stood at least five foot seven or eight, and was probably my weight, which on her was considered slender. Her hair was cut in a similar style to her mom's and I wondered if these were new cuts. Her hat was also a small pillbox which I suspected her mother must have loaned her for the occasion.

June had spoken to me. I knew this because my mind registered that the background conversation had ended with an inflection and then silence. Also, Barb nudged my foot.

I looked at June and smiled. I felt the warm flush creeping up my neck. "I'm sorry, Mrs. Weber, I was lost in thought."

"That's all right, dear. Please, call me June. I was explaining to Barbara that I remembered you had called, wanting to speak to my husband. Did you ever get an answer to your question?"

I hadn't planned on bringing that up; not two days after she'd buried her husband. I wasn't sure how I should answer. "Um, yes, in a manner of speaking. I was able to research some old files."

A woman stopped at our table to greet us. She passed out program booklets for the table. "Our speakers are almost ready to begin. If you'd like refreshments, better get them now. They won't be serving during the presentations."

I stood up and offered to get refreshments.

"Thanks, Grace. I'll have herbal tea, whichever they have." I looked at June.

"I asked Jennifer to bring me a cup of tea on her way back."

"I'll be right back." There were quite a few women in line so I changed course to the ladies' room. I knew it was down a narrow hallway. I turned the corner and was surprised to see the outside door at the end of the hallway opened. I moved closer and saw Jennifer Buckner standing outside talking to a man.

More than talking, she appeared to be arguing. She stood with her back to me but it was apparent in the way she clenched her fists at her side that this wasn't a pleasant conversation. I couldn't see the man clearly from my angle. He stood about Jennifer's height and her hat perched high enough to effectively block his face.

When he stepped toward her, poking his finger high on her shoulder, I coughed and rattled the door to announce my presence. Jennifer whirled around, a look of apprehension on her face. She seemed relieved when she saw me.

"I was about to close the door. Glad I didn't lock you out." I smiled at her as though her tryst were perfectly normal.

The man who had been advancing on her turned away abruptly, mumbling, "Later, we're not finished."

Jennifer didn't respond. She moved slowly toward me. When she passed me I touched her arm. "Are you okay? Was he bothering you? Do you know him?" I was ready to call the police and about to tell her so.

"He was bothering me but I know him. He's my husband."

The look on my face must have encouraged her to explain.

"Things have been difficult with my dad's death and taking care of my mother. Lloyd doesn't understand about family. He didn't have a great childhood."

I didn't understand what she meant. "He's upset because you want to spend time with your mother?"

She blushed and shook her head. "No. It's about money. It's always about money. My father's will—" She stopped and took a short deep breath, not the kind you take when you're going to spill your guts but the kind you take when you're closing the subject and moving on.

"Forgive me for babbling. We should get back to the table. Were you going in or coming out?" She motioned to the ladies' room door.

I wasn't surprised by her change of course, only by how smoothly she did it. She looked as calm and pleasant as when we'd met fifteen minutes ago. "I'll join you in a few minutes. Please tell Barb I haven't forgotten her drink order."

At that comment her smooth demeanor shifted. Her eyes flooded with concern. "Please don't mention seeing Lloyd."

It seemed a little late to be seeking her mother's approval; they'd been married for years. Her eyes pleaded. I tried to read more into her request. Was he abusive? Did her mother know and want her to leave him? I nodded my head. "I won't."

She smiled and squeezed my arm before she left. I was good to my word about only taking a few minutes, but by the time I re-entered the room most everyone had taken their seats. The room looked like a field of wildflowers with colorful blooms nodding and bending in greeting to each other. True to Barb's prediction there wasn't a bare head in the crowd.

I quickly picked up two beverages and made my way through the tables, mindful not to bump the flora and fauna atop most heads. My brothers would have called it flotsam and jetsam. Three women had filled out the open spots at our table. I'd have to introduce myself during a break. Jan Pauli's place remained empty.

Barb gave me a "where have you been?" look and I flashed a smile. I caught Jennifer's eye. We exchanged a tiny nod. The obligatory tap on the microphone focused our attention on the mistress of ceremonies.

"Good morning, ladies. Welcome to our Fall Fling! I want to take a moment to acknowledge everyone who worked on…"

My mind wandered to my encounter with Jennifer as the M.C. droned. *Money. She said it's about money. No, she said it's always about money. That's a big difference. He's an ex-con, she's a successful businesswoman, maybe he's spending too much of her money. She mentioned her dad's will. If John Weber hated his son-in-law but loved his daughter, what would he do? What could he do, with his wife still alive?*

The polite applause lasted seconds as our speaker stepped up to the podium. "Good morning. My name is Helen Gurrie and I am thrilled to be able to talk to you today about preparing our bodies and beings for the winter months using massage, aromatherapy, and flower essence-based products."

I agreed with the massage. I wasn't sure about the other two. Busy volunteers moved between the tables distributing handouts and individual jars with our names on a label on the lid.

"What you are receiving now is a facial cream specially formulated for your skin type based on the cards you turned in. Has everyone received their jar?"

I had a jar with my name on it. I could only assume that mine was generic since, a late attendee, I had not filled out a card. I opened the jar and sniffed. "*Mmm,* gardenia," I whispered.

June lifted her nose out of her jar. "Mine's lily." She held out her jar to me and we switched. Barb opened hers and crinkled her nose. She passed it to me. Two of the women, Fran Ledbetter and Joanne Schuster, opened their jars, traded sniffs, then passed them around.

"Please don't open the jars until it is time for your facial. The contents are fresh and work better if you keep the jars sealed."

The other two who sat with their hands folded over their jars looked at June. She had been slow in passing the jars around and now all five opened containers were grouped in front of her. Jennifer, who was probably too preoccupied to care about the scent, giggled as her mother quickly grabbed lids, screwed them on, and passed them back.

"Since the response to this event was so high, we thought it best to divide the program in half. Ladies at tables one, three, and five will move into the adjacent salon for their facials, tables two, four, and six will remain seated to enjoy

Ava Deutsch's program about medicinal plants and common curatives. At noon we will enjoy our tea and then the tables will switch for their afternoon programs.

"Those of you moving to the salon, please leave your hats at your seats. Remember to bring your jars."

We were at table three. I dutifully left my homemade head-piece on the chair and followed the crowd to another level of the building that housed a salon. I admired the way the club involved several local businesses in this event. Nice planning; Schwarze and Krieg probably handled it.

Six young women, all wearing lab coats over black slacks, waited for us. The black stitching over the pocket of the coat spelled *Pour Vous*. They split our group. Half of us would get shoulder and neck massages and soft music, while the other half enjoyed facials and aromatherapy.

We went in pods of three with one clinician. I was in the first pod. She seated me, June, and one of the women who hadn't opened her jar, in comfortable leather chairs. She adjusted each chair-back so the top supported right below the shoulder blade. We had forty-five minutes per pod to enjoy a neck and shoulder massage and a paraffin wax hand treatment. As she finished each of us, she adjusted the chair to support our back and tipped the chair down. She ended each massage by placing a warm gel mask, filled with the scent of lavender, across our eyes.

When the third in our pod finished we were asked to relinquish our chairs to the next pod and so on until it was our turn for the facial. I was amazed and impressed by their ability to move us through so quickly. It moved like a cattle drive, but it felt so good I could barely *moo*.

As soon as the clinician applied my cream I knew it wasn't gardenia. I didn't want to make a fuss. I had Barb's. I remembered the pungent smell.

The facial could be booked as a religious experience: a

deep cleansing and removal of impurities, a stringent resolve
to stay pure, and finally, a calm soothing peace. On that
thought I must have drifted off. I felt a touch on my shoulder.

"It's time to move." The chair adjusted to a sitting position.
The soft voice belonged to the clinician. She smiled when I
focused my eyes.

"*Mmm,* another hour?" I sat up and took in a deep breath.
"Okay, I'll go peacefully." I stood up and felt the room tip a
little. I put my hand on the chair. "Whew. Little dizzy there."

"That can happen after a massage and facial. You may be
dehydrated. Let me get you some juice."

I shook my head. "I'm okay. Just a split-second swoon;
got up too fast." I smiled to show her how much better I felt.
"Thank you, it was wonderful." I put out my hand and folded
a tip into hers.

I heard a small cry and turned to see June slump back into
her chair. Apparently the dizziness had hit her too. I rushed
to her side.

"June, are you all right?"

She struggled to stand.

"Don't try to get up. I was dizzy too. It'll pass. I'll get you
some juice."

"I am a little late with one of my pills." She removed a
small ceramic box from her purse and picked out a yellow,
oval pill. "Maybe that's the problem."

Rachel appeared at my side with a glass of thick peach-
colored liquid. She handed it to June.

"Papaya. It will help."

June swallowed her pill and drank down the juice. She
seemed better. She stood up slowly and stayed up.

"Let's go back to the dining room. I think we need nour-
ishment."

She smiled and nodded. I offered her my arm. We walked
slowly down the hallway. "I guess these old bones are too

brittle for pampering. It's a good thing it wasn't a complete massage. They'd be moving me out on a gurney." She leaned toward me and said, "Don't tell Jennifer. She worries about me." June patted my hand to seal the deal.

I had news for her—they worried about each other. I nodded in agreement.

The presentation on medicinal plants and their curative benefits was well-liked if the applause we heard as we entered the room was any indication. We returned to our table moments before the soup course arrived.

A placard near the centerpiece described the garden-fresh luncheon menu. Squash soup, blended endive and red leaf salad, warm French rolls with shrimp cheese spread, chilled medallions of chicken served over dill rice, and for dessert, flourless chocolate cake. The menu sounded delicious. Too bad no one at our table got to eat.

THIRTY-EIGHT

JUNE WEBER TOOK a spoonful of her soup, gagged, and toppled out of her chair. Her body hit the floor with that kind of thud that tells you it was dead weight. Jennifer screamed and the woman on the other side of June pushed her chair back so hard she tipped forward out of her seat. Women rushed forward shouting.

I called to Barb. "See if you can help. I'll call 9-1-1." I pushed my way through the women coming at me. I heard Barb's voice above the noise requiring everyone to stand back and give June air. *Way to go, Barb.*

In my single-mindedness to find a phone I almost collided with Ava Deutsch.

"Sorry. Where's the phone?"

Ava gave me a peculiar look. Her eyes widened and her mouth opened slightly.

"June Weber has collapsed. Where's the phone?"

My urgent words wiped that look from her face and replaced it with one of action.

"In the hallway near the ladies' room. On the left side."

That would mean retracing my steps through the crowd of excited women.

Kris Guill approached Ava. "I called 9-1-1 from my office. They should be here any minute."

I heard sirens and was grateful for their quick response. June Weber hadn't looked good. The paramedics rushed her to Edwards Hospital. Two policemen arrived shortly after the paramedics. They asked everyone to return to their seats.

A second medical team checked each table to ask if anyone felt ill.

Barb and I returned to our table. June's place, marked by a yellowish stain around her tipped soup cup, had an ominously vacated look, like someone who had rushed away, never to return. Jennifer must be crazy with fear. First her dad, now her mom. I squeezed my eyes shut and prayed for her. I knew what it meant to lose a mother.

"Grace, are you okay?"

My eyes flew open. Barb's face showed concern. "I'm fine. Just thinking, actually, praying."

I looked around at what had been chaos moments earlier and saw groups of women at each table talking quietly or staring into space. Some women held their hats on their laps, some still wore them. I rolled my eyes up and saw straw. Barb had already removed hers and I did the same. It seemed frivolous.

A police officer approached our table. I had a feeling we'd be first. He smiled and waited for a police technician to collect June's soup cup before he sat down at Jennifer's place. "Ladies, I'm Officer Joe Walton. Can you tell me what happened?"

One at a time, we described what we saw. I told him that June wasn't feeling well when we returned from the salon. The woman who had fallen out of her chair confirmed that June looked sweaty. She thought maybe the steam treatment had affected her. I hadn't thought of that. Steam opens your pores but it could have an adverse reaction if you have high blood pressure. Wouldn't she have known that?

While the others were answering, I noticed all the soup cups were collected. No one else seemed ill. How could the soup affect only June? She couldn't have been the only one to eat it. We weren't the first table served.

Some of the women were staying to finish lunch and a

shortened afternoon program, probably most of the club members. Barb wanted to leave. *Fine with me.* We rode back to Pine Marsh in silence. I was surprised at how June's collapse affected me. I'd only known her for a few hours, but I liked her. In some ways she reminded me of how I thought my mother would have reacted to a "spa day" if we'd ever had that opportunity.

The change in the feel of the road signaled that we were crossing the bridge into Pine Marsh. I didn't see the ambulance tucked up at the top of Lily's driveway until we were in front of the house.

THIRTY-NINE

BARB PULLED OVER to the curb in front of the house. The paramedics were bringing Ric out on a gurney. An oxygen mask covered his face. Pete Peterson saw me and waved me up.

"Oh, my God, what happened?" I looked down at Ric. His eyelids fluttered when he heard my voice. With what seemed an enormous effort, he opened his eyes. His dark eyes looked fringed with gray like a frost creeping from within to freeze his life. His eyes closed. The paramedics lifted him into the back of the ambulance. One turned to look at me and Peterson.

"You go; I'll follow in my car."

I climbed into the back and barely sat down before the ambulance backed out of the drive and turned for the exit. I stayed out of the way as the paramedic connected leads to Ric that would send information ahead to the hospital. She finished and moved away, clearing a spot for me. I picked up Ric's hand. It was hot. I expected it to be cold like his eyes. The unexpected warmth made me feel better. I held his hand until we reached Edwards Hospital.

It wasn't until they were bringing Ric into the ER that I realized the driver had been one of the medics that answered the 9-1-1 call at Jefferson Hill. I approached him.

"I was at a luncheon earlier. You answered the call there, an older woman?"

"Oh, yeah. All the hat ladies." He looked at my head.

"The lady you brought in. Did she, I mean is she…"

He understood. "She was alive when we brought her in."

My shoulders relaxed. "Thank you."

"We barely finished the paperwork on her when we got the call for him." He jerked his thumb back toward the ER. He must have done a quick review of the circumstances in his head. "Oh, say, I'm sorry. Is that guy your husband…or something?"

"Something," I answered. I wasn't going to elaborate.

Peterson came through the ER entrance.

"What have they said?"

"Nothing, they put him in there." I motioned toward a cubicle. "What happened, Pete? Did he fall?"

"No. It's some kind of sickness. I got your message and went on over. He took forever to open the door; I was deciding how to break in when he opened it. He stumbled onto the porch and collapsed. His skin was hot but he wasn't sweating. He kept fading in and out; seemed delirious. I called 9-1-1 from the kitchen."

"When I talked to him this morning he complained about being achy and dizzy. I thought the physical therapy had wiped him out. Thank God you went there."

"I wouldn't have gone if you hadn't called."

A nurse who had been filling out a chart at the triage desk asked us a question. "Are you talking about the patient brought in from the luncheon?"

"No, we came in with Ric Kramer." Peterson pointed to the cubicle.

"I was at the luncheon where Mrs. Weber collapsed. Can you tell me about her condition?"

"She's been admitted to ICU. I'm sorry, unless you're family that's all I can say."

"I understand. Why did you think we were talking about Mrs. Weber?"

The nurse seemed hesitant now, as though she had spoken out of turn.

Peterson pulled his identification from his pocket and gave her the obligatory flash. "If there's anything you know you need to tell me."

Magic badge. It could have said "dog catcher" but it worked.

"I don't know anything. I overheard the symptoms you mentioned. They're similar to hers. I thought that's who you were talking about."

"I saw June Weber when they took her out. She was sweating profusely and not delirious." My tone invited her to respond. Apparently my tone didn't carry any weight. She merely raised her eyebrows in a "wouldn't you like to know" expression.

But I did know. Her look also said, "that was then, this is now," as if she had shouted it. Ric and June had similar symptoms only hours apart. That meant that they had the same disease. What kind of illness would strike a strong man in his thirties and a spry woman in her seventies?

Except Ric wasn't that strong anymore. He was on medication and his lungs had sustained damage from the fire, weakening his immune system.

June was on medication, too. She'd taken something during our spa time. Her age would be against her. They both seemed vulnerable.

I turned to tell Peterson my thoughts but he'd walked across the room to another desk. He stood on the visitor side and leaned over most of it to use the phone. He hung up the phone and nodded to the woman behind the desk.

"Who'd you call?"

"I've called for a detective to come out here. If I followed what that nurse said and didn't say, it looks like we have a coincidence. A big one."

"You mean both of them getting sick with the same thing? I thought so, too. I mean, what are the odds?"

"Exactly," he interrupted. "I don't like those odds."

And I didn't like the implication. Two people becoming sick from the same virus was one thing. Two people being *made* sick? That was bizarre. I didn't like bizarre.

FORTY

"GRACE!" THE WORD exploded from his mouth.

I whirled at the sound and stood open-mouthed as I watched Harry stride toward me. Several heads had turned at his shout but that was nothing compared to the looks that must have shot around the ER when I rushed into his arms.

I couldn't speak. My chest burned from holding my breath. I let the sobs and the air seep from my throat until I could inhale freely. His arms tightened around me. The warmth from his body mingled with the tension of mine and slowly relaxed me. He stroked my hair and murmured over and over, "Grace, forgive me. I'm so sorry. Forgive me."

I could hear the catch in his voice. His reaction was more serious than disappearing for six days. Had it been only six days? I lifted my head and looked into his soft blue eyes. "I was with Garza when he got the call. It said you were here."

I heard the panic in his voice. "It said you were ill, rushed from a luncheon. The message said it didn't look good. I begged Garza to bring me to you. God, Grace." He put his hands on either side of my face and kissed me.

I lowered his hands to my lips. "How awful for you. I'm fine. It's June Weber and Ric." My voice cracked on his name.

"Kramer's sick?"

I nodded and let go of his hands. "He looked terrible. I don't even know how to find Karen." Harry's look was a question. He didn't know yet. "They left for Europe to meet their daughter. She said she'd call when they were on their way back. I'd like to stay here…in case."

Harry nodded. "I'll stay with you."

Detective Garza, who had been respectful of our reunion, stepped forward now. "That won't work, Mr. Marsden. I only brought you because of the message. Since your wife is fine I've called for a squad to take you to the station so you can be processed."

Harry looked like he was about to argue, but caught Peterson's look and stayed quiet. He held me for a moment and kissed the top of my head. "I'll be back to sit with you as soon as I can." He turned to Peterson. "I want to hire you to stay with Grace until I can get back here. Will you do that?"

"That's already the plan." He shook hands with Harry. Garza escorted Harry to the waiting squad.

"Thank you," I said.

Peterson stared at me. I felt uncomfortable under his scrutiny.

"Like I said, already my plan." He didn't smile, only stared.

Garza returned carrying a tray with three cups of coffee and various packets. "I thought we could use some."

My hand reached for a Styrofoam cup. Peterson took his and then suggested we move to the waiting area. He put his arm around my shoulders to guide me. It felt wrong. I stopped walking and feigned looking around.

"Tissues. I need a tissue." I walked away from him to the nearest desk. Hospitals always had tissues. "May I?"

The nurse nodded and I pulled two from the box.

"Okay," I said briskly as I sat down between Peterson and Garza. "I'm all set."

"Mrs. Marsden, you were at the luncheon. Did you see anything unusual? Did Mrs. Weber eat anything different from the other women? Drink anything different?"

I sat still and closed my eyes to reconstruct the day from the moment I met her. I walked my mind through the two hours I'd known her. I opened my eyes, prepared to answer.

"She took some kind of medication and drank a glass of papaya juice. That's the only thing different."

I hoped he wouldn't ask about anything unusual. I didn't want to tell him about Jennifer and her husband. It couldn't have anything to do with this and I didn't want her to be bothered by this bulldog with a badge.

"Good, I'll have that checked. Anything unusual happen?"

My hesitation was a giveaway if my eyes weren't already purple.

"Mrs. Marsden?"

"I saw her daughter having an argument with her husband. They were in the little courtyard outside the back door."

"Could you hear the argument?"

"Not really, mainly mumbling." *That's not lying. He asked if I could hear the argument.*

"Did her daughter see you?"

"Ah, yes. I made a noise so they'd notice me. He left and she came inside."

"Did she offer any explanation for the argument?"

This guy is good.

"Yes. She said it was about money."

"What about money?"

"I don't know any more. She stopped talking about it and asked me not to tell her mother."

"Nothing else?" He waited with his pen poised over his notebook.

"Nothing."

He stood up. "Thank you, Mrs. Marsden. If you think of anything that might connect Mrs. Weber and Mr. Kramer, please call me."

I watched him walk away and realized that as much as I disliked him I didn't want to be alone with Peterson who acted so different from the man I'd met almost a year ago. He'd always been so cheerful and sweet. Maybe becoming involved with *Mayhem & Murder, Inc.,* as Ric once referred to Harry and me, had soured his disposition.

I bounced out of my chair as he pulled his closer. "I'm going to get another coffee. Can I bring you one?"

"I'll walk with you. I've got something in my car I want to show you. I'll bring it in."

At least he didn't ask me to go out to his car. We parted company in the foyer. I found the vending machine and hunted in my purse for change. I knew I had quarters. I was still fishing around, about ready to dump the contents on the table, when I felt someone behind me.

"Allow me." Peterson leaned forward and to the right so he could drop in four quarters. His head leaned close to mine. I kept my head down and my eyes focused on the opening in the vending machine. I watched the cup drop, the coffee fill and pulled it out as soon as the last drop dripped. I hurried back to the waiting room wondering how to handle this new development.

Jennifer Buckner walked toward me. She seemed to be moving on automatic pilot, her feet carrying her while her eyes saw nothing.

"Jennifer? It's Grace Marsden. We met this morning."

She focused on me and nodded.

"How is your mother?"

"Not good. They don't know what's wrong. I needed to stretch."

"Here, sit over here." I led her to the table. "Take this, I haven't touched it." I guided her hands around the coffee cup. She took a sip and put it on the table.

"Thank you." She seemed to notice our surroundings for the first time. She looked at me in confusion. "Why are you, I mean, did someone else from the luncheon get sick?"

"No. A friend of mine was brought in right after your mom. He's sick too. The symptoms are similar."

Peterson sat down at the table. He balanced two cups of coffee on top of a sheaf of papers. I reached for the cups and set them down. He must have seen me give up my cup and have gone back for another. This was the Peterson I remembered. I started to introduce him to Jennifer, but realized it wasn't necessary. I'd forgotten he'd grown up in Lisle.

"Hi, Jen. Been a long time."

"Pete. It's good to see you." She looked at both of us.

"My friend is his partner." I figured the simpler the better. I also figured this was my chance to try and find out Ric's condition. I left them to catch up.

My encounter was of the prickly kind. The charge nurse didn't care who I was, but rather who I wasn't—a relative. She refused to give me any information. She would only repeat that he had been admitted to ICU.

I felt the frustration first as a tingling in my fingers and then as a twitch that had to be acknowledged. I sat down with my feet tucked up under me on one of the couches, no easy accomplishment in a sheath dress. I closed my eyes and tried to take calming breaths, keeping my head back against the cushion. Sometimes if I could relax fast enough I could calm the urges.

My brain whizzed along a path above the quagmire of this week, touching points then skittering away before it became entangled. My obsessive mind demanded order. I kept taking deep, cleansing breaths, forcing my brain into slow motion. Slowly, a pattern emerged. Greed; more greed. Fear; more fear. Death; more death.

I sat up quickly, certain I was on to something. My thick hair swung forward across my face when I rubbed my temples with my fingertips. Instinctively my fingers moved upward through my hair and down to the ends where I could twirl the strands between my thumb and first two fingers. I sat with my feet flat on the floor leaning slightly forward, staring at the low table covered with magazines. The more I twisted my hair the more a pattern emerged. The more a pattern emerged the harder I twisted my hair.

I winced when I twisted a few strands from my scalp. *Stop it. You're losing control.* Like I didn't know. A bright orange length of cording plopped on the table.

"Try this, darling."

Harry stood before me. I jumped up and bumped around the table to reach him.

"Is everything done? Are you free?"

"I'm free to stay in town. David had everything arranged when I arrived. I went home to change and bring you something more comfortable." He held out a bag.

"Perfect. I was going crazy in all this." I waved a hand up and down the front of me.

"Funny, I was going a little crazy looking at you in all of that." His grin filled me with joy. I stretched up to kiss his mouth. I had intended a quick smooch, but the hunger I felt on his lips drew me into a long, hard kiss; its intensity taking both of us by surprise. The look we shared confirmed the feeling.

"I'll be right back."

"I brought the files and notebook I found on the counter. Looks like you've been sleuthing. I need to know what you've been up to."

I opened the bag and pulled out the files and swollen notebook. "Peterson has some files too. We, Ric, Peterson and me, were going to meet tonight to compare our research."

"I can't believe those two would let you get involved in a murder investigation." Harry's voice raised in anger. "What were they thinking? Especially Kramer; I thought he…knew better."

I swallowed hard knowing what Harry had been about to

say. Now was not the time to defend anyone, including myself. I handed the files to Harry. "Give me five minutes."

Safely locked in a stall in an empty restroom, I leaned my
forehead against the metal door. Slowly, without complete
awareness, I lifted and let my head fall against the door. *One,
one thousand, two, one thousand, three, one thousand, four,
one thousand.* The thumping sound filled my head with calm;
forced the scurry in my brain to slow.

Harry had moved to where Peterson and Jennifer sat. I noticed that Peterson had moved his chair so close to Jennifer's
that their thighs touched. *So much for worrying about him;
looks like he's moved on.*

I sat down next to Harry and immediately put my hands
around one of the cups of coffee on the table. I felt this would
be a long night. I apologized for taking so long.

"No problem. I'm getting Harry up to speed." Peterson
shuffled some of his papers into a different order.

Harry sat with his hands in his lap, his gaze fixed on the
papers in front of him. He was either furious with me for
getting involved or furious with himself for abandoning me.
When he looked at me I knew. The remorse I saw in his eyes
caught at my heart. He'd let me down, in a big way, and he
knew it. The part of me that I hoped went only skin deep
wanted to see him stew. The better part of me couldn't stand
to see him upset.

I slipped my hand under the table and lifted his left hand
from his lap and up to my face. I rubbed my cheek against
the back of his hand. "You're here now. That's what matters."
His eyes thanked me.

Jennifer cleared her throat and stood up. "I'll be right back.
I want to let the nurse know I'm out here."

Peterson sensed good timing. "I've spent some time com-
bining Ric's research and my notes. We've got a timetable
for the events, but gaps in our theories. We know Schoebel

was a convicted sex offender. We think he killed a young girl who went missing the summer of 1978. I was away courtesy of Uncle Sam when that happened. My mother was living in Oak Park by then but I remember her writing something about 'kids not being safe anywhere.'

"That would be the time frame of when the trunks were stored at the antique store on Ogden and the Book Nook News. I found out that Schoebel did some work for both places. He could have made extra keys or he might have been in the store and knew the girl from town. Eventually, everybody goes to the Book Nook.

"My money is on him killing the girl there. Kids always thought the basement was creepy but kind of cool. I remember a few of us getting in trouble when we tried to sneak down there to look at the rumored grave. There's a section in the basement left uncovered by cement to provide access to the water pipe. As a kid we liked the grave theory better.

"It would have been easy to lure Amanda to the basement and kill her. Using the trunk was easier than trying to carry her upstairs and out the door. The report never mentioned a search of the basement. She was supposed to be with a friend on the other side of town when she disappeared. That friend told the police that Amanda had been acting strange, not spending as much time with her as a best friend should. The police searched the homes and wooded area in that neighborhood, but had to consider the runaway theory, too."

Peterson stopped talking when Jennifer returned.

"My research came up a little different." I opened one of the folders. "The receipts weren't clearly marked on which trunks we retrieved from which location, but I think the two high trunks came from Antiques on Plank. Also," I paused to make sure I really wanted to put this on the table, "I think that Amanda could have been killed by her boyfriend Karl Deutsch and her body hidden in the trunk."

"Karl Deutsch?" Peterson's surprise wasn't as complete as I thought it would be. He looked like he was considering the idea. "I did hear he was her boyfriend."

"John Reeder told me he noticed a change in Karl that summer. Told me—"

"Excuse me?" Jennifer's voice interrupted. "Are you talking about Amanda Jhanson? If you are, you're wrong. Amanda's not dead or at least she wasn't that summer."

Mine and Peterson's looks must have been mirror images. Neither of us found our voices before she continued.

"It's true she disappeared, but she turned up in some hippy colony in Florida. Ran off with three kids she'd met earlier in the summer. She got pregnant by one of them. The family didn't find out she was alive until five or six years later. They moved to Florida to try and convince her to leave the commune. I think by then she had three children. Amanda was over eighteen; she stayed. Her mother essentially wrote her off and tightened the reins on the younger sister. I don't know who's in the trunk, but it's not Amanda."

I sat back in my chair. "How could people not know this? Why wasn't there an update on the computer site?"

"I only know because Mrs. Jhanson confided in my father. She wanted him to drive to Florida with them and examine Amanda to see if she had been drugged. I guess they thought they could involve the police. Once they determined her lifestyle and the possibility that she worked in the commune growing marijuana, they kept quiet for fear she'd be arrested and convicted."

"The report said she was missing, a possible runaway." Peterson rubbed both hands over his face. "If the body isn't Amanda's then what's Schoebel's involvement with any of this? Or Deutsch's?" He tilted his head toward me.

"Whose body is it? The other missing person, the seventy-two-year-old?"

I shrugged my shoulders. "We're back to square one. For all we know the skeleton could be the remains of the sobbing spirit that haunts the Jefferson Hill mansion."

"If it is, that would leave Schoebel out; he wasn't that old." Peterson's face registered the chagrin I felt.

Harry spoke up. "I don't think we can leave Mr. Schoebel out entirely." His tone was tentative like he was thinking things through as he spoke. "I walked outside to talk to him after the trunk was opened." Harry turned to me. "Sorry I popped out on you but I saw Schoebel take a key off the ring he was holding. He looked around as though he wanted to hide it somewhere. He caught me looking at him. I followed him outside to ask him why he wouldn't open the trunk. I knew he could have. I thought he might have had an idea of what was inside.

"He looked a mess. Extremely nervous, biting his lip, shifting from foot to foot. I knew he had to be involved. I asked him for the key he took off the ring. He said he couldn't talk to me there but to meet him in a half hour at the back entrance to Antiques on Plank. I couldn't get him to budge. I certainly didn't raise my voice. I don't know why anyone reported otherwise. Who did report it?"

"Our new cleaning lady; well, almost cleaning lady."

"What?"

"It's another long story. Jan Pauli was going to be our cleaning lady but she backed off the job when I insinuated that Ava Deutsch could somehow be involved. She was appalled that I would drag the good lady into this mess. She reported seeing you argue with Schoebel."

"I'd like to talk to her."

"Me too, but she's in the hospital, here in fact. Her car went down the embankment coming across the bridge to Pine Marsh. She's in intensive care."

"How convenient." Harry's tone sounded skeptical.

"Oh, that's not all. I found out that Schoebel and Pauli were married."

"Our prospective cleaning lady was married to the sex offender that I ran down? This is too much coincidence."

"They weren't married long before his first conviction."

"First conviction?" Jennifer's voice quivered. "He had more."

Peterson answered. "He served three years for his first conviction and while still on probation he violated his parole by molesting a twelve-year-old girl. He did fourteen years at Joliet. When he got out he moved to Lisle and became a model citizen until his death. However, when they searched his apartment after his death they found videos of child pornography. They checked the photos for local kids. No one from the area, he bought the sick stuff, didn't produce it."

"He worked at Jan Pauli's company. She'd gone on to build a successful company after her divorce. I don't know if she felt sorry for him or wanted to keep their marriage a secret. After meeting Jan, I'd say he blackmailed her to keep her secret."

"How much of a secret was it? You found out." Jennifer had a point.

I thought about it and slowly a reason formed. "I wondered about that, too. No one would go looking for that connection unless it would be news. I heard that Jan Pauli retired early from her company, sold it to someone who was going to take it public. What if she was concerned about disclosures or information that would come out if she took her company public? It wouldn't look good to have an ex-husband who was a convicted sex offender on the payroll. When she sold her company, he lost his job.

"We know he had an income stream from somewhere or someone. The story I heard was that Jan is an eccentric and loves her free time and that's why she chooses to clean houses. She has an innate business sense and has built up her cleaning service. She may have been paying him to continue his silence. Who would hire a cleaning lady with a convicted sex offender for an ex-husband?"

"And who could open locks," Harry added.

"Wow, I hadn't even thought of that."

Peterson took a deep breath and exhaled. "I think the Lisle Police should be looking at Jan Pauli as a suspect in Schoebel's murder."

The surprise on my face must have shown.

He continued. "Think about it. She was at the depot that night. She may have heard him tell Harry that he had something to tell him, show him. Maybe he was going home to get a copy of their marriage license." He looked at me; his voice took on an excited tone. "You said you found a record of their marriage. Did you look for a record of divorce?"

I caught the excitement. "No, I didn't look. I assumed she divorced him when he went to jail."

"An ex-husband jailbird is one thing, but a current one is different."

Jennifer's gasp wasn't loud, but we all heard it. In that instant I remembered that her husband had been incarcerated for some kind of fraud. Peterson must have realized it, too. He swiveled to face her.

"Jenny, I'm sorry. I wasn't thinking." He looked desperate for her understanding.

Her eyes brimmed with tears but her voice held firm. "It's all right. I know you didn't mean to hurt me. I understand why this woman would try to keep that secret. I always die a little when my husband's past surfaces. In a sense, I'm doing exactly what she did; paying him or at least providing him with a lifestyle he couldn't afford on his own."

She bowed her head and I could see tears slipping down her cheeks. I slid a napkin across the table to her.

It took enormous courage for her to speak up. This was a

woman of values and ethics who took her marriage vows seriously even though she'd been yoked with the tremendous burden of disappointment and regret.

Peterson slipped his hand over hers. His attention didn't appear to be the awkward flirting he'd tried with me. His intent seemed sincere. I smiled at what I sensed might be a beginning for them.

Harry picked up the thread of the newest theory. "If this Pauli woman killed him, is she the one who broke into the office to steal the file on Schoebel? Is she the one who trashed our kitchen? Why?"

"If she wanted to keep her marriage a secret, she might have thought I had some information about it. Liz kept bragging to everyone how I ferreted out the trunks. She teased that no secret would stay buried with me on the trail. I thought it was funny at the time, but maybe Jan took it seriously."

"How many people knew about your powers of research and persistence?" Harry smiled at his words.

"Liz brought it up a lot. The *Naperville Sun* did a story on the event and gave me some space; how I found the trunks, my background as a reference librarian, that kind of stuff. I think Liz was excited by the unusual circumstances in our lives lately. She thought I led an interesting life, until she thought I was weird and fired me."

Harry's eyebrows lifted.

"I'll tell you later."

"So, everyone knows you are a good researcher. Pauli doesn't want that bit of info coming to light so she breaks into the office to remove any notes on her and Schoebel. The story probably came out right before the event so she wouldn't have known you might know until then. How did you meet her?"

My voice raised in excitement when I answered. "She was waiting downstairs at the office building supposedly to clean up the mess once the police left. She let me know she cleaned houses early in the conversation. Do you think she's the one who broke into our house?"

Peterson and Harry both nodded their heads.

"It makes sense, darling. She wanted to make sure you didn't have anything at home."

"It doesn't make sense. Only the kitchen was trashed. Nothing was touched or missing anywhere else. And if someone were trying to remove something in secret, why make a mess? It was the same at the office; only when we cleaned up did we realize that papers and folders had been moved."

"Like someone wanted you to find something that you'd ordinarily have no reason to find?"

I looked at Harry and answered slowly. "Yes, exactly like that."

"What is it? You've an odd look on your face. What else did you find?"

I didn't know how Harry could read me so well. I'd always blamed the Druids in his ancestry.

"After the second break-in, I found a key in the mudroom."

Harry turned to Peterson. "You told me there was one break-in."

"Actually three. Jan claimed she found the prescription bottle of warfarin sodium in our kitchen. When Jeffers and I walked in she had it in her hand. He took the bottle to the lab. I never got a chance to tell anyone about the mudroom. I thought it was Jan Pauli."

"Jan Pauli again. I'm liking her better and better for this murder."

"Peterson, this doesn't wash. If she killed Schoebel who ran her down and why? Sounds like whoever killed the doctor," Harry paused to look at Jennifer. He inclined his head slightly in respect, "may have run down Pauli. Same M.O."

Peterson turned to Jennifer. "I found out something from

your father's autopsy. He was struck by the car but that isn't what killed him."

Jennifer crushed the napkin she'd been holding between her hands. "What do you mean?"

"The report showed that your dad bled to death. The M.E. thought it a little odd that there was so much blood loss based on the injury. He ran additional tests and found a high level of Coumadin in his blood."

"My father took that for his heart. It's a blood thinner—" Jennifer looked at me. "Did you say the bottle said 'warfarin'?"

I nodded.

"That's a generic name for Coumadin."

Jennifer's face crumbled into sobs. "Oh, my God. Oh, my God." She put her head in her hands and moaned. I jumped up and went to the water fountain with my cup. I dumped the contents and filled it with water.

Peterson had his arm around her trying to calm her. She kept rocking and moaning. I put the cup down in front of her and Peterson tried to get her to sip at it. Jennifer lowered her hands and accepted the cup. She took a gulp and immediately coughed, dribbling some of the water down her chin. I expected more tears. Instead a pained, but clear look appeared in her eyes when she spoke.

"I don't know about the woman, but I know who killed my father. It was my husband." She stated that as matter-of-factly as if she were commenting on the weather.

"Jenny, you're upset. I understand that—"

"You don't understand. When we got here last week Lloyd and my dad got into a huge fight over the usual—that Lloyd was living off me. The tension made it impossible for us to stay; we moved to a hotel.

"My father was furious with an investment that Lloyd had made without telling me. I found out about it after he'd lost thousands of dollars. I shouldn't have told my father. Dad said he knew of only one way to make sure Lloyd couldn't lose my inheritance and that was put it in a trust for me and my mother.

"Lloyd went crazy, ranting and raving about my dad and his 'holier than thou' attitude, his 'too good for my little girl' attitude. Don't you see?" She turned to look squarely at Peterson. "Lloyd was a pharmaceutical salesman. We were in their home on and off during the week. He could have switched the pills, the dosage. With the Coumadin levels too high, a hard bruise could cause internal bleeding.

"I thought Lloyd was trying to make amends, be considerate of my feelings when he sided with me on not wanting an autopsy done. Now I know why. Oh, Dad." She broke at that point and put her head down on her forearms.

Harry motioned Peterson to lean toward him and he lowered his voice. "Best call your contact at the station. They should be alerted."

Quiet as he was, Jennifer's head shot up. She wiped the tears from her face using the backs of her hands. "Wait. If he did that to my father, maybe he did something to my mom?"

It was something to consider. He had been there. The argument made sense now. She'd said: *it's always about money.* "I know he was there, but how could he have done anything? You're thinking poison, right? No one else has become ill; other than Ric."

"Kramer has the same illness?"

"It looks like it. There's no link between them. None."

"No apparent link. If they have the same symptoms there has to be a link."

Peterson had left the table. Harry moved his chair to face Jennifer.

"Anything different with your mum this week? Did she receive anything in the mail? Try a new product?"

Jennifer kept shaking her head. "Nothing. We had our hair

cut for Dad's funeral, but that was three days ago. Nothing. Today's luncheon was the first thing we did since his death."

"The facial. Your mom had a facial today."

"Grace, that won't fit. Ric didn't have a facial."

There had to be a connection. Harry put his hand over mine. I felt the calm from his hand. *His hand. That was it!*

"It's the honey." I nearly screamed in my certainty. "It's the honey. I gave the honey to Ric to use. It was in the kitchen cabinet. He said it smelled funny. I didn't give it a thought. Someone put something in the honey. We've got to get it and have it tested."

Peterson walked into the room accompanied by Sergeant Royal and Detective Garza. He led the way to the table. "I was on the phone with the station when they walked in."

He introduced Jennifer to them and pulled over two more chairs. They remained standing. "I'd rather do this at the station." Nancy Royal looked sympathetic but firm.

Jennifer and I both shook our heads. "I'm not leaving my mother."

"I'm staying too."

Royal and Garza exchanged glances and sat down. Garza pulled a report from his pocket. "When Mrs. Weber was admitted, she had a small container of face cream in her purse. We're having it tested. We were told all the attendees at the luncheon were given one?"

"Yes," I answered. "The women had filled out some type of questionnaire about their skin and the herbalist created a PH-balanced and appropriately scented face cream for them. I was a last minute attendee so mine was generic; smelled of gardenia."

"Wait. Yours smelled of gardenia? How did you know it was yours?" Nancy Royal leaned forward.

"My name was on the lid. Each person's name was on their lid." I felt the blood drain from my face. They noticed.

"What's the matter, Grace?"

"The lids. At the table we opened our jars. Several of us including June passed them around and sniffed them before we were told not to open them because they would lose moisture and freshness. I knew mine was gardenia. June put the lids on and gave them back. When they did my facial I thought it didn't smell as much like gardenias; smelled more like the one Barb had but I didn't want to make a fuss."

"You're saying your jar ended up on Mrs. Weber?" Royal knew how to turn a phrase.

I looked at Jennifer. I nodded my head.

"Gracie, you're the link." Harry's voice was so low I almost didn't hear him. "The cream and the honey. They were meant for you." His eyes glinted with anger and his face hardened like stone. I felt the cold fury. Everyone did and I'm sure they were thankful it wasn't directed at them. "Some sick bastard tried to poison you."

The blood left my face before it rushed back with a vengeance. I felt the heat and pressure as the blood surged through my head. I heard Garza asking where the honey was now and Peterson answering. I heard Royal use the radio on her jacket lapel to contact someone about getting ready for another lab test.

Then it went quiet.

FORTY-ONE

I FELT THE cool cloth on my head and a gentle stroking on my cheek. I opened my eyes knowing I'd see Harry. His stony visage had been replaced by concern. He smiled and leaned forward to kiss my cheek.

"Gracie, girl. You had me worried."

I tried to smile to reassure him. My lips couldn't make the curve; they flat-lined and I clamped them tight to keep from crying. Scary enough that someone wanted to hurt me, but two people had become ill, maybe would die because of me.

"*Shh,* it's not your fault."

No one was in the cubicle with us. He gave me another kiss and then pushed aside the drawn curtain. "She's awake," he said.

A nurse came in and lifted my wrist. She timed whatever it is they time and lowered my arm to the bed. "Pulse is fine. Any pounding or dizziness?"

"No. I feel fine. I'd like to get up."

She helped me into a sitting position and swung my legs over the side. "Stand up slowly."

I did as I was told. "Thank you."

She smiled and left the cubicle. Harry put his arm around me and we went out to the waiting room. Everyone who'd been there before I fainted had left. Peterson and Garza left for Lily's house to retrieve the honey. Royal went to check on the warfarin and Lloyd. Jennifer returned to her mother's room.

We were almost at the table when I glimpsed someone moving down the hallway.

"Harry! That woman. She's the one from the depot. Stop her!"

My cry alerted her and she ran for the door. Harry's stride overtook her quickly and he grabbed her from behind. She struggled to free herself.

The nurse called security and within seconds a guard helped Harry subdue her. She had quieted and seemed resigned to her capture. She looked bigger in the long cape and cowl collar that she'd turned up around her ears.

I walked toward her hoping that answers would be forthcoming. Instead, only more questions.

"MAEVE? WHAT IN heaven's name are you doing here?"

Harry turned to me. "Grace, why did you shout for me to stop her? It's Maeve."

"Who?" Then I remembered the bee lady.

Security hadn't let go of her arm. "I'm sorry, officer," Harry started, "We know this woman, there's no problem. My apologies."

"Be more careful next time. Got everyone worked up." He let go.

"Thank you. Come with me, Maeve. You've some questions to answer."

One question was answered when she turned around. I looked into the face of a Deutsch.

I could hardly contain myself but I stayed quiet until Harry brought her to the table. "Grace, this is—"

"Eva Deutsch," I finished for him.

They both looked startled. She wasn't as pretty as she had been in the pictures I'd seen.

"Grace, what are you saying? This is Maeve Flood."

"She has called herself that since 1978 but her real name is Eva Deutsch."

The woman in question stared at me like I had announced the plague as something good.

"Grace, Aunt Mildred has known Maeve for thirty years, at least." He looked at Maeve for confirmation. She stared at me. The more I looked at her the more I saw the differences. It was like looking at Ava Deutsch, but she wasn't identical; not like the photo. Close, too close to be a coincidence. The answer came as though someone had lifted the top of my head and poured it in. *Potato, patato, highwater, flood. Highwater, Hochwasser, waters, flood, whatever.*

"You're not Eva. You're Magda."

She didn't respond for a moment and then nodded her head.

"Who is Magda?" Harry was the only one left in the dark.

"Magda is the triplet Deutsch sister that everyone thinks died during the war. Her nanny, Hilda Hochwasser, went back to Germany with her right before war broke out. The report the Webers received informed them that Hilda's home had taken a direct hit from a bomb and that everyone had been killed."

Harry stared at Maeve in astonishment. She smiled at him. The corner of her mouth lifted unevenly, marring the effect. Her smile, a pale imitation of the megawatt grin I'd seen in the photos of her sisters, disappeared.

Her speech came slow and deliberate. "Where to begin?"

I had a feeling we were about to hear a story that had never been told.

"It's true that the Hochwasser home was destroyed. I survived. They found me under the rubble. I had broken bones and some burns." She passed her hand slowly over her upper chest and face.

I thought of how her life had started and how she'd been abandoned by her grandfather. Her life didn't get easier in Germany. She'd gone through hell while her sisters lived in the lap of luxury. I felt sorry for her.

"The neighbors had children and problems of their own. No one seemed anxious to take on the care of a damaged child. Julia Penny, an Englishwoman at the hospital who'd stayed behind to help in the children's clinic where I'd been brought, took a liking to me.

"When it became too dangerous for her to stay she left for England and took me with her. She knew my name was Hochwasser and she translated it into English as Flood. There was no translation for Magda. She named me Maeve. She explained my appearance in the village of Baulfield as her sister's daughter come to stay in the country to escape the blitz in London. The few people we knew assumed my scars were from a London bombing raid. When I grew older she told me my real name and my family history as she knew it. I could barely remember Hilda, but I knew she hadn't been my mother. I knew I had lived in an English-speaking country before Germany. It hardly mattered. I loved the English countryside. The climate strengthened me inside and out.

"Julia started keeping bees and chickens. She taught me how to plant a garden and how to collect wildflowers for medicine. We were self-sufficient.

"She treated my burns with potions she made from the flowers. One day she tried the honey mixed with the flowers. The results were astounding. Julia was convinced that if she'd known the right combination earlier she could have healed all the scarring. There was nothing to be done for my mouth—nerve damage probably from the bombing."

My voice almost blurted the truth: that she'd suffered that damage within minutes of her birth.

"Julia died a few years later and I stayed on. So many children were left on their own after the war. I was nearly seventeen, grown, by most standards. I stayed on with the bees."

Harry shook his head. "What a fantastic story."

"It's the truth. You believe me, don't you?"

"It won't be up to me to make that judgment. The police will have to determine that."

Her eyes widened. "The police? But I haven't done anything wrong. I've been trying to help." She looked at me. "Your back door was open. I wanted to leave you what I'd found. I didn't know you were alone."

"Why didn't you talk to me?"

"I was going to but as I walked in and was about to call out, I heard a scream like a banshee. I jumped and knocked over a container; it hit the floor and spilled; I dropped the key and ran."

"What key would that be?" Detective Garza's voice startled all of us.

Maeve, I couldn't call her Magda, turned her soft eyes on the detective's stern face. "The key I found in the dirt after I saw that man who was killed being helped across the back of the smithy shop."

We all jumped at her comment. Garza spoke first.

"You saw Schoebel? What do you mean 'helped'?"

"I mean the person held him up; half walking half dragging him like the chap had too many pints in too short of time, if you get my meaning."

"Who, who did you see with him?"

"I couldn't see; too far and too dark. I wasn't the only one there. One of those costumed people stood much closer. Dressed like the station master, he was. Hasn't he come forward?"

Garza shook his head.

"I can tell you, though, that it wasn't Harry. The person I saw wasn't nearly as tall or broad." With that sentence a burden lifted from my shoulders.

"How do you know Mr. Marsden?"

"I know him through his Aunt Mildred. I gave him some honey to help his burns." She pointed toward his hands.

"You made the honey that Mrs. Marsden had in her home?"

"The bees made the honey but I added the flowers. Yes."

"In that case, I'm placing you under arrest for the attempted murders of Ric Kramer and June Weber. Stand up and place your hands behind your back." Garza moved out of his chair and behind Maeve before I could speak.

"Harry, do something. He can't arrest her."

Harry looked at me like I'd taken leave of my senses.

"Grace, she tried to kill you or at best make you sick."

Maeve, who'd gripped the table in shock, spoke. "I never did. To anyone. I don't know anything about those people. And I only went to see Mrs. Marsden to try and help."

She looked into my eyes. "Oh, please. I didn't do anything."

Garza had lifted her from the chair and pulled each hand behind her back. The *click* of the handcuffs sounded painful. I cringed as Garza read her her Miranda rights.

"Call David. She doesn't have an attorney." My eyes pleaded with Harry.

"Bloody hell." Harry left the room but returned immediately with Nancy Royal and Peterson.

"What's going on? Who's she?"

"Our poisoner. She admitted to tampering with the honey she gave Marsden who in turn gave it to Kramer."

"Who poisoned the cream?"

"Are you certain about the poison?" Harry asked.

"We don't know exactly what kind of poison but the lab confirmed there is an alkaloid substance in both containers. Toxic when absorbed through the skin. Immediately deadly if ingested. The lab called the center for poison control in Atlanta and they are determining what serum will work. In the meantime both patients are receiving new medication to combat the effects."

"Maeve didn't do this. You said the poison was deadly if ingested. Maeve knew I'd never use her honey as a sweetener. Why would she tamper with the honey?"

I seemed to have scored a point.

"We took the liberty of checking the sugar and Sue Bee honey in your kitchen and any sugar and honey from Mr. Kramer's kitchen when we picked up the jar. Do you drink your coffee black?"

I knew Royal knew the answer. She'd seen me drink coffee. "Yes."

"Then, you may have been the target, Mr. Marsden." She turned to face Harry. "The sugar bowl and honey bottle were laced with the same alkaloid poison. There was no poison in the sugar or honey at the other house."

"Me?"

"If you were set up to take the fall for Schoebel's murder, as it is becoming apparent that you were, what better way to make sure that you didn't clear your name than to kill you and let you take the rap to your grave?"

"Wouldn't that be a tad suspicious, indicating I'd been innocent all along?"

"Yes, but now the murderer had one more degree of separation from the original crime which could have made the search more difficult if not impossible."

"It's becoming apparent that Maeve had nothing to do with the poisoning. Do you have to arrest her?"

"Not this moment." Garza unlocked the cuffs.

Maeve rubbed her hands in relief. Her wrists showed some chafing. She reached into her deep pocket and pulled out a small jar. She unscrewed the top, dipped her finger inside, and dabbed the cream on her wrists, one, then the other.

Peterson leaned forward. "Can I see that?" He reached for the jar and sniffed it.

"The one Kramer used smelled awful. I wouldn't have used it."

"He didn't know what it should smell like. He experienced what he expected. If Mrs. Marsden had mentioned that it smelled sweet then he would have questioned its merit when it smelled bad. He only knew it healed and sometimes we erroneously believe that something must taste bitter or smell bad or cause pain to be of benefit. Nature doesn't heal that way."

Peterson handed back the jar. "They look identical, but one's a killer."

FORTY-TWO

"THAT'S IT! OH, GOD. That's it." I shook Harry by the arm and about hugged Peterson. "I know who's in the trunk. And if I'm right there is only one person who would have killed Schoebel."

"You convinced me that Pauli killed Schoebel to stop the blackmail." Peterson looked confused.

I'd seen it all in a moment of crystal clarity, but now the pattern clouded and faded. I had to braid to get my brain to slow down and follow. The orange length of cord materialized in my hands before I knew it.

I could sense more than see Royal and Garza staring at me. Peterson had seen this before. I didn't sense that Maeve thought this strange. She put her hand on my arm as I braided and I felt a soothing sensation like a low vibration penetrate my mind.

The pattern came into focus.

"Eva Deutsch is the body in the trunk," I blurted out louder than I intended. The nurse and security guard, who had stayed nearby, looked startled.

I lowered my voice. "It all makes sense and this is the only way it makes sense. Everyone thinks Ava is so sweet. What if she was tired of being the nice sister? What if Eva's behavior after the will came out was the last straw? I mean she's not Mother Theresa. Eva threatened to ruin the business, her charities, everything that she held dear.

"What if they argued? Maybe she didn't mean to kill her. Maybe it was an accident and she hid the body in one of those old trunks. Once she made up the story that Eva had left the country, she didn't want to take a chance on moving the body. Years went by and her life went on the way she wanted. She became reclusive, maybe afraid to be around too many people who knew Eva.

"Did anyone check with Eva's accountant to see if any money changed hands? Has anyone ever seen them in the same city since that summer? If they both have an interest in antiques isn't it likely that someone would see them at the same auctions?"

I thought my logic irrefutable. During my explanation, I had seen skepticism grow in their eyes, only to be replaced by a dawning of agreement. Now their eyes looked resigned; not the look I expected. I felt like I'd missed something. I looked at Harry.

"What is it? It makes sense, doesn't it?"

"It makes perfect sense."

I could hear the "but" coming.

"If it makes sense that Ava killed Eva, then it also makes sense that Eva killed Ava," Harry said.

Garza nodded his head. "Maybe Eva wanted more than what Ava was willing to give. Maybe she'd always resented her sister for holding back on money, limiting her to a budget. With Ava gone and Eva in her place, she'd have all the money. It could work both ways. And how do we tell who's alive and who's dead?" Detective Garza asked.

"Records. They must have kept records. Even though they were twins, they had to have had different childhood illnesses, maybe broken bones. Maybe different DNA?"

Harry shook his head. "With identical twins the DNA is identical. I don't think that would be any help."

Royal answered my first question. "John Weber, the twins' physician in their childhood, was killed the day he did an autopsy on the skeleton. The shed behind the Weber home that he used for storage was broken into and vandalized the day of the funeral. Boxes were ripped open, papers scattered everywhere. We thought kids did it. Now I'm willing to bet if we looked for Deutsch records on Ava and Eva we'd come up empty."

"So it fits that after the body was discovered, she'd have to eliminate any way to identify the body as her sister. That meant killing the one man who might remember which little girl had broken something and then destroying the records he'd kept."

"I thought Lloyd killed Weber?" Peterson asked.

"Yes and no," came Royal's cryptic reply. "We found a fingerprint on the inside of the bottle from the Marsden home. Easy to match up with Lloyd Buckner's prison file because we knew whose print to look at. However, he has an alibi for the time the doctor was hit.

"My guess is he was waiting for the increased dosage to do its job. I checked with the M.E. and he speculated that with the amount in his system he might have bled out in another two days. The doctor's death may have been attributed to accidental overdose, his own error in filling the prescription. Lloyd's plan to kill him slowly was trumped by our murderer who didn't know that and couldn't wait."

"Who are you charging with his murder?"

"The D.A. is working on charges. It's too convoluted for me. We picked up Buckner before I came here. He's spending the night in our jail. I wanted to let his wife know."

Peterson offered to go get her.

The charge nurse walked briskly to our table. I thought she came to throw us out. She smiled instead and told us that the helicopter from the poison center had landed on the roof and delivered the serum for June and Ric.

Commotion at the ER door drew our attention. One paramedic pulled the gurney through to the trauma unit while the other related the patient's vitals and circumstances.

"Female, bullet wound to the head. Hemorrhaging, possible brain swelling—" The door closed behind the cart.

A Lisle police officer entered the ER. He made a beeline to his sergeant. "Neighbor heard a shot, called 9-1-1. Looks like she flinched."

"Any sign it wasn't attempted suicide?"

"Anything's possible, but it doesn't look like it."

"Who is she?"

Maeve had gripped my arm when the cart had passed us. I think she knew the answer; I think we all did.

"Wallet says, 'Ava Deutsch.'"

FORTY-THREE

Maeve jumped from her chair and ran after the cart. "Please let me see her, I'm her sister." Her voice sounded so full of pain I felt tears spring to my eyes.

She spent twenty minutes with her sister. When she returned, her eyes were swollen and her sobs uncontrollable. I'd brought tissues and water to the table and now guided her to it.

"Maeve, I'm so sorry. Here, sit down. We'll help you through all this."

"How can you help me through killing my sister?"

Her statement brought everyone's head up and Royal's notebook out.

"Are you confessing to shooting your sister?"

I lashed out at her. "Don't be ridiculous. Your own officer called it suicide."

"He said it appeared to be suicide."

Maeve spoke softly. "I might as well have put a gun to her head. I didn't know, didn't understand. I saw her tonight. Before I came to the hospital I went to see her. I'd come in the back way. She was sitting at a small desk. She had a bottle out and was pouring herself a drink. I didn't want to startle her; I wanted her to know I was there.

"I spoke to her from across the room. 'Hello, sister. I've come a long way to find you,' I said. She leaped up from her chair and backed away from me. I tried to calm her. 'I know you never expected to see me but I've thought of nothing else all these years.' She cringed and put her hands in front of her. She kept whispering, 'No, no, you're dead.' I took a step toward her. She turned and ran down one of the aisles. I hadn't meant to upset her, terrorize her. I called out that I was leaving, but that I'd come back. I only wanted to talk to her. Instead I pushed her beyond her limit." Maeve broke down, sobbing.

I put my arm around her shoulders. They lifted and fell with each sob. Soon she stopped crying and took a sip of water.

Nancy Royal spoke gently to her. "The nurses said she mumbled something they couldn't make out. Did you understand her?"

Maeve nodded. "She said 'listen to the bones' and 'forgive me.'" Maeve looked on the verge of tears, but she swallowed hard and drank more water. "I think she was asking my forgiveness for killing me."

My heart lurched in my chest when I heard the first part of the message. Had Ava left that message to frighten me or to plea for her capture? Was she already so unraveled that she couldn't decide to kill again or kill one last time?

"Ms. Flood, did your sister name you? Did she call you Ava or Eva?"

"I wish she would have known me as Magda, to know one of my sisters knew I was alive." She shook her head. "I'm sorry, that's all she said."

THE POLICE HAD turned Ava's house and business upside down in the following hours. They found a strongbox hidden in her home that unlocked with the key Maeve had. The box contained identification and a current passport in the name of Eva Deutsch. They suspected that Schoebel had stumbled on the knowledge of the murder and had been quietly blackmailing Deutsch. At his bank they found photocopies of the same records in his safe deposit. His bank records showed modest deposits every three months over the last twelve years, which indicated he'd hadn't known from the beginning. He'd had his orders from Ava not to open those two trunks. He must have panicked once the body was discovered, thinking he'd be a prime suspect and that she could slant the investigation toward him. When Harry followed him out, Schoebel considered him a chance to strike first.

Ava Deutsch's car was impounded and technicians were able to match the paint on her car to paint flakes found on John Weber's clothes. We couldn't be certain, but after much speculation we determined that both Harry and I had been targets. There had been some thought that June might have been a target since she had been her husband's nurse, but she had stopped assisting him after the accident with the babies.

All the jars had been collected and checked. No other jar had the toxin. Ava's research of medicinal plants gave her as much knowledge of poisonous ones. It hadn't been difficult for her to extract what she needed from easy-to-find garden plants. Ric and June were unfortunate "collateral casualties," as the report indicated. Both were recovering and expected home in a few days.

Ava seemed to have been a master of misdirection. They had questioned Jan Pauli about the false report she made and found out that Ava had threatened to implicate her in Schoebel's death by revealing her secret, which would provide a great motive and ruin her business.

Pauli admitted that she had suspected Lloyd Buckner of dosing the doctor. She cleaned for the Webers and had been there when the first argument took place. The next week, she'd seen Lloyd sneak from his in-laws' bathroom and then later she'd spotted the odd bottle on the vanity in Lloyd's ditty bag.

After Dr. Weber's death she felt certain Lloyd and the bottle had something to do with it. They had moved back in with June. Jan had used the pretense of cleaning the house for the friends that would visit after the funeral, to sneak into the bathroom and remove the bottle. She wanted someone to know about the medication but didn't want to get involved. She had overheard Karen and Nick talking about the break-in when she first visited and decided to copycat that crime by arriving early to lightly trash my kitchen so the bottle could be found.

After she left, she'd decided to come back and confess her lie and explain her idea about Dr. Weber's death. She didn't want Lloyd to go free. She'd been so anxious to come back and tell me that she hadn't paid attention to the narrowing road. She said she'd been trying to open a bag of tortilla chips and released her seat belt to reach the bag when she lost control of her car. She panicked and hit the accelerator and veered off the shoulder down the embankment.

In addition to a master of misdirection, Ava was also capable of using her surroundings to her advantage. The police could only speculate that she had used the bat from Harry's car after she heard Schoebel arrange to meet Harry. Further testing of the bat indicated bits of gravel from the parking lot and a sticky substance that turned out to be a piece of the honey sticks that a vendor had been selling during the event. That combination indicated that the bat had been on the ground. They had found a thin leather glove near where they estimated Harry's car had been parked. The match was found in Ava's house. She more than likely hid next to his car when she heard the exchange. She noticed the bat and used it.

It wouldn't have been difficult for her to half drag, half walk a stunned Schoebel to her store where she finished the job. She waited for Harry to drive up and pushed the corpse into the car's path. It would have been easy for her to slip away behind her store.

The police found the remote from Harry's car in her store. That explained how she got into the house to poison the honey.

The police also had a theory about my attack at the depot. Royal was pretty certain that what had slowed the movement of the bar Ava had swung at me was the fact that her sleeve snagged on a nail in the wall. She couldn't explain the cold air I'd felt, but she had the explanation for the message no one sent. She believed that Ava did stumble against the key and set off a few dots and dashes. In Royal's further questioning of Joe he admitted that he hadn't actually heard "help me" but rather an "h" and "p." His imagination filled in the rest. Royal seemed convinced she had the only logical explanation. I wasn't sure it was as logical as all that, nor would I want it to be.

The extended Deutsch family had been shocked by the news of the murder-suicide. They would be planning a double funeral for deaths fourteen years apart. They were burying the sisters together but waiting for the extensive laboratory testing to tell them, if it could, which dates to use for which sister.

MAEVE HAD ASKED us to meet her at her hotel the next day for a cup of tea. Harry and I went early. We took a table near the window in the atrium. Harry ordered tea for three. Our server had laid the service, filled our water goblets, and settled the teapot on the table before we spotted Maeve.

Harry stood up and pulled out her chair. She sat down and rubbed her hands together like a child in a candy store. "This is lovely." She pulled a small bottle of honey from her purse and dribbled some into her tea. She smiled at me and cocked her head toward Harry. "A man to keep hold of. The bees know a good one."

I wasn't certain if she was teasing about the bee thing, or if she was, as Harry's family would say, daft. It didn't matter; she was sweet and harmless. I smiled back. "I intend to." I slipped my hand under his.

He leaned toward me and brushed my temple with a soft

kiss. We had enjoyed a wonderfully affectionate homecoming once he'd had some sleep and I'd had some food. Harry had removed any misgivings I had about his being drawn closer to Lily.

"I'll tell the bees their honey had some help from your 'honey.'" Maeve chuckled at her bee humor.

Harry and I burst into laughter. It felt good to be laughing; healing came with it.

"Maeve, has your family's attorney contacted you?" Harry asked.

"So nice to have a 'family,' such a lovely word. I spoke with him this morning. I have an appointment to meet with him after our tea." Maeve's voice quavered. I felt so sorry for her; she'd come here to meet her sister.

Maeve's answer to Harry's question brought me back from my thoughts.

"I've known about my sisters for a few years. I found out through one of those odd occurrences that you know must be destiny. I'd been up to London, which I rarely did, to see about putting some of my honey in a posh beauty care sort of shop. I'd seen their adverts in the local paper and contacted the store manager. My cottage and the hives both needed some restoration. I'd hoped to sell enough to make the repairs.

"In their window I saw a placard with this remarkably familiar photograph. Ava Deutsch would be a presenter that afternoon talking about *The Power of Plants*. Of course, I stayed for the talk and all the while she spoke I remembered snatches of long forgotten conversation and decades-old glimpses of little girls in party dresses. I didn't dare speak to her, but I took the pamphlet about her."

"Is that when you subscribed to the *Lisle Sun?*" She seemed surprised that I knew.

"Yes. I thought I'd learn about my sisters that way. There were many articles; Ava was in the news quite a bit." She turned to Harry. "When I met you and found out you lived in Lisle, it was as if an occult hand had brought us together, not only your hands. That is when I made up my mind to come across.

"I came straight to her shop once I settled in. The shop was closed but I saw a light on. I thought she might be in the back. I went round and the back door was unlatched. I went in but didn't feel right about it so I left and came over to the event I'd read about."

"You must have set off the silent alarm that notified the police, although the police said an electrical glitch had been responsible. An officer came to get Ava. Her absence is what gave Hannah the edge to get the trunk."

"I saw when she left. I knew she wanted the trunk. I had some grandiose idea that I would win the bid and present the trunk to her. Silly, wasn't it? I mean, she didn't know me, probably wouldn't have cared."

"It wasn't silly, but I'm glad you kept hidden." Harry's voice was low and serious. "You would have been a threat to her, Maeve. She killed once because of greed and then twice more to hide the first. As first-born you would have been entitled to the lion's share, of everything. She would have found a way to kill you, too."

Maeve shivered; her eyes filled with tears. "I should never have come. I didn't want the money. I was daft to think I could waltz into their lives, as though fifty years hadn't happened. I should never have come. She died because of me." Maeve put her hand up to her mouth to hold in sobs.

"She committed suicide, Maeve. Her greed sickened her with remorse. I think she knew the police would put it together; maybe even hoped they would."

Maeve's attempt to meet her sister had convinced the guilty sister that her dead sibling was back from the grave she'd locked her in fourteen years ago. She had already gone beyond sanity. Maeve's choice of words had reinforced the illusion that she had returned from the dead.

Her crying slowed. "It was my fault. I never should have come."

"No, Maeve. You were right to come. You have family here; nieces and nephews and cousins. They'll want to know you and they'll love you no matter how many years have passed because that's what families do. Give yours a chance." I hoped Harry understood I was talking about us as much as Maeve. I would be meeting Will next week. Karen and Hannah were arriving midweek with their daughter. Our family additions were precious and welcome, as much as I hoped Maeve would be to her family.

She sniffed into a hankie she pulled from her pocket. A few more sniffles and sips of tea and Maeve regained her vigor. "I think I'm ready for that solicitor. Thank you both for all you've done for me. I don't know how to repay you."

"You already have." Harry flexed his hands.

Maeve finished her tea and stood to hug each of us in turn. I whispered to her, "Thank the bees for us and tell them Harry and I and our son will visit next summer."

Her eyes widened and her crooked smile beamed.

"The bees will be pleased."

* * * * *